The Carriagemaker's Daughter

***Other Five Titles
by Amy Lake:***

The Earl's Wife

The Carriagemaker's Daughter

Amy Lake

Five Star • Waterville, Maine

Five Star First Edition Romance Series.

Published in 2002 in conjunction with Alison J. Picard Literary Agent.

Set in 11 pt. Plantin.

Printed in the United States on permanent paper.

Library of Congress Cataloging-in-Publication Data

Lake, Amy, 1952–
    The carriagemaker's daughter / by Amy Lake.
       p. cm. — (Five Star first edition romance series)
    Sequel to: The earl's wife.
    ISBN 0-7862-4013-X (hc : alk. paper)
    1. Governesses—Fiction.   2. England—Fiction.
    I. Title.   II. Series.
    PS3562.A374 C37 2002
    813′.6—dc21   2001058593

The Carriagemaker's Daughter

Chapter One

The position of governess is a respectable one for a young lady with an impeccable reputation and few expectations.

Helène let her portmanteau drop to the snow at the side of the road and sighed, rubbing her arm. It was not that the bag was heavy—her belongings were pitifully few—but the two miles or more from the coach stop to the Sinclair estate was a long way to carry something so unwieldy. Even as cold as it was on this late November afternoon, she was beginning to perspire.

Helène peered down the road uneasily, noting that it would soon be dark.

She wondered again why no one had met the coach, since the letter detailing her travel arrangements must surely have arrived at the estate by now. Yesterday's early morning start from a gloomy, soot-ridden London had been bad enough. Then there was the day and a half spent crammed in a mail coach with an odd assortment of other passengers, a number of whom were not particularly clean. The lecherous comments from several of the men, the incessant arguments over whether or not to keep the windows open—

It wasn't an experience she cared to repeat. And the inn they had stopped at last night! She was still scratching from the bed bugs.

In short, Helène was in no mood for excuses. Perhaps she should plan a set-down to give Lady Sinclair when she finally arrived at Luton Court.

How dare you—
I am not accustomed to being treated—
The Prince will be informed of your outrageous—
Helène repressed a tired giggle, imagining the scene. She would say nothing of the kind, of course. She needed this position, and an impoverished spinster of evidently humble family had no business complaining about anything to the likes of the Marquess and Marchioness of Luton.

You are a governess, Helène reminded herself. They are Quality. You may not like the rules but you do have to play by them. She rested a few more minutes, sitting on the portmanteau, before getting to her feet and trudging on. It had been a mistake to stop, she decided. The struggle to carry her bag had taken her mind from how hungry she was, and now her empty stomach clamored for attention.

Botheration. Helène winced as the strap dug cruelly into her hand. *If only I had a rope,* she thought. *I could tie one end around my waist and one end to the portmanteau and drag the blasted thing behind me. Through the snow and mud and all.*

It would hardly matter, since she couldn't be any dirtier than she was already after a day and a half in the mail coach. Helène's thoughts moved to an uneasy consideration of her appearance. A governess was not required to be a fashion plate—in fact, it was discouraged—but her employers had every right to expect a reasonably tidy appearance. Helène wasn't sure she still qualified in that respect. She had lost weight in the stress of recent months and, although the brown merino wool had some years of service left in it, the dress now hung loosely around her waist.

I look like I'm wearing a sack, thought Helène gloomily. And not a very clean sack, at that. The revolting man sitting next to her in the coach—the one who kept pretending to brush dirt from her bodice—had not been careful with the greasy chicken he was eating—

Best not to think about him. But her skirts still showed the evidence of his noonday meal. Helène stopped and set the portmanteau down once again. She pushed the hood of her cloak aside and felt her hair. It was impossibly tangled, as usual, and half of it seemed to have fallen down around her ears. She rearranged several hairpins, jabbing blindly at the heavy mass in yet another futile attempt to wrestle her curls under control. She found little else to be cheered by in her appearance—her nose was a bit too long, her mouth too wide, her brilliant green eyes too bold—but Helène harbored a secret pride in her hair. Glossy and thick, its deep auburn color complemented the warm ivory of her complexion. Unbound, the silky locks fell in curls past her waist.

"I'll be cutting it off any day now, you daft girl," her father had told her, time and again. *"Hair like that is the sign of the devil, don't you know, and a waste of time for the likes of you. 'Tis not like there's to be suitors banging at your door—"*

Helène grimaced at the memory, though his words had been said affectionately, in jest. She never believed he would carry through on his threat. Still, in London, hair was only one more commodity, and if she could have convinced her father to eat a bit of meat, she would have cut off the tresses herself and sold them for a fine hock of lamb. But in the last few months of his life Nathaniel Phillips had wished for naught but his ale.

At the thought of food Helène's stomach growled, and she glanced down involuntarily at the bodice of her dress. A sapphire ring was pinned carefully in the lining, its large stone hidden from the waning rays of the November sun.

If she had known of that to sell, 'twould have been food for a year.

Helène walked on as the sun sank lower in the sky and the

surrounding hills took on the bluish cast of a winter's evening. The broad hills and meadows of Bedfordshire were beautiful in the twilight, but Helène was feeling the first glimmering of fear. She really did not want to be outside after dark on a cold November's night. Her exertions no longer kept her warm, and her feet especially felt the cold, her toes almost numb, even through the leather of her half-boots.

What could Lady Sinclair have been thinking, to risk her new governess freezing to death before she'd even arrived? She didn't know the district, and it was certainly possible, thought Helène, that she might miss the turn-off to Luton Court in the dark. Perhaps she had missed it already! Her heart began to pound and she forced herself to breathe slowly. No matter how bad the situation, it would never do to panic. Now think—had she passed any cottages along the road?

No. She'd seen not another living soul or habitation since the coach had driven away.

But how much farther could it be? How long had she been walking?

Helène cursed herself for being a fool and not demanding more assistance from the coach's driver before he left. But the man had been ill-tempered and rude and she'd been certain someone from Luton would arrive at any moment.

Stupid. Stupid, stupid girl, to go haring off from the coach stop with no plan in her head other than she would soon find Luton Court conjured up in front of her. Should she continue walking? Should she attempt to find some kind of shelter for the night? Deep in contemplation of her precarious circumstances, Helène didn't hear the rider as he approached. Suddenly—

"H'yah!"

An enormous chestnut stallion was almost on top of her.

Rearing up, its forelegs flailed the air as Helène backed away. She tripped over the portmanteau and fell hard to the ground.

"H'yah!" The rider yelled and the horse reared again. Helène rolled from under the plunging hooves, gasping as her hood fell back and snow cascaded over her face and down her neck. She managed to scramble off the road, but without her luggage. Down, down came the horse and she watched, horrified, as the portmanteau was trampled into a muddy, crumpled heap.

"What the devil?" she thought she heard the man shout. What the devil, indeed! The rider brought his mount under control and Helène shakily pushed herself to her knees. She started to brush the snow from her hair, taking care to keep clear of the stallion, which was still fitful and stomping. The man swore, in a steady voice, using a number of words that she found unfamiliar.

That's a surprise, thought Helène, her mind recovering from the fright. *One would have thought I'd heard them all by now.* She clambered to her feet and glared up at him.

"What in heaven's name are you about?" said the man. The cursing had stopped but the voice still betrayed his irritation. A deep voice. Strong. She looked up at him without speaking, half-dazed from the shock of being nearly trampled under-hoof.

"Standing in the middle of a public road like that!" he continued. "Young women with no common sense shouldn't be allowed out on their own."

Common sense—! Indignation cleared Helène's thoughts.

"And gentlemen who can't keep charge of their animals shouldn't be allowed on a horse," she snapped, brushing more snow out of her hood and off her skirt. Her heart was pounding from the encounter and she hoped the man couldn't see that her hands trembled. What a nasty, disagree-

11

able person! She finished removing the snow and eyed her skirt in annoyance. A number of mud stains now competed with the chicken grease on the front of the brown wool. Heavens, at this rate she'd be lucky if Lady Sinclair allowed her into the house.

The stallion sidled nervously and neighed. Helène looked up to see the man staring down at her, an expression of amusement on his face.

"I'm willing to concede the point," he told her, "but only because it's too cold to stand here and argue. Come, where's your home? I'll take you back—"

He stopped suddenly and looked down at the portmanteau, as if seeing it for the first time.

"What's all this?" he asked her. "If you are running away, *mademoiselle*, I must inform you that the middle of November is a poor time for it."

Helène sighed. *"Pour vrai, monsieur,"* she told him. "I'm sure you are correct. But as it happens, I am en route to my employer's estate, and I am no more eager than you to stand here and discuss it in the cold. Now, if you will excuse me—"

She bent down to pick up the battered portmanteau, keeping a wary eye on the restless stallion. But the man, who had cocked his eyebrow at her refined accent—or perhaps the scrap of French—muttered something under his breath and dismounted to stand in front of her. She found herself looking up into a pair of deep brown eyes.

"Your employer's estate?" He looked nonplussed. "The *Sinclair* estate?"

"Yes, as it happens." She tried to push past him but the man was immovable, a broad-shouldered rock in her path.

"Pardon me, sir," she said, hoping that she wasn't addressing some high-in-the-instep aristocrat. "But I really must be on my way."

Almost before she knew he had moved, he plucked her portmanteau from her hands. She found herself lifted up and deposited, as if she was no more than baggage herself, side-saddle on the stallion.

"Hang on," said the man.

"Sir!" she said. "I must insist that you release me this instant." Helène looked down, thinking to jump, but the ground seemed to be a very great distance beneath her feet. She hesitated.

"It would be much easier if you could sit astride," said the man. He swung himself up to sit behind her. "This business of putting both feet on the same side of the horse is absurd."

Helène turned to stare at him. *"Monsieur,"* she said. "I assure you, I do not wish to be on this monster of an animal in any position at all. Now, if you will please assist me—"

"Don't be a little fool. You'll freeze before you reach Luton, and, as it happens, I'm going there anyway. Now sit still."

He clamped an arm around Helène and, as she started to object, uttered a soft clucking sound to the stallion. The horse sprang forward immediately into a smooth trot and Helène swallowed her protest. Now what? The man's forearm was like an iron vise around her middle, and she seemed to be in contact with more of his body than she really ought to be. Even riding sidesaddle she was nestled snugly against the man's thighs, her back held firmly against his warm chest.

"Sir, I must protest—"

"I don't suppose we could continue this conversation at some later time?" said the man. "Alcibiades and I have had a long day, and idiotish young women weren't part of our plans."

"Oh! But—"

"Hush," said the man, without emotion. "Be glad you'll

not be found a month from now, frozen in a drift of snow."

There was no reply to that. The arrangement was undoubtedly most improper, but Helène couldn't summon the energy to complain any further. She supposed that she had once been as dewy-eyed and innocent as any young miss, but the last year in London had left her with few girlish fantasies. And who was there left to care anymore, whether it was proper or not?

It actually feels rather good, Helène decided, releasing her breath in a drawn-out sigh. Warm. If he really is going to Luton Court then so much the better. If he isn't . . .

She decided not to think about that possibility. The man somehow inspired trust, despite his abrupt manner. Helène stole a glance at his face and discovered that he was looking down at her with a peculiar, rather intent expression, which quickly gave way to a half-smile.

Warm brown eyes—

Helène held his gaze for a moment and tried not to blush.

"I can't imagine that even Lady Sinclair is hiring French-speaking scullery maids these days," the man said. He had apparently decided that some conversation could be tolerated. "So you would be . . ."

"The new governess."

"Ah. The governess."

"And you are—?" asked Helène.

"A house guest."

After this meager exchange, nothing further was said. The stallion trotted on, his stride fluid and steady, as the twilight became night and a light snowfall began. She watched the flakes descend, dusting the horse's mane and glinting like bits of silver fire in the moonlight. Any sound from the surrounding woods was muffled and heavy in the snowfall. Soon the horse and its rider seemed the extent of Helène's world, everything else unreal. Despite the renewed gnawings of hunger she felt comfortable and . . . and safe.

Papa. Papa, wake up.
I've brought the doctor. Papa—

Helène's head came up with a jerk and she realized she had dozed off. *Good heavens,* she thought, sitting up a little straighter. *I hope I wasn't asleep for long.* The road had narrowed, and the muddy ruts were smoothed over with a good layer of gravel. A regular planting of trees lined the sides—columnar beech from the look of it, although in the fading moonlight of a winter's evening, she couldn't be sure. *It must be very pretty here in the summer,* thought Helène, muzzily. *I wonder what the gardens are like at Luton Court. Will there be any statues?* She thought of a statue she had seen once of the Greek Apollo—quite shockingly naked—in another garden, another place. Strange to think of a man's body as beautiful. Helène's eyes began to close again. *His arms are so strong . . .*

Wake up, she told herself, straightening again and taking a deep breath. Wake up. You don't want this . . . person to think you are the type of woman who falls asleep in the arms of any stranger she happens to meet. Indeed not.

Mayhap we are poor, her father had told her more than once, *but the Phillipses have always been respectable.*

A bit of wishful thinking, perhaps, these days.

Their silent journey continued, the horse's stride never faltering, the man seeming to take no notice of her at all. Although she was content for the most part to be ignored, Helène began to contemplate the appearance she would soon present to the marquess and marchioness, and she decided to risk voicing one complaint. She turned to look up into a strong, craggy face. The man raised his eyebrows.

Faint heart ne'er won fair maiden, Helène could hear her father saying. 'Twas not the most logical adage for her current situation, but it would have to do. She took a deep breath. "Your animal has destroyed my portmanteau," she told the man, her voice firm. "I'm sure my things are ruined."

"Your clothing?" His voice sounded skeptical.

"Yes, my *clothing!*"

"Clothing of the sort that you are wearing now?"

Helène narrowed her eyes. Was the man short of wit? "What other kind of clothing would you suppose?" she asked him.

"*Mademoiselle,* I must say that if the contents of your bag are similar to the costume you are wearing at present, it can hardly be much of a loss."

The tone of his voice betrayed amusement, but Helène was in no mood to be teased. Well! she fumed. This was the outside of enough. Run down in the middle of a public road, accosted, her baggage ruined—and now insulted. Helène's temper, never under the best of control, flared, and she tossed her head at him.

"Sir, I will thank you to put me down at once!"

"Certainly."

A twitch on the reins, the horse stopped—and Helène found herself lifted to the ground.

"Good evening to you, *mademoiselle,* it was a pleasure to have been of some service."

Her mouth agape, she stared at the rider in speechless fury as he rode off at a smart trot, and without a glance behind. He was out of sight around a curve in the road before she realized he still had her portmanteau.

"Oh! Of all the despicable, odious, *pig*-headed—!" She stomped after him, only to discover—as she rounded the curve herself—that Luton Court stood in front of her, lights burning from every window, and the front entrance not fifty yards away.

Surely Harrison has arrived with the luggage by now, thought Lord Quentin, anticipating the pleasures of a hot bath and fresh clothing. He dismounted wearily from Alcibiades and tossed the reins to the waiting groom. The stallion snorted and stomped but Charles ignored him. He was gazing back in the direction from which he had come, watching, through the heavy snowfall, for a small figure to appear.

"Will you be wantin' this . . . item, milord?" asked the man, and Charles turned to see the governess's portmanteau in his hands. The groom looked bemused, and Lord Quentin could only imagine what he thought of the torn and muddy bag.

"Yes—well, no." Charles was about to tell him to give it to the housekeeper with directions to hold it for the new governess, who would be arriving very shortly. But it had been a long, cold day, and he was tired, and he doubted if he could summon coherent instructions for the portmanteau.

"Oh, just give it here," he said to the man. Charles dropped the bag on the steps, where it landed with a muddy squelch. The chit ought to see it there, he thought. And it would avoid any awkward explanations to Mrs. Tiggs.

"Very good, milord," said the groom, carefully paying no further attention to the bag. He led Alcibiades away and Charles took one last look down the Sinclair's long front drive. Ah, yes. There she was now. He turned and bounded up the staircase to the house.

By the time Helène reached the steps of Sinclair Court she was as cold as before and much angrier. Left without help or transportation—twice!—by the high-and-mighty Sinclairs and now their high-and-mighty houseguest! Pah! Helène conveniently chose to forget that the rider had obviously known she was only yards away from Luton Court when he set her down. The Quality! They were anything but, in her mind.

She trudged up the steps, thinking dark thoughts about gentlemen on horseback, and rapped smartly on an enormous double door. To her surprise, it swung back at once, and an imposing white-haired man stepped out, staring down his nose as if he had detected a noxious odor.

"Kitchen help applies to Mrs. Tiggs," said the man, pointing somewhere off to her left. He started to close the door.

Tired as she was, Helène stood her ground. "I am Helène Phillips, the governess," she told the butler. "And you are—?" She almost laughed at the man's reaction to that little piece of impudence. For a moment he looked too flustered to speak.

"Ah, yes," he said finally, recovering. "Miss . . . Phillips." He intoned the words as if her name was painful to his throat. "Come this way please. I assume your luggage follows you?"

Her luggage. Blast and damn, thought Helène. The man had said he was a house guest of the Sinclairs, but she'd seen no sign of her portmanteau. What could she tell the butler? *Pardon me, but one of your guests rode off with my bag?* She murmured a vague agreement, hoping that the missing item would soon appear. The butler, who offered nothing more in the way of conversation, was already walking away at a brisk pace, and Helène had some difficulty scrambling to catch up.

What is wrong with me? she wondered. *I feel so weak.*

They made their silent way through an enormous entrance hall, complete with potted palms twice her height and bust after bust of English literary figures. There was Marlowe, and Edmund Spenser . . . Goodness, what a disagreeable expression on *his* face. Helène was only half aware that she had

18

stopped to look at the poet, and when she glanced around, the butler was nearly out of sight. She hurried after him. The entrance hall seemed to stretch on forever. Her legs felt leaden, and twice she stumbled over marble that was polished smooth as glass.

Finally, just as Helène thought she could walk no further, they came to a grand staircase, also of marble and adorned with wrought iron balusters. The butler started up without a glance back. Helène followed him, her heart pounding, each step swimming before her eyes in a sea of exhaustion. Halfway up the staircase she paused to catch her breath.

"Come along, Miss Phillips," commanded the butler.

"Yes—"

A long gallery, well-lit by candles and richly carpeted, greeted her at the top of the staircase. Under less trying circumstances the carpet might have impressed Helène with its plush elegance, but it was no easier to walk on than the marble had been. The butler, now yards ahead, had stopped before a set of double doors. This, to Helène's relief, was their destination.

The butler knocked loudly, and a petulant voice responded with a complaint that Helène did not catch. They entered the perfumed and dimly lit room, and Helène saw a woman lying on a velvet chaise lounge in front of the fireplace clasping a compress to her forehead.

"Your ladyship," said the butler.

"Who is this, Telford?" asked the lady, glancing at Helène with a *moue* of distaste. "I don't interview the scullery girls, you silly man. Take her to Mrs. Tiggs."

"Miss Phillips, milady," said the butler. "The governess." He turned on his heel and walked out. The woman looked up at her in surprise. She was a small woman and very pretty, Helène supposed, if you happened to be partial to soft brown hair and a pouting, rosebud mouth. The marchioness—for Helène couldn't see how this woman could be anybody other than Lady Sinclair—sat up and frowned. She gave a sigh of disgust.

"I am Helène Phillips, ma'am," said Helène meekly, common sense prevailing over her irritation, at least for the moment.

"Such a headache, you have no idea," said Lady Sinclair, lying back on the chaise with another sigh. "Well, this is all very inconvenient. You were to come today, you say? I don't remember any such thing."

"Lady Sinclair, I'm sure you must have received my letter—"

"And what in heaven's name are you wearing?" added the woman, glancing again in Helène's direction and sniffing audibly. "This is quite, quite unacceptable. You must change into decent clothing at once. What will people say? Why on earth we must have a new governess only weeks before Christmas I will never understand, and I'm really much too busy to be bothered—"

She continued in that vein for some time, and Helène heard her out in silence, wondering what she might be able to do about her clothing. She possessed a rose sarcanet that was marginally more fashionable than the brown wool, but it was hardly winter wear. And this was assuming she found her portmanteau, and assuming her clothing hadn't been trampled into rags under the hooves of that brute stallion.

"Oh, never mind," said the woman, with another martyred sigh. "Mrs. Tiggs can sort you out."

"The children—?"

"Go and ask Mrs. Tiggs. I'm sure Alice and Peter are around somewhere."

Lady Sinclair closed her eyes and waved Helène away.

Helène stood there for a moment, debating whether this was the appropriate time to discuss the terms of her service with the Sinclair family.

" *'Tis best to begin as you mean to go on,* " her father had often told her, one of the few pieces of good advice he had had to give. If this was the marchioness's usual attitude toward her employees, Helène doubted that her own temper would survive unnoticed for long.

But you've never been a governess before, she reminded herself. Perhaps this is how they are always treated.

She stood for a few more moments, wavering, then turned and left the room. The woman did not glance up and Helène shut the door behind her with just a tiny bit more force than necessary. What now? The long upstairs corridor seemed to stretch on forever, punctuated with one closed door after another, and the butler was nowhere in sight.

What an odd house this was. Helène, deciding she was going to have to find the redoubtable Mrs. Tiggs on her own, started to retrace her steps.

"I trust you found your luggage," came a newly familiar voice.

She whirled around to see the man from that afternoon standing behind her, his eyebrows cocked in question. Helène resisted the impulse to step back and catch her breath. It was the first time she had seen him out of his riding cape, and although he was only somewhat above medium height, he was powerful in build. Broad shoulders, muscular thighs tautly encased in fine breechcloth—

"Mmm. My luggage?" said Helène.

His thighs are really none of your business, she reminded herself. She concentrated for a moment on his face. The man was not handsome in a conventional way. His nose was long and had a slight crook to it, and his face was . . . it was very . . .

Rugged, Helène decided. His clothing was of the finest quality, but the man didn't look like a fashionable London gentleman. He looked less tame. His thick brown hair was of medium length and arranged carelessly, with several locks falling over his forehead. She could find no fault with his eyes, however. They were a deep brown and—

Helène blinked. She had been staring, she was sure of it. How mortifying. Was the man speaking to her?

"I beg your pardon?"

"Yes—did you find your portmanteau? I left it on the front steps."

"The front steps!"

"You couldn't possibly have missed seeing it." The man shrugged. "Well, never mind—it will turn up eventually. The thing is hardly likely to be stolen."

She was dirty, and exhausted, and suddenly very annoyed.

"Well, I *did* miss seeing it," Helène told him. "Apparently I was lucky to even be allowed to set foot on the sainted front steps, and my chances of finding anyone to help me find a place to *sleep* in this house, let alone find my poor, trampled portmanteau—"

Helène stopped to catch her breath. She had lost her temper again, she thought miserably. The second time today.

The man shrugged again. "As you say. But would you have preferred explaining to Mrs. Tiggs how I ended up with the thing?"

Mrs. Tiggs again.

"I would have preferred that you hadn't taken it in the first place!"

"*Taken* it—"

"Lord Quentin!" interrupted a high, breathy voice from the doorway.

Helène turned around to see the marchioness standing with arms outstretched. Lady Sinclair advanced toward the man and flung her arms around his neck.

So he *is* a lord, was Helène's first thought.

"Oh, Charles," cooed Lady Sinclair, "tell me you've come to stay. I've been so dreadfully lonely." Helène could hardly avoid noticing that her ladyship's bosom, only half covered by the thin material of her dressing gown, was now pressed closely against the man's chest. She wondered if it was accepted practice for the ladies of the *ton* to walk about *en déshabillé*. Her own father—

"Hello, Celia," the man said, and Helène could have sworn she saw a flicker of disgust on his face. The lady, undeterred, continued her enthusiastic embrace, and if it hadn't been for that brief flash of expression Helène would have concluded that they were lovers. She was turning to leave—it was high time to find Mrs. Tiggs—when she heard the man's voice.

"Celia, perhaps you could introduce me to your new governess. I believe she is in some need of assistance."

"Oh, Charles, simply *look* at the pathetic creature!" said Lady Sinclair, waving her hands vaguely in Helène's direction. "I can't imagine why Jonathan hired such a girl, her reference was *quite* inadequate. I've half a mind to turn her out this instant, she's dressed *abominably*, Charles. It's a disgrace to the household. You have no idea what I endure here, absolutely no idea—"

Helène didn't hear the rest. She stood rooted to the carpet, a strange buzzing in her ears, and wondered if this is what it felt like to faint. Ridiculous. She had never fainted before.

I just need something to eat, thought Helène. *I need to find Mrs. Tiggs.* She tried to take a step but the hallway contracted

and skewed sideways around her. A figured rose carpet . . .
plush, soft . . .

The buzzing grew louder. She heard an exclamation of annoyance, somewhere in the far distance, and then even the
carpet disappeared.

Chapter Two

Lord Quentin pushed Celia away and caught the girl as she fell.

"Charles!" screeched Lady Sinclair.

The governess—although of more than medium height—weighed next to nothing, Lord Quentin discovered. He could feel the bones of her hips as he cradled her against his chest, and, if the bodice of her dress had not hung so loosely, he guessed it would be a simple matter to count each of her ribs. For the first time he looked closely at the girl's face and saw the signs that he had missed earlier, signs familiar to him from three wretched years on the Spanish peninsula.

The chit was half-starved. Charles was suddenly furious with Celia.

"Oh, just leave her there and I'll call a footman," the lady was saying. He looked at the marchioness blankly, unwilling to believe that even Celia could be that callous. But no—

"I'll have James take her to the kitchen," said the marchioness. "Cook will feed the girl and send her on her way first thing tomorrow. Of all the cheek, to show up at Luton looking like that. Really, Charles, she's filthy! How can you stand to touch her?"

Lord Quentin considered his options. He had no idea where the girl's room might be and, all things considered, it was entirely possible that Lady Sinclair had never bothered to have one prepared. His own bedchamber, on the other hand—as a frequent visitor to Luton—was not far away down the adjacent hall. He started to push past Celia.

"Oh, Charles!" protested Lady Sinclair, but, seeing the

frank determination in the set of his shoulders, she changed tactics in an eyeblink. She laid a well-manicured hand on his arm to stop him as he passed and flashed a disarming smile, the invitation written plainly on her face.

"Don't be so tiresome, Charles." Her voice was warm, honeyed. "James will collect the silly girl in a minute. Come, tell me all about London . . ."

Celia motioned toward the open door of her rooms.

Lord Quentin hesitated. What had gotten into Celia? She'd always been a flirt, but this brazen invitation—as a married woman—was not her usual style. Despite the long journey and the unconscious, rather grubby woman in his arms, Lord Quentin's body was quick to respond. Lady Sinclair had been toying with the neckline of her gown as they spoke, and at this point very little of her bosom was left to the imagination. Vivid memories of previous visits to Celia's boudoir before her marriage sprang forcefully to Lord Quentin's mind.

Lady Sinclair leaned closer, and Charles realized the answer to his own question as the scent of a fine sherry wafted in his direction.

Celia was drinking again. Poor Jonathan.

The girl stirred in his arms. "Papa," she said, and then something too soft for him to hear.

Somebody's daughter. He sighed, and, ignoring Celia, carried the governess toward his rooms.

"Charles!" the marchioness cried, watching him leave. "You can't take her into your rooms! She's—she's . . . unclean!"

"Call Mrs. Tiggs," he called back to her.

"Oh! I'll do no such thing! If you're so smitten with that odious . . . *creature,* take care of her yourself. " Celia flounced away, slamming the door to her suite.

Charles knew this was bluff. The marchioness would call

the housekeeper—and quickly—if only to remove the governess from his bedroom.

Lord Quentin laid the girl down on the silk coverlet. He checked her breathing—strong and regular—and would have unfastened the stays on her dress if the garment hadn't already been little more than a loose sack. There was nothing else he could do for her at the moment. The years in Spain had familiarized him with all manner of bullet and bayonet wounds, but hunger was a different problem. He sat down to wait for Mrs. Tiggs.

As expected, the housekeeper arrived within minutes, clucking loudly. She took one look at the woman lying unconscious in the middle of Charles's large, four-poster bed, and rang for a footman.

" 'Tis the governess, milord?" she asked Charles. "Telford said—"

"It would seem so."

"Taken ill, milord?"

"Hungry, I should think."

"Hungry!" Mrs. Tiggs looked astonished for a moment; then she nodded and set to work, muttering imprecations under her breath.

"Not that I'm complainin', you see," she told Lord Quentin, gently wiping the girl's forehead with a moistened cloth, "but 'twould be better t' my way of thinkin' if a body was informed when someone new comes t' the door."

Lord Quentin frowned. "Are you saying that no one knew that a governess had been hired?" That would be just like Celia, he thought.

"No, milord. Well, yes, milord. Didn't know she was t' be comin' today. Last girl left over a month ago."

"Ah." Charles considered this for a moment. "There was

a previous governess?"

"Aye, milord," said Mrs. Tiggs. "This one'll be the third."

"What happened to the first two?"

Mrs. Tiggs shot him a sharp look. "Well, now, 'twouldn't be my look out, would it? But both of them was pretty and young, and as near t' quality as makes some people nervous, if you get my meanin'."

"Ah." Celia's resentment of any other pretty woman was well-known. But Charles still wondered at the unconscious girl's physical state. Was Lady Sinclair hiring from the poorhouse now? Or was this merely Jonathan's attempt to appease his wife's jealousy?

He looked at the governess's face, where the clear ravages of recent hunger—dry, cracked lips and sunken cheeks— couldn't erase the charm of thick lashes, black against smooth skin, and a wide, sensual mouth.

She might have been lovely, thought Charles. If she had been a lady.

"Not that I need the warnin', you understand," continued Mrs. Tiggs. "All my rooms are in order and 'twould have been a simple matter—"

Lord Quentin nodded his agreement. "I dare say."

"And the poor girl, half froze t' death, I just don't know—" Mrs. Tiggs chattered on, smoothing tendrils of the governess's hair back from her face. The thick mass of auburn curls gleamed in the candlelight. "Ought t' be wakin' up by now, t' my way of thinkin'."

The governess moaned. Her eyelids fluttered open, then closed again, and Charles caught a glimpse of clear green eyes.

"Mrs. Tiggs," said Lord Quentin.

The woman looked around. She looked surprised to see him still sitting there. " 'Tis no need for you t' stay, milord."

"Mmm, yes. Well, it is my room."

"Eh? Oh, right you are, right you are. Well, 'twill just be a minute—"

"Mrs. Tiggs, I think the young woman will appreciate a light meal when she awakens. Perhaps you could send for some tea."

"Just be a minute, milord, James'll be movin' the girl t' her own room in a trice."

The girl. Charles was suddenly curious. "Does anyone know her name?"

"Miss Helen Phillips, I believe."

Miss Phillips. Twice the chit had been in Lord Quentin's arms, and she was now lying on his bed, but it seemed almost improper to know her name. As if some odd intimacy had been established, thought Charles, and immediately banished the thought. He didn't need a compromised governess on his hands.

A burly footman scratched at the door. "Mum?"

"James, take Miss Phillips to Miss Fitzpatrick's room." Mrs. Tiggs took another look at the governess, who was stirring again. "I believe she'll need t' be carried. You can do that, can't you, James?"

"Mum?" The footman looked confused. "Miz Fitzpatrick?"

"Now, James," the housekeeper said, as if speaking to a child, "you remember Miss Fitzpatrick, don't you?"

He nodded. "Yes, mum."

"And you do remember where her room is?"

The man looked unhappy. "Miz Fitzpatrick ain't here no more."

Mrs. Tiggs nodded. "Yes, quite right you are. Very good, James. But if she *was* here, do you remember where she would be?"

"Oh. Oh, yes, mum." James nodded vigorously.

"Good. Take Miss Phillips t' *that* room, do you understand? I'll follow you in a minute."

"Yes, mum."

The footman picked up the governess as if she was a delicate piece of porcelain, nearly weightless, and left. Mrs. Tiggs followed, pausing at the door to send Lord Quentin a speaking look.

"James is a good lad. He wouldn't do anythin' t' annoy Miss Phillips, if you take my meanin', milord."

"Ah." Charles nodded.

"And I'll see that she gets some nice hot tea."

"Something to eat, too, Mrs. Tiggs."

"Yes, milord."

She left, and Lord Quentin was not to see Helène Phillips again for the remainder of that day.

Amanda Detweiler reclined on the fine brocade of a chaise lounge and watched Lady Pamela Sinclair put the final touches to her *toilette*.

"London is simply too dreary this time of year," she remarked. "Everyone swathed in layer after layer of scarves and smelling of wet wool."

"Indeed," said Lady Pamela. "Would you have them freeze, instead?"

Lady Detweiler considered this seriously. "I believe I might," she said finally. "A score fewer bird-witted females would have made Lady Jersey's *musicale* last night entirely more bearable."

Pam laughed. "I must beg to differ. With Sally's choice of a soprano, last night was destined to be intolerable."

"Mmm. I concede the point."

"But it's only a few more days in town. We'll be at

Luton Court by Sunday."

"I understand that Charles Quentin will be joining the party this year," said Amanda.

"As he does every other year."

"The countess said he may have arrived there already, in fact. On his way to Tavelstoke."

"Mmm," said Pamela. She looked at herself in the mirror, frowned, and started removing hairpins. White-gold hair fell in heavy waves around the faultless oval of her face.

"I have always thought him as handsome as any man of our acquaintance," continued Amanda. "Excepting the Earl of Ketrick, perhaps."

"Mmm." Patiently, Pamela arranged layer after layer of silken curls atop her head, fixing them in place with the pins. The reflection of her wide, aquamarine eyes stared back at her from the mirror. "Beastly things."

"Men?"

"Hairpins."

"Ah." Lady Detweiler pursed her lips and blew out her breath in annoyance. "Pamela."

"Yes, darling?"

"It's been almost a year."

"A year?"

"You know very well what I mean. Edward and Claire were married over a year ago. You've been avoiding the male of the species ever since."

"Surely not." Lady Pam turned around and flashed Amanda a mischievous grin. "I assure you, I still find men perfectly fascinating—"

"Then why on earth—"

"—in theory."

Amanda gave an unladylike snort. "Men are no good in theory, my dear. Only in the flesh."

31

Pam laughed. "Have you been talking to my sister-in-law again?"

"Hmph," said Lady Detweiler. She shook her head at Pamela. "Well, I do know one thing. If you can't be bothered with Charles Quentin, I'm sure there will be more than one woman at that houseparty who will be. And I assure you, their interests will *not* be theoretical."

"Mmm," said Lady Pamela.

Lord and Lady Sinclair kept city hours even at Luton, and Charles judged that he was not too late for dinner. He arrived in the huge, Pompeiian-red dining room to find Jonathan and Celia chatting with Viscount Dreybridge and his young bride. The Viscount was a distant cousin of the Sinclairs, if Lord Quentin's memory served. And there was Lord Burgess, making calf-eyes at a voluptuous beauty. Ah—Lucinda Blankenship. Lord Quentin smiled, thinking that Jerry was well on his way to making a cake of himself—as usual.

Several other guests were scattered about the room, a number of whom he knew by sight but not acquaintance. Of the ones he did—well, there was Lady Harkins, she of the formidable bosom and sharp tongue. A true dragon, she was; widowed these twenty years and spending every moment of it the soul of propriety and the terror of every debutante. Lord Quentin could remember Lady Harkins's comments on the occasion of Jonathan and Celia's marriage, and wondered how she came to be invited to Luton. Some connection of the late Lord Harkins, no doubt.

Charles wandered over to the small *table du vin*, which was set with a sparkling assortment of crystal decanters. Two more Sinclair cousins—Sir Clarence Frost and Lady Jenkins—stood chatting by the fire, but it seemed that the marquess's younger sister had not yet arrived at Luton. Charles, who claimed an acquaintance with Lady Pamela Sinclair through his long friendship with Jonathan, was disappointed. Lady Pam shared his disinclination to make *ton* society the whole of life, and Charles realized that he had been counting on her presence for intelligent conversation.

Soft laughter from Miss Blankenship floated across the room, and Charles turned to see Lord Burgess whispering into her ear. This was quite improper, earning a glare from both Lady Harkins and the marchioness, the latter displeased to find the interest of any male fixed elsewhere than on herself.

Lady Sinclair was easily roused to competitiveness, especially on her home turf. Perhaps her attention would now be diverted to Lord Burgess, thought Charles, feeling an odd mixture of relief and concern. Celia's flirtatious attentions were flattering, of course, and for the most part harmless.

Except when she was drinking. Charles had no desire to be the cause of a row between husband and wife; nor, he should think, did Lord Burgess.

The marchioness looked his way, and her eyes narrowed. Her gown was a clinging, high-waisted silk that claimed only a wisp of material for its bodice, and the candlelight cast intriguing shadows on the fabric of the skirt, faintly outlining the curves beneath. Charles reflected, once again, that Lady Sinclair could make more out of the edge of propriety than any other female he knew. She held his gaze, giving him a slow smile that Charles felt down to his toes. Damn the woman, anyway. He certainly had no intention of taking up where they had left off before she became the Marchioness of Luton. No matter how tempting it might be.

"Lord Quentin," purred Lady Sinclair. "Do join us."

From Celia, in her current state, the invitation sounded more like a threat. Charles smiled blandly and poured himself a glass of whatever wine was closest to hand. In truth, he should be damning the drink rather than the marchioness. Celia could be volatile and jealousy incarnate—but she was no tramp. Indeed, since her marriage to his close friend Jonathan, Charles had seen a more vulnerable side to the marchioness, and watched as a touching loyalty grew toward her sometimes difficult husband.

Was her loyalty returned? Jonathan loved his second wife, Charles was sure, but recently—with the estate taking so much more of his time—it had seemed a cool, absent-minded sort of affection. Which was typical of Jonathan's nature, to be sure, but hardly of Celia's.

Perhaps it was the lack of fervor in her husband's approach that had driven her back to the wine, and to this distracted prowling for men. Perhaps Celia was still convinced she didn't quite deserve her good fortune . . .

Celia had been the young widow of an obscure baronet when she married Jonathan Sinclair, himself a widower with two children. It had been a whirlwind, tempestuous romance—the talk of London society that season, and Celia the subject of much acid comment from disappointed mamas.

A shockingly forward, penniless baroness! And the Sinclair fortune—oh, my dear, it's too much to endure.

The new Lady Sinclair had a certain reputation to overcome, as well—at least in certain quarters. Lord Quentin knew, as did a fair percentage of the gentlemen of the *ton*, that the marchioness had not entered into her present marriage without first enjoying what several of the more vigorous London bucks had to offer. Charles, to some current regret, had been one of them. Returning from three years of war, the stench of blood, gunpowder, and Spanish dust not yet erased from his mind, he had been ready for a taste of the first ripe peach to fall from the tree.

And Celia had been at her glorious, sensual best that London season. They had enjoyed a number of . . . encounters together, and even now Lord Quentin had flashes of memory that left his heart pounding and his mouth dry. He wondered how the marquess had survived the past year and a half. Celia was a tigress.

"Charles, I'm becoming quite vexed with you," said Celia, pouting that he had not joined them. "Do you know, Lord Burgess, that Lord Quentin once refused to dance with me at the Duke of Lincolnshire's ball?"

"Surely not," said Lord Burgess.

" 'Tis true. He insisted that Jonathan have the second waltz, even when everyone knows—"

As Celia prattled on, Miss Blankenship caught his eye and sent him a wink. Impudent chit! thought Charles, but he couldn't help a small smile. Lucinda Blankenship was near to a hoyden, and since she had become engaged to Lord Netherfield—

"Charles, old man. I hear you're on your way to Tavelstoke within the sennight," said Lord Burgess, interrupting his thoughts.

Charles heard Celia's sharp intake of breath.

"Indeed," he replied. "My father's recent illness left affairs unsettled at the estate, and the steward has requested my assistance."

"But surely that can wait until after the holidays," said the marchioness, her eyes glittering, her lips set in a rosebud pout. "And Tavelstoke is so close—you could be there inside of the day."

"I'm afraid not, my lady," said Charles. "But if all goes well, I should be able to return shortly after Christmas."

"After Christmas—! But Charles . . ." began Lady Sinclair.

"Now, don't fret, my love," said the marquess, joining the

conversation. Lord Quentin thought he heard a stifled snort from Miss Blankenship. "I'm sure Lord Quentin will return as soon as matters are settled."

"But—"

"The earl now resides in London, does he not?" Lady Jenkins broke in smoothly over Celia's pique, and Lord Quentin offered her a grateful smile.

"Yes," he told her. "My father and his wife are greatly content these days, but his health is still poor. They prefer a quiet life in town."

Lady Jenkins, like most of the *ton*, probably knew all there was to know about the Earl of Tavelstoke's recent history. "I'm so glad to hear he is happy," she told Charles. "They both deserve every bit of it."

"Indeed," said Miss Blankenship. She turned to the marchioness with an ingenuous smile. "As you know yourself, Lady Sinclair, it is marvelous fortune for an *older* widow to find such joy in a second marriage."

Lord Burgess was seized with a sudden fit of coughing, and Celia rounded on Lucinda with poorly concealed fury.

"And what, pray tell, would you know about—"

There was a loud knock at the door. "Dinner is served, milord," announced Telford.

And not a moment too soon, thought Lord Quentin, hearing several faint sighs of relief. Charles was beginning to realize that his week at Luton Court might prove less relaxing than he had hoped.

Chapter Three

*The governess shall have no object of more than
the most basic of accommodations.*

"Miss?"

A soft voice broke into the last moments of sleep, and Helène woke to the unbelievable, mouth-watering aroma of hot chocolate. In those first moments she had no idea where she was.

"Miss?"

Helène pushed herself up in the bed. A young girl stood in the doorway to the room, holding a pot of chocolate and a plate of cheese scones. At the sight of the scones, one thing was clear to Helène.

She was no longer in her father's house.

"Miss, I'm ever so sorry t' be wakin' you, but Mrs. Tiggs said as what you must be hungry—"

Mrs. Tiggs?

"—an' she tried t' get you t' eat summat last night, but you was so tired—"

Last night?

"—an' I was t' see you got these."

"Thank . . . thank you," said Helène.

The girl bobbed a quick curtsey, set the chocolate and scones on the nightstand and left.

She must be a parlour-maid, thought Helène. But where am I? Feeling the scratch of wool on her skin, she realized that

37

she was still wearing the brown merino dress. Someone had removed her shoes and covered her with a goosedown duvet during the night, but she had no memory of any of it.

Helène looked around. A small room, but pleasant enough, with two large windows set into one wall, and a washstand between them. The windows faced east, she thought, from the sunlight pouring in. A small rug covered a portion of the well-scrubbed floor, and the bed was fitted with a decent set of linens and a plump duvet.

Sheer bliss, thought Helène, bouncing slightly on her bed, and noting that the mattress was firm and not the least bit lumpy.

Where was she? Deciding that the matter would be best addressed on a full stomach, Helène directed her attention to the scones. Her eyes closed at the first bite, threatening tears. The scone, still warm, was the best food she had tasted for a year, and two or three more quickly disappeared. Then she swung her legs over the side of the bed and sat for several rapturous minutes, sipping hot chocolate. A rather unpleasant, muddy-looking bag sat on the floor next to the washstand, and Helène frowned, wondering where she had seen it before.

Her portmanteau. With that realization, memories of the past two days flooded back. The coach ride from London. The long walk to Luton Court. And . . . and a gentleman on horseback.

"Oh, dear," moaned Helène. "My clothes." She sprang from the bed and almost fell, the room spinning around her.

The dizziness—an aftermath of hunger—was a recently familiar sensation, and Helène lowered herself to the floor, where she sat, head in hands, until it passed. Eventually she felt well enough to explore what might be left of her portmanteau. She crouched down at the side of the bag and gingerly pried it open. The two nightgowns on top were smudged with dirt and showed some evidence of the stallion's hooves, but, to her relief, the grey wool walking dress and rose sarcanet appeared intact. She looked around for a place to hang them, and noticed a large mahogany tallboy against the far wall.

Lady Sinclair must expect her governess to be well dressed, thought Helène. Her own selection of clothing would be dwarfed in the dresser, but it couldn't be helped. *Pretty is as pretty does,* she could almost hear her father saying. Helène suspected that this sentiment would be lost on the Marchioness of Luton.

Lord Quentin was usually at his best in the early morning, but he had awakened today in an irritable mood, his head aching from a great deal too much brandy the night before. Whatever had possessed him to plan this extended stay at Luton Court? It had seemed like a good idea at the time—a short respite with friends before the work awaiting him at Tavelstoke. A respite—ha! How could he have been such a fool? Jonathan Sinclair he counted among his oldest and dearest of friends. But the marchioness . . .

Celia presented a problem. Charles inhaled deeply at the sudden, energizing memory of their latest encounter, only a few hours earlier, in this very room.

He and Jonathan had talked deep into the previous night. For the most part the marquess spoke and Lord Quentin listened, as was usual between the two of them, but at one point Charles attempted, cautiously, to raise the subject of Celia's drinking.

Jonathan had seemed surprised and hesitant to recognize the marchioness's impulse toward the bottle when she was unhappy or bored.

"Everyone drinks too much in the country," had been his casual response. "I shouldn't be too concerned."

Had he truly not noticed Celia's behavior? Charles could only conclude that Jonathan had immersed himself in estate business to the exclusion of other matters. This was not unusual for the owner of an extensive property, of course, but perhaps other men did not have wives as demanding as Celia.

After the marquess retired, Charles had remained in the library to finish off a decanter of brandy, and finally—long past midnight, and long past the time he would have preferred to be asleep—he had made his way quietly to his room. The late hour should have sufficed to avoid a further confrontation with Lady Sinclair. But no sooner had he closed the door to his chambers—

Charles threw back the covers and bounded from bed, almost upsetting the steaming pot of tea left by his valet some minutes before. He jerked open his wardrobe door, feeling it was essential that he be out of bed and dressed immediately. A ride was what he needed. A nice, long gallop in the early morning cold.

He had discovered Celia Sinclair in his bed last night, smiling and—as he was shortly to understand—unclothed.

"Charles. Finally," the marchioness had cooed. "You can't imagine what I've suffered, waiting here for you."

Her voice slurred, and he could see that peculiar glitter to her eyes that—in Celia—signaled tipsiness.

"Lady Sinclair," Charles had replied, his voice as cheerful and matter-of-fact as he could contrive. "You seem to have lost your way."

"Mmm," she responded, and stretched, cat-like. "I think not."

The coverlet slipped from her shoulders and Lord Quentin caught sight of one rose-tipped breast. Celia's breasts were, as he knew from experience, magnificent.

"I believe this is my bedchamber." The words came out in a croak.

Celia smiled and hiccuped softly. "Oh, I may be in the wrong bedchamber, my lord, but I assure you that this is very much the right bed."

"Celia—"

"Don't be such a spoilsport, Charles. You know Jonathan doesn't care." A hint of pain surfaced in her voice.

Lord Quentin decided to make an attempt at reason. "I'm sure he does," he told Celia. "I know that Lord Sinclair cares very much."

"Bosh," said the lady. "Not a bit." She tried, unsteadily, to rise, clutching the bedclothes around her. "Just a fast bit of tumble," she purred. "Or two. Something to see you through the next few weeks."

The bedclothes slipped from her hands, and Celia stood before Charles tipsy and hopeful, entirely naked. She was, he admitted, the most exciting, sensual creature he had seen in some time. Her skin glowed warmly in the candlelight, and her hair was slightly damp, as if she came fresh from her bath. Celia always smelled wonderful, Charles remembered. Newly bathed, a light sprinkling of perfume . . .

"Mmm," she murmured, moving forward to put her arms around his neck. "I know just what you want."

Seeing the bed behind her, Charles had a flash of memory, the memory of another woman who had been in his rooms today. In the present circumstances it was a distraction, as good a straw to grasp as any. He took the marchioness by the shoulders. "Celia," he said slowly, "what happened to the new governess?"

She giggled and hiccuped again. "Who?"

"Miss . . . Miss Phillips. Has she recovered?"

Celia frowned and sat down on the bed. "Oh. Her. Well,

you ought to know better than I! She was in *your* room." The marchioness sniffed suspiciously. "Oh, heavens, don't tell me she was lying on this coverlet!"

Seeing her distaste, Charles felt wicked inspiration strike. "I believe she was sick on it only twice."

"Oh!" She glared at him. "Never mind that," she said. "It's a thick carpet, and I've no objection to the floor."

"Celia. What happened to Miss Phillips?"

"Oh! A pox on the stupid chit! I don't know what happened to her and I don't care!" Her voice petulant, betraying impatience, Celia stood and tried to run her hands down his arms. To his amazement, Charles felt nothing.

"Mrs. Tiggs had James move her to her own room—"

"Well, there you have it, then. Mrs. Tiggs took care of her," said Celia.

"—but has anyone checked on her since?"

She shrugged.

Charles felt suddenly weary and was losing the energy necessary to humor the marchioness. "I've had a long day, Lady Sinclair," he said. "I think it is past time for you to leave."

"Charles," said the marchioness, "you think too much."

"I dare say you are correct."

Celia straightened up, yawned, and unexpectedly gave in. She laughed softly. "Oh, darling, very well. You win this time." Grabbing her silk wrapper she fastened it swiftly around her waist. "There'll be other nights, you know."

"Hmm," said Charles, and the marchioness—wobbling slightly—left.

Helène found a rather nice woolen shawl in one of the drawers of the tallboy. It didn't clash too dreadfully with the sarcanet, and she tried a number of ways of arranging it about her shoulders for best effect. A lace fichu tucked into the bodice would have helped even more, thought Helène. A small mirror above the wash basin revealed collarbones that jutted alarmingly from under her pale skin.

It would have to do. She sat on the bed and finished the last of the cheese scones, sighing in contentment. Her stomach felt reasonably full for the first time in . . . months, anyway. Perhaps being the employee of a great house wouldn't be so bad. Helène wondered how old the Sinclair children were, and what the family expected of a governess. Her father, of course, had been no help with these details.

"But I cannot leave you!" Helène protested. "Bedfordshire is two days journey from the city!"

"A day and a half, m' love, a day and a half," said her father, a flicker of his usual bonhomie in evidence through the devastation of his illness. " 'Twas your Aunt Matilde's dyin' wish, as you know well."

"Father, I know nothing of being a governess."

" 'Twas arranged long ago. Now, run along—" Her father began to cough, and Helène helped him sit up in the bed. When the spasm was over, he spoke again, gently—

"You know I never meant for you t' be a servant t' some miserable toff. Tears me up inside, it does. But I'm near t' gone—"

"Father—"

"Ach, did I raise you t' be a ninny? I'm dyin', and in London you'll be set a whore—or you'll starve."

At the memory of his voice, tears started to Helène's eyes. Her father was capable of speaking with a refined accent, learned—so Aunt Matilde said—during the years her mother was alive, but during times of stress, and then sickness, his speech returned to its hardscrabble roots.

Did I raise you t' be a ninny?

Nathaniel Phillips had worked hard and fought to give his daughter everything he could, and they had made do quite nicely—father, daughter, and aunt—until the last years had brought a double calamity. First, Matilde's consumption had taken much of their money, and then, this past year, her father's own illness had finished the rest. Helène's aunt had originally spoken of a situation with the Marquess of Luton not long before her death, and later it had seemed a wonderful idea; a chance, even, to send a bit of extra money back to her father in London. But Helène had been unable to leave him in town, sick and alone, and it was not until Mr. Phillips was clearly dying, and the last few pounds of their savings nearly gone, that she had summoned the nerve to write Lord Sinclair.

'Twas arranged long ago—

She had thought her father's words no more than the fantasy of a sick man but, to Helène's surprise, her request for a position was accepted almost immediately. So here she was, a governess in Bedfordshire. But where were her charges? And why had no-one enquired about her presence?

And why would a marquess have been willing to hire an impoverished and inexperienced young female, sight unseen? The arrangement was most odd. She supposed it was not impossible that Aunt Matilde had maintained some friendships among the *ton,* still—

Helène shook her head, banishing these worries for the moment. "Well begun is half done," she murmured to herself, echoing one of Mr. Phillips's favorite maxims, and thinking that there was no more time to waste on questions or regrets. She would perform her duties at Luton as best she was able. What else could she do?

Taking a deep breath, Helène reached once more into the soggy portmanteau and fished out a small book. It was a well-used, dog-eared volume, bound modestly in red buckram and inscribed with gold lettering:

Conduct and Deportment for the Modern Governess
by Miss E. A. Chaldecott

Helène had found Miss Chaldecott's manual in one of London's many second-hand book sellers the day before she left for Bedfordshire. At a shilling and six pence it was almost beyond her means, but she had raided a long-hoarded stash of pennies and made the purchase, eager for any guidance in her new profession.

She wondered who Miss Chaldecott was, and whether she had been a governess herself. Surely if the book had been published it must contain reliable information. Helène turned to the first chapter hoping, if nothing else, for brevity. She was not disappointed.

"The position of governess in the well-born household is quite straightforward and of two-fold disposition," wrote Miss Chaldecott. *"First, you are to instruct the children according to the wishes of their parents. Secondly, you are to keep the children from the eye and ear of these same parents, and to attract as little notice as possible yourself."*

Perfect, thought Helène. "Attract as little notice as possible—" There was nothing she would like better. She read for a few more minutes. Miss Chaldecott seemed to have no high opinion of the basic common sense, not to mention the morals, of the average governess.

"A governess who finds herself in an incommodious condition

must expect to be thrown out at once, without reference."

An incommodious condition? Helène could hazard a guess as to the meaning, but since she had no expectation of attracting male notice, she read quickly on.

"You may hope to have few friends, if any. The common servants are below your touch, and the family, above it."

Few friends . . . It seemed to be a dreary occupation, but, considering her life during the past few months, dreary might be a step in the right direction. Sighing, Helène laid the book on her nightstand. If she was to accomplish any of Miss Chaldecott's directives, it would be necessary to *find* the children. Gathering the shawl from the tallboy around her shoulders, she determined to find the housekeeper—Mrs. Tiggs?— and ask for help.

Helène heard, just then, a soft scratching at her door. She pulled it open and found herself looking into the friendly, open face of a burly young man.

"Miss . . . Miss Phillips?" He seemed confused.

Helène recognized his odd costume—a silverish jacket and sky-blue breeches—as house livery. A footman, she supposed, having little first-hand experience of servants in a great household.

"Yes?" She smiled at him, and was rewarded with a great, ear-splitting grin.

"Hmm, Miss Phillips, I'm James."

"How do you do?" said Helène, hoping that the footman could give her some assistance. "Am I being summoned?"

"Miss?" James was clearly confused.

"Yes, well . . . how can I help you?"

"Help me?"

A more straightforward approach was needed, decided Helène. "James," she said, "why are you here?"

This produced the desired effect. "Ah, yes, miss. I'm t'

take you t' Miss Alice and Master Peter," said the footman, adding, "If you please?"

The children. Well enough, then.

"Excellent," she told James. "I'm entirely at your disposal."

"Miss?"

"That's fine, James," said Helène. She pulled the shawl tightly around her shoulders. "Lead on."

James headed down a narrow corridor, dimly lit with tallow candles. Helène watched carefully for small details in their surroundings, in hopes of being able to find her way back to her bedchamber. Her bedchamber . . . Helène realized that she had no idea of how she had arrived in that room in the first place. How strange. Well, there was no help for it now since James surely didn't know.

After making several turns, and descending a narrow staircase, they arrived in a carpeted hallway that seemed more familiar. A tall, dark-haired man turned the corner a few steps in front of them, and stopped for a moment, staring at Helène. Memory flooded back and, blushing hotly, she found herself rooted to the spot.

The man on horseback. The man who had stranded her in the snow—

His eyes flicked dismissively over her dress as he passed by James and Helène without a word. How rude—! Her chin went up of its own accord, and she resisted a sudden, childish impulse to turn around and stick out her tongue.

James remained oblivious. "Here you are, Miss Phillips," he said, as they approached a double door of polished beech. The footman smiled cheerfully, relieved, she suspected, to have successfully accomplished his task.

"Thank you very much," she told him. "This is the nursery, I assume?"

"Oh, yes, miss," said James—and the door burst open.

"Is she here? Is she here, James? Is this her? Oh, please, miss, are you our new governess?"

Two shining, eager faces looked up at Helène as if she was the long-awaited answer to prayer; one small girl, perhaps six or seven years of age, with blond ringlets falling almost to her waist, and a somewhat younger boy with a smudge of dirt on his nose. Both children were bouncing with excitement.

"She's beautiful!" declared the little boy. Helène found herself much charmed. At least a child could be counted on to look past outward trappings—

"It is her, isn't it, James! It is!" said the girl.

"This is Miss Phillips," said James. "Miss Alice, Master Peter, say your howdos."

"How do you do, Miss Phillips!" came the duet.

"I am quite well, thank you," said Helène. "And I am very glad to meet you—" She happened to glance at the footman and saw that James looked worried.

"I'm . . . I'm sorry, miss," he said, "but I wasn't told anything else—"

"We'll be just fine, James," said Helène. "You may leave. The children can show me around the nursery."

"Oh, yes, please, Miss Phillips!"

And so, bouncing and chattering happily, they did.

What a dreadful costume, thought Charles, watching the two children disappear with the young woman into the nursery. What could Jonathan have been thinking, to have hired such a drab for a governess? That dress is even more unfortunate than the dirty sack she was wearing yesterday. She's entirely too thin—

Lord Quentin stopped himself, realizing that a woman who'd apparently not had enough to eat for months could hardly be expected to have money for clothes. Frowning, he wondered whether Celia would attempt some contrivance to dismiss her. But, what was it Mrs. Tiggs had said about the two previous governesses?

—pretty and young, and as near t' quality as makes some people nervous, if you get my meanin'—

Perhaps the marchioness would actually welcome a female so little able to steal the attention from herself.

Still, someone in Miss Phillips's position was expected to be of respectable family—the younger daughter of some country squire, perhaps—and the girl clearly did not qualify on that account. Good breeding was more than elegant cheekbones, or long, auburn hair and green eyes . . .

Bother it all, where was he? Charles found that he had walked straight past the door to his own rooms while in contemplation of the various shortcomings of the dowdy and unsatisfactory Miss Helène Phillips.

Chapter Four

The week at Luton passed quickly for Charles, with evenings reserved for various amusements and the days spent closeted with the marquess in his study. Jonathan had little feel for the practical matters of country life, and this past year had been a bad one for both the barley crop and the lambs, leaving the marquess even more distracted than usual by matters of business.

'Twould have been better, Charles thought, if the marquess would tend to his wife and let the steward worry over the sheep. But Jonathan wished to keep much of the work in his own hands, and frequently sought Lord Quentin's advice on the running of the Luton estate. This was not an aspect of their relationship that Charles always enjoyed, and he rued even more the absence of Jonathan's sister, Lady Pamela. Superior to Lord Sinclair in wit, Pam could be counted upon to sway her brother in matters of common sense.

Charles dealt with Celia by the simple expedient of retiring immediately after each night's entertainment—and locking his door. Lady Sinclair pouted prettily during the day, and bided her time. Charles knew that he had not heard the last from the Marchioness of Luton.

If Lord Quentin occasionally wondered how Miss Helène Phillips was faring in the nursery he did not admit it to himself. Jonathan never mentioned the girl and had quickly changed the subject with a bored wave of his hand, the one time Charles had asked about her.

"Mmm, yes. I'm sure she is doing quite well, quite well, I'm sure . . ."

Charles had seen the governess a few times in passing, and the glances she bestowed upon him on these occasions were decidedly cool. The nervy chit. Miss Phillips was dressed as poorly as ever, and Lord Quentin felt that she showed far less embarrassment about this than she ought.

On the day before he was to leave for Tavelstoke, Lord Quentin's morning ride took him farther afield than he had intended, and it was past noon before he and Alcibiades were once again in sight of the house. Snow had been falling off and on for most of the week, but there had been little wind, so that Luton Court and its surroundings now lay spread out below him like a Christmas fantasy. Luton was not the equal of Tavelstoke in the restraint or refinement of its architecture, of course. The numerous balconies and bay windows of the main hall—combined with copious amounts of iron-work scrolling—suggested, if anything, a rather baroque sensibility. Still, at times like this, one sensed what the builder must have had in mind. The estate looked marvelous, gleaming in a blanket of snow.

Sunny or not, the winter's chill had crept through the thick wool of his cloak, and Charles found himself anticipating a good fire and a glass of warmed brandy. He clucked at Alcibiades. Removing his feet from these cold boots would be worth braving yet another episode of Celia's pique when she learned that he still planned to leave on the morrow.

As he approached the stables, Charles heard all manner of odd noises from beyond the larger paddock—squeals and shrieks, and other . . . thudding sounds that he couldn't identify. Leaving the stallion in the care of a senior groom, Charles rounded the corner to find two small, snow-covered children and one equally snow-covered adult, in the middle of some kind of altercation.

What was this?

"Miss Helène! Watch out!" A child's voice—

A snowball, launched by the smaller of the two children, landed squarely in the middle of the adult's back. A woman, Lord Quentin now realized. A burst of feminine laughter rang out as she turned and released a missile of her own. More shrieking and whooping from the children, but Charles's attention was now diverted. The hood of the woman's cape had fallen back, revealing the slightly disheveled figure of Miss Helène Phillips.

Alice and Peter. The governess. Of course.

Thud. Giggles erupted from the direction of the two children, and Charles looked down at the front of his fine, many-caped riding coat in shock. He had been hit by a *snowball*.

Afterwards, Lord Quentin could never explain why he became so angry. Snowball fights were a regular feature of his own youth, and these were Jonathan's children, after all; he had known them from infancy. Only last summer he had played swing-the-monkey with Peter until his arms ached, launching the boy again and again into the river and getting drenched for his troubles.

Undoubtedly, his reaction would have been different if the children had been the only participants. But the sight of the governess raised his ire. *She* was involved, and how dare she—

"Oh! My lord!" said Miss Phillips, pushing a tangle of curls back from her face and dropping him a brief, snowy curtsey. Her nose was red from the cold, and Lord Quentin had the impression she was hiding a smile. The two children had rushed up and were peeping out at him from behind her skirts, still giggling.

"Lord 'Wentin," said the smaller child, only now recognizable as Peter— "Lord 'Wentin, come have a snowball fight with us! It's fun!"

That was quite enough.

"Peter—" began the governess.

"Your father has not employed Miss Phillips for the purposes of fun," stated Charles.

Good grief. Had he truly uttered something so rudely pompous? The words hung in the cold air for a moment's shocked silence. The governess frowned, and Charles, despite his inner chagrin, gave her a quelling look. Alice and Peter stared at him, their eyes wide and anxious. Lord Quentin found this reaction even more annoying. He wasn't an ogre. Children adored him!

"I'm quite sure Lord Sinclair would have no objection to his children stretching their legs," said Miss Phillips, finding her voice. "They've spent the entire morning indoors." Her tone was unrepentant, and Lord Quentin became convinced that the governess was laughing at him. This was unacceptable.

"You know nothing of the matter, *mademoiselle*," he said.

"Of what matter?" came her retort. "I know nothing of my own profession?"

"Apparently you do not!" Charles, provoked, now decided that it was time to put this headstrong young woman firmly in her place. "This is Luton Court, not the local London middens, and these are the children of a marquess. I should report this questionable behavior to Lord Sinclair."

Alice started to cry. Miss Phillips—who had narrowed her eyes at his peremptory words—bent down to comfort the girl.

"Hush, sweetheart. It's all right."

"But— He said—"

"Take Peter in and warm up. I'm sure Mrs. Tiggs will have fresh scones and raspberry jam for you, if you ask please."

The sniffling stopped.

"Come on, Peter," said Alice, and the two children—chins thrust into the air, refusing to look in Charles's direction—ran off toward the house. The governess's watchful gaze remained on them until they reached the kitchen doorstep; then she rounded on Lord Quentin with blazing eyes.

"You can't possibly be that much of a prig!" she said. "Alice is but seven years old! Peter is five! Should they have no time whatsoever to play?"

Charles, who had just begun to consider that one or two things he had said might have been a bit unfair, felt the renewed flare of anger.

"Whether they play or not is hardly your decision," he told her. "As the marquess's friend, I can assure you that Lord Sinclair would want to be consulted—"

To his surprise, the governess looked suddenly uneasy.

"Lord Sinclair has not yet spoken to me concerning his children," she said slowly. "Nor has Lady Sinclair. I am carrying on as I think best."

"Not spoken to you—?" Lord Quentin stopped himself. That was indeed odd. Jonathan had never doted on his children—tending toward the same cool detachment with which he recently favored his wife—but it was not like him to ignore their care in the hands of a new governess.

And as for Celia . . . Charles had heard the marchioness say on several occasions that young children made her nervous. She had tried, he knew, to make some approach to Alice and Peter, but with little success. They seemed to sense the marchioness's discomfort, and had yet to welcome their stepmother into their lives. Lady Sinclair had probably thought her husband should be the one to sort out a new governess. Why had he not?

"The marquess is a very busy man," he told Miss Phillips,

trying to think of some excuse that might make sense. "He will no doubt consult with you as his schedule permits. In the meantime—"

"In the meantime, I shall do as I see best for the children. And what I think best is none of your affair."

Lord Quentin looked down his nose at her, glaring. He had little previous experience with governesses, but he was the heir to an earldom, and she was—she was nobody.

"I think you will find that I can make it my business in short order," he told Miss Phillips. "And that the Marquess of Luton will be a great deal more interested in my opinion of the matter than your own. So I would suggest—"

He stopped abruptly, unable to believe his eyes. The girl, with a defiant expression, had stomped her foot, and started to walk away. No one in Charles's experience had ever dared walk away from him while he was still speaking.

"Miss Phillips, I am not through—"

"Lord Quentin." The governess stopped, turning to address him. He caught a flash of green, angry eyes. "Lord Quentin, I'd like to ask a favor of you."

A favor! Charles forced himself to rein in his anger and ignore those eyes. Lud, but the girl could be beautiful. He cocked an eyebrow at the governess, saying nothing.

"When you speak with Lord Sinclair concerning my . . . position, please tell him that both his children are marvelously bright and making an excellent start to their studies. Peter's maths are perhaps a bit weak, but he's very young and I've no doubt he will come right along. Alice will be speaking French like a *parisienne* within the year."

"Miss Phillips—"

"And they have both been very lonely. If he wishes to dismiss me it would be best for the children if I were replaced as soon as possible." The governess turned on her heel and left.

★ ★ ★ ★ ★

What an insufferable man! Helène, fuming, tramped through the snow and back into the house. Make it his business! Well, he had certainly done *that*, hadn't he, the pompous, condescending . . . jackass! She cursed Lord Quentin *sotto voce* all the way to the nursery, trying to drown out the little voice carrying an undercurrent of stark fear.

If the marquess dismissed her, she had no place to go.

"I wish you'd stay, old man," Jonathan told Charles. "Celia has been on about it for days. She'll be devastated if you leave before Christmas."

Indeed, thought Lord Quentin, with an inward sigh. He had yet to decide if the marquess was so wrapped up in current estate matters that he didn't notice his wife's growing flirtatiousness, or saw it and remained indifferent. The two had once been much in love, he knew. Had the glow faded so quickly from their relationship?

Perhaps Celia had carried her games too far.

"Branscomb has sent me a list of improvements needed over the next year," Charles informed his friend. "Some of them should really be in place before the coldest months. Indeed, they should have been done well before now."

"Another few weeks can make no difference, surely."

"Unless 'tis your cottage missing a piece of its roof."

"Mmm." Jonathan nodded, but Lord Quentin knew he was unconvinced. Cottages? Roofs? Luton's roof did not leak, why should anyone else's do so? Charles did not believe that Lord Sinclair was completely wanting in intelligence—he had managed to survive Oxford after all—but he was stolid and unimaginative in his thinking. Latin had provided fewer problems for the marquess than literature and its confusion of fictional characters.

"I'll be back shortly after Boxing Day," he told Jonathan. "Father saw to the servants' gifts personally, and I'll do no less."

Tradition and duty were two aspects of a nobleman's life that Lord Sinclair comprehended very well. "Of course," he said, surrendering the point with grace. "Celia and I will look forward to your return."

"Ah. Yes," said Lord Quentin. He left the library shortly afterward, not realizing until much later that he had never mentioned anything to Jonathan about the governess.

Helène relaxed back into her bed with a contented sigh, all thoughts of a certain high-handed lord forgotten for the moment. She looked at the supper tray, realizing that she had—oh, the wonder of it all—left a bit of meat pastry uneaten. Three meals that day, and tomorrow, too, no doubt! An entire wax candle at her disposal, and a warm, clean bed.

All that I lack, thought Helène, *is a book. I'm not complaining. But with an entire candle, and without Papa to see to in the middle of the night, when he came home roaring and jug-bitten from the Cook's Goose—*

Helène took a slow breath, her pleasant mood threatening to evaporate. Her poor father. Her poor, charming but often imprudent father. Convinced to the last that he could once again, someday, be a "Purveyor of Fine Équipage" to the mighty of the *ton.* Even as he sickened, and they marched down to their last few pounds and bits of jewelry to sell.

Nathaniel Phillips had been a puzzle to many who knew him. Orphaned as a boy, raised by a country parson and his good wife to have fair manners and a share of book learning, he had eventually been apprenticed to a carriagemaker in London. Years of providing fine carriages to people who were no better in wit than himself, but who would barely deign to touch his hand, had left him untouched until her mother died. Then the bitterness had surfaced, and in force—

No. She didn't want to think about Papa right now. If she was to be thrown out into the snow tomorrow she could still enjoy tonight. A nice, long book was all that was missing, and Helène was determined to find one. The library, according to Alice and Peter, was almost directly beneath her own room, two floors away, and if she used the back staircase it should be easy to slip in and out unseen. Helène felt convinced that the fine lords and ladies of the house would now be doing—well, whatever it was that they did in the evening. Playing cards, perhaps. Or gambling large sums of money on trifles. Surely not reading.

The Luton Court library struck Lord Quentin as the most unexpected part of the marquess's estate. There were times one could swear Jonathan didn't have two thoughts in his head, but with regard to books Charles could detect no fault in his friend's judgement. The collection of medieval illuminated manuscripts, for example, was marvelous. All under lock and key, of course. Charles's interest this evening was in something more prosaic, something to lull him to sleep.

The slightest breath of a draught stirred the fire, and Lord Quentin looked around to see—

The devil take it. Lady Sinclair, still dressed in her evening gown—thank heavens—but with hair *déshabillé*, closed the library door. She set the lock and stood eyeing him without a word.

Silence. It seemed to stretch on forever.

"Good evening," said Lord Quentin *en fin*. He made no move to approach the marchioness and suddenly felt quite tired of the whole situation. Had the marchioness expected to find him here? Was she dipping deep yet again? "I was about to retire, so I shall leave you in peace."

"Oh! Well, there's no need to run, my dear," said Lady Sinclair, with a light laugh. "I'm in search of fresh reading material, not you."

"Afraid the books might escape?" said Charles, with a pointed glance at the locked door.

"Pah!" Celia's mouth turned down in a pout. "Charles, I can't see the problem. It's not as if Jonathan pays the slightest attention to anything I do—"

Lord Quentin wished that just *once* Jonathan would listen to his advice concerning women. "I'm sure that the marquess—" he began, but Celia waved her hand in furious dismissal.

"I don't want to hear about the marquess," she cried. "Not tonight."

Drink, and the lateness of the hour, had combined to make her rather cross. Charles was annoyed himself, not the least with Jonathan. Lady Sinclair was a beautiful woman, and—as he well knew—a delicious bed partner. How long did the marquess expect him to act the saint?

Still, the rules of the game must be followed; honor and loyalty to one's friends, and even consideration for the lady in question, who was no doubt once again drunk. Charles summoned self-control. There was really only one way to convince Celia that he was not interested. A cruel way, perhaps—

"Please excuse me, my lady," he said. "I find that I've lost all interest in present company."

It was a lie as he spoke it. Nevertheless, the words hung in the air, certain to infuriate, and the marchioness responded in kind.

"Not interested! What humbug! Who do you think you're looking for Charles? A milk-and-water miss who'll take your money and do her duty in bed? I'm the only woman who appreciates you for exactly what you have to give."

Lady Sinclair had edged toward Lord Quentin as she spoke; she now stood only inches from him and raised her arms to wrap around his neck. Charles braced himself, hardly breathing, refusing to give her the satisfaction of seeing him react. There was enough truth in the marchioness's words to make him uncomfortable. He had never met a woman who entered into the spirit of a physical relationship more enthusiastically than Celia Sinclair. He'd often thought that marriage to the type of schoolroom female she had just described would be nigh unsupportable.

He was not currently considering marriage, of course. A lifetime of feminine protests and shocked glances, sharing a bed with a wife who flinched at his every touch. It had never struck Charles as a situation to be much sought after.

He studied Celia's face, seeing the doubt and uncertainty that belied her outwardly brazen manner. Lady Sinclair had traded on her charms all her life. She knew no other path of communication with the opposite sex, and was, in consequence, ever vulnerable to them. One could almost feel sorry—

The marchioness frowned. An unpleasant thought had apparently just occurred to her.

"Unless you're having a bit on the side," said Celia, her voice becoming petulant. "I know you, Charles, you're never long without company." She paused, obviously running through the list of possible candidates in her mind. "Who *is* it? Lucinda Blankenship wouldn't dare cross me—"

"As you say."

Lady Sinclair gasped suddenly and stepped back from him. Charles started to straighten his neckcloth, thought better of it.

"Oh! It's that governess, isn't it!" cried Celia, pointing a shaking finger somewhere in the direction of his chest. "You've taken that . . . that *girl* to your bed!" Her voice rose to a screech. "Well, I won't have it Charles, do you hear me? I simply won't have it! I'll sack her at once!"

For a moment, Charles was too stunned to reply. The governess! Why had the marchioness picked Helène Phillips, of all people, as the object of her jealousy? He was both stung by the accusation that he would bed a chit of that class—there were rules about such behavior, as well—and outraged that Celia would threaten to dismiss her on his account. His anger grew. He was tired; tired and ashamed of the temptation he still felt each time he looked at Celia. The woman was married to his best friend, and this was enough—

"I've no interest in some dirty little nobody," he drawled, the only response he could think of that might divert Celia's attention from the unfortunate Miss Phillips. Charles forced himself to keep his voice low and calm. "But I've also no interest in you." He moved toward the door.

"I'll discharge her without reference! I can promise you of it!"

"Go right ahead," Lord Quentin shot back. "And also explain it to Jonathan, if you will. I could hardly care less." He twisted the key in the lock, opened the door and left, shutting it firmly behind him.

"Oh!" cried Celia. "Oh!" Other words seemed to escape her. She picked up a porcelain vase from the mantle and threw it at the door, where it shattered. She stomped angrily across the room, and then also left, slamming the door.

Helène heard the library door close a second time, and let out a deep, shaky breath. Perhaps her heart would stop pounding in a few minutes, and she might dare to leave her hiding place. There had been plenty of room behind one of the floor-length velvet drapes that covered the library windows, although she had been shaking so much she was sure that Lord Quentin or the marchioness would notice.

Stupid. Why had she bothered to hide in the first place? It might have been a bit awkward, of course—meeting Lord Sinclair, or one of his guests at such a late hour—but a bit of awkwardness would have been far preferable to the scene she had just overheard.

Some dirty little nobody. Tears threatened, and she dashed them away in annoyance. One more arrogant, self-important lord and his odious lady. And to be threatened with dismissal twice in one day! The position of governess seemed a great deal less secure than one might have imagined, and Helène wondered if either Lord Quentin or Lady Sinclair would really take their complaints to the marquess. Surely if she was to be insulted on such a regular basis, Helène would never survive, for her temper would break and she would tell these people just what she thought of them.

Some dirty little nobody. She didn't care what a man like that thought. She just didn't care.

In the evening of the next day Lord Quentin rode through the gates of Tavelstoke, and for the first time allowed himself a sigh of relief. He had gotten a late start and it had been a long, cold ride, and he was very glad to be home. Alcibiades, who only minutes earlier had been showing signs of fatigue, was now almost prancing in anticipation of warm stables and a double measure of oats.

"Hang on, old friend," Charles told him. "Stevens will have you fixed up in a trice." The stallion nickered softly in reply.

The house loomed in front of him, the brickwork and slate roof luminous in the rays of the setting sun. Tavelstoke

Manor, large and formally laid out as it was, was a welcome refuge after the week at Luton Court. His spirits lifted, as always, at the sight of the tall, sash windows framed with a tracery of honeysuckle vine. Charles had spent almost nothing of his childhood here; still, it was home.

Unfortunately, 'twas often a quiet home now, even with the three score servants needed to maintain the estate and its grounds. The old earl had ever disliked traveling, and, being fond of the London entertainments, these days rarely left town. Charles missed his father; despite having almost no interests whatsoever in common, they rubbed along together quite well. He was almost equally fond of his stepmother, knowing that Susannah had saved the earl from a lifetime of melancholy after the desertion, and later death, of his mother.

It would be a lonely Christmas indeed without them.

You needn't stay here long, a niggling voice reminded Lord Quentin. The marquess expected him back shortly after Christmas, and this time for an extended stay. Charles sighed. Luton Court was acclaimed for its winter house parties, and they often lasted near to February. An entire month under the same roof as Celia Sinclair? It was an alarming thought, but Lord Quentin decided he would worry about it later. The steps of Tavelstoke Manor rose immediately before him, and he threw the reins to the waiting stable boy. Alcibiades was led off and Charles barely managed to find his own rooms, and remove his boots, before falling into bed, soundly asleep.

There would be other, more restless nights in the weeks to come, nights when the image of Celia Sinclair would take up residence behind his eyelids. And he would find little relief when, on occasion, the marchioness faded from his mind, only to be replaced with the likeness of another woman, a slender chit with auburn hair and green eyes.

Chapter Five

The morning light streaming into the bedroom windows assured Lady Pamela that she was now at Luton Court, and no longer in the sooty pall of London. The winter light in town never streams anywhere, Pam thought to herself. It limps along, if one is lucky. She pulled on a silk wrapper and opened the doors to her small balcony, feeling invigorated, as usual, by the country air. Even the *contretemps* with the coach yesterday—a trace had snapped and caused a horrible tangle that had taken ages to sort out—was fading quickly from memory. Luton Court at Christmas was warmth and security, one unchanging tradition in an occasionally tumultuous life.

Why do I feel so lonely? Pam asked herself, and then stopped, a *frisson* of shock traveling the length of her spine. *Lonely? I'm here at Luton, with family and friends—of course I don't feel lonely.* She looked out at the distant hills, covered in gleaming caps of snow. The holidays had been magical for the children of the country household. Pamela remembered waking to the hush of an early Christmas morning, creeping downstairs to see the huge linen-draped tables that had appeared overnight, as if by magic, in the grand entrance hall. Tables of gifts and of every kind of food and drink, including one entirely devoted to spun-sugar candies, covered the marble floor. She remembered the thrill of anticipation, a happiness almost too great to be endured.

Things seemed different as an adult. Oh, Jonathan was glad enough to see her, Lady Pamela supposed. Even Celia had managed a smile or two of greeting, followed almost immediately by complaints about the lateness of the hour. Pam and Amanda's arrival had been delayed well into the evening as a result of their carriage mishap, and Celia, as they were shortly to discover, was still in high dudgeon over Lord Quentin's departure earlier that day.

"He's gone," Lady Detweiler had told her, wandering into Pamela's sitting room last night, one hand cradling a huge snifter of brandy. At Luton less than an hour, Amanda had wasted no time in securing the latest *on dits* from her maid. "Left for Tavelstock just this morning."

"Who's gone?" Pam had been supervising the unpacking of several trunks of clothing; her attention was currently diverted by the sight of a rip in the hem of a fine watered silk.

"Charles Quentin, you goose, who else?"

Lady Pam yawned and set the dress aside. Her own stitching was as fine as any abigail's; she'd repair the small tear tomorrow herself. "Jonathan said that he would need to be spending some time at the estate. The old earl, you know."

"Yes, well yawn all you may, I don't see any likely candidates in the remaining lot."

"Likely candidates? What about Lord Burgess? He's had a *tendre* for you for ages, you know."

Jeremy Burgess and Lady Detweiler enjoyed a mutual loathing. It was an old joke, and Amanda sputtered. "Pah. We are not talking about me as you know full well. And as for Lord Burgess—"

"Well, I think we should. Now, Viscount Dreybridge is no longer available, but—"

"Fustian. How long will he be gone, d' you think?"

"Viscount Dreybridge? He's still here."

"You," said Amanda, "are being deliberately obtuse. Well, never mind. Lord Quentin will be back on the new year, although dawn tomorrow wouldn't be soon enough for your dear sister-in-law. Let's hope she hasn't scared him off permanently."

"Charles should be able to handle Celia."

"You'd think so, wouldn't you? What is it about men, anyway? Even the intelligent ones seem to lose all power of reason at the sight of a plump pair of breasts."

"I don't know what it is," sighed Pam. "I wish I did."

Lady Pamela now shut the balcony doors, and returned to the dressing room to complete her morning's *toilette*. Amanda wouldn't be out of bed for another hour, at least. This would be a good chance to find her brother and catch up on the family news.

Hélène tramped back to the house through a bright carpet of new-fallen snow. She had woken up early that day, feeling a sudden urge to explore her new home. She had seen almost nothing of the larger grounds of the estate since her arrival, and a morning of good exercise had proved exactly the activity to raise her spirits.

Bright sunlight pierced the cold morning sky, and the crisp air was pleasant enough if you'd spent the past hour climbing to the top of the nearest hill. The grounds of Luton had stretched like a glittering wonderland below her, the Lea River a crystalline ribbon running to the north of the main gardens. A thick woods of pine nearby looked particularly inviting, and she planned to explore it later that week.

Hélène brushed at her skirt, which showed the evidence of a recent encounter with knee-high snowdrifts. Her mood, which had fallen precipitously after the scene she had overheard in the library two nights before, was now almost cheerful. If she was fated to be a governess, there were surely worse places to be.

But the hour or so out in the fresh air had flown by, and Alice and Peter would soon be ready for schoolwork. Helène kicked up flurries of snow with each footstep as she hurried along. She should have just enough time to return to her room and exchange the heavy cloak for a shawl before meeting the children in the nursery.

Lady Pamela found her brother tucking into an enormous plate of cheese scones and bacon.

"Good morning," said Lady Pamela to the marquess. They were both early risers, and often had the breakfast table to themselves.

"Mmph," replied Jonathan, over a mouthful of bacon. Then—"I rather doubt it."

Pam laughed. "Don't tell me Celia is still cross over Lord Quentin's early departure. Too dreary even for her!"

This comment on his wife's petulant nature went unremarked by the marquess. "No, the latest crisis isn't Charles, as a matter of fact. It's the new governess."

"Miss Fitzpatrick?"

"Celia sacked Miss Fitzpatrick weeks ago," said her brother, reaching for another scone. "I insisted she be replaced before the holidays."

"And the new governess is even prettier?" The entire household was aware of Celia's jealousy of attractive young women.

Jonathan laughed. "Not prettier. Dirtier."

"Dirtier!"

"Yes. She showed up unexpectedly from London, standing on the front steps, practically in rags. Celia claimed she smelled like greasy chicken."

Lady Pamela stared at him.

"Apparently, her attire has not improved in the meantime, and Celia has been complaining without interruption."

A new governess—employed from where? Town? It's fortunate that I arrived no later, thought Pamela. Between Jonathan and Celia, the poor woman might have ended up back out in the snow. But what was this about dirty clothing? She cupped her chin in her hands and thought for a moment.

"Jonathan," she said at last. Her brother looked up warily.

"Mmm?"

"Jonathan, what do you mean she showed up out of nowhere? Didn't you send the coach for her?"

"Mmm. The coach?"

"Yes, the coach. Where did she come from? London? Good heavens, Jonathan, don't tell me she traveled on the *mail coach*."

"Oh. Yes. Well, no. Many people have their own coaches these days, you know—"

Pamela snorted. "I'm sure a governess has no such thing. Are you telling me this poor woman walked all the way to Luton from Cotter's post? In November?"

The marquess appeared flustered. "I really don't think—"

"Oh, Jonathan." Pamela sighed. Her brother was a kind soul at heart, but sometimes incredibly obtuse. So accustomed was the marquess to a life of privilege that problems such as poverty and hunger simply failed to register. The steward and tenants of Luton Court had long since learned to broach any major requests for assistance through Lady Pamela. Although a generous landlord in his own, erratic way, Jonathan sometimes forgot that such creatures as tenants existed.

Pam stood up suddenly. "Where is she?"

"Where is who?" asked Jonathan.

"The governess!"

"Ah. Well, you see, I'm not sure—"

Closing her eyes, Lady Pamela blew out a long puff of breath. "Oh, bother it all. Never mind. I'll talk to Mrs. Tiggs myself." She left the room in a flurry of skirts.

The marquess watched Lady Pamela leave. 'Twas a shame he hadn't thought to send a coach, he now realized. But the letter from Miss Phillips announcing the time of her arrival had been delivered almost a fortnight ago, and he never seemed able to remember such details for long.

And it wouldn't do for him to take a personal interest in the governess. Jonathan remained sitting at the table for some time, his ostensibly worried expression slowly replaced by a half smile. He had chosen his words with care. He knew his sister, and felt confident that Miss Helène Phillips would presently be in good hands.

Pins in mouth, Helène was attempting to marshal her hair back into some sort of order when she heard a soft knock at her door. James? she wondered. Or perhaps the maid, bringing a fresh set of linens. Jabbing in the last hairpin, and hoping everything would stay in place for at least the morning, she walked over to open the door.

"Miss Phillips?"

Aphrodite, come to life, thought Helène. The woman standing in the doorway was dressed in a simple white morning gown of fine muslin. Her hair was a dazzling golden hue, and piled in thick ringlets on top of her head. She was smiling at Helène.

"Miss Phillips?" she repeated.

Helène realized that she had been staring in a most impolite manner. "Yes . . . Yes, my lady?"

"May I come in?" asked the goddess.

"Oh. Oh, of course . . . my lady," said Helène. "I'm afraid there is no chair."

The woman looked around and laughed. "Pah. A nice enough room, I'm sure, but *not* for the governess. You'll have to forgive Mrs. Tiggs, Miss Phillips. She was only acting according to her previous instructions. Apparently the last two governesses used this room. I can't imagine why . . ." She hesitated. "Well, perhaps I can. Let us say that the nursery at Luton Court is bothersomely close to the marquess and marchioness's suite."

"The nursery?" Helène brightened, thinking that at last someone was taking an interest in the children. But who was she?

"Yes. Of course, that's where you will stay as well. Not *in* the nursery, you understand." The lady smiled. "There are some very nice rooms next door. Quite convenient, but you will still have some privacy. Alice and Peter are well-behaved children, I dare say, but you'll not want them in your pocket every hour of the day."

Alice and Peter. How well did this person know the children? Who was she? Helène was about to ask when the woman noticed her portmanteau.

"Is this your bag?" she asked, sounding dubious.

"Ah, yes, Lady . . ." Helène trailed off.

"Oh, I beg your pardon!" The woman gave a another throaty, musical laugh. "It's the fault of Luton, I'm afraid. Every time I'm here for more than a day I become as hare-brained as my brother." The woman held out her hand. "I'm Pamela Sinclair, the marquess's sister."

"My lady." Helène dropped what she hoped was a serviceable curtsey.

"Oh, posh," said Lady Pamela. "You're the governess, not a scullery girl. I have high hopes for you, by the way. Sensible conversation, that sort of thing. Now come along and I'll show you to your rooms."

Helène hesitated.

"Oh, and leave the bag here, I should think. One of the footmen can collect it later."

Lady Pamela awoke sometime in the uncounted middle hours of the night, the dream so vivid that for a moment she thought herself back in London. She felt for the candle on her nightstand, but it had guttered out.

How odd, thought Pam. How very odd.

The old marchioness and her daughter were riding through Hyde Park. Pamela was a child of—seven or eight?— and she was in high alt to be allowed a carriage ride during the fashionable hours of the afternoon. It was a glorious day in the late spring, leafy green, the smells of London for once left behind. Pamela was restless. She wanted to jump down from the carriage and run through the daffodils, chasing butterflies. She wanted to climb a tree. Her mother rarely allowed such things.

"Oh, look, Mama, isn't it beautiful?" Pamela pointed—

A woman and a man in a carriage, painted gaily, silver and cream. Pamela had never seen these two people before. The man was handsome, his eyes sparkling with merriment. The woman was impossibly beautiful, red hair piled on her head in thick, shining curls. She inclined her head toward his, her hand resting on his shoulder, and Pamela heard the sound of male laughter. As the silver and cream carriage approached, the old marchioness hissed in anger—

The child Pamela wanted to talk to them. It was the most important thing in the world, to be able to talk to them. The adult

71

Pamela remembered that she was dreaming. She turned to her mother, to remonstrate, even as the child looked again toward the red-haired woman in the carriage . . .

The dream collapsed in a swirl of green and silver. The woman was Helène Phillips.

Chapter Six

The governess must be dressed well enough to be a credit to her employers, but in no wise well enough to be mistaken for one of them.

"Miss Phillips! Miss Phillips!"

Two small children ran across the room, both trying to jump into her arms at the same time. Helène heard soft laughter, and realized that Lady Pamela was already in the nursery. Alice and Peter adored their aunt, and for the last several weeks—ever since Lady Pam had arrived at Luton for the holidays—she had spent nearly as much time with them as had Helène herself.

"Careful, you two," said Helène, smiling down at Alice and Peter. "You wouldn't want to give your aunt the impression that I'm not teaching you manners."

"Indeed," said Lady Pamela, with another laugh. "I should be required to give your governess a severe scold if that were the case."

"Oh, no, Miss Phillips!" they chorused. The two sat down at the small study tables, doing their best to appear angelic. Alice was the tidy one, her blond hair held neatly behind her ears with a ribbon, her pinafore starched and clean. Peter, on the other hand, could never stay in proper order for long. Already this morning he had managed to acquire several smudges on the front of his shirt and one on his nose.

"We're ready for our schoolwork, Miss Phillips!"

In Peter's case, her name sounded more like "Miss

Phiwips" but then, Peter was only five and a half. His pronunciation drove seven-year-old Alice half crazy with frustration. She was forever trying to correct her younger brother, even though Helène had carefully explained about the stages of growing up, and how different children learned proper pronunciation at different ages.

"But he's saying it wrong!" Alice would wail.

"Someday Peter will say it correctly," Helène replied. "We just have to be patient."

"But Miss *Phillips!*"

Under direct attack Alice would argue the same point indefinitely. Fortunately, she responded well to re-direction. "Come now, show me your new drawings," Helène would say, and she would be diverted at once.

"Miss Phiwips! I made drawings too!"

And so it went. November had given way to December, and now the Christmas holidays to the new year. As she fell into bed every night, Helène wondered how two small children could be so exhausting. Miss Chaldecott was silent on this point, as she was with regard to such difficulties as "What to do when the paint pot spills all over the carpet" and "How many times a five-year-old boy might reasonably need to visit the privy closet in the course of a single afternoon." Helène still consulted the handbook from time to time, but she now entertained doubts that Miss E. A. Chaldecott had ever met an actual child.

It was of little matter. However poorly she might have been prepared for it at the beginning, Helène enjoyed her employment as a governess and began to consider herself a modest success at the task. The children were well-mannered and agreeable. They rewarded Helène's efforts with cheerful affection, and she had grown enormously fond of them both.

The continued absence of direction from Lord Sinclair

was her only real concern. He had requested a single interview with Helène since her arrival, a brief exchange in which he had stared at her intently and asked only if she needed any additional supplies for the children's education. He had since visited the nursery on a few occasions, and Helène was given to understand from Alice and Peter that their father was a somewhat distant, albeit stable and comforting, presence in their lives.

It was often so in the *ton,* of course. And at least Lady Pamela could be counted upon to spend time with her niece and nephew. Helène counted it a stroke of luck that the marquess had such a sister.

"Peter, come here for a moment, please."

An apron with several deep pockets had proved to be an essential part of a governess's wardrobe. She pulled a small square of linen from one of the pockets now and wiped the smudge from Peter's nose.

"Umph," he declared, screwing up his eyes and trying to wriggle away.

"The nose is much better. I suppose the shirt will have to wait." She set the boy down and went to gather materials for the morning lesson.

The Sinclairs' "schoolroom" was attached to the nursery suite and had proved to be an inexperienced teacher's dream; warm and airy, and stocked with every provision imaginable. Books, art supplies, and lesson slates were all neatly arranged and marked according to the abilities of each child. Whatever the problem had been with the previous two young women, thought Helène, it hadn't been that they were incompetent. With the schoolbooks as a guide, and two children eager to be helpful, she had managed to make a creditable start as a governess.

Maths and their letters in the morning, before tea.

French after lunch—

"I can see that you will be admirably busy," Lady Pamela was saying. "I shall return for tea. Behave yourself for Miss Phillips, children, if you please."

"Yes, Aunt Pamela!"

Helène set Peter to practice drawing his letters while Alice, as usual, was content to read, and the nursery was, for a time, blessedly quiet. She spread the skirts of her new, fern-green cambric day gown and sat down at the teacher's desk, content to watch the children at their tasks. Her small charges were slowly returning to the discipline of day-to-day schoolwork after the holiday just past. Helène herself had played only a small part in the festivities, for Christmas was a private, family affair at Luton Court. Alice and Peter had been Helène's only responsibility as far as gifts were concerned, and both were delighted with what she had contrived to make for them; their name in illuminated script, flowing with golds and scarlet and deep blue inks, on a fine sheet of parchment. The parchment and inks had been rooted out from among the schoolroom supplies.

"Oh, Miss Phillips!" Alice had said, her eyes brimming with tears. "It's the most beautiful thing I've ever seen!"

That was gift enough for Helène.

Alice and Peter were not the only cause of Helène's current satisfaction. Her situation had been generally much improved since Lady Pamela's arrival, and not only in the matter of her new rooms, which were spacious and well-appointed. Lady Pam had insisted that she be allowed to dine with the family and guests, and that the library and stables be open to her.

The marquess's sister had also declared, to Helène's blushing embarrassment, that a governess must be properly clothed. The battered portmanteau was dragged to the middens, along with every scrap of clothing it had once held, as she took on the task of providing Helène with a new wardrobe. Lady Pam was energetic, competent, and armed with a comprehensive knowledge of the latest London fashions. She ignored the governess's every protest, using the Christmas holidays as an excuse.

"These are my own clothes! I'm not ashamed of them!" Helène had said at first, mulish. This was a bouncer, of course.

"No one said anything about being ashamed," replied Pamela. "We are talking about clothing here, not morality. One's dress should be a matter of enjoyment."

"Enjoyment for whom? I'm the same person no matter what I wear!"

"Humor me," said the unflappable Lady Pam, holding a length of silk shawl up to Helène's face. "Yes, this color suits you very well."

Further objections to the scheme got no further, as Lady Pamela apparently brooked no compromise on the subject of clothes. Several days after that conversation a *modiste* had arrived—one Madame Gaultier—and Helène was summoned to Lady Pamela's sitting room for fittings. Every piece of furniture was awash in cambrics, calicos, and silks.

"She is too thin, neh?" said the dressmaker, taking an appraising look at the governess.

"I think we should allow some room for increase."

"Very good, my lady. Now, as for the number of walking gowns . . ."

"I can't pay for this!" Helène protested.

"Of course you can't," said Lady Pamela, holding a lilac silk up to Helène's face. "I can."

"You! But what will Lord Sinclair say?"

"We won't tell him, will we?" said Lady Pam. "And I can assure you that he isn't likely to notice a thing on his own."

"But—"

"Stand still."

Helène continued to argue until Lady Pamela told her that the gowns were to be her Christmas gift, and if Helène continued to fuss about it in such an unbecoming manner she, Lady Pamela, would order twice as many.

If *Madame* Gaultier could speak a single word of French, Helène was the Prince Regent. The *modiste* had, however, a good eye for the flattering cut of a gown and was remarkably quick as well. The cambric gown Helène wore today, for example, had been made up within hours. Grosgrain ribbons of a deep green set off the high waist, and the skirt sported lines of tucking along the hem. The bodice was gently fitted, and although the neckline was not low cut it showed Helène's bosom—and here no one could complain of her figure, thin as she still was—to great advantage. Anyone could feel pretty in a dress like that, and, despite Helène's objections, the fern-green cambric was only one of several new *habillements* now gracing her wardrobe.

The latest addition was a grey silk evening gown with a gauze overskirt, simply cut and eminently suitable for a small country ball. Here Helène had tried to put her foot down, but Lady Pamela had been adamant.

"A beaded reticule and matching gloves in addition, I should think," she told Madame Gaultier, as the *modiste* took careful notes in a tiny, precise hand. "To be made up within the month."

"Trez bien, mam'zelle."

"You are wasting your time!" protested Helène. "What

are the chances of my being invited to a ball? And can you imagine the marchioness allowing me to attend?"

Lady Pam looked at her archly. "I wouldn't be so sure about your chances. And don't argue with your betters."

This last was uttered in Pamela's flawless imitation of Lady Sinclair's voice at its most petulant. Helène stuck out her tongue.

"C-O-W," spelled Peter, his lips pursed in concentration. "Cow! It's cow, Miss Phillips!"

"Very good, Peter," said Helène.

Alice was unimpressed. "It's only three letters! Can't he read anything bigger than *that?*"

"Hush, Alice," said Lady Pam, who had arrived for tea. "He's only five."

"I bet I could read more than stupid old cow when *I* was five!"

"Could not!"

"Could too!"

"Could *not!*"

"Alice. Peter," said Helène softly. The children immediately quieted, and Peter went back to his picture-book.

"I wish I knew how you did that," commented Lady Pamela. "I thought we'd be hearing 'could not' and 'could too' for the next hour."

"I regret to disillusion you, but it's not always successful."

"Ah."

The two women sipped tea and chatted quietly in French. Lady Pamela enjoyed the habits and patterns of this language as much as Helène, and they both felt it was a benefit to the children to hear natural conversation *à la française*. Not that they always paid much attention. Alice, with sketch book in hand and a look of artistic concentration on her face, was attempting to draw Peter as he played with his blocks. It was a hopeless task.

"Sit still, Peter!"

"I can't!"

"Miss Phillips!"

"Helène," began Lady Pam. There was a mischievous look on her beautiful face. "Do you have any particular plans for the remainder of the afternoon?"

"Only French, I believe. Alice is progressing exceptionally well—"

"The sun is shining today, as I'm sure you've noticed," interrupted Lady Pam. "One might *almost* call it warm." Helène noticed that the children's ears had perked up.

"I might call it warm as well, my lady, except that it is so cold, " replied Helène. She cocked an eyebrow at Lady Pam.

"Oh, fustian," said Pamela. She sighed theatrically. "You know very well what I mean. The children can't stay indoors all winter—they'll be positively peaked by February. And 'tis a perfect day for a good tromp through the snow."

A lack of patience for book-learning was Lady Pamela's one besetting weakness. She was intelligent without being the least bookish, a combination which baffled Helène. With such a grand library at her disposal—! But Lady Pam could never see a child quietly at work in the schoolroom without wanting to set them outside "in the good fresh air," and in this she became Helène's ally. The governess no longer worried that the next snowball fight would lead to her dismissal from Luton.

"Well, Peter does have a prime case of the fidgets these days," Helène admitted. "I suppose French can wait until tomorrow. Although—"

"Miss Phillips! Oh, yes, *please*, Miss Phillips!"

Too late. Alice and Peter, with the acute hearing children

use only when adults are trying to conceal something from them, crowded around Helène, their faces shining in anticipation.

"Oh, very well," laughed Helène. "But only if your aunt agrees to join us."

"Aunt Pamela! Aunt Pamela!"

Helène looked at Lady Pam and grinned.

Lady Pamela watched Helène making a row of miniature snowmen with Alice and Peter in the late afternoon sun. She felt satisfied with the changes that the past few weeks had brought in the girl's looks. Miss Phillips was filling out a bit, and her skin had the healthy glow that came with wholesome food and enough of it. No one would ever find fault with that hair, and combined with the new wardrobe, the governess now made a more than tolerably attractive figure. Still, there was one aspect to the situation that troubled Lady Pam.

'Twas all very well to provide someone with proper clothing. Easily done, in fact, if one had money and taste. But, now what?

"She's a governess," Lady Detweiler had reminded Pam the night before. "A very intelligent governess, to be sure. But what is the chit to do?"

Lady Pamela had already considered this at some length. "I can't imagine anyone really wants to spend their life moving from house to house," she told Amanda. "Only becoming accustomed to one family and then—gone. She should get married."

"Pray remind me of the reasons that marriage would be an improvement," was Amanda's rejoinder. "Besides, like it or not, she isn't *ton*. You can't marry her off to the first besotted viscount that comes along."

Pragmatic as always, Lady Detweiler had the right of it.

The usual younger son would never do in this case. The boy might be swayed by Helène's beauty, but the family would never allow the match. No, it would need to be someone of more mature years, in charge of his own life, and possessed of adequate income. Lady Pamela wrinkled her forehead, mentally reviewing the marquess's list of guests. Now that Christmas itself was past, there would be a steady stream of new arrivals, and the return of at least one older friend of the family.

Celia had been in alt last night, Pam recalled, ever since word had arrived that Lord Quentin would be returning to Luton Court at almost any hour.

Charles Quentin. Lady Pamela's fingers, encased in a rabbit's fur muff, tapped out a thoughtful tattoo. Jonathan's friend had been a regular visitor at Luton for years; she knew him well, although no romantic spark had ever flickered between them. Still, Lady Pamela had found Lord Quentin to be intelligent and, like herself, possessed of both a wicked sense of humor and a more than average appreciation for the more blatant absurdities of the *ton*. But as a possible husband for Miss Phillips? No, it was impossible. Charles was the future Earl of Tavelstoke—

"Good heavens, have you run mad to be outside in this weather?"

Pamela turned around and burst into laughter. Lady Detweiler was picking her way through the snow, an expression of distaste on her face.

"It's only snow, Amanda."

"Nasty, cold stuff I've always thought. And not a decanter of sherry in sight. What's the point, my dear?"

Pamela pointed at Helène and the children, who were now engaged in adding sprigs of yew to the top of each snowman's head. The effect was somewhat antler-like. Snowreindeer? wondered Lady Pam.

"Yes, well it's all very charming and pastoral, I'm sure. Can we go back in now? I've been stuck all alone with your sister-in-law. She's in an absolute tizzy over Lord Quentin."

"Lord Quentin?" Lady Pam asked Amanda. "Has he returned already?"

"No, but he will be arriving any minute, according to Celia. She can hardly sit still. I am quite convinced her *decolletage* is getting more outrageous by the day. This morning's gown is positively alarming, I'll have you know. Lord Quentin could stick a *grapefruit* down there, if he had half a mind—"

Pamela erupted into laughter once again.

"—and a very large grapefruit, at that. D' you suppose," added Lady Detweiler, "that she intends to continue this absurd flirtation? Although I can't imagine why I should care."

"I believe she . . . knew Lord Quentin before her marriage," replied Pam.

"Indeed. Why does Jonathan not put a stop to it? She'll end up in real trouble one of these days."

Lady Pamela sighed. She had wondered the same thing. Of late, her brother's affection for his wife seemed even cooler and more distant than usual. "I don't know," she admitted to Amanda. "He must see her insecurity. I believe she would not behave near so badly if . . ." Screams of laughter erupted from the direction of the snowmen and Pam broke off, her attention diverted once more to the children and their governess. "Amanda, does Helène Phillips remind you of anyone?"

Lady Detweiler had the best memory for faces of anyone in Pam's acquaintance. She glanced at the girl, then looked at her more carefully for several moments, frowning. "No . . . I don't think so." But Amanda sounded unsure.

"I keep thinking I've seen her somewhere before."

"In London, perhaps?"

Lady Pamela hesitated, closing her eyes. A memory, a hand's breadth out of reach—

"I don't know," she finally said. "There's something about her face, and that hair, that seems so familiar . . ."

Hooves sounded close by, muffled by the snow. Pam and Amanda turned to see a horse trotting down the long front-court drive. The size of the stallion identified its rider even before they could clearly see his face.

"Speak of the devil," said Amanda.

It was indeed Charles Quentin. He stopped in front of Pamela and Lady Detweiler, swung down from his mount, and doffed his hat.

"Welcome back to Luton, Lord Quentin," said Pam. "I hope your journey was uneventful."

"Lady Pamela. Lady Detweiler. I took advantage of the full moon and left Tavelstoke before dawn this morning. I'm delighted to see you taking full advantage of our fine weather."

Amanda snorted. Pamela winked at Lord Quentin. "I believe that Lady Detweiler has taken about as much advantage of the weather as she can endure," she told him.

"Oh, come now," said the lord. "Look at how much Alice and Peter are enjoying themselves—" He stopped abruptly and frowned.

Helène had been gathering another armful of 'antlers.' She reappeared now from behind the yew hedge, a slender figure in a brushed-wool pelisse of deep forest green. A matching shawl was cast loosely around her neck, and a mass of glossy auburn curls shone in the winter sun. She looked, thought Pam with satisfaction, like any proper young lady. Lord Quentin was staring blankly at the governess.

Pamela and Amanda exchanged looks.

"Who—?" began Lord Quentin. Then—"I don't believe I've been introduced to your new guest." He looked a little puzzled, as if he realized he should know her.

"Of course," said Lady Pamela. "Miss Phillips!" she called to Helène.

Miss Phillips? The governess? Charles looked at the girl as she walked slowly toward them, trying to put this rather dashing young woman together with the person he had last seen wearing little more than rags. How could he have forgotten that she was so pretty? Thick auburn hair set off a perfect, creamy complexion. A wide, sensual mouth and brilliant green eyes—

The eyes met his. He drew in a sharp breath.

"Lord Quentin," said Lady Pamela, "may I present Miss Helène Phillips?"

The girl obviously remembered who he was. She gave him a quick, veiled look and dropped into a deep curtsey. Watching Miss Phillips's hands flick her skirts out into a wide circle, a quick rustle of fabric over the surface of the snow, Lord Quentin was amused. It was apparently quite possible, he saw, for a curtsey to convey irony. The chit had some spirit.

"Miss Phillips is Alice and Peter's new governess."

She was rather young, he realized, with shock. Perhaps nineteen or twenty years of age. Hunger had added several years to her appearance.

Wide green eyes regarded him steadily. "Lord Quentin and I have already met," Miss Phillips said. "In fact, I last saw him at this very place."

Charles was briefly perplexed by this remark. Then—

"Of course." He smiled at the governess. "The snowball

fight. Between Miss Phillips and the children. Quite a charming sight, although I believe Peter was besting you."

It might have been a peace offering, but the intended recipient did not waver. "You didn't find it charming at the time, as I recall," she told him.

"Well, perhaps—"

"Although I suppose it was an improvement over our previous encounter."

There was a moment's silence. Lady Detweiler, eyebrows lifted, was looking at Lord Quentin with something approaching a smirk.

"Indeed," Lady Pamela said, waiting for Miss Phillips to explain.

"Yes. He threw me off his horse and stole my baggage." Flashing a wide, innocent smile, Helène Phillips turned and walked away, calling for the children.

"Alice! Peter! Time to go in!"

"Oh, no, Miss Phillips!" came the expected reply. "A few more minutes!" But the governess was ready for them.

"Hot chocolate!" she called. With squeals of delight, the two small figures ran after her, and they proceeded in single file back to the house, two bouncing children following their energetic, green-eyed teacher.

Silence reigned for a moment, punctuated only by occasional stomps and snorts from Alcibiades.

"Well, Lord Quentin," Amanda finally said. "You certainly seem to have a way with the young ladies."

Helène raised a spoonful of soup to her mouth and chanced a surreptitious glance at Lord Quentin. How could she have forgotten how handsome the man was? It was appalling, her heart seemed to want to go *thump* every time he looked her way.

Which was fairly often. Helène felt the breath catch in her throat as Charles Quentin's eyes once again met hers. His lazy smile startled her, and she looked back down at her soup in confusion.

Drat the man. And what had she been thinking, to be so rude to him that afternoon? But he had stood there, staring, and then had the *nerve* to mention the snowball fight, as if—

As if what? asked a little voice. He was charming about the snowball fight.

Charming! Ha! Lord Quentin's charm was exactly the problem, thought Helène. To be so . . . so *agreeable,* after he had threatened to have her dismissed!

"Charles, dear, pray tell me what you are finding of such interest at *that* end of the table," demanded Lady Sinclair. She was staring at Helène with a small frown.

The governess bit back a grimace. Lady Sinclair had the eyes of a hawk, and Helène didn't much care for the feeling of being watched. The woman had never been uncivil to Helène—at least not after that first day—but she had clearly been displeased by Lady Pam's insistence that the governess dine *en famille.* Even a well-dressed governess.

Lady Sinclair seemed to like me better when I wore near rags, thought Helène. *Could she be jealous?*

What an absurd thought.

"In *my* day," the elderly Lady Harkins informed the group, "the governess ate alone in her rooms. Such new-fangled notions, marchioness. I confess I am quite shocked."

"I quite agree, my dear Beatrice," said Celia. Her voice dropped to a stage whisper. "But it's Lady Pamela, you know. Such kindness toward the unfortunate."

Lady Pamela was engrossed in a conversation with Sir Clarence and missed this comment, but, even from her position as the least exalted guest at table, Helène could sense

Amanda Detweiler's ears perk up. Skirmishes between Celia and Lady Detweiler seemed to be a frequent occurrence at dinner. Helène was secretly amused by this—as, she suspected, were a number of the other guests—but she worried that any defense of "the unfortunate governess" might backfire to her own harm.

The marchioness could not dismiss Lady Detweiler. She could certainly dismiss Helène.

"Did you say unfortunate, Celia?" Amanda's voice dripped honey. "To be working as your governess, I assume?"

There were suppressed male chuckles. Helène blushed, and Lady Sinclair glared at Lady Detweiler.

"And what would you know about governesses, Lady Detweiler?" she asked. "Not having any children of your own, of course."

"I know very little, thank goodness."

"Ah—Well."

According to Lady Pam, Celia was forever needling Amanda with small barbs about her unmarried state, and never seemed to catch on that the exercise was futile. Lady Detweiler had enjoyed a number of discrete liaisons with well-placed gentlemen over the years, but she had no interest whatsoever in marriage. Her feelings on children—*les petits horreurs*—were even more unequivocal.

"Perhaps Miss Phillips could explain her method of instructing the children in French," broke in Lady Pamela, smoothly. "It's really quite intriguing."

"French?" said Celia, startled. "The girl doesn't know any French!"

Helène bit her lip. Stay seated, she told herself. Stay seated and take another spoonful of soup. Remember the soup? It's quite delicious.

"Well, she ought to!" an indignant Lady Harkins was saying. "In my day a governess was required—"

"In *your* day, Lady Harkins—"

"Celia—"

Several people began talking at once, with Lady Sinclair's complaints still audible.

"Jonathan, I demand to be told—"

Helène never knew how Charles Quentin managed to make his voice heard over the general babble of voices. But suddenly all was quiet, and everyone—good heavens, everyone was looking at *her*.

"*Mademoiselle,*" said Lord Quentin. "*C'est vrai, vous avez une méthode unique d'enseignement?*" The words were spoken coolly, his eyebrows raised in question, and Helène received the impression that he was expecting her to—what? Flee from the room? Break down in tears?

He's testing me, she realized. *What a bothersome man! They aren't his children, after all. What does he care whether I speak French or not?*

"*Ce n'est pas dire grand-chose,*" she told him. "It is nothing so very wonderful. Alice and Peter are very bright, as well. We merely attempt to learn the language naturally, as would a young French child—"

"*Et les tout-petits?* And the little ones? They are happy with this?"

"*Mais oui. Vraiment, en point, c'est tout.*"

Lord Quentin asked a few more questions, and the governess unconsciously followed his lead in slipping from English into a rapid, idiomatic French. Had she been watching her employer, Helène might have thought to worry, for the marchioness was weak in languages, and could no longer follow the conversation. Lady Sinclair grew quietly furious.

★ ★ ★ ★ ★

Lord Charles Quentin finished another glass of brandy and stretched out his legs in front of the library fire with a contented sigh. Whatever Jonathan's failings might be, second-rate brandy wasn't one of them.

"Going t' bed now, old man," said his host, his words slurred. The marquess had matched him glass for glass, but Jonathan never had the head for liquor that Charles did. He was quite drunk, and Lord Quentin could imagine the headache his friend would suffer from on the morrow.

"I'll be off soon, myself," Charles assured him.

The marquess made his unsteady way to the door. Lord Quentin decided to wait a bit longer before retiring to his rooms, and poured himself another glass of brandy. The fire crackled with heat, the library was rich with the familiar smells of book leather and vellum . . . Perhaps his eyes closed for a moment. He was upstairs, preparing for bed. An auburn-haired beauty was lying on top of the coverlet, completely undressed. He was immediately aroused and she reached for him, smiling—

Charles eyes popped open and he sat up with a start. Why was he dreaming about the governess, for pity's sake? He had enough trouble as it was with the lady of the house.

He sat back in his chair.

Miss Phillips *was* attractive. Still thin, of course. 'Twas little more than six weeks since she had arrived at Luton Court, and she'd been half-starved then. Still, she had cleaned up nicely. That gown tonight had hinted at rather delectable breasts, and a narrow waist . . .

And that wide mouth with the ripe-red lips. It would be no hardship to take her to his bed, thought Charles. No hardship at all. Lord Quentin found his thoughts threatening to warm to this topic, and he shook his head to clear it. Celia. He should be making plans to avoid Celia, even though he knew that resisting her for one night wouldn't solve anything. The lady was persistent.

Still . . . Charles was honest enough to admit that his present situation was not altogether the marchioness's fault. Her husband seemed intent on ignoring her, and she must have sensed that Lord Quentin was tempted, that the memories of their previous encounters sometimes came too vividly to mind.

As his thoughts continued to wander down various unsettling pathways, the image of Helène Phillips arose once more before him. He envisaged her walking into the library, her auburn hair falling in long curls past her waist. She was wearing a lilac blue silk wrapper over a cambric nightgown, the candle in her hand illuminating a dark fall of eyelashes with golden light. She was smoothly curved, luscious—

He heard a soft cry of surprise and looked up. Miss Phillips was standing there with eyes wide, evidently quite real.

Chapter Seven

"I beg your pardon, Lord Quentin," Miss Phillips said, backing away from him toward the door. "I had no idea—I didn't know—"

She looked delightfully vulnerable in the silk wrapper. Almost unconsciously he rose and advanced toward her and she backed away more quickly, never taking her eyes from his face. Then her heel caught in the long hem of her robe. She swayed, fighting to keep her balance, and tumbled to the floor in a jumble of white cambric and lilac blue silk.

"Good heavens." Charles had caught a quick, tantalizing flash of ankle as the girl fell. He stepped over to where she sat and reached down to—

"I'm quite able to get to my feet unaided, thank you." The girl's tart comment stopped Lord Quentin. She got one hand underneath her and scooted away from him, *derrière* to the Aubusson carpet, until she had backed herself into a sofa. Then she clambered onto the cushions, clutching her wrapper with one hand.

Charles studied her, amusement warring with chagrin. The girl was frightened. She was *en déshabillé,* true, but that would hardly explain the degree of anxiety he saw in her eyes.

The silly chit had no reason to be afraid of him! Lord Quentin was annoyed. This is a piece of missish nonsense, he decided. How dare she look at him as if he were about to spring at her and rip off her clothing? He had no reputation as a cad, and he was certainly not one of those gentlemen who bedded low-caste girls against their will.

"I was just returning this . . ." The governess trailed off,

92

her voice trembling. She glanced at the library shelves, and he realized that she had a book in her hands.

Ah. It isn't fear, Charles decided. It's guilt. Something about that book is making her nervous. An idea struck Lord Quentin, probably not the most sensible idea he could have conjured up, but one that was a complement to his own recent thoughts. Perhaps it was a book of . . . indecorous nature. Of course! No doubt Jonathan had a few such volumes, and she had been curious.

He must give the girl a lecture, Charles decided. She had no business with that sort of thing, assuming she even understood what she was looking at, and if anyone was to discover the book in Miss Phillips's possession it might prove embarrassing to the marquess.

"May I see?" He held out his hand for the volume she was clutching, and, after a moment's hesitation, the governess gave it to him.

He looked at the title and blinked in surprise. The *Letters* of Pliny the Younger. In Latin. Charles thought back to the first time he had seen Helène Phillips—half starved, dressed nearly in rags. It was most unaccountable. Lord Quentin frowned.

"How is it that you read Latin?"

"My aunt . . . my aunt taught me."

"Your aunt!"

The disbelief in his voice brought a spark to Miss Phillips's eyes. "It is no offense for a governess to read a classical language."

"No, but—" Sitting down beside her on the sofa, Lord Quentin tried a different tack. "I imagine Lord Sinclair would approve. Surely you are not forbidden the library?"

"No," she replied, blushing. "But I was unsure if the marchioness . . ." She hesitated.

Charles nodded. "Unsure if Lady Sinclair would be . . . mmm—"

". . . *comfortable* with my presence here," she finished, clearly relieved that he understood.

"Especially when you are reading Latin histories." His grin was conspiratorial. "The marchioness's Latin is worse than her French."

"Oh, surely not—" She stopped herself, and blushed again.

Charles laughed. " 'Tis true. But there should be no need for you to prowl around the house late at night. The library is a public room. I will ask the marquess—"

The girl flinched as if struck.

"What is it?"

"Ah. Well, you see . . ." Miss Phillips was obviously hesitant to continue. Charles smiled in encouragement.

"As I explained earlier—"

Earlier?

"—Lord Sinclair has spoken to me only briefly. About the children." Another blush. "He has not . . . given me any further details as to my position here, or what is expected of me. Lady Pamela has been most kind, of course, but . . . but I've not wished to be forward in my assumptions."

As she had explained earlier? Lord Quentin was baffled by her words until he remembered the day of the snowball fight. But that was a month ago! Had Jonathan still not properly interviewed the girl? What idiocy was this?

Come to think of it, Charles reflected, there was something very havey-cavey about the entire arrangement between the Sinclairs and Miss Phillips. For one thing, a marquess did not hire starving young women dressed in rags for a governess. For another, starving young women did not generally speak the king's English, nor have Latin and French at their disposal.

It was a puzzle. Celia had said that it was Jonathan who had insisted on hiring a new governess, but surely the marchioness must also have had a hand in the decision. Mrs. Tiggs had as much as told him that the previous two governesses had been too pretty and well-bred for Celia's tastes. Perhaps she had chosen a girl unlikely to inspire jealousy.

How ironic it would be, thought Charles, if that was indeed Lady Sinclair's reasoning, for the young woman's appearance was now little short of stunning. Still . . . Miss Helène Phillips could hardly be quality, no matter how many languages she spoke.

"Please excuse me, Lord Quentin. I must return to my room." The governess smiled hesitantly, and he found himself strangely reluctant to see her go. A few more minutes could surely do no harm, and he was intrigued by the curves hinted at by the soft draping of her wrapper. Slippered toes peeped out from under the silk hem—

Ah. Well. Charles forced his attention back to the book in hand.

"Are you truly interested in Pliny?" he asked, the first suitable question that came to mind. The governess looked up at him warily, as if trying to judge the sincerity of his interest.

"Not Pliny himself. Elder or younger, that is," she finally answered. "But in the history of ancient Rome, and all of the Italian peninsula. His description of the eruption of Vesuvius, for example—" Miss Phillips stopped, but her face had come alight with these words, her eyes flashing green fire. The effect was rather delightful, and Charles wanted to see it again.

"I've always found Rome one of the most intriguing cities of the continent," he told her, forgetting for the moment that the governess could hardly have visited it herself. "Marble columns falling over into dust, the ruins of the Forum filled chock-a-block with people selling everything from cheap trinkets to fish. But I suppose, if you've lived with such glories your whole life, they become part of the background—"

He stopped. Miss Phillips had been staring at him with an expression Charles could hardly interpret. When she spoke it was with a dreamy quality, unselfconscious, almost as if he was no longer there.

"Oh! It would be marvelous to see the Forum!" cried the governess softly. "And the Pantheon and the baths of Caracalla! To stand on the steps of the Curia and imagine Cicero speaking in that very place—" The governess halted abruptly and sighed, and her gaze shifted from his face. When she spoke again her tone was matter-of-fact.

"At any rate, I find it more enjoyable to read contemporary accounts of ancient life than the current scientific books. Although—" she added hastily, as if Charles would be offended at this dismissal of modern scholarship, "I am sure they are of greatest interest to the experts."

"Dull and dry as bug dust, actually," said Lord Quentin. "It makes one surprised that anyone wants to visit Rome these days, if they've read more than a page of, say, Liddell. Or Scott."

Miss Phillips was startled into laughter. "Oh, no!" she said. "To think all these years I've been feeling guilty that I found him pompous and . . . and rather long!"

"Interminable," agreed Charles. "Although usually accurate, one must admit." They chatted comfortably about Rome for several minutes more, Miss Phillips once again charming in her animation. She was, Lord Quentin discovered, curious, intelligent, and well read. He hadn't had a more enjoyable conversation in months.

Careful, old man, said the little voice, reminding him that the girl was, after all, only an employee in this house. He could do as he wished, of course, but it was highly inappropriate for Miss Phillips to form an acquaintance with one of the guests.

"How did it happen that you are a governess here?" asked Lord Quentin, and then was surprised when the girl answered. He hadn't intended to speak aloud.

Miss Phillips took a deep breath. "My aunt . . ." She hesitated. "My father and my aunt arranged the position." All animation left her face, and the wariness returned.

"Your father?"

"Nathaniel Phillips. He died . . . not long ago."

"Ah," said Lord Quentin. The name rang no bells with him. But then, there was no reason to expect that it would.

"I really must leave—"

Miss Phillips leaned forward to adjust the strap of her slipper. Charles caught a glimpse of *décolletage,* and all thoughts of Roman ruins or Latin histories flew straight from his head. Although she was still rather slender overall, the girl's breasts looked to be spectacular. Charles felt the first twinges of desire.

A pretty little nobody with, as far as he could tell, no family interested in her welfare. Lord Quentin had always preferred to take his pleasures among the more mature ladies of the *ton,* ladies for whom the rules of the game were well understood. Young nobodies weren't generally his style, and—Pliny the Younger notwithstanding—Miss Helène Phillips was well down the social ladder. But the governess had piqued his interest. Charles wasn't sure he cared to examine his feelings any more closely than that. She was . . . interesting, that was all, and an opportunity that he was currently at liberty to explore. A dalliance would certainly make his stay at Luton Court more satisfactory.

The girl shifted on the sofa, as if to rise. "Pray excuse me, my lord. It is quite late, and—"

Perhaps Miss Phillips could be persuaded to engage in an occasional tumble during the next few weeks. She was only a governess after all, and he was the heir to the Tavelstoke earldom. The girl would probably be delighted to receive his attentions. And it would take his mind from the persistent temptation presented by Celia Sinclair.

"Miss Phillips," he began. She looked up, and Lord Quentin found himself staring into wide, questioning eyes.

"My lord?"

"Hmm." He was suddenly unsure of himself. It rankled. "Ah. I trust you've found your accommodations satisfactory?"

"My accommodations?"

"Well, yes. And the children? They are advancing well in their studies?"

She looked at him as if he had lost his mind. "They are doing quite well, thank you," she said finally. "Alice and Peter are delightful."

"Ah."

"Now, if you will excuse me—"

Charles took a deep breath. Why was he hesitating? He couldn't remember what he had planned to do or say. His attention seemed captive to her eyes, to the cascades of auburn hair about her shoulders, the bruised ruby lips—

"My lord!" protested Helène Phillips.

Charles had leaned forward to kiss her. The governess, heedless of the honor being bestowed upon her, was pushing him away. She was no match for his strength, of course. He took her hand.

Long, slender fingers.

A bell of warning sounded, softly, somewhere in the back of Lord Quentin's mind. He ignored it and concentrated on the fingers, bringing each one to his lips for a taste. Heat flowed through his veins, his groin tightened, and he heard Miss Phillips murmur another protest.

She tried to snatch her hand away; he allowed it, moving his own hand to stroke her hair. He watched her reactions carefully, seeing first confusion in her eyes, and then—

And then his own desire, mirrored there. He was sure of it.

The chit wanted him, thought Charles, exultantly. And no innocent, surely. Well, this would be easy.

Lord Quentin was going to kiss her. Helène, although having no previous experience in the matter, was quite sure. The nerve of the man.

Her eyes closed in a moment of confusion, and she found her lips brushed very softly with his. Then Helène's arms moved around his neck, and she returned the kiss, hearing him groan softly. His hand was moving—good heavens, his hand was moving against the back of her neck and down the silk of her wrapper, stroking softly.

Time slowed, Lord Quentin kissed her again and again, and Helène swam in honey. He had pressed her into the sofa cushions and his movements were becoming . . . odd. Insistent and disturbing. She heard his voice whispering against her ear.

"Relax. Everyone else has retired to bed."

Relax?

What was happening? What was she doing? Helène struggled to sit up, to push the man away from her.

"Easy, my sweet—"

"I am not your sweet!"

Crack! Her hand flew forward of its own accord, and she slapped him roundly across the face. Helène gasped and buried her face in her hands, sickeningly aware that her temper had once more gotten the best of her, aware that it was her own fault. She could hardly claim seduction. Not when she had gone to the library of her own accord, dressed only in nightgown and wrapper, and sat right there, on the sofa, letting him make love to her—

At least, that's what she *thought* Lord Quentin had been doing. A country girl might have been able to explain things more clearly, but Helène was town born and bred. She had witnessed more than she ought in the back streets of London, but as for details . . . the details were still obscure to her.

Heavens. Helène finally shook off her paralysis and looked up. Lord Quentin was watching her with hooded eyes. He seemed unperturbed by the slap and his gaze raked over her once again, following the hollow of her neck down to her *décolletage*. Helène put her hand up to cover . . . whatever it was that had captured his attention. He leaned back against the cushions and she felt a shiver that had nothing to do with the temperature of the room.

"I must ask your forgiveness, *mademoiselle*," said Lord Quentin. "Pray do not be alarmed. I was carried away by the brilliance of your eyes—"

Helène, for reasons she could hardly begin to explain, burst out laughing.

"My *eyes?*" she managed to say.

Lord Quentin looked startled. He had been leaning forward on the sofa, his hand reaching for hers, but now he checked himself. "I fail to see what is so amusing," he told her.

"Oh! I'm terribly sorry," she said. "It's only that I'm not accustomed—"

She stopped, searching for an explanation that wouldn't make either of them sound foolish. But Lord Quentin abruptly stood up.

"There is no need to elaborate, *mademoiselle*," he said. "I will bid you good night."

Helène saw that he was offended and, for some reason, this struck her as even funnier.

"Oh, my lord," she said, hiccuping with the effort not to laugh, "I'm . . . I'm *honored*, truly I am."

"Yes," said the lord, drily. "I can see that you are." He turned on his heels and walked out.

"What's wrong, maman? Who is she?"

Lady Pamela sat up in bed with a start. Never one to be troubled by nightmares, she was perplexed by the lingering touch of anxiety, feeling it float slowly away as she came fully awake. Why, after all these years, did she dream about that day in Hyde Park? And why did she associate the woman in the carriage with Helène?

Does Helène Phillips remind you of anyone?

The girl was a riddle. In some ways—the wardrobe she had arrived with, her shyness in company—she seemed less than what a governess ought to be. But in other ways she seemed much more. Her accent, for example, was impeccable, and few members of the *ton* could match the fluency and ease of her French. Grammar could be obtained from books, but the rest—Where could the girl have learned it?

Lady Pamela slid out of bed and walked to the balcony, tempted, despite the cold, to step out into the velvet black of the winter's night. Luton in winter. The stars blazed cold fire, far more magnificent than one ever saw through the smudge of London's winter air.

Helène had spoken little of her past. Her father had been a carriagemaker, and a reasonably successful one, it seemed, until his illness. Her mother was dead—

Her mother. A shiver went through Pam as a fragment of

her dream came to mind once again. That afternoon in Hyde Park . . . The old marchioness had been an intensely social creature, always happier in London than at Luton Court. An extended promenade through the park was *de rigeur* for any sunny day, and Pamela enjoyed the rides, especially as her mother knew *everyone*. But Lady Sinclair had been very angry with her daughter on this occasion.

"Who is she maman? She's beautiful."
"Pamela, stop this hen-witted fussing at once!"
"But maman—"
"I've told you before. She is no one."

Chapter Eight

A governess with any need to conceal her past is earnestly to be pitied.

Lady Detweiler, for reasons that were initially unclear, arrived at the breakfast table in advance of eight o'clock that next morning. Pamela and the marquess watched her entrance with a mixture of amusement and alarm. Grumbling loudly, eyes shielded against the soft morning sunlight with an enormous chicken-skin fan, Amanda was the picture of beleaguered misery.

"Heavens. Couldn't you sleep?"

"Can someone please explain to me," complained Amanda, making her way immediately to the samovar of coffee, "this fanatic interest in fresh air during the winter. I *cannot* comprehend it. As if it wasn't bad enough that it's cold *outside*."

"If you're trying to tell us that your rooms are not warm enough," said Jonathan, "ask for an early fire to be laid."

"Pah. The maids have to rest sometime, I suppose."

The marquess chuckled and Lady Pamela hid a smile. That was Lady Detweiler all right—all bark and no bite. Pam had never known anyone who grumbled as loudly as Amanda, or who was as genuinely considerate of the servants.

Lady Detweiler grimaced at the sight of Jonathan's plate, piled high with slices of ham and smoked pork sausage.

"We shall be killing the poor pigs left and right this winter, I see."

103

"This is hardly an unreasonable breakfast," protested Lord Sinclair, who never seemed to catch on to Amanda's teasing. "You should see what Lord Burgess eats."

"Lord Burgess," she told him, "is an ox. I can't imagine what all this is doing to your digestion. It must be perfectly demoralized by now."

Lady Pamela snorted.

"Reynolds, pour another cup of coffee for Lady Detweiler, if you please," the marquess instructed the waiting footman.

"Indeed," said Lady Detweiler. "I shall need it to fortify myself for the contemplation of those sausages."

Eventually Jonathan left to prepare for a much-anticipated day of grouse hunting, leaving the two women with the break-fast salon to themselves. Lady Pam had been deep in thought for some time, choosing to ignore Lady Detweilers's good-nature abuse of her brother.

Last night's dream had continued to nag at her. The woman in the carriage . . .

"Out with it," commanded Lady Detweiler.

"Hmm?"

"You are wool-gathering over something. A shocking new scandal? Or is that too much to hope?"

"Amanda, do you remember the story about the Duke of Grentham's elder daughter?"

"The Duke of Grentham?" Lady Detweiler sat back in her chair and sipped a third cup of coffee. "Ah, yes. Torrance. He disowned the girl, as I recall. Married a cit."

"Exactly. What was her name?"

"Hmm." Amanda pursed her lips. "Something like . . . Oh, yes. Guenevieve. Quite a shocking choice, in my opin-ion."

Lady Detweiler had idiosyncratic notions on the subject of Christian names. Pamela forged ahead. "Did you ever see her?"

"Guenevieve Torrance?" Amanda paused. "The old duke must have banished her a good twenty years ago."

"At least," agreed Pamela.

"Well, darling, I may be a tad bit older than you are, but that still makes me in the neighborhood of ten when dear Guenevieve sacrificed everything for *l'amour*."

L'amour. Pamela thought back to the old scandal. She had been very young, of course. If it hadn't been for that day in Hyde Park—

"What happened to her, d' you suppose?" mused Lady Detweiler.

"I believe she stayed in London," said Lady Pamela. "For a few years, anyway."

"Well, you seem to know a great deal about it." Amanda blew out a sigh and reached for the pot of marmalade. "I confess myself defeated in this case—simply too long ago. How mortifying. The duke's chit and that . . . What was he, anyway?"

"I'm not sure. Some sort of tradesman."

"Handsome beyond compare, I suppose."

"Yes," said Pamela. "I believe he was."

That day passed more slowly than usual for Helène. Lady Pamela did not visit, being required to consult with the staff regarding further holiday preparations. The custom at Luton Court, as with many noble houses, was to hold most of the holiday affairs *after* the new year, Christmas itself being fairly quiet and reserved for family. As the first week of January drew to its close the pace of household activities increased, along with the general level of noise. Various thumpings and bangings from the rooms below announced that the servants were preparing the largest ballroom for the traditional *bal*

d'hiver. The marchioness had been in full cry for days, direct-
ing troops of servants in the placement of ever more decora-
tions and the laying in of vast quantities of food. The Yule
tree, which until Boxing Day had stood solitary and
undecorated in the middle of the Great Hall, was now fes-
tooned with quantities of silver and gold netting, bits of tin
cut into the shape of stars—

—and popped corn. The marchioness had the tree strung
with ropes of this corn, a newly-fashionable import from the
Americas. Showing more interest in the out-of-doors than
Helène would have expected, Lady Sinclair had impatiently
explained to Alice and Peter that the strands of popped corn
would be later thrown out onto the snow for the birds. In the
meantime—

"You can eat it!" Peter confided to her.

"Surely not," said Helène, fingering a small piece of the
fluffy white stuff.

"You can! 'Sgood!"

Helène had difficulty keeping Peter away from the tree after this, although he promised her he would only eat the bits
of popped corn that "the birds don't want."

"Miss Phiwips. Miss Phiwips, I'm *hungry.*"

"You just had breakfast! Miss Phillips, he just ate!"

"Did not!"

"You did too!"

Not unexpectedly, with the ruckus of preparations for the
houseparty and ball only a floor away, the children were having difficulty concentrating on their schoolwork. Helène's
mood was little better; she felt fidgety and out-of-sorts. Nothing to do with Lord Quentin, of course—she'd banished any
thoughts of *that* gentleman from her mind. But the morning
dragged on, with the children quarreling at the least provoca-

tion, and eventually Helène gave in. Alice was allowed to set out her new collection of watercolors—a gift from Lady Pamela—and Peter happily occupied himself with his beloved wooden blocks.

At mid-morning there was a great commotion—horses whinnying, good-natured shouting and so forth—from the front courtyard. The children jumped up and ran to the windows.

"Oh! Father's going hunting," said Alice. "Poor birds."

"Papa never shoots any birds!" crowed Peter. "He misses!"

"I know *he* always misses, silly," said Alice, "but one of the other gentlemen may hit something."

Helène smiled at this bit of innocent chatter. She came over to the window—only to shoo the children away—and happened to catch a glimpse of the group below.

He was unmistakable among the others, both in the broadness of his shoulders and the way he carried himself. She watched for a moment until, incredibly, he turned around and looked straight up at the nursery windows. He doffed his hat.

"Oh, look!" said Alice, waving madly. "He sees us! Look, there's Lord Quentin, Peter! Hallo! Hallo!"

"Lor' Wentin'! Lor' Wentin'!" contributed Peter.

"Look, Miss Phillips, he sees us!" But Helène, blushing miserably, was already in full retreat. The rest of the day passed without further incident, although later, the governess could scarce remember anything she or the children might have accomplished.

Helène plopped down on her bed and sighed, thinking of the evening meal shortly to come. It was ironic, considering that she had been often hungry only months before, that she now anticipated the marquess's table with something like dread. Five and six courses, night after night! No wonder these people slept until noon. It was exhausting.

Of course, if she didn't eat dinner with the family and guests she would have no reason to wear one of her beautiful new gowns. Helène opened the wardrobe and hesitated, wondering how long it would be before the marchioness stopped frowning at the sight of her. The nicer the garment, it seemed, the deeper the frown. Lord Quentin, on the other hand . . .

Bother Lady Sinclair. And bother Charles Quentin, what did she care what he thought? Feeling rebellious, Helène selected a rose tabby with lace-trimmed sleeves and a simple beribboned waist. Lady Pamela had insisted the tabby was unexceptionable for a governess, but there was no ignoring the rather low neckline. *Tant pis!* She would dress as she pleased.

Celia stood in the doorway to her husband's rooms, her eyes showing the red cast of a recent bout of tears.

"Jonathan," she began, and waited, but Lord Sinclair was reading his newspaper and showed no sign that he had heard her.

"*Jonathan.* Who is this new governess? I must know."

Her husband looked up, his expression mildly questioning. "The new governess? Her name is Miss Helène Phillips, as I recall."

Celia's eyes widened in anger. "Don't patronize me! I'm not a fool!" she cried. "Who is she? Some daughter of an old friend, you said? I think not. She appeared at our door nearly in rags!"

"I should think you would have no more complaints about *that,*" said the marquess, returning his attention to the newspaper. "Her new clothing is quite respectable," he added. "Charming, really."

This last remark was ill-chosen. The marchioness stamped her foot.

"Charming! Oh!" she said and flounced out.

Jonathan sighed. Perhaps it had been a mistake to accede to Pam's request that the governess join them at dinners. Celia's jealousy, he could see, was in full cry. And he was not prepared to explain Helène Phillips. At any rate, not yet.

Lord Quentin, it seemed, had also taken special care in dressing that evening, and Helène tried not to stare. A neck-cloth tied in the simplest of knots set off the fine black wool of his jacket, and his pantaloons, also black, showed his well-muscled thighs clearly. The pantaloons were secured with silver buckles of classical design; they glittered every time he moved or shifted his weight, and she found herself more aware than she liked of each small movement.

Helène reminded herself sternly that Charles Quentin was of no interest to her. None at all. Now he was saying something to Lucinda Blankenship, who laughed prettily in reply. Well, she is certainly welcome to him, thought Helène. She had spoken to Miss Blankenship on a few occasions and found her quick with a catty remark but otherwise lacking in wit.

He is laughing at me, thought Helène. *I'm sure of it.*

The dinner eventually provided some relief for her discomposure. She found herself seated to the left of the agonizingly shy Viscount Dreybridge, so that a great deal of effort was required on her part to further the conversation. It kept her mind occupied and out of more dangerous waters.

"Are you en-enjoying your s-stay at Luton, Miss Phillips?" attempted the viscount. Kind eyes blinked owlishly from behind a pair of alarmingly thick spectacles. The viscount and viscountess—his cheerful but equally shy wife—were favorites of Helène, as they seemed oblivious of her low consequence and would often talk to her, if haltingly. The pair were newly married and, although they had no family as yet, the viscount had strong opinions on child-rearing which he could sometimes be coaxed to voice.

"I—I quite believe," he told Helène, "that children should be allowed free discovery of the world around them. Let them—let them discover that they must wear shoes, for example, by bruising their toes. Or learn their maths by counting the apples fallen from a tree."

"How should they learn to read?" asked Helène, genuinely curious.

The viscount hesitated. "Perhaps," he allowed, "one might employ books. But—but it seems to me that a stick, used to draw in the dirt—"

He halted in confusion. Helène smiled and, taking pity on his lordship, launched into an extended description of Alice and Peter's daily schedule. This brought them in good order all the way through to the fish.

But as she spoke, Helène's mind occasionally wandered, followed by her gaze. Whenever, by merest chance, her eyes met Lord Quentin's he looked . . . amused. So be it, thought Helène, feeling indignant. She'd done nothing to be ashamed of, and if he thought that she was *amusing,* that was just too bad. Helène acknowledged her naivete in many things, but she wasn't stupid, and she wasn't about to be some fancy lord's bit of fun. Lord Quentin could take his rugged, handsome face, and those deep brown eyes, and his broad shoulders, and—

And take them somewhere else. She wasn't interested.

He was seated next to the marchioness, of course. Lady

Sinclair seemed to laugh delightedly at Lord Quentin's every remark, and it was beginning to grate on Helène's nerves.

"Miss?" The footman interrupted her thoughts, proffering a dessert tureen of *blanc mange*.

"A small portion, thank you."

"Yes, miss."

Her eyes glanced up again of their own accord, and she saw that he was still watching her. She blushed. Lady Sinclair was eyeing them both—she said a few words to Lord Quentin and then turned away. The marchioness did not look pleased.

After dinner the gentlemen were left to their port, and Helène followed the other ladies into the drawing room. It was her habit to remain there only briefly, for politeness, and then retire for the evening, although Lady Pam had asked her more than once to stay.

"I believe Amanda and I are in danger of boring each other senseless. We are in urgent need of fresh topics of conversation."

"Indeed," added Lady Detweiler. "It would be a mercy to have someone new to talk to. If Celia mentions her close family connection to the Duke of Bucchleigh one more time . . ."

Helène demurred. "The marchioness looks daggers at me every time I remain more than a few minutes."

Amanda snorted. "I dare say she's worried you might start speaking in French."

"Ah. *Certainement pas.*"

But this evening was to be different. Lady Sinclair had never sought Helène's company in the drawing room, but tonight she approached the governess almost immediately, wearing a small, tight smile.

"Miss Phillips, I've been anxious to have a word with you."

"Your ladyship?"

"Yes. Well—"

Perhaps it was Jonathan's remark, or the number of times that Lord Quentin had glanced in Helène's direction during that meal. Perhaps it was only the wine. Whatever the reason, Celia's instincts, generally excellent in social niceties, now led her into murky waters.

"That is a beautiful gown you are wearing, Miss Phillips," the marchioness said.

Helène stiffened and resisted the impulse to glance downwards. The neckline of the rose tabby showed more *décolletage* than anything she had worn before; even so, it was no lower than that of any other woman in the room. Including Lady Harkins.

Well, perhaps Lady Sinclair's intentions were benign. Helène smiled tentatively and said, "Thank you, my lady. You are most kind to notice."

"Indeed," said Celia. "One might almost say your wardrobe is *fashionable*. Quite fine, in fact, for a governess."

"I must thank Lady Pamela for the loan of her *modiste*," said Helène. "Madame Gaultier has remarkable taste." Despite the compliment, she was uneasy at Lady Sinclair's attention. Something in the tone of her voice . . . Helène noticed that Lady Pamela and Lady Detweiler had ended their conversation with Lucinda Blankenship and were turning their attention to the marchioness.

"Ah, yes. Lady Pamela is too kind." Celia's eyes glittered. "But my dear, I'm truly afraid that—in this one instance, you understand—she may have led you astray."

Helène was confused. "My lady?"

"That neckline, you see," explained the marchioness. "Quite unremarkable for a woman of higher class, of course. But for *you* . . . Well, I'm sure you understand what I mean."

"I'm afraid I do not," declared Helène. "Pray enlighten me."

"It looks . . . rather whorish."

Silence descended on the room in an eyeblink and was just as quickly broken.

"Celia—"

"Lady Sinclair—"

"Chit deserves it, I daresay. These governesses nowadays—"

Even Lady Dreybridge attempted to say a few, nervous words. Lady Pamela had moved to Helène's side and was telling her something that she couldn't hear. That buzzing sound again. Helène grabbed a deep breath and held on, refusing to faint for the likes of Celia Sinclair. Other people were talking, but she didn't—

"Pray excuse me," she said, finding her voice and looking directly at the marchioness. "I'm afraid I do not find the present company entirely to my liking."

Celia hissed, Lady Harkins gasped. "Of all the impertinent—!"

"Miss Phillips, allow me to accompany you," urged Lady Pamela, the words low and soothing. "Lady Detweiler and I—"

"I'm quite all right," she said to Pam, knowing she sounded ungracious, knowing it wasn't Lady Pamela's fault.

I am not interested in your help. I have no use for any of you, for your world, for your notions of Quality—

The buzzing returned. Helène fought it and managed to make her way out of the room. At the doorway she paused, and looked at the marchioness. Lady Sinclair stared back at her, a smile half-seen at the corner of her mouth.

"Please inform Mrs. Tiggs, " said Helène, "that from now on I shall require my meals brought to my room."

★ ★ ★ ★ ★

"Oh look, maman. It's the pretty carriage . . ."

Pamela turned toward the marchioness with a child's trusting eyes. Something pretty—surely her mother would like that. The phaeton was a warm cream, the wheels picked out in silver. Fit for a princess, thought Pamela, who was staring at the red-haired beauty sitting atop, laughing, head inclined gracefully to the man at her side.

How she would like to ride in a phaeton!

The man said something to the woman. She smiled and touched his arm.

"Pamela. Come here."

Pam skipped after a butterfly, pretending that she hadn't heard her mother's call. Daffodils underfoot, the scent of French lilac in the air—

"Hello, child."

It was her. The lady and the man had dismounted from their phaeton and were walking barefoot through the long meadow grass, hand in hand.

Barefoot!

Pamela stared goggle-eyed at them, and was about to speak—

"You're Helène," she said.

The woman shook her head. "No," she said. "I'm not Helène."

"But—"

"Pamela." Her mother's voice again. "Come here at once!"

"But maman!" Pamela cried. "It's Helène!"

The red-haired woman had something to tell her. She was sure of it.

The candle was just guttering at her bedside when Lady

Pamela awoke. She lit another candle and sat in bed for a long while, thinking. Eventually she got up, throwing a wrapper over her nightgown.

It was time to have a talk with Helène Phillips.

Chapter Nine

Once upon a time—

—there was a rich and powerful duke who had two beautiful daughters. The younger daughter, of sweet and caring disposition, had contracted a disease in childhood and one leg was crippled as a result. She walked with only the slightest of limps, but her parents were ashamed of her nonetheless, and did not allow her to participate in society. Having no sons, the duke and his duchess fixed all their hopes on the elder, who, strong-spirited and independent, was yet expected to marry into high station, in accordance with her parents' wishes.

One day a new carriage arrived at the duke's town home. Cream and silver, it was the most beautiful carriage in all of London, and it was to carry the older daughter that night to the first ball of her coming-out season. The duke escorted the girl outside to show her this marvelous equipage, feeling all the pride of a man who is able to provide every luxury for his family.

"You will be the belle of the season," he told his daughter. "No one will outshine you and you shall have any gentleman you wish."

"It's very beautiful, Father," replied the girl, dutifully. But she was looking at something other than the plush cushions or the velvet drapes. The carriagemaker wished to see at firsthand the pleasure of his customers in a task so finely accomplished. He stood next to the cream and silver coach, one hand gently stroking the bright paint. He was tall and handsome, and the duke's daughter saw past his plain clothes to the

warmth and admiration in his eyes.

The governess had been bewildered by Pam's appearance at her door in the middle of the night and then frightened by Lady Pamela's first question.

Who are you? Pam had asked without preamble. *Who is your mother?*

She was insistent, and eventually, sighing, Helène gave in. The story she told Lady Pamela was both extraordinary and heartbreaking.

"That young man . . . he was your father?" Lady Pamela asked. She was sitting cross-legged at the end of Helène's bed, her feet tucked under the duvet.

"Yes. He was a master carriagemaker. The best workmanship, the finest materials . . . My father insisted that the patron's horses be brought to him, that only if he could see the team could he design a proper carriage 'as a harmonious whole.' But he worked little in the last year."

"He's no longer alive?"

"No." Helène hesitated. "He died shortly before I accepted the position at Luton."

"I'm so sorry," said Lady Pam. She frowned. "And your mother had already passed away?"

"My mother . . . my mother died many years ago. When I was still a small child."

"Good heavens. Did you live alone? Was there no other family to turn to?"

"There was my aunt—"

When the duke discovered that his daughter had developed a tendre *for the carriagemaker he was at first amused. The idea that she could be serious in her fondness for the young man never entered His Grace's head, and he merely forbade her from ever speaking or writing to him again. When they ran off together, in the cream and silver carriage, the duke forbade her name being mentioned in his presence. When his younger daughter continued to insist on it, he sent the girl away, at barely fifteen years of age, to one of his minor country estates.*

The carriagemaker's business thrived. The ton, *even while they condemned His Grace's child as unworthy of her name, flocked to buy her husband's wares. 'Twas the latest fashion, to drive a coach built by the man who married the daughter of a duke. The carriagemaker and his bride moved into a new home, comfortable and with a pleasant prospect, and they lived in great happiness for some time. But the duke's daughter could not quite forget her parents, nor—after the birth of her own daughter—cease to wish that her mother and father could someday hold their first grandchild in their arms.*

Helène faltered over these last few words. "My mother never told me any of this, of course," she told Lady Pam. "I don't even remember her. But my aunt lived with my parents almost from the start—"

"The younger sister?"

"Yes."

"Hmm," said Pamela. She was still mulling over something Helène had mentioned earlier. The Duke of Grentham had no sons?

The duke's younger daughter was, in her own way, as strong willed and persistent as her sister. Now in the country, free of her father's interference—and with plenty of time on her hands— she sent a message to the carriagemaker and his wife. A correspondence began and soon a plot was hatched between them. The sisters would meet in town and, babe in arms, and proceed to-

gether to see the duke and duchess.

Their father would certainly be reconciled, thought the sisters. For who could resist the sight of a rosy-cheeked baby girl . . .

The duke was enraged. The duchess cried and begged him to stop, but he listened to no one. He threw his daughters out of the house and followed them down the front steps and into the rain, berating them furiously as the sisters tried to return to their carriage. That same cream and silver coach—! At the sight of it, the duke's anger took a ferocious, violent turn. There was an edged iron bar sitting discretely to the side of the front door, placed there for the convenience of any guest needing to scrape bits of the London street muck from his shoes. The duke picked it up—

"Dear Lord," breathed Lady Pamela.

—and advanced toward the carriage. By the time he was through, and had collapsed panting, head in hands, on the curb, the beautiful coach had been smashed to bits. Leaving the horses with the groom, the two sisters walked home in the pouring rain; slowly, with Matilde's limp, and Guenevieve sheltering the babe with her cloak. The carriagemaker's wife took ill with the grippe a few days later, and weakened by sleeplessness and her sorrow, she died within the fortnight.

Neither of the sisters ever saw their father or mother again.

Pamela and Helène sat in silence for several minutes. The fire had burned low and Lady Pamela prodded it back to life. She was thinking about the red-haired woman she had seen that day in Hyde Park. Lady Guenevieve Torrance. Guenevieve Torrance Phillips. Helène's mother.

Ironically, it had been the old marchioness who had ensured that her daughter would remember the couple in the

119

cream and silver carriage. Exquisite as Helène's mother had been, Pamela would no doubt have quickly lost interest and returned to the pursuit of butterflies. But the Marchioness had hissed cold fury—

"Pamela, return here at once!"
"But maman!"
"At once!"
Embarrassed, Pamela returned to the carriage. But as she walked away, the red-haired lady winked at her. It was as if she knew.

"And your aunt, I suppose, taught you French—"

"—and Latin. Apparently, my grandfather had felt some guilt that Matilde was unable to participate in society, and tried to make it up to her with a fine education. Until she ran away, she had the tutors one might expect of a duke's son."

"And Matilde lived with you until she died?"

"Yes. About a year ago. My father's business was not what it once was, but we were comfortable enough until then. I think my aunt kept Papa in check. But as her illness worsened, what he didn't spend on her medicine began to go for ale. And then he became ill himself, of course."

"How did you hear of the position at Luton Court?"

"I'm . . . not entirely sure. Aunt Matilde mentioned it first, and later my father said that it was her dying wish . . ." Helène faltered. "I was surprised when the marquess offered me the position. Could my aunt have known him?"

Lady Pamela was wondering the same. But she now turned her attention to another, smaller mystery.

"Is that your mother's ring?" She had just noticed the band with its sapphire that Helène was twisting on her finger.

"It belonged to my grandmother. My father said that a messenger came to the house one day, about a month after my mother died. He gave a parcel to Aunt Matilde; it was the ring. There was no note . . ."

"It's beautiful."

"My father didn't give me the ring until the night before he died. I would have sold it if I'd known. Even though he said it really belongs to the new duke . . ."

The new Duke of Grentham, thought Pamela. Of course. Of course, there must be a new duke—

The governess interrupted her thoughts with a question. "Did you really know my mother?"

"No . . ."

"What is the matter, maman? Didn't you see the carriage? Isn't it beautiful? The lady smiled at me!"

"Don't talk nonsense, child."

"She did! She did! And she winked! Who is she, maman? Who is she?" Pamela bounced up and down on the carriage seat, willing her mother to turn around and look. Maman must know them. She knew everybody. Perhaps Pamela could have a ride in that wonderful coach . . .

"She is no one."

"But maman!"

The marchioness's next words were clipped, uttered in an icy tone of voice that her daughter had long since learned to dread.

"She is Guenevieve . . . Phillips. You are never to speak to her, do you hear me? Never!"

"Helène."

"Umm?" Helène was staring, unseeing, into the fire.

"This changes everything, you know."

"Why?"

"Well, your grandfather. The Duke of Grentham." Pam bit her lower lip, thinking. "Whatever your mother's sins in the eyes of the *ton*—"

"My mother was guilty of nothing more than falling in love with a good man!" cried Helène.

"I am not disagreeing with you," said Lady Pam. "Nevertheless, it will affect your position, your standing in society. Your father was a cit, of course, and you may not be able to marry as you would otherwise—"

"No. Nothing is changed." Helène found, to her embarrassment, that she could not keep the tears from flowing. "My parents are dead and I am exactly the same person that I was before. I am content to earn my living, and . . . and to perdition with the *ton!*"

Lady Pamela blew out her breath, thinking that she had been as guilty as anyone of making certain assumptions about Helène because of her station in life. So easy to dismiss her situation, to fly in like some shining goddess of plenty, bearing lace and silks for the poor governess. It was a lowering thought, to find herself in league with every punched-up dandy and simpering female of the *ton*. Miss Helène Phillips. Only a governess!

Pamela Sinclair was no hypocrite. She enjoyed the perquisites of wealth, enjoyed the comfortable homes, the beautiful clothes—and if she was diligent in certain activities for the benefit of the poor, well, it was simply her acknowledgment of *noblesse oblige*. On the other hand, Lady Pam had never countenanced the *ton*'s easy assumption that an individual outside of their ranks was somehow less than human. She never mistook the circumstances of her birth and breeding for anything other than the sheerest luck.

"But think," she told Helène, "you might *want* to marry. A duke's granddaughter will be forgiven much. You could make a reasonably good match of it.”

“And live among the people who drove my mother to her death?”

Lady Pamela was silent for a moment.

“I’m sorry,” said Helène. “I didn’t mean you, of course.”

“I understand that,” replied Lady Pamela. “But you see, you *do* mean me. Me and Amanda—and even Alice and Peter, for that matter. I can sympathize with your bitterness. But even if the *ton* sometimes acts like a pack of sheep—”

Helène laughed.

“—it is still made up of individuals. Don’t damn us all. ’Tis an individual you would marry.”

Helène shook her head. “I wouldn’t know where to start. Besides, being a governess isn’t that bad.”

“Here, no. Even Celia has her moments, and annoying as she can be, you’ll never starve at Luton. But all children grow up, and the next position may be much less to your liking.”

“I’ll manage.”

“Not to mention that you have one exceedingly serious fault for a governess.”

“What?” cried Helène, aghast.

“You are very attractive.”

Helène looked up at her in confusion.

“Oh, don’t be naive,” said Lady Pam. “Surely Lord Quentin isn’t the first man to take notice of you, whatever your wardrobe.”

“Lord Quentin!” Helène blushed hotly. Lady Pamela merely raised an eyebrow.

“Yes, Lord Quentin. Don’t tell me you haven’t . . . well, never mind. I would write you an excellent reference, of course, but I can imagine there are any number of young wives who wouldn't have you in their house."

"Wouldn't have me in the house!" Helène was outraged. "I can assure you that the puffed up gentlemen of the *ton* hold no interest for me!"

Lady Pamela laughed. "As you say," she told Helène. "But I won't hold you to it forever."

Lady Detweiler, of course, was still awake.

"Thank goodness," she told Pam. "I'd thought you'd retired hours ago. I'm like to die with boredom if you continue to insist on sleeping through the prime of the evening. D' you suppose James could bring us a bit of brandy?"

"It's half-past two in the morning," said Pamela, handing Amanda a decanter.

"Just as I said. Is this Jonathan's best? Marvelous. Now tell me you are here because you have gossip."

"Well, as a matter of fact, yes." She recounted her conversation with Helène. Lady Detweiler was suitably impressed.

"The Duke of Grentham's granddaughter!"

"Yes," said Lady Pamela. "Guenevieve Torrance was her mother."

"I don't remember talk of any grandchild."

"Apparently the old duke cut anyone who dared suggest that he even had daughters," said Pam. "I don't think Helène's birth was much known."

Amanda burst into peals of laughter. "So our dear Lord Quentin has formed an attachment to a duke's chit and doesn't even know it! When will you tell him?"

"I'm not sure I will."

"Pish-posh. Of course—"

"Do you think he is really developing a *tendre* for her? They've hardly had the chance to speak more than a few words together."

"Haven't you been watching him at dinner?"

"Mmm."

"Well I have. And I would guess," said Amanda, "that they've *spoken* together more than you might think."

Lady Pamela walked over to her writing desk. She sat down and thought for a few minutes, chin cupped in hands. Should she tell Jonathan what she knew? What was he likely to do? Or Celia?

No. Not yet. Pamela hunted through the desk and managed to find one pen without a broken nib. She took out a sheet of writing paper.

Dear Mr. Witherspoon, wrote Lady Pamela, explaining her present requirements to her man of affairs.

Chapter Ten

A governess takes no interest in men.

Helène opened the door quietly and looked out into the hall. Here and there a lone beeswax candle burned in its sconce, but there was no sign of human activity. She mentally reviewed the path she would follow to reach the library, and wondered how likely it was that she would encounter the marchioness or, heaven forbid, Lord Quentin. Surely it would be too great a coincidence to find him there again. It was after midnight, and holiday activities had kept the household busy the entire day. Even the energetic Lord Quentin must be a'bed by now.

Oh, fustian, said a little voice. Why should you care if he . . . if someone does see you? He admitted himself that you've as much right as anyone to borrow one of Lord Sinclair's books.

She and the little voice had been arguing all evening, and part of her found its logic appealing. There was a part of her, in fact, that thought it might be highly agreeable if she *did* find Charles Quentin in the library.

Lady Pamela had said that he was interested in her. Helène would have dismissed this idea out of hand if not for the way he had kissed her. As if he wanted to drown in her lips . . .

Heavens, what nonsense. Blushing, Helène went to the mirror, and decided she was satisfied with what she saw. She was still a trifle thin, but she had filled out during the few

126

weeks at Luton, and her skin was smooth and no longer chapped at the first hint of cold. Helène fussed briefly with her hair, wondering if she dared leave it down for the evening's excursion. The nightgown—

The nightgown would have to be changed. Helène wasn't sure what Lady Pamela had been thinking, to ask Madame Gaultier to put together this particular confection. The neckline was nearly indecent, although the cream silk did feel marvelously smooth on her skin. She couldn't imagine why she even had it on, really. Much too flimsy for a winter's night.

You'll have the wrapper on, said the voice. Don't be a ninnyhammer. Just go.

Helène stood, indecisive, in the middle of the room. She intended only a short trip to the library, hardly a minute's time, she knew exactly the volumes she wanted—

A soft knock on the door startled her, and she stared at the door for a moment, frowning. Lady Pamela retired at an disgracefully early hour, according to Lady Detweiler, whenever she was at Luton. Alice or Peter? Helène's heart skipped a beat, wondering if one of the children had been taken ill. Peter had the sniffles that morning, but surely the nanny would have informed her earlier if—

Another knock. Helène opened the door to see . . . Charles Quentin. He was holding a volume of Tacitus.

"You've been avoiding the library, and I should think you're bored silly by now. May I come in?"

This was an outrageous request, and he surely knew it. If she allowed a man in her rooms—at midnight, yet!—the marchioness wouldn't be too far wrong to call her a whore.

"No!" she hissed, allowing herself one covetous glance at the Tacitus. "Are you mad? Lord Sinclair will dismiss me!"

"Oh, is that the problem?" he said, flashing her a grin.

Helène felt trapped. "Well, I can assure you that neither he nor the marchioness will ever find out."

"No, that isn't the problem! Go away!"

"*Mademoiselle—*"

They both heard it at the same time. The sound of footsteps on the staircase at the end of the hall. Celia Sinclair's voice.

"You planned this!" hissed Helène, furious.

"No, as a matter of fact, I didn't." Lord Quentin looked over his shoulder, and she sensed that he was worried. "Don't be a ninny. Let me in or there really *will* be a fuss."

"Oh, bother it all!"

She stood aside and Lord Quentin nipped in, closing the door very softly behind him. For a long moment he stood silent, staring at her. Helène realized she was still wearing only her nightgown. She was both embarrassed and livid.

"What do you think you're doing?" she asked him. "Do you think I can afford to lose my position here?"

"Quiet," he hissed back at her. "Celia will be gone in a moment, and then I'll leave."

"What if someone saw you at my door? What if someone sees you leave? The marchioness—" Helène stopped, realizing that she was about to say something very unflattering about Lady Sinclair.

"The marchioness will have you hung by your toes from the ramparts, yes, I know." Lord Quentin grinned.

"All very easy for you to laugh at!" Helène was finding it difficult to express the extent of her outrage in a whisper. "You and rest of your precious *haut ton*. Your idea of a large problem may be a poorly tied cravat, but I can assure you, *monseigneur,* that losing my position here is no—"

He stepped forward and stopped her tirade with a kiss.

"Mmph!" said Helène, trying to push him away. The kiss

was gentle but his hands on her back were . . .

"Mmm," said Helène.

Why did this man exert such an effect on her? Helène tried to fix her mind on her predicament—the fact that he had no business being in her room, that she would be ruined, dismissed—but nothing she could think of at that moment made his mouth and his hands feel any less wonderful.

"Shh," said Lord Quentin. His lips left hers and trailed softly across the line of her jaw to the hollow of her neck. She heard a soft *thud* and realized that the volume of Tacitus had dropped to the floor. Helène stopped pushing. She began to sag, unresisting, feeling her body sink into a pair of strong arms.

She was hardly aware that Lord Quentin had reached behind her to turn the key of the door lock. He lifted her as if she weighed nothing and carried her to her own bed. Helène felt the soft cotton duvet at her back and then she was floating, aware of nothing more than his hands on her back, his lips trailing across her collarbone. She clutched at the fine wool of his jacket as he shifted his weight onto the bed. A soft sigh escaped her lips.

"Mmm," said Lord Quentin. He seemed to be in no more prudent or sensible a frame of mind than Helène. She saw his eyes close, and felt his hands moving hotly over her breasts. He murmured words she could not hear.

Her nightgown was little more than a wisp of fabric, and Helène could feel every muscle of Lord Quentin's chest as he crushed her against him. His hands descended to her lower back, then returned to her breasts.

They lay together on her bed for some uncounted time, and Lord Quentin's caresses became gradually more insistent. Helène felt herself sinking deeper and deeper into the duvet. A voice inside her said that this was no more than a dalliance for him, lasting perhaps no longer than a night or two, and that she could never be happy with a relationship of that kind.

Or could she? His hands felt better on her body than anything she had imagined. What did it matter, after all? Who was there to care what she did? Lord Quentin was kissing her again, passionately, urgently, and as an experiment Helène touched the tip of her tongue to his lips.

It was as if she had set him on fire. He moaned and shifted fully on top of her, fumbling at the buttons of his breeches.

"You are so beautiful," he murmured into her ear, "I wish—"

The rest of his words were lost in another moan, and the effect would perhaps have been more romantic if she hadn't immediately heard her father's voice—

Pretty is as pretty does.

"Lord Quentin," said Helène, struggling to sit up. "Please."

"No one will find out," he gasped, nuzzling at her breasts. "I promise you no one will find out."

Who was there to care what she did?

She cared.

Charles was no longer thinking clearly. He was no stranger to the *boudoir,* of course, and the position he now found himself in—entwined with a gorgeous woman on top of a bed—was a position he had been in many times before.

But the beauty on this occasion seemed to be having second thoughts, and Lord Quentin was having difficulty bringing himself under control. Damn the chit, anyway, had she bewitched him? He couldn't even look at Miss Helène Phillips without becoming aroused. And now . . .

And now they were in her bedroom, the whole night ahead

of them, and his mind was awash with desire. Desire was all he could think about, all he could feel.

He needed her more than he remembered needing any woman before.

"Lord Quentin, please," said the girl. She pushed weakly at his chest.

He rolled away from her and stretched out on his back, feeling irritable, very irritable. How could the blasted girl ask him to stop now?

Charles had conveniently forgotten that only a few minutes earlier he had essentially forced himself into Helène's room. At the moment his thoughts were focusing more on the fact that he was the heir to an earldom and she was merely a governess. She ought to be *jumping* at the chance to be . . .

To be what? He hadn't thought much further ahead than the next few minutes. Perhaps that was the real problem. Miss Helène Phillips was an intelligent woman. Too intelligent to engage in a brief affair, especially with Celia on the prowl, perhaps waiting for an excuse to be rid of her.

Charles recovered his equilibrium, and was cheered by a sudden inspiration. Helène Phillips would become his *mistress*. Of course. They would need to be discreet until he was able to return to London, but certainly she would be delighted at the prospect, and be willing to—

To indulge him. Tonight. Right now, in fact.

He endured an almost painful tightening of his groin at the thought. She would be delighted, overjoyed! And what woman wouldn't be, to be the mistress of Lord Charles Quentin? No more worries about money, about letters of reference, about Celia Sinclair—it was the perfect solution, for both of them. He would settle Miss Phillips in a fine London townhouse, and spend night after night after night . . .

A small, incoherent sound escaped his lips. Helène was

saying something . . .

"Lord Quentin!"

Charles realized that he had been idly caressing her breasts with his hand. He grinned at Helène and leaned over her so that she was pinned on her back between his arms. Her thick auburn hair spread out in waves over the coverlet and every curve of her body was limned by the thin silk chemise.

"I have an idea," he began.

"Lord Quentin, I must insist you let me up immediately! I'm terribly sorry that I didn't say so at once, but—"

"Mmm," said Charles. "You look adorable when you are angry."

It was true. Miss Phillips's eyes flashed green fire and her mouth formed an "o" of protest. He kissed it. Following a brief tussle—which Charles found almost unbearably stimulating—the girl pushed him away and sprang from the bed.

"Get *out!*" cried Miss Phillips, when she could finally speak.

"For heavens sake, keep quiet!" warned Charles, wincing and rising to his feet. He hoped that nobody had been passing by in the hallway at that particular moment.

"It's rather late to be concerned about my reputation, don't you think?" Her voice had returned to a whisper, but she was still agitated, and Charles was nearly out of patience.

Damn it all. If she would only calm down, he could describe to her the many advantages of becoming his mistress.

"Let me suggest—" he began.

"No!" in a fierce whisper.

"But if you'll only listen for a moment, and allow me to explain—"

"I am *finished* listening to you for this evening, my lord."

"Miss Phillips!"

The voice, from the hallway outside the door, brought their hissed conversation to an abrupt close. Celia's voice. Lord Quentin thought furiously for a second, and then mimed sleep to Miss Phillips.

Wide eyed, she pointed at the bed in question.

No. No, that wouldn't do. She would have to answer the door—

"Miss Phillips!"

—but not in *that* nightgown. Charles looked around, noticed her wrapper and threw it to the girl. He motioned to the door. She shook her head, violently, pointing at him. Oh, for the love of—

"*Miss Phillips,* are you in there?"

There was no help for it. Charles moved silently across the room to the wardrobe and squeezed in, quietly pulling the door closed. Of all the ridiculous—! He'd hardly touched the girl, and here he was, hiding in the closet like a love-struck twenty-year-old. Lord Quentin prided himself on the discreet and dignified nature of his *affaires de coeur.* Crouching in a wardrobe had never been necessary before, and he was highly annoyed with the stubborn Miss Helène Phillips for making it necessary now. If she had only kept her mouth shut and let him explain—

He heard the door open.

"Miss Phillips, *what* is going on in here?"

"I beg your pardon?"

Don't let her in! thought Lord Quentin, wishing that he could somehow send signals through the wardrobe door.

"I'm quite sure I heard a man's voice in this room, Miss Phillips. I'm asking for an explanation."

"A man's voice?" The governess, to Charles' relief, sounded genuinely sleepy and confused.

"Yes!" From the sound of it, Celia was still standing in the doorway. Lord Quentin could imagine the marchioness's frustration at not being allowed a clear view of the entire room.

"I beg your pardon, my lady, but you must be mistaken. I've had a terrible headache this evening—" The governess broke off suddenly and Charles heard a sound of annoyance from Lady Sinclair.

"Miss Phillips, really, I'm sure you don't expect me to believe—"

"Mmm." A soft moan. That must be the girl, thought Charles. What was happening?

There was a loud thump, followed by a moment's silence. Then—

"Oh, bother it all."

The door slammed shut and a lengthier silence ensued. What on earth had happened to Miss Phillips? Lord Quentin was very tired of being hunched over in a woman's wardrobe, but he had a healthy respect for Celia's cunning. She might wait at the doorway, listening. . . .

Another long minute went by, and then Charles heard soft footsteps. The wardrobe was flung open and Miss Phillips stood there, eyes blazing, in silence. She motioned toward the window.

"Your exit, I believe, my lord," she hissed.

Lord Quentin shook his head. He'd climbed out of a few *boudoir* windows in his rambunctious youth, to be sure, but it was a method used more for speed than stealth.

"Too noisy," he whispered back.

"C'est tant pis," she retorted. "By the time they find you in the bushes nobody will be able to prove which window you came from. Tell them you were trying to climb into Lady Harkins's room and she pushed you away. Tell them anything—I don't care. Just get out."

"What happened?" he asked her, stalling. "I heard something fall."

"I fainted. Again."

"You really fainted?"

Miss Phillips looked disgusted. "Of course not." She had grabbed his wrist and was yanking him toward the window.

Lord Quentin chuckled. "Good job."

"Well, I certainly didn't do it for your approval. Now, please go."

Charles decided an offer of *carte blanche* could wait until the next morning. The girl was overwrought. He eyed the view from the window. A ledge several feet below, then a drop into a bank of yews. Well, he had climbed down from worse.

"Until tomorrow then, fair maiden," he told her, pretending to hold a hat in his hands and making a sweeping bow.

Was that the hint of a smile? He preferred to think so. But the governess watched, silent and impassive, while he climbed out the window. As he hung, swaying, from the ledge, about to drop to the turf below, Lord Quentin heard the unmistakable click of a window latch being closed.

Charles smiled to himself. Impudent little vixen! He was beginning to think that Miss Helène Phillips was a woman of whom one might not easily tire.

Chapter Eleven

Alice and Peter, faces shining and hair full of snow, caught up with Helène as she returned to the house from her morning walk. Lady Pam trailed behind, grimacing with the effort to keep her skirts held above the ever growing drifts of snow.

The children began talking at once.

"Oh, Miss Phillips, did you hear—?"

"Miss Phiwips! We're going to—"

"Let me tell her!"

"No! You *always* get to tell her *everything!*"

"No, I don't!"

Helène could see another snowball fight brewing; fortunately, Lady Pamela had now joined the group.

"I'll tell her, if you please," said Lady Pam. Both children looked downcast. "Oh, don't be little fussbudgets. You're going to need to warm up first anyway, so go ask Nanny to help you out of those clothes. I believe Cook is making poppyseed cake today."

Peter's eyes lit up. "Yes, ma'am," he and Alice responded, and they bounced off.

"Tell me what?" asked Helène, after the children reached the house without further conflict. "And isn't it a bit early for Alice and Peter to be outside?"

"Pah!" said Lady Pamela. "They were too excited at the news." She gestured to the scene around her. "And besides, this is new-fallen snow! You cannot expect children to remain inside when there is new-fallen snow!"

Helène laughed. "And the news?"

136

" 'Tis the cutting of St. Raymond's tree on the morrow."

"St. Raymond?"

"A long story. But the short of it is, that although the men usually cut the tree by themselves, this year Celia has decided we should make a 'snow-picnic' of the event."

"Lady *Sinclair* suggested—?" She and Lady Pamela had started walking back to the house; Helène now stopped to stare at Pam in disbelief.

"Don't look so shocked. I'm sure Celia ventures outside from time to time. I understand she has a fine new winter outfit, complete with an enormous rabbit's fur muff."

"And—?" suggested Helène, not quite believing that a new muff was enough to convince the marchioness to brave the elements.

"And, there will be a ride on the hayrack, where I believe it is traditional for the gentlemen to make sure the ladies are kept warm."

"Ah."

"Ah, yourself," said Lady Pam. "You will be joining us, of course."

"Hmm," said Helène. They had almost reached the kitchen door. The two women stood on the stoop and brushed snow from their skirts, inhaling the unmistakable aroma of almonds and poppyseed.

"I think not," she finally answered Pamela. "Nanny is too old to go, of course, but surely one of the footmen could be assigned to watch Alice and Peter."

Lady Pamela lifted her eyebrows. "You will *not* be asked to keep charge of the children," she told Helène. "They will be well occupied. Besides, 'twill be harmless fun. Amanda has been convinced to join us, so we can easily contrive to help you avoid Celia."

"Even so." Helène managed a great, theatrical sigh. "I'm

sure the children will be delighted to escape their taskmistress for an afternoon."

"Taskmistress?" Lady Pamela sniffed. "To be sure, one can see how much Alice and Peter despise you."

Helène was forced to laugh. "No, I don't mean that . . ." She hesitated, the reason for her reluctance to join the party not something she wanted to admit even to herself. It was one thing to *know* that the very beautiful Lady Celia Sinclair had fixed her interest on Charles Quentin. It was quite another to watch it happening. A cold evening's ride in a hayrack? She could already see Lady Sinclair and Lord Quentin huddled together, almost hear Celia's protests—

"Oh, Charles. My hands are so cold."

Helène shook her head. Botheration. Why should she care whose hands Lord Charles Quentin chose to warm? His activities were a matter of indifference to her, after all. Nevertheless . . .

Lady Pamela had seen the warring emotions on Helène's face and her perception was, as always, acute.

"You aren't really worried about the children, are you?" she asked Helène—and then, without stopping for a reply— "You're worried about Celia and Charles Quentin."

"No! Well, that is, of course, the marchioness is not overly fond of me. I try to stay out of her way."

Lady Pam nodded. "And Lord Quentin?"

Helène found a bit of snow still clinging to her skirt. She brushed it away. "What about Lord Quentin?"

Lady Pamela studied Helène closely. The governess was blushing, despite herself.

"Helène. Tell him."

"No."

In the end, the choice of whether or not to join the next

day's activities was made for her. Shortly after Helène returned to her rooms, a footman arrived with a note from the marquess, requesting that she accompany the party to a "St. Raymond's Day Tree-Cutting And Snow Pick-nick." Helène assumed that her presence was required only to mind the children, being unaware of a conversation between Lord Sinclair and Charles Quentin in which her name figured prominently. At any rate, there was no avoiding it now, and she comforted herself with the thought that she would scrupulously avoid Lord Quentin, and certainly *not* speak with him.

The day of the "pick-nick" dawned clear and cold, but there was happily little wind. Helène, who had never before dined *al fresco* in the middle of winter, anticipated being miserably chilled, but she had not counted on the ingenuity of the marchioness when physical comfort was at question. The party gathered in a sheltered clearing at the edge of a small forest of Scotch pine. An army of servants had preceded the guests, trampling the snow into a smooth, flat surface and laying huge rugs over the ground. Comfortable winged-back chairs, each with its own set of wool blankets, were clustered about, with heated bricks to be used as foot-rests. Several bonfires blazed away at the edge of the clearing, and the guests stood chatting as footmen circulated with cups of mulled wine.

An overwhelming quantity of food, all served in the highest style on silver platters or in crystal bowls, was laid out on linen-draped tables, with chafing dishes to keep various dishes warm. Alice and Peter were in alt, running circles around the party, flopping backwards in the snow to make angels, asking everyone in earshot, over and over, "Which tree? Where is it? When can we cut the tree?" The marchioness tried to shoo them away, only to be countermanded by her husband. Childish fun, it seemed, was to be allowed.

Celia Sinclair stood out from the rest of the group in a long fur-lined pelisse of scarlet wool, the red in bright contrast to the white and green of her surroundings. The other ladies were similarly arrayed, if less colorful. Helène was astounded to find each of them in possession of appropriate and stylish cold weather garments, as few of the women had previously exhibited any interest in the out-of-doors. She herself was only adequately dressed in her forest-green pelisse, covered on this occasion with a mantle of grey wool borrowed from Lady Pam.

The mantle had earned her a curt remark from Lady Sinclair.

"My goodness, Miss Phillips, I hope that association of colors will not frighten the horses."

Make up your mind, thought Helène. Do you want me to be well dressed or not? But she was enjoying the day too much to worry about the marchioness.

"Miss Phillips! Miss Phillips!"

The children ran towards her with the news that they had discovered a "big river" nearby. A *river?* The Lea flowed through the northern part of the estate, but that was some distance away. Still, feeling uneasy about Peter's common sense with flowing water, Helène followed them through the woods to have a look.

"See, Miss Phillips! We told you!"

The children had reached the bank of a small creek that flowed in twists and turns down a wooded, rock-strewn slope. Partially frozen over, the creek sparkled in the sunshine against the green background of pine. Bare sticks of willow poked through the ice near the edge of the stream, and the sound of the water was a soft murmur in the otherwise silent woods.

Peter threw a pebble onto the ice. Parts of it seemed solid.

Helène had heard of people . . . skating on rivers. She had
seen a pair of the odd shoes in a shop once, high-laced leather
with a piece of polished metal on the soles, somewhat like the
runner to a sled. But one could hardly skate on something like
this, surely it wasn't smooth enough—

It was a very small creek, really. Peter threw another rock,
apparently content to stay well away from the edge of the water. Alice was complaining that Helène had not allowed her to
bring her sketchbook. She began drawing something in the
snow with a stick. The burble of water was almost hypnotiz-
ing. Helène took a small step forward, imagining what it
might be like to glide over a river of ice.

"You *are* a little fool, aren't you?" teased a male voice, almost in her ear.

Helène jumped. One foot slipped as she turned around,
and she began to fall. Immediately, a strong arm wrapped itself around her waist, hauling her upright and away from the
creek's edge. She looked into the eyes of Lord Charles
Quentin. He was smiling.

"What are you doing? Let go!" Helène tried to extricate
herself, but her captor was unyielding.

"Alice. Peter. Go back to your father." Lord Quentin's
arm was still around her waist. He motioned the children
away from the creek.

"But Lord Quentin!" protested Alice. "It's pretty!"

"I'm sure the marquess can arrange for James to bring you
more hot chocolate," he told her. "And Alice—"

"Yes, sir?" said the girl.

"We wouldn't want your father to scold Miss Phillips,
would we?"

"Oh no, sir!"

"Why would Father scold Miss Phiwips?" asked Peter,
eyes wide.

"Because she almost fell into some very cold water. Your papa might not think she was clever enough to be your governess, doing something as foolish as that."

The mock seriousness of his tone was lost on both children, and Peter looked up at her with a shocked expression.

"Oh, for heaven's sake!" said Helène.

"We won't tell!" said Alice.

"Good. Now off with you." They trooped away obediently, but Lord Quentin did not loosen his grip. Helène stopped struggling and stood, rigid and furious, feeling his breath warm in her ear.

"You are no longer joining us at dinner," he said. "Why is that?"

"I did not 'almost fall into cold water!' " she told him, choosing to leave the playfulness of his words unacknowledged. "Are you mad? I wouldn't even have slipped if you hadn't startled me!"

"You've entirely the right of it," said Lord Quentin. "I do apologize."

Startled by his answer, Helène found herself with nothing else to say. "Very well," she muttered, finally. "Now be so good as to let me go—"

"You haven't answered my question."

She was beginning to feel a little weak in the knees. Lord Quentin's body was strong and warm against hers, and Helène felt his lips nuzzling the top of her head.

"I prefer to eat alone."

"I don't believe you."

Her body betrayed her, insisting that it wished to remain standing there enfolded in his arms. But . . . what had Lord Quentin just said?

"I don't care what you believe," Helène retorted, and, pushing his arms aside with sudden strength, she stomped away.

★ ★ ★ ★ ★

The marchioness had decided that champagne was *de rigeur* for a winter's picnic, while the marquess preferred the warmth of brandy. Consequently, both were offered in addition to the wine, in liberal portions, and by mid-afternoon the greater number of the guests were somewhat unsteady to foot. Lady Sinclair was in her element, shrieking with laughter at every jest or *bon mot* from the gentlemen, and had attached herself quite firmly to Lord Quentin's side.

"Doesn't the marquess notice anything?" Helène asked Lady Pamela and Lady Detweiler, and was promptly embarrassed to think she had voiced such an impertinence aloud.

"An excellent question," answered Amanda. She shrugged. "I believe much of what Celia does is indeed *designed* for her husband's notice. But Jonathan's attention seems quite difficult to catch, these days."

"Can't he see what she's doing—?" Helène stopped. Both women were looking at her with raised eyebrows.

"He?" Lady Detweiler asked the girl. "The marquess? Or Lord Quentin?"

"I—well—" She blushed. *What is wrong with me?* wondered Helène. Mooning over an arrogant, conceited lord as if she believed in fairy tales! The shy governess and the handsome earl-to-be, living happily ever after in some ivy-covered castle. Well! Celia Sinclair could just *have* him, every last bit of him, because Helène was finished with such nonsense. She'd sooner marry a *footman*.

"Why are the gentlemen cutting down a tree?" she asked, focusing her attention on a less aggravating subject.

"Oh, don't get me started," begged Amanda.

Lady Pam laughed. "In a word," she said, "tradition."

"In a word," said Amanda, "a parcel of male nonsense."

"Isn't that what I just said?" Pamela turned to Helène.

"All of the local countryside was once wooded. But even before the modern century began much of the forest was gone. Used for cottages and firewood, I suppose. One of the early marquesses tried to forbid the cutting of timber on estate property—"

"But it's a very long story," interrupted Amanda, motioning for one of the footmen's attention. "D' you suppose Celia thought to bring any sherry?"

"Yes," said Lady Pam. "Well, to shorten things a bit, each year the gentlemen of the household cut one large tree—"

"Drunk as a lord, every one of them. It's a wonder no one's ever been killed."

"—and present it to the people of Luton-on-Lea on St. Raymond's Day," finished Lady Pam. "There's a very nice ceremony in front of the church, that sort of thing."

"Ah."

"Don't forget to tell her the part about the donkey," said Lady Detweiler.

Viscount Dreybridge approached Helène a short while later, wondering if he might "borrow" Alice and Peter for a "scientifical experiment."

"I—I believe," he stammered, "I believe that children have a natural . . . instinct for geometry. Figuring the height of that tree, for example. We will employ the So—Socratic method, and—"

"Alice is but seven," said Helène. "Peter is five. Surely they are not ready for geometry."

"No, no!" said the Viscount, undeterred. "It is a perfect age. They have no previous misunderstandings of scientific methods to overcome. Now adults, on the other hand—"

He rambled on. The children adored the viscount and were agreeable to the project, so, with some misgivings,

Helène gave them leave to go. Accepting a small glass of mulled wine from one of the footmen, she stood in front of one of the bonfires. The heat was almost painful on her cheeks, and Helène hoped some of the warmth would find its way to her toes.

"I will teach you to ice-skate, if you wish." The soft voice was right behind her, and Helène had just enough presence of mind not to jump. Lord Charles Quentin. Of course. He stood grinning, his hand already at her elbow.

"The Lea is often frozen thickly enough by the middle of January," he added. "But you must promise never to go near it without me."

He steered her over to the far side of the bonfire. It would be churlish to refuse his company, thought Helène, and so she went unresisting, but with a worried glance in the marchioness's direction. Lady Sinclair looked displeased. Wonderful, thought Helène. He amuses himself with the hired help for a scant few minutes, and I have *her* looking daggers at me for the rest of the afternoon.

"I appreciate your offer, my lord," began Helène, hoping, as she told herself, to be rid of him quickly. "But I really don't think—"

"We haven't finished our conversation," said Lord Quentin, as if she had not spoken.

A conversation! Is that what he called it? Helène felt a twinge of annoyance at the man's high-handed manner. "I don't recall—"

"And I will continue to plague you until you have heard me out."

"Then by all means, my lord," said Helène. "Let us finish at once. You have my entire attention."

Her heart had begun to thump alarmingly, and her thoughts raced. Why was he here? Was he playing some game with her—or with the marchioness? Perhaps his attentions were all to make Lady Sinclair jealous, and Helène no more than an expendable pawn.

Yes, decided Helène. *That* was undoubtedly the reason for his interest. Even the other night . . . was it a coincidence that Charles Quentin appeared at her door moments before they heard Celia? Suddenly this seemed very unlikely, and Helène's annoyance changed to fury. How like the Quality, to assume other people had no feelings!

"What is it?" she heard Lord Quentin ask. She turned to see an honest question in his eyes. Helène had never been skilled at hiding her emotions, and she realized that much of what she was thinking must have been mirrored in her face.

" 'Tis all a good game to you, I'm sure, my lord," she told him. "But I am not playing."

"A game?" He had the grace to look confused.

"Aye," said Helène. "But I pray you, choose someone else to gain Lady Sinclair's jealousy. I'm afraid I could not muster enough interest to make the charade convincing."

There! Let him think again, if he was so convinced she was easy prey.

Lord Quentin shook his head and chuckled quietly.

"What Celia thinks should be a matter of indifference to you, Miss Phillips," he told her. "As it certainly is to me."

Helène shot him a disbelieving look. "Ah, but you are mistaken, my lord," she said. " 'Tis a matter of great concern to me, if I have a position at Luton Court, or must needs return to an uncertain future in London."

The fire blazed up for a moment, a shower of sparks falling out into the snow. They stepped back and once again Helène felt Charles Quentin's strong arm at her back. A chill ran through her that had nothing to do with the weather.

"Your future is not uncertain."

Startled by the odd intensity of his words, Helène looked up at Lord Quentin. His brown eyes were warm and compelling, and she forced herself to turn away.

"No," she answered. "No, I indeed hope not. Now, if you will excuse me—"

"Don't go." He placed both hands on her shoulders. Helène fancied she felt the marchioness's stare knifing into her back. She attempted to back away but his grip was strong, his fingers decidedly intimate even through the heavy wool of her cape. She felt short of breath, and angry at herself for her own, mindless reaction.

Foolish girl.

"I understand your concerns," Lord Quentin was saying. He spoke in a near whisper. "But I have a . . . an idea."

An idea? What was this?

"I can imagine no idea of yours which would be of any help, my lord," she whispered back. "Unless you have children in need of a governess."

There was silence for a moment. While the fire crackled and warmed her cheek, the other sounds of the party—the murmur of conversation, the clatter of silver—seemed to fade. Abruptly, as if the knowledge had been transferred directly into her soul, burning there like a brand, she knew exactly what idea Charles Quentin was talking about.

Helène turned to face him. She raised her eyebrows. "Ah. I see. I've been a bit of a slow-top, I suppose. You mean to offer me *carte blanche?*"

It was plain speaking. Lord Quentin appeared momentarily disconcerted, then he smiled at Helène. "Perhaps I've been too forward. But I had the impression—the other night—that you do not judge me . . . repugnant to your sensibilities."

The words spoke of hesitation and doubt. But Helène saw amusement in Charles Quentin's eyes, and she realized that he felt sure of himself. Sure that she would say yes.

"You are a beautiful, intelligent woman. You are wasted here—"

"And I should find my true worth in your bed?"

Lord Quentin blew out a slow breath. Perhaps it now occurred to him that he was approaching his subject in an awkward way.

"Your pardon," he finally said. "I do not mean to imply that your worth lies only in your . . . mmm . . ."

"Physical attributes?" supplied Helène. "I am glad that you admit some possibility of other talents on my part."

"You misunderstand the nature of what I am suggesting."

"Misunderstand *carte blanche?*" Helène spat back. "I think not." Her voice was sharp, her pique rapidly mounting. Perhaps it was her very real attraction to the man that added fury to the insult. She longed to slap him, to hurl curses at that smiling, arrogant face. But a public scene was unthinkable. Helène was aware that Lady Sinclair was watching every gesture between herself and Lord Quentin. Even if the marchioness could not hear the words—

She forced herself to speak calmly, as if they were discussing nothing more than the height of the tree selected to be cut for St. Raymond's Day.

"Let me assure you, my lord, that I do not find you personally repugnant," she told Lord Quentin. "Only your idea of proper employment for a respectable female."

"Don't be so quick to dismiss the idea. Is *this* what you aspire to in the way of employment? Alice and Peter are pleasant enough children, I dare say, but—"

"They're quite wonderful, actually."

"—but this cannot be what you wished for your life. It is customary to settle a certain sum of money on one's . . . mistress. You would never need work again, even if our relationship . . . mmm . . ."

"Even after you send me on my way? 'Tis a pleasant thought, I admit."

"You are deliberately twisting my words!"

Helène noted, with satisfaction, that the gentleman was now just as angry as she.

"This conversation is over, my lord. Whatever you may think of governesses, " she told him, "I can assure you that we are not whores."

"Miss Phillips, I never meant—"

"You never meant!" Helène knew that Lady Sinclair still watched them, knew, too, that it would be no difficulty for the marchioness to guess the source of conflict between Lord Quentin and the governess. She was past caring. "Oh, my lord, you meant *exactly* that!"

His eyes blazed. "I can assure you, Miss Phillips, that any mistress of mine is no whore."

"We disagree, then, on the plain meaning of an English word."

"You would have your own establishment in town. Clothing, jewels, anything at all. Most women in your station would jump at the chance to better themselves—"

"To *better* myself!" Helène's voice rose, her fury suddenly complete. She could feel the guests—and Lady Sinclair, certainly—turning to look at Lord Quentin and herself. Disaster loomed, inexorable and hungry.

"Miss Phillips! Miss Phillips!"

Alice and Peter appeared at her side, tugging on her cape. Lady Pamela was close at their heels and Lady Detweiler— Helène noticed, from the corner of her eye—had engaged the viscountess and Lady Harkins in animated conversation.

"Miss Phillips! Aunt Pamela said we can help cut the tree!"

"Cut the tree?" Helène was all at sea for a moment. What tree?

Lord Quentin proved faster to respond. He looked at the children and frowned. "I'm sure your father will let you watch us, but—"

"Sorry," interjected Lady Pamela, moving quickly to Helène's side. She sent a speaking look to Lord Quentin. "Best I could think of on the spur of the moment. Now, Alice—" She turned her attention to the girl. "Please explain to Peter that when I said help *cut* the tree, what I meant was—"

"But, Aunt Pamela!"

"You *said—!*"

"Alice. Peter." Helène's voice was soft. The children immediately stopped arguing and turned their attention to her. Lord Quentin chuckled.

"How do you *do* that?" asked Lady Pamela.

"When the gentlemen are ready to cut the tree, you may watch, but only if you are standing next to me and holding my hand."

"Yes, Miss Phillips," chorused Alice and Peter.

"Now, come along. The fire has made me quite thirsty, and I shall need you to help me find some hot chocolate." Helène left Lady Pamela with Lord Quentin and, one child in each hand, walked away without a backward glance.

"Lord Quentin, a word with you if I may," said Pamela Sinclair.

The gentlemen had selected a well-formed pine not too far from the clearing and were now rallying to the cause, bearing axes and a two-man timber saw. Men and their traditions!

However much she may have reassured Helène, Lady Pamela had always worried that the St. Raymond's Day tree-cutting was an affair ripe for disaster. Amanda was quite correct about the amount of spirits that were generally consumed. But the marquess had undergone a long apprenticeship during their father's day, and her brother was generally trustworthy in matters of straightforward labor. This year, as it happened, they also had the Viscount Dreybridge, who was a dab hand with an axe. The viscount and Lord Quentin had remained more sober than some of the rest and Jonathan now set them to work.

"Alice! Peter! Come to mama, darlings."

The voice, against all expectation, was that of Lady Sinclair. She stood as close to the working group of men as she dared, with her rabbit's fur muff in one hand and champagne in the other, and called for the children.

"Good heavens. What is Celia going on about now?" was Amanda's comment. "Is she trying to add 'maternal' to her list of talents?"

"I should say so," said Lady Pamela.

"I don't think she's that good an actress."

"She does try with them, you know," added Pam. "And I suppose she's noticed that Charles is fond of children."

It was true. Alice and Peter, with the unerring instinct of the young, had discovered that Lord Quentin was the one gentleman of the party with a gift for play. He'd been flat on his back making snow-angels with them earlier, and his coat still sported the evidence.

"If Celia thought the children were the key to Charles's affection, I dare say she'd be down in the snow herself," said Lady Detweiler. "Did you decide to tell him, by the way?"

"Mmm?"

"Don't be coy," said Amanda. "Did you tell Lord Quentin

151

that he's been making free with the granddaughter of a duke?"

Lady Pam sighed. She'd known for weeks that Charles found the governess attractive, but something else had happened between the two of them today.

"No," she told Lady Detweiler. "And I don't think I can—"

"Oh, for pity's sake, why not!"

Lady Pam considered this. "For one thing, Helène specifically asked me not to."

"Pish-posh. She can hardly be twenty—what does she know?"

"Nineteen, I believe. But for some people nineteen is as good as thirty. Perhaps she would prefer to be loved for herself."

"Idealistic nonsense. What on earth would it mean? No one is ever loved for themselves. Their looks, their money, their connections, yes, but—"

Pamela laughed. The subject of true love never failed as a source of skeptical comment from Amanda.

"So, what was it?" asked Amanda.

"What was what?"

Amanda threw up her hands. "How can we gossip if you won't pay attention? What *did* you tell the illustrious Lord Quentin?"

"That if he was the cause of Helène's dismissal, I should have Jonathan call him out."

That was too much even for Lady Detweiler. She snorted. "D' you want your brother killed? Besides, wouldn't the marquess be the one who had dismissed her?"

"Mmm," said Lady Pam. "That's a point. But Lord Quentin assured me that there was no mischief afoot."

Amanda groaned. "I shall despair of you yet. She's a

woman. He's a man. Of course there will be mischief."

As the men prepared to make the final, uphill cut on the St. Raymond's Day tree, Lord Sinclair rounded up the more inebriated and instructed them to stay out of harm's way. The marchioness kept Alice and Peter at her side, and the best Helène could do was to stay as close to Lady Sinclair as she dared.

"*Evoe!*" shouted the marquess, an ancient Luton battle cry. An ear-splitting report rattled the ground and bounced off the nearby hills, and the tree—slowly, as if sinking through water— began to lay itself down on the hill. Helène watched in mixed trepidation and awe. She had never seen anything so large . . . fall. The tree continued its descent for what seemed like minutes, tearing branches from neighboring trees with a *crack crack crack*. Then came a thunderous crash that she felt through her feet, and finally, abruptly, silence. Peter, entranced by the huge cloud of snow flung into the air by the tree's impact, slipped from Lady Sinclair's grasp and dashed forward. But the pine, although horizontal, was not at rest. It shifted slightly and began to roll.

"Peter!" cried Helène. She ran forward to grab his arm, and caught it—

—too late. The boy fell, his feet slipped under the trunk, and down they went in the snow. Helène tried to cover Peter's body with hers. Above them echoed the terrific noise of a branch splintering as the tree continued to shift . . . then, again, silence.

Lord Quentin was wielding the final cuts of the axe and did not see Peter run forward, turning around only at Helène's cry. The boy and the governess went down in a flurry of snow and breaking tree limbs as the tree continued to roll—only another few inches, but it seemed to take an eternity. He could see a small foot . . .

Why had she let go of the child's hand? Lord Sinclair was already on his knees in the snow, digging, and in the next moment Charles and the viscount were at his side. The party was a babble of confusion. The men worked furiously, with Alice crying in the background, Lady Pamela comforting her, Celia wailing some complaint—

A second foot appeared, then the green wool of a woman's cape.

"Take care," said the marquess. "There may be broken bones."

"Papa!" Peter's face appeared from under the cape, followed by an arm. He was scratched but otherwise unhurt and Lord Sinclair lifted him gently away from the tree. Lady Detweiler retrieved the boy, and the men returned to Helène, who was still motionless in the snow. Her breathing was regular, however, and there was no obvious injury. Charles carefully felt the back of her neck.

"Miss Phillips," said Jonathan. "Miss Phillips, you must wake up."

"Mmm," came the murmur. Her eyes fluttered open, and she stared at nothing in particular.

"Cold," she said, eyes threatening to close.

"Miss Phillips," said the marquess. "We will assist you directly, but we must know if you can move your legs."

This had some effect. Another second's silence, then Helène struggled to sit up in the snow.

"Do not move," commanded the marquess.

"I am quite fine," she told him, coming to her senses. "And yes, I can move my legs—and feel them, too. They are very cold. Now if one of you gentlemen would be so kind—"

She extended her hand. It was at this moment—he

couldn't have explained the impulse, he only knew that the scare had left him angry and shaken—that Lord Quentin lost his temper.

"You harebrained little fool! You could have been killed! What were you about, not keeping a good hand on the boy?"

Helène hesitated. The marquess, who knew what had happened, and who wished to have a word with his wife before discussing the matter with anyone else, sighed and rubbed the bridge of his nose. He shrugged at Helène.

"You're quite right, my lord," said Helène. "It was very foolish."

This stopped the tirade. "Indeed," muttered Charles, and he stalked away.

Lord Sinclair had an extended, private conversation with his son while the rest of the men sawed off the remaining branches and then roped the tree to a team of horses. The head groomsman was in charge of walking the team to the village, dragging the pine behind them through the snow, while the rest of the party prepared for the evening's ride in a hayrack. Peter had objected loudly and at length to missing this portion of the day's entertainment. In the end, Helène and Pamela tucked him and Alice snugly into the hay, covered them with a pile of blankets, and watched for the three or four minutes it took before both children were soundly asleep.

The other guests crowded after them into the racks. Lady Sinclair and Lord Quentin sat together, and although it was difficult to see much in the dark—the torches being reserved for the benefit of horses and driver—Helène caught occasional snatches of their conversation. It was more than she wished to hear. The marchioness had, by this time, imbibed a very large quantity of champagne, and she was a giggly, affectionate drunk.

"Tonight," she thought she heard Lady Sinclair whisper. But Helène didn't catch Lord Quentin's reply.

Chapter Twelve

The governess can expect immediate dismissal for any of the following indiscretions . . .

Charles paced back and forth in his bedroom, trying to convince himself that his current state of nervous agitation was in no way his own fault. Two wives under one roof—wasn't that the ancient symbol for disaster? And even if neither of *these* two women was actually married to him—

Blast and damn. A man wasn't meant to live like a monk, whatever the monks might think about it. It was unnatural. But the woman he wanted . . .

The woman he wanted had just turned down his offer to make her his mistress. He could still hardly believe it. A blasted governess! And he was the heir to the Earl of Tavelstoke! She was really too low-born for him in the first place, he didn't know why he had even *considered* offering her *carte blanche.*

No. No, it had been a mistake from the first. He had any number of ladies—baronesses, countesses, the odd duchess—willing to dance to the tunes he played. He'd had no complaints, he could have his pick—

You don't want your pick of the current crop of bored *ton* wives, said the little voice. You want Miss Helène Phillips, impoverished cit, currently employed as governess by the Marquess of Luton.

More fool you.

Footsteps sounded in the corridor outside. Lord Quentin stared at the bedroom door, knowing that at any moment Celia Sinclair could waltz right in. She had done her best to tease him in the hayrack, going so far as to attempt to unbutton his trews, whispering outrageous suggestions in his ear at the same time. It had left him feeling unsettled.

"Relax," Celia had murmured. "I'm only trying to get warm."

"Celia. Please."

A certain amount of such carryings-on was expected, of course; in the black of a January night it was difficult for anyone to see whose hands went where. People crammed into the racks for warmth after an afternoon of brandy and mulled wine—it was almost traditional, really, for some bit of scandalous behavior that was forgotten on the morrow. The marquess was nowhere near and the blankets were a camouflage—

"Mmm," said Celia.

—but he was aware of a certain auburn-haired chit, sitting next to Alice and Peter in the back of the rack.

Aware that she could hear them, if she wished. And Lord Quentin suspected that Miss Phillips was, indeed, listening.

"I believe he's offered her *carte blanche*."

Lady Pamela warmed her feet in front of the bedroom fire. The hayracks had been snug enough, with all those blankets, but it had been a cold night. Her toes still felt numb.

"Has she accepted?" asked Lady Detweiler, who was warming up in her own way, sipping brandy from an enormous snifter.

"I think not."

"Smart girl. *Carte blanche* for a duke's granddaughter? He should marry her."

"I rather imagine he thinks it's a generous offer for a governess."

"All the more reason you should tell him the truth before he makes a bigger fool of himself," retorted Lady Detweiler. "He must be absolutely smitten. Celia was practically inside his trousers tonight. Why else would he put her off?"

Lady Pamela sighed. "Well, she is married—"

Amanda snorted.

"—and Jonathan is his best friend. Charles Quentin has rather definite ideas about honorable behavior."

"I've never known a man whose sense of honor trumped his breeches."

This earned her a snort of laughter from Lady Pamela. "You are," she told Amanda, "the one truly cynical woman of my acquaintance."

"Absolument."

All things considered, thought Pam, it had been a pleasant day, although she felt a chill when she thought about the accident. In her mind's eye she could still see Peter running toward the fallen tree, Helène trying to catch him. Pamela knew as well as her brother did that Lady Sinclair had had the charge of Peter when he slipped away, and she was furious with Celia for allowing Miss Phillips to take the blame. She had tried to talk to Helène afterwards, but the governess was adamant that—as far as *she* was concerned—there was nothing to discuss.

"It will all be forgotten in a day or two," the girl had insisted. "Anything I say now would only antagonize Lady Sinclair."

There was some truth to that. Lady Pamela decided, for Helène's sake, not to force the issue. "You may be right," she told the governess. "I'm not happy with it, but at least Jonathan saw. He knows."

"I will be content with that."

But did Lord Quentin know? Helène never asked. Charles had certainly shunned the girl for the remainder of the afternoon, and had not demurred when the marchioness insisted that he accompany her in the hayrack. Fool of a man, decided Lady Pam, forgetting for the moment that she herself had warned him against compromising Helène.

And compromising Lady Sinclair? If Celia continues to be so bold in her current pursuit, thought Pamela, we really will have a scandal. She turned around and looked at Lady Detweiler, frowning.

"Do you think Jonathan cares at all about Celia? They seemed so much in love at first, but I'm no longer quite sure."

"Hmm." Amanda considered this. "I think she has a certain vivacity and quickness of spirit that he admires. But your brother tends to be somewhat distant in his affections, and I think it frustrates Celia that he does not fawn over her as if they were both seventeen."

"And so she flirts openly with Lord Quentin, hoping to draw Jonathan's jealousy—"

"—only to find that *Charles* has his eyes on a French-speaking governess."

Lady Pamela laughed. "Yes, well, much as I think Celia behaves abominably at times, I do feel a bit sorry for her."

"Sorry—!"

"Indeed. Jonathan may seem the docile, oblivious husband, but I can witness to his fundamental stubbornness. We used to have contests when we were children to see who could keep a piece of fresh horseradish in our mouth the longest—"

"How revolting," said Lady Detweiler.

"—or who could climb out the nursery window and crawl closest to the edge of the roof. You know, that sort of thing. Now I'm a reasonably obstinate individual myself—"

"I hadn't noticed," was the dry reply.

"—but Jonathan always won. In trying to make him jealous, Celia may have found that she's bitten off more than she can chew."

"Which would explain the tooth marks on Charles Quentin."

The lord in question spent a restless night dreaming confusedly of an auburn-haired marchioness with green eyes. The dream had been very vivid, and he awoke feeling rather out of sorts with the world and in serious need of female companionship.

He lay in bed thinking that this was all Helène Phillips's fault. Well, to the devil with her, he'd given her the opportunity of a lifetime and if she didn't care for his offer, there was always Celia Sinclair. Or . . .

Charles briefly considered the other female houseguests. Lady Pamela was out of the question, Amanda Detweiler too sharp tongued, the viscountess too young and in love with her husband, Lady Harkins . . . Lady Harkins was unimaginable. Charles shook his head irritably, knowing that it didn't matter how many other women graced the marquess's table. He only wanted the one.

This would not do. He had never been at the beck and call of a female and he wasn't going to start now. If Miss Helène Phillips thought she could play amorous games with him, set him to running after her, she would be surprised. From now on, Charles told himself, he would treat her with the coolness befitting her station. Ignore her, certainly—she'd had her chance. It was over.

He dressed on his own and managed a quick breakfast before visiting the stables, only to find, as if his own thoughts had conjured her up, the stubborn, unappreciative Miss Phil-

lips there before him. Lady Pamela was giving her a riding lesson in one of the smaller paddocks.

An unusual occupation for a January morning, to be sure.
But the paddock was sheltered from the wind, and the two
women seemed happy enough, so fully occupied with their
mounts that they had not noticed him. Charles at once forgot
his resolution of not an hour previous and found a spot where
he could watch them without being easily seen.

"Steady now," Lady Pamela was saying. "Take a tighter
grip on the reins. There—good."

Helène Phillips was no rider. Charles found himself holding his breath as she maneuvered the mare along the paddock
fence, wobbling slightly but seemingly unafraid.

"Lean forward slightly." Another admonition from Lady
Pam. "No—stay over the withers."

Miss Phillips leaned forward and, despite her unsteady
seat, stroked the mare's neck. Charles found his eyes wandering to the cut of her riding habit, which fit snugly over pleasing curves. What was a governess doing with such an outfit?
he wondered, not knowing that the habit was another gift
from Lady Pam. And, come to think of it, why was Pamela
teaching the girl to ride at all? It wasn't a skill her profession
demanded. The Sinclair children would be taught to ride by
. . . by the grooms, probably. Someone with experience.

Jonathan's sister happened to glance his way. She said
something to Miss Phillips that Lord Quentin could not
catch, and the girl shook her head vigorously. Charles told
himself that he had no reason to think they were talking about
him. Still, it rankled. He watched the lesson a bit longer and
then slipped away to saddle Alcibiades.

You're doing a fine job of ignoring the chit. Charles didn't
bother to answer the little voice. He was thinking that Miss
Phillips was progressing quickly as a horsewoman, and that it

would be no time at all before she might accompany him on an early morning ride. This was an energizing prospect. Lord Quentin mounted Alcibiades and headed off, urging the stallion into a gallop the moment they were out of sight of the stables. The image of the wine-red fabric of Miss Phillips' riding habit as it clung tightly to her form was imprinted on his mind, and Charles found himself imagining what it would be like to take it off, button by tiny button.

Sooner, rather than later, he would prefer.

His thoughts turned to the traditional methods of wooing a mistress. Christmas was only weeks past; perhaps it was not too late for a gift. A nice piece of jewelry might be exactly the way to warm the heart of the stubborn Miss Phillips. But nothing too flashy. A pearl necklace, or a fine locket watch. 'Twould be no more than the work of a few days to ride into London and visit the appropriate shops. He imagined fastening a necklace around Helène's smooth neck, imagined her lying on the bed beneath him wearing only pearls. . . .

Charles shifted in the saddle. The little voice reminded him that Miss Phillips did not seem the type of woman to be swayed by gifts. But what nonsense! he told himself. If gifts would not do she simply must be made to see reason. There was no comparison between a life as his *cher amie* and her current position as a governess, ever at Lady Sinclair's beck-and-call.

Or even worse, he realized, feeling a sudden, cold pricking at his heart. On some other estate. Some household where she would be fair game for any randy lord-of-the-manor that happened along, unable to voice a protest for fear of being dismissed. At the thought of those randy lords Lord Quentin's expression hardened. He knew more than a few, and more than one young buck who considered governesses a particular delicacy.

"Much better than a scullery maid, my good man," he remembered Lewisham saying, "and bother all the rules. Who would believe the chit, anyway?"

He would draw Terence Lewisham's cork, thought Charles, the very next time he saw that odious, brass-faced scoundrel.

After the St. Raymond's Day tree cutting, Helène made a real effort to avoid the notice of Lady Sinclair, whose frown deepened each time she saw the governess. Helène assumed—correctly, as it happened—that Celia knew Lord Quentin had made her an . . . offer.

Why does she care? wondered Helène. *She couldn't possibly think that I would accept.* Besides, if the scene in the hayrack was any indication, the marchioness might well be Lord Quentin's lover already. Her ladyship didn't seem to allow minor considerations of propriety to stand in the way of pleasure. Helène would have thought that other members of the party—the marquess, at least, or even Lady Harkins—might have objected to Celia's behavior, but this did not appear to have occurred.

Can he truly be fond of her?

Helène remembered the flicker of disgust she had seen on Lord Quentin's face when the marchioness had embraced him those many weeks ago. It had seemed real, but perhaps her ladyship improved on closer acquaintance. It must be so, thought Helène, shivering in a sudden chill. She couldn't help but notice that Lord Quentin was now avoiding her. He had barely spoken to her on the occasions she happened to see him walking past the nursery. This had happened several mornings in a row. Disturbing to the children, Helène decided, and she made it a point to close the door.

On another occasion, Lord Quentin chanced to be outside

on the same afternoon Alice and Peter built a snow fort on the front lawn. He had watched the children for some time, but without exchanging more than a handful of words with Helène.

Not to mention that he was often attached to Lady Sinclair's side these days, the marchioness laughing and smiling her delight.

I don't care if she is his lover, Helène told herself, but the declaration failed to convince.

He offered you *carte blanche*. He would never have said that to a lady, it was an *insult*.

All true, thought Helène. So why did she feel so empty? She was warm, well-dressed and fed, and spent her days teaching two wonderful children. How could she even imagine that any man was worth all that?

Worth her reputation. Worth her integrity.

Worth everything, came the reply, and Helène was not quite sure if it was meant as yea or nay.

She really should go to bed. The hallway clock had barely chimed eight, but fatigue was claiming her earlier and earlier. The pace of activity at Luton had, if anything, increased since St. Raymond's Day, with the formal *bal d'hiver*—the centerpiece of the winter holidays at Luton—being held in little more than a week. More guests arrived by the day, and Helène had needed to keep a particularly close eye on Peter. This afternoon Lady Sinclair had caught him sneaking popped corn from the tree and there had been a row, which had ended with both children in tears.

"Miss Phillips, your duties are in the nursery," Celia had said, "with the children. I should not need to worry about them being always underfoot."

"But we aren't—!"

"Yes, my lady," Helène broke in, quashing Alice's protest.

165

Under the circumstances, staying in her own rooms as much as possible was probably the safest choice. Helène had never much liked confinement, however, and if she escaped the marchioness's notice she would escape Lord Quentin's notice as well. She needed to see him, to show him . . . what?

That I don't care, decided Helène. *If he leaves Luton Court without seeing me again, he'll never know how much I don't care.*

With those thoughts in mind, and telling herself that the family and guests were still at dinner, Helène made the short trek downstairs. *More* mistletoe, she noted, once safely behind the library doors. It seemed that Christmas trimmings remained for some time at Luton Court. Sprigs of the funny, grey-green leaves, embellished with tiny velvet bows, still hung from every conceivable place in the house, and a few not-so-conceivable ones. Helène had been kissed once by the Viscount Dreybridge—who blushed mightily and gave her a quick peck on the cheek—and *twice* by young Lord Cantingham, a recent addition to the party's numbers. But not Lord Quentin . . .

At the thought of that particular lord, Helène found herself blushing at nothing in particular.

Drat the man. She refused to behave like a moon-struck girl, and it was hardly likely that Charles Quentin would ever seek her out again, mistletoe or no.

"Good evening, Miss Phillips. Bored with Tacitus already?"

Helène whirled around. She had not heard Lord Quentin enter, but there he was, looking dreadfully handsome in an afternoon coat of dark grey superfine, the fabric stretched tightly across his broad shoulders. Helène felt his presence in the room as a physical blow, and her thoughts scattered. She glanced up involuntarily, cursing the blush that was stealing once again across her cheeks.

"My lord," she said to him, with a small nod of her head. Why was he not at dinner? If Lady Sinclair had noticed his absence—She must leave at once, but Lord Quentin stood immobile between her and the door. His eyes were warm and brown, and they seemed to bore into the core of her being.

This would never do. "Please excuse me," said Helène, forcing her feet to move. She moved around his lordship, head high, her heart pounding so hard she was sure he could hear it.

"Please don't," said Lord Quentin, reaching out to catch her arm. "You've been avoiding me the past few days, Miss Phillips. I'm not leaving this room until you tell me why."

She had been avoiding *him?* Well, if that was to be his claim, thought Helène, she was happy to oblige.

"You're quite mistaken, my lord," she told him, "I've no need to avoid you."

"No need—?"

"You've been so happily employed elsewhere that it would be quite needless for anyone other than Lady Sinclair to go to the bother."

He grinned.

Charles heart leaped to his throat, and he could have laughed for joy. Indifferent, was she? 'Twas closer to jealous! And how fortunate that he had thought to visit the library this evening. He had tried to put the girl from his mind, truly he had, but now there would be no need. He found himself eager to sweep away every obstacle, to grant her this one more chance to be sensible—

Miss Phillips did not seem aware of her good fortune. She favored him with a frown.

"If you are quite finished with my arm, my lord, I am needed in the nursery."

He released her but did not move. "Alice and Peter," he told Miss Phillips, "are currently asleep in their beds, with Mrs. Hawkins in the next room. As they always are at half past eight."

The governess took a quick, ragged breath. "Nevertheless," she began.

"And I believe that this is a ball of mistletoe."

Miss Phillips glanced overhead, stepped back—

There was no mistletoe just at that spot, as it happened. Lord Quentin didn't care. He reached around the governess's waist with one strong arm, and pulled her to him. Slender, tall, she fit snugly against his chest, the top of her head even with his chin. He bent down to kiss her.

The chit was stubborn, and Charles was prepared for at least a token resistance. But he knew his own strengths, and he was confident that he had the means to persuade Miss Phillips. She was not indifferent to him—he was sure of that, whatever she might say—and he had thought to overwhelm her, to bury every protest under his lips.

But Lord Quentin was in no ways prepared for surrender. Helène Phillips sagged against him, melting into his arms in a manner that sent fire roaring through his veins. He caught her up and carried her to one of the large library armchairs, murmuring words of longing and hunger against the silken curls of her hair.

Nothing had ever felt this good. Nothing.

He held her against him within the close confines of the chair. "Helène. Helène," whispered Lord Quentin. Visions of the house he would buy her in London flashed through his mind, the bedroom they would decorate together, the bed in which he would spend every minute of his evenings and nights—Charles could have cried out in his triumph. She would have him now, they could leave within the week.

Helène twisted in his lap, a fresh torment that scattered all thought. She was saying something . . . He forgot about London townhomes and concentrated on the feel of warm skin under his hands. Charles sought her neck with his mouth. Her hair, coming loose from its pins, cascaded down in heavy waves. He was lost, unseeing, drowning in the fragrance of her hair, his fingers tracing the curves of her shoulders, her breasts. . . .

Charles heard nothing more than Helène's breathing and his own, and uncounted minutes passed in their embrace. Then—

The governess gasped, stiffened—there was a draught of air—

"Dear Charles," drawled a familiar voice. "How very amusing."

Celia Sinclair stood inside the doorway to the library, a half-smile playing over her lips.

Chapter Thirteen

"Miss Phillips!"

Helène had been setting a slate of maths for Alice; she turned to see Lady Sinclair at the nursery door. The children stared at their stepmother in astonishment, for a visit from the marchioness was a rare event.

"Miss Phillips, a word with you if I may." Celia's words were clipped and cold.

"Yes, your ladyship." The governess levered herself from the tiny schoolroom chair. She brushed down her skirts and hesitated for a moment, looking at Alice and Peter. The events of last night's scene in the library were fresh in her mind, and Helène was expecting a painful interview—but she had not been prepared for Lady Sinclair to issue the summons in person, nor so soon.

The marchioness had already turned to leave.

"In my rooms at once, Miss Phillips."

"Yes, your ladyship." The governess turned to the children. "I'll be back in a few minutes. Alice, continue with a second page of maths. And help Peter, if you please."

"Yes, Miss Phillips." The children looked worried. "But—"

"Now, don't fuss. I'll return presently."

"Yes, Miss Phillips."

The marchioness set a smart pace down the hallway, and Helène hurried after her. She had wanted to run, last night, run fast and far from Luton Court and never return. But

Charles Quentin had caught her in strong arms as she lurched to her feet. He had stood to face the marchioness with Helène—miserable, white as chalk—clamped to his side.

"*Celia,*" *Lord Quentin had said, sounding calm, assured, and—to Helène's astonishment—almost cheerful. "How delightful to see you.*"

The marchioness ignored his words, and addressed Helène. "Miss Phillips, this is outrageous conduct!"

'*Twas ever the woman to be blamed! Helène hardly knew if she attempted a reply. She felt the muscles of Lord Quentin's arm tighten, heard his voice.*

"*Miss Phillips is very tired and not feeling quite well, as you see. I will escort her to her room, and then you and I can discuss matters.*"

"*There is nothing to discuss! She will be dismissed immediately on the morrow.*" *Lady Sinclair stopped abruptly. Something in what Lord Quentin had just said had apparently caught her attention.*

You and I can discuss—

"*Oh,*" *said Celia. She sat down on one of the library sofas and waved a hand in airy dismissal. "Very well. I shall wait.*"

"Peter," said Alice, "stay right here." The girl carefully wiped chalk dust from her desk and put her slate back in its holder.

"Why should I?" asked the boy.

"Because Miss Phillips told us to! I need to find Aunt Pamela."

"Why?" Peter was standing up now, too, clearly about to demonstrate that his sister was in no way the boss of him.

"I just do."

"I'm going too!"

171

Alice hesitated. She was a realist where her brother was concerned. "Well, come along then. I think we should hurry."

Lord Quentin and Helène had walked in silence up the grand staircase and down the long, carpeted hallway to her room. He kept one hand on her elbow, the other firmly pressed against her back, and although his physical presence was comforting, Helène found she had nothing to say to him. She hesitated at the doorway. He looked down at her, a half-smile tugging at the corner of his lips. A lock of brown hair had fallen over his forehead, to almost boyish effect.

He looks, thought Helène, like a young man who's just been caught behind the barn with the milkmaid. A bit chagrined, per-haps, but not truly embarrassed. As if the situation was hardly worth the worry.

This thought did not improve her mood.

"Miss Phillips. Helène." Lord Quentin leaned forward, his hand raised to stroke her hair. She backed away. "Please do not distress yourself—"

"I'm fine," she told him. "You've no need to fear hysterics."

"I'll speak with Lady Sinclair."

This was too much for Helène. "I believe, my lord," she said, "that you have spoken to Lady Sinclair entirely enough for my taste already."

"And, if it's necessary, the marquess."

The marquess? Worse and worse! She'd had very little conver-sation with Lord Sinclair after their first interview; nothing be-yond a few words and the occasional tip of a hat. But his smile had always been kindly, and to have Lord Quentin discuss these cir-cumstances with the marquess, as if she was some errant school-girl—

"Lord Sinclair and I will sort everything out," Lord Quentin

172

was saying. *"You needn't be concerned that—"*

"Oh, no, my lord," said Helène. *"Please spare me. I've no desire for any more gentlemanly assistance."* She flung open the door and tried to shut it behind her but Lord Quentin was there first, his hand firmly against the jamb, blocking her retreat.

"You do need my help," he said. *"And, like it or not, you shall have it."*

"Pah!" said Helène, and, pushing him away, she closed the door in Lord Quentin's face.

"Miss Phillips, it pains me to say this."

The marchioness had collapsed into a chaise lounge the moment they entered her rooms. Sighing deeply, her hand pressed against her forehead, Lady Sinclair was the picture of wounded sensibility. Helène was unmoved by the small drama being enacted for her benefit, and she stood in silence, determined to remain calm.

She had spent long, sleepless hours the previous night, turning her few options over and over in her mind. She could return to London. But to what? With her father dead, there was nothing left in town for Helène.

Or find another position as governess. Perhaps, with Lady Pamela's help, it could be done.

Helène had tried not to think of the third possibility. Had *he* planned all of this? Had Lord Quentin known that the marchioness would follow him to the library? Helène would be dismissed, of course, and he would be waiting, her savior knight, ready to spirit her away to her new life as his mistress. The word did not sound so terribly bad, really. Better than—alone.

"Miss Phillips!" The marchioness broke into Helène's thoughts. She had clearly expected some protest from the governess; there being none, Lady Sinclair impatiently renewed her attack.

"Do you understand the seriousness of your offense?"

"You have not explained the cause of your displeasure," replied Helène. "Surely even a governess is allowed a semblance of private life."

Not according to Miss Chaldecott, of course. Helène knew that her claim was presumptuous, even absurd, but she felt calm. With very little to lose, she would not be so easily frightened.

Lady Sinclair attempted it, nevertheless. She rose from the chaise, and stamped her foot.

"I won't have it, do you hear me? I won't have this hoydenish conduct in my household! Your behavior as an example to the children is appalling—"

My behavior? thought Helène, and although she did not say this aloud, Lady Sinclair could read the governess's face. The marchioness erupted in fury.

"I wish you to pack your bags at once! You will not spend another night under this roof, Miss Phillips, I shall talk to Lord Sinclair *immediately*—"

"As you wish," said Helène. She turned and walked out.

"Aunt Pamela! Aunt Pamela!"

The children had finally found their aunt in the music room, where Lady Pam was working on a particularly difficult passage in Mozart's second *phantasie*. She turned to smile at them.

"You've come just in time, little ones. I'm making a hash of this run, and I think it's just time for some cocoa."

"Oh, but Aunt Pamela!" Alice ran forward; she and Peter started talking at the same time.

"Lady Celia came to the nursery—"

"Miss Phillips went with her—"

"She looked *mad!*"

"Miss Phillips told us we had to stay—"

"Alice. Peter." The children, still bouncing in their impatience, fell abruptly silent. "Excellent. Now, please tell me precisely what happened—"

"Lady Celia—"

"Miss Phiwips said—"

"—one at a time. Alice, you may begin."

Lady Pamela found Lord Quentin in the solarium, examining one of Jonathan's cymbidium orchids. He looked up at her approach and smiled.

"All right, I'll confess it. I'm hiding," said Charles.

"From Celia or from me?"

Lord Quentin seemed to see something in her face and realize that this was not amiable banter. He frowned. "Do I have reason to hide from you?"

Lady Pam drew a death breath and bit her lip. She had not had time to think carefully about what she should say to him. Charles Quentin had been Jonathan's friend since their school days. She had believed him to be an honorable man. But by whose definition of honor? The current situation did not need to be his problem. A lord could walk away from Miss Helène Phillips without a glance back, and there would be few in the *ton* to question him.

He will never marry her, thought Lady Pamela. He will think of his father's own life—and worry—and walk away.

Fool.

"I've just spoken to Miss Phillips," said Pam. " 'Tis disheartening to see you hidden away when she is even now packing to leave."

"I suppose it's all over the house." Lord Quentin sighed.

"Well, it can't be helped, I suppose—"

"Can't be helped? Indeed, I should think—"

"—but Miss Phillips has no need to pack. I've already talked to Jonathan."

Lady Pamela sat down on the edge of a rattan chaise and blew out a long breath. "Explain to me, if you will, exactly what you hope to accomplish by talking to my brother."

Lord Quentin looked at her in surprise. "Well, Miss Phillips won't be dismissed, of course. I've explained to Jonathan that I was very forward in my advances—"

"I dare say."

"—and that Helène was too much the innocent to . . . well, that I was too insistent—"

Lady Pamela regarded him with narrowed eyes. Men! Living in their own little world of rules and technicalities, honor and gentlemen's agreements. She had decided long ago that the sex was incapable of thinking more than a day or two into the future. How else could one explain duels?

Of course the marquess would accept Lord Quentin's explanation. Of course Helène would not be dismissed. Lady Sinclair might make her life miserable on a daily basis, but she would be warm, well-fed, and have a roof over her head.

Then, the day the Sinclair household arrived in London for the Season, everything would change. A bit of exchanged gossip here, a lowered voice there . . .

Helène's reputation would be ruined. And, ironically, if word ever got out about her parentage it would almost make matters worse. A penniless duke's granddaughter with a spotless reputation, even as a governess, was one thing. But once the *ton* wags were finished with the story—

Just like her mother, they would say. Shameless and wild!

"You," Pamela told Lord Quentin, "have badly mistaken the matter."

"I think not. I can assure you—"

"You think not at all! The problem Miss Phillips faces extends far beyond her current employment at Luton Court."

"I do not understand."

Lady Pam paused, considering her words. She was not so concerned about Helène's chances of finding another position as a governess, of course. The girl's ancestry should be made known, and she should marry. But this was not an explanation she could yet give to Charles Quentin.

"Her problem lies in wait, perhaps years in the future," said Pam, choosing the easiest excuse. "Eventually Helène will need another position as governess—"

"Years!" said Lord Quentin. "The *ton*'s memory is measured in hours! 'Twill all be long forgotten—"

"How well," said Lady Pamela, "do you know Celia Sinclair?"

Silence greeted this remark. Lord Quentin took a deep breath. "What do you want me to do?" he said in frustration. "I've offered her *carte blanche,* as you must know. She wouldn't have it."

"Offer her marriage."

The words hung in the air between them. Lord Quentin uttered a low sound, whether of disgust or despair Pamela could not tell, and turned away.

"I can't," he said, his attention now fixed on the orchid.

"You mean you won't!"

"I will be the next Earl of Tavelstoke within a few years. You know as well as I that it would never do."

"And Helène would be your countess. Her French certainly outclasses most of the *ton,* but I dare say they'll manage to survive."

"It doesn't matter how many languages Miss Phillips speaks. She's still a tradesman's chit. It would be disrespectful to my family—"

"Disrespectful!" Lady Pamela faced him, fighting the urge to stamp her feet. Damn Helène's pride! If she could only tell him—"What about the disrespect of offering *carte blanche* to an innocent of not yet twenty years?"

Lord Quentin started to pace. There was very little room among the various plants and bits of garden statuary that filled the solarium; Pam held her breath as he almost knocked over a large St. Francis. He looked up at her, hesitated, and then—

"I don't understand." He stopped, began again. "You yourself had a . . . relationship with Edward Tremayne—"

Lady Pamela was not accustomed to blushing. She did so now, unaccountably flustered to have past events brought so abruptly to mind.

"I understand your meaning," she told him, "but—"

"And you've suffered nothing of it," continued Lord Quentin. "Your former circumstances are never spoken of, and you are accepted everywhere."

"Don't be a fool. It would be a very different matter for Helène."

"I suppose you have the right of it. But—being a mistress . . . cared for, protected. . . . It isn't the worst life in the world, is it?"

"No," she answered him, slowly. "It isn't the worst life in the world."

They were silent for several moments. Lord Quentin sighed. "Do not concern yourself with Miss Phillips' reputation," he told Lady Pamela.

She again narrowed her eyes.

"I will speak again to the marchioness," he added. "I'm quite sure I can convince her that the consequences to this particular piece of gossip will not be to her liking."

★ ★ ★ ★ ★

After this interview Pamela sought out Lady Detweiler, and the two of them hurried to Helène's room. They found the governess sitting on her bed and staring forlornly at the door of her wardrobe.

"My brown merino has been lost," she said. "But I cannot take any of your beautiful gowns with me—"

"Helène—"

"I don't suppose anyone would object if I took a single walking dress . . ." The girl's voice trailed off.

Pamela and Amanda exchanged glances.

"Helène," said Lady Pam. "Listen to me. I have not spoken to Jonathan as yet, but let me assure you that nothing will come of this. You will *not* be dismissed. I give you my word."

The governess looked up at them. A trace of anger sparked as she said, "I'm afraid Lady Sinclair was clear on that point."

"You must trust me. Lady Sinclair will be overruled," insisted Pamela. She hesitated, then added, "—and I did speak to Lord Quentin just now."

Helène stood up and walked to the window. She turned to face the two other women.

"And—?"

"He has repeated his offer of *carte blanche*," said Lady Pam.

Helène flushed. She didn't need to hear the words, as she had already seen the truth in Lady Pamela's face. He would not offer marriage. She would not accept anything else.

"Helène," began Lady Pam.

"Please," said the governess. "I don't want to hear any more."

"I believe he does care for you, however. Do you care for him?"

Lady Detweiler raised an eyebrow. She had remained uncharacteristically silent during the present discussion, and Pam could feel her frustration. Amanda tended to think of men as temporary amusements. Marriage had never figured into her plans.

"I . . . I thought perhaps I did," began Helène. "But—"

Lady Pamela sighed. She could not see her way to encouraging a nineteen-year-old maiden to accept an offer of *carte blanche*.

"This is all stuff and nonsense. Tell him," said Lady Detweiler. "Or I will."

"Amanda—"

"Oh, no!" exclaimed Helène. The governess looked at Lady Detweiler. "You wouldn't!"

"Don't be too sure. Now, child," said Amanda, "our dear Lady Pamela is the soul of tactfulness, which is why you really need me here. This is not a game. Celia did not much take to you from the beginning. If Charles Quentin had bedded her—"

"Amanda."

"—but as it happens, he did not. And I believe the marchioness prefers the excuse that his attentions are focused elsewhere, rather than believe that he has no interest in *her*. So she now truly dislikes you and would not be adverse to seeing your reputation in tatters."

Helène looked shocked. "Is this true? But why—?"

"Jonathan will resist dismissing you, I am sure. But Celia may eventually convince him that his children should not be taught by the subject of such gossip. One way or the other, it will be difficult to find further offers of employment from the worthy matrons of the *ton*. Now, Pamela will hire you as a companion—"

Helène turned her attention to Lady Pam, who nodded.

"—and if London society continues as devoid of intelli-

180

gent conversation as it has been this past year, I may fight her for you. So you needn't starve. Nevertheless—"

Amanda stopped. She glanced at Lady Pamela, who shrugged. "Nevertheless. Lord Quentin is handsome, intelligent, and wealthy. You are young and beautiful, and, as it happens, the granddaughter of a great duke. Is this—" Lady Detweiler made a sweeping gesture—"is this all you want from your life?"

Chapter Fourteen

Celia claimed the headache and remained abed for the rest of that day, so Lady Pamela decided it was safe to put off her interview with Jonathan until the morning. She had long considered it impossible to obtain sensible conversation from her brother in the evening; he tired easily, and his head for spirits was appalling.

The next morning she dressed hurriedly and went down to breakfast. The marquess was sitting alone, as usual, his plate piled high with food.

"Jonathan, I must speak to you," she began. Lord Sinclair stopped his attack on a rasher of bacon and looked up. Something flickered in his eyes, too briefly for Pam to identify, followed by an odd moment, a sense of communication between them. As if he knew something . . .

"Pah." The marquess waved an airy hand, and the moment was over. "If you are here to ask me to dismiss the governess," he told Pam, "I've already told Lady Sinclair that it is out of the question. Miss Phillips stays."

Pamela, frowning, sat down. "Dismiss her? Of course not! I'd come to ask you to allow her to stay, as a matter of fact. Alice and Peter—"

"Well, there you have it, then," said Jonathan. "The difficulty is resolved. Now, Celia has decided that we must have orange trees in the ballroom—"

"Jonathan, please listen to—" Pam broke off. "*Orange* trees?"

"Complete with hanging fruit. She has become quite

insistent on the matter."

"I doubt even Lady Sinclair can convince the hothouse trees to set ripe fruit in January."

"The fruit is to be tied on. Can you," said the marquess, "please convince her to see reason?"

Several more bleak, sunless days passed. The snow continued, the drifts piling so high around the house that the coal boys—as Helène was told—began daring each other to jump into them from the windows of the servants' attic. The marquess had expressly forbidden this, and Helène kept a careful eye on Peter. She continued her duties in the schoolroom, cheerful and unworried for the sake of the children, and waited for a summons to Lord Sinclair's study. She was still convinced it would come, no matter what the assurances from Lady Pamela. Perhaps he only waited to dismiss her until the houseparty had broken up.

Or had Lady Sinclair said nothing? Helène occasionally wondered if Charles Quentin had, indeed, managed to silence her; and if so, what had been the price of his success. The guests seemed to treat her much as before. Lady Harkins harrumphed at the sight of her, of course, but the attitude of the others ranged only between common partiality and indifference.

She was careful to avoid Lord Quentin, who, to Helène's surprise, persisted in his attempts to speak with her. On one occasion he had showed up at the door to her room just as she was dressing for breakfast. Helène had refused him, furious.

"Are you mad?" she had hissed. "I wouldn't let you in if the Prince himself came marching down that hall. Now go away!"

His hand had remained firmly on the door frame. "Don't be such a goose," he said, flashing his charming, knee-weakening smile. "We have matters to discuss, and you can't hide in your room forever."

"Don't be so sure!" Ignoring the smile, she closed the door—narrowly avoiding his lordship's toes—and collapsed onto her bed with a sigh.

Wasn't she in enough trouble already? The man was cork-brained to continue pestering her with Lady Sinclair practically within earshot.

Fortunately, the evening of the *bal d'hiver*—the great Winter Ball of Luton Court—was drawing closer. Perhaps the marchioness would soon be too busy to pay further attention to Lord Quentin or Helène.

From the windows of the solarium Charles watched Miss Phillips as she returned from her morning walk. The governess leaned down to brush snow from her skirt and a long tendril of hair escaped from its pins. Lord Quentin's breath caught in his throat.

The girl stood up just as Lord Cantingham passed by on his way to the stables. He gave Miss Phillips a friendly wave, and Charles was glad to see this evidence of her continued good reputation. It seemed that his second talk with the marchioness had accomplished its purpose.

Celia had been drunk the night she discovered Charles and Helène in the library, and in no mood for sensible discussion upon his return. He had endured her tears and threats for over an hour, and could do little to mollify her. But on the following day—

"Think about it," he had told Lady Sinclair, catching her at afternoon tea. "You've made no secret of your own interests,"—this was as much honesty as he dared with her— "and you'll look a fool. Out-flanked by a mere governess!"

Self-interest was the best approach with Celia, to whom

being publicly spurned would be the greatest of humiliations. There had since been no hint of gossip. Now, as for his see-sawing relationship with Miss Helène Phillips . . .

Charles closed his eyes. No other woman had ever affected him in this way. She amused and exasperated and intrigued him all at the same time, and he desired her so much—

He desired her so much that every morning he woke up and felt his heart beating with cold pain because Miss Helène Phillips was not lying in his arms. It would be no hardship, thought Charles, no hardship to see her in his bed each day, her long auburn hair spread out in waves over the pillow, the smooth skin of her breast turned up to his waiting mouth—

They would spend part of each year in travel. Rome was first on the list, of course, but he was sure that Helène would enjoy Athens, as well. And the islands of the Peloponesus, Miletus, perhaps even Crete.

He had seen many of these places on his own, but to visit Rome with someone you love, someone who was intelligent and thoughtful—

Someone you love? The small voice professed shock. Charles ignored the comment, but another followed on its heels.

And how, naged the little voice, *would the* Countess of Tavelstoke *occupy herself during all of this pleasant to and fro-ing with one's mistress? And one's children, as well—where might they be?*

Lord Quentin frowned. He was fond of children of every age and had imagined himself the father of a large brood. Unlike some of his class, Charles planned to take an active part in their day-to-day lives. But with a mistress occupying so much of his time . . .

Offer her marriage.

No. No, there must be some other answer. Marriage to

Miss Helène Phillips would never do.

Helène would have been happy to never leave her rooms or the nursery again, but Alice and Peter needed fresh air as much as ever, and she refused to make them suffer for her own peace of mind. They usually spent an hour or more of each afternoon outside, adding to the children's "snow castle" behind the main stables. By now the castle was an elaborate structure, and even Lady Detweiler occasionally braved the elements to admire the latest addition. Viscount Dreybridge was a frequent visitor, effusive in his comments on the children's grasp of engineering and architecture. Crenelated walls surrounded a snowy keep, their turrets washed down with buckets of icy water until they sparkled in the sun. The structure even boasted a *donjon*—Peter's favorite—dug deep into the snow beneath the "great hall."

Lord Quentin, despite Helène's unspoken protests, had volunteered as a castle-builder on several occasions, and was the children's favorite for his skill in the intricacies of design. Blocks of ice now encased one of the main walls—Lord Quentin's idea, of course—and it was Lord Quentin who had engineered a trip to the Lea with several footmen to demonstrate the proper technique used in cutting these blocks from the river. Whenever he joined them, his thick brown hair tousled in the wind, his eyes twinkling with good fun, Helène would declare it time to return to the nursery. But, as ill luck would have it, either Alice or Peter would just then require Lord Quentin's help with some bit of the structure, and it was one thing after another until Helène admitted defeat.

She was always polite to him for the children's sake, and on these occasions Lord Quentin never attempted private conversation. All to the better, the governess reminded herself.

He was wonderful with Alice and Peter. Seeing him on his back making angels, or grabbing Peter in one arm to fling him, giggling delightedly, into a snow drift—well, one would never imagine his behavior only weeks ago when hit by a snowball, nor guess what a proud and overbearing man Lord Quentin really was.

The morning of the ball dawned sunny and cold. Helène was determined to ignore the evening's festivities, and had resisted all attempts by Lady Pamela to convince her otherwise.

"The marchioness," said Lady Pam, "will be so occupied in fawning over the male guests that she will never notice that you are there."

Helène was not so sure. "Even without Lady Sinclair glaring at me," she told Pamela, "I would dread it."

"Why?" Suddenly Lady Pam stood up, putting one elegant hand melodramatically against her forehead. "Oh! What an idiot I've been! Can you dance?"

Helène laughed. "As it happens, yes," she said. "My aunt, despite her leg, was a good instructor, and my father grew rather skilled himself. But it doesn't signify. Who would ask me?"

"Well, Jonathan, for one," said Pamela. "He seems to be the last person Celia would care about. And then there's Viscount Dreybridge, Lord Cantingham . . . Oh, and Lucinda Blankenship's brother has finally arrived. Robert, Rupert—something like that. He's quite nice, strange to say."

And Lord Quentin? But it was a name that remained unspoken by both.

"I appreciate the kind thoughts," Helène told Lady Pamela, "but, no. And I'm terribly sorry about the grey silk."

This was the evening gown that Madame Gaultier had made for the ball. Helène had tried it on more often than she wished to admit; tried it on and waltzed around her bedroom with her hands resting lightly on the arms of an imaginary gentleman with deep brown hair.

"Pah," said Pamela. "I don't care a ha'penny about the gown. 'Tis your happiness—"

"Then don't ask me to attend."

Lady Pam sighed. "Very well," she told the governess, "I won't."

Helène now sat quietly in the nursery schoolroom as Alice and Peter practiced their letters, thinking about how very happy she was not to be attending the Luton Court *bal d'hiver*. Such nonsense, really. All the fine ladies bedecked in their finest jewelry, the men in buckled breeches, everyone whirling about the dance floor of the largest ballroom, drinking champagne and eating inordinate amounts of food.

Helène had never been to such a ball. She had always imagined they might be rather . . . wonderful.

There came a scratch at the door.

"Miss Helène?"

"Hello, James," she said, as Peter attached himself, as usual, to the footman's coattails.

The young man looked nervous. "Ah, Miss Helène?"

"Yes, James?" She smiled in encouragement but did not attempt to prompt him further, having learned that patience was the only answer. The footman was not terribly clever in remembering complicated instructions, but he was kind, dutiful—and persistent.

"Ah. Lord Sinclair, that is, the marquess—" James stopped and took a deep breath. "Lord Jonathan Sinclair requests your presence in his study," he finished in a rush, and stood beaming at her.

Helène's mind went momentarily blank. Lord Sinclair? In his study? It had been days now, days since the incident in the library. She had been waiting for this summons, knowing it would come. Still, she was not prepared. The governess rose slowly to her feet and looked down at Alice and Peter. The children seemed unperturbed.

"James can stay with us while you talk to Father," said Alice, barely looking up from her slate. "Don't worry, I promise we'll be good."

"Ah. Miss Phillips."

Helène had only once before entered the marquess's study, at the time of their first interview. She advanced slowly, marveling again that Lord Sinclair could accomplish any work whatsoever in such magnificent surroundings. Huge, heavy tapestries hung on the wall behind his desk and the floor to ceiling windows showed snow-capped hills in the distance. The desk itself was ornately carved and polished to a mirror finish, but it held surprisingly few papers.

"My lord?"

The marquess looked up, his expression kind, but with an odd edge, as if he was guarding something, something he should have told her all along . . . Helène blinked, wondering at her thoughts. Lord Sinclair said nothing for several more, slow seconds, and Helène, not knowing that she stared, decided that there was something familiar about his face. Lady Pamela, she realized. It is Lady Pamela's face, re-told in the planes and rough edges of the male. A handsome face, clean-shaven, with his sister's aquamarine eyes, and Pam's white-gold hair seen here in a darker, ruddier hue.

"Mmm," said Lord Sinclair. "Ah. Yes, well the Winter Ball is tonight, you know . . ."

Helène, half expecting instant dismissal, was at sea. The ball? What was this?

" 'Tis very exciting for the children. You will accompany Alice and Peter—"

"Ah. Yes, of course, my lord." Helène blushed furiously. She should have realized that she would be responsible for the children! But they were so young, surely it would be too late—

"—but they are to stay no more than three-quarters of an hour."

The governess nodded. "Very well, my lord."

She curtsied and turned to leave, her mind leaping to the evening ahead. The ball! No one would dare object to her presence if she had Alice and Peter in tow. But 'twould be for less than an hour, Helène reminded herself. She could wear the grey silk gown, perhaps with a bit of ribbon threaded through her hair. Her blush deepened. Charles Quentin might see her, thought Helène, even if only for a moment.

"And Miss Phillips . . ."

The governess had turned to leave; she faced Lord Sinclair once again.

"James will then take Alice and Peter to Mrs. Hawkins. You are to remain at the ball."

Helène stared at him. "But—Lord Sinclair—"

"This is my express wish."

Helène did not dare to argue. He doesn't mean it, she told herself. He can't really mean it. She was convinced that Lord Sinclair had barely noted her existence before today, after all. And what would the marchioness say?

Lord Sinclair cocked one eyebrow.

"As you say, my lord," said Helène.

Alice and Peter seemed unsurprised at the news.

"You'll need time to dress," said the girl, looking at Helène with wise, seven-year-old eyes. "So you needn't bother with us. I can dress myself, and Nanny will tend to Peter."

★ ★ ★ ★ ★

Helène stood before the mirror in her bedroom, regarding her appearance with a critical eye. Her auburn hair was set off by the deep, shimmering grey of the silk gown. She had initially objected to the color, but Lady Pamela and Madame Gaultier had insisted. They were right, of course.

Scalloped lace trimmed the neckline and sleeves and set off the smoothness of her skin to advantage. Otherwise the gown was free of ornament, calling attention only to the woman wearing it. Any misgivings she had originally felt about attending the *bal d'hiver* were fading, and if she could only stop this pounding in her chest—

"Miss?"

Helène looked up to see Lady Pamela's maid standing in the open doorway, holding a long string of pearls.

"Milady said as I'm t' help you with your hair," said Jeannie.

"Oh, I don't think . . ." Helène was a bit confused by the girl's arrival. She'd had no chance to consult with Lady Pamela over the marquess's command that she attend the ball.

"Milady said I'm t' do your hair," repeated the maid. She looked mulish, and Helène realized that she must have instructions not to be refused.

"Well," said Helène, "I suppose." Even a lowly governess knew of Jeannie's reputation as a hairdresser; she could see the girl eyeing the *coiffe* she had attempted on her own with what looked perilously close to pity.

"Hmm," said the maid. "I think 'twould be best if you sat down."

With a few deft movements the girl loosened every strand and ringlet of Helène's hair and started over. She brushed out the auburn curls with confident strokes, and then piled them

191

atop the governess's head, managing to secure the whole arrangement with a few, well-placed pins. Unlike Helène's own attempts, the maid's arrangement felt as if it might stay in place. Jeannie fussed for a few more moments, and then—

"My goodness," said Helène. Deep auburn curls framed her face, with a few wispy tendrils softening the strong lines of her cheekbones. The difference was astounding and, magically, there was now a strand of pearls interwoven within the shining tresses. "My goodness. Thank you."

"Hmm," said Jeannie, standing back from the governess and examining her handiwork with a practiced eye. " 'Twill do very nicely, I think."

After the maid disappeared, Helène was left to pace nervously, wondering how long it would be before she could seek out the children, and what she might do to quiet the beating of her own heart. 'Twould be mortifying if a fit of apoplexy prevented Miss Helène Phillips—a nineteen-year-old governess—from attending the Grand Winter Ball.

Thump. Thump. Helène's pacing carried her over to the small washstand and there, at the side of the basin-and-ewer, was the ring. It flashed blue fire in the candlelight; she picked it up and turned it over in her fingers.

Her grandmother's ring. Given to her by her father, but far too late, only hours before his own death. He must have known she would have pawned it, as she had pawned all of her aunt's jewelry—

Papa. You need the medicine.

Ach, you daft-witted gel, I'll be dead soon enough without the leeches havin' their hand in it—

It was a gorgeous piece, the huge sapphire brilliant in its clarity and color and set in an ornate band of gold. The stone told of a family that needed nothing from its members other than loyalty, nothing from the outside world beyond its admiration. An old family, proud . . .

Everything her father, in his final, bitter years, had professed to hate. Helène slipped the ring on, thinking—just this one time.

Sell this ring if you must t' keep you from the poorhouse. That much they owe you. Her father's last words had been bitter with the sober knowledge that he had not provided more for her.

Chapter Fifteen

A governess is well advised to avoid grand society affairs of whatever kind.

"Miss Phillips! Oh, Miss Phillips, you look *beautiful*." Alice clapped her hands together in delight, and the look on Peter's face was enough to make Helène feel like a princess.

"Thank you," she told them, glad for their innocent, uncomplicated enthusiasm. "Alice, your dress is very pretty. And Peter, you look exceedingly handsome tonight." The children beamed. Peter was still in short pants, of course, but proudly sporting a small neckcloth tied "just like Papa." Alice wore a simple adaptation of a lady's evening gown, with a rustling, white cambric overskirt and a fichu of lace at the neckline. They were both quite charming; a tribute, Helène knew, to Lady Pamela's efforts entirely. The marchioness had declared herself too busy to be bothered with children's clothing.

"Now come along. Your father will want to us to be early, so we can choose a good spot."

Thankfully, the marquess had not insisted that Alice and Peter join him and Lady Sinclair in the reception line. Helène's idea was to pick some out-of-the way nook where the three of them could watch as the various lords and ladies of the party made their entrance. The *bal d'hiver* at Luton was not only for the houseguests, she had discovered; the local gentry were invited as well.

" 'Twill be," announced Peter, in his chirping, little-boy voice, "a sad crush indeed!"

Helène shepherded the children down the long hallway to the grand staircase, and from there to the ballroom. She focused her attention on Alice and Peter, resisting the impulse to scan the crowd for . . . a familiar face. She was the governess with her charges, and that was all. None of the guests presented any special interest to her.

Lord Charles Quentin entered the ballroom and began circling its perimeter, searching for the one young lady he most wanted to see.

The marquess himself had insisted that Miss Phillips attend the ball. Jonathan had offered no explanation for this decision to Lord Quentin, nor had he mentioned anything about the incident in the library. This was discomfiting. It was possible that Celia, for reasons of her own, had said nothing to her husband. The marquess was notoriously absent-minded, of course. . . .

Charles would still have preferred the chance to set matters straight with his friend. But could he? What else might Lord Sinclair know?

He had gone to the marquess's study two evenings past, intending to clear the air. The two men had sat drinking brandy far into the night, and Lord Quentin had been about to broach the subject of Miss Phillips when the marquess spoke first.

"The children adore their governess," said Jonathan. "Corky little chit."

The comment had appeared from nowhere. Charles sat up and stared at him, wondering what to say.

"Ah. Yes—"

"I've insisted she attend the ball. It won't do, old man, won't do at all."

Charles sat up even straighter. It won't do? Could Jonathan mean his offer of *carte blanche* to Miss Phillips? If so, why had he not mentioned it before now? A sudden, chilling prospect sprang to Charles's mind: Jonathan challenging him to a duel over the governess. He himself would delope, of course, but the marquess was such a terrible shot that he might actually hit something, possibly even Lord Quentin.

"Mmm?" offered Charles, still trying to frame an appropriate response. He had wanted to clear the air, after all—

Jonathan looked up owlishly, as if unsure of what they had been discussing.

"Miss Phillips?" prompted Lord Quentin.

"Ah, yes. Well," said Lord Sinclair, "I think it's time she went out a bit in society."

The ballroom at Luton Court was, as Jonathan fondly described it, "of singular and curious formation." The product of some previous marquess's scheme of Modern Architecture, the room was square, not overly large, and flanked on all four sides by a colonnade which opened, to the east, onto the terrace of the formal gardens. As the dancers tended to remain within the center area, the portion of the ballroom beyond the columns was the site of constant moving to and fro, and free for assemblages of gossiping mamas and young men who'd had too much to drink.

Lord Quentin had first met Celia Sinclair—Celia Penrose, as she was then—in the Luton Court ballroom. The festivities on that occasion had continued very late, and as the strains of the last waltz faded he had led the young, widowed baroness into one of the darker corners of the colonnade. Or had Celia taken him? That evening was confused in Charles's mind, although the hours later spent in the lady's bedroom were an uncomfortably vivid memory.

But it was not the marchioness that he searched for now. A slender chit, with shining auburn hair—

Lord Quentin turned, and there she was.

Helène Phillips stood quietly at the edge of the west colonnade, a lovely young woman elegantly clad in an elegant grey silk gown, her hair arranged in a cascade of ringlets, pearls glistening through the curls. An excited, bouncing child held on to each of her hands.

"Lord Wentin! Lord Wentin!"

Miss Phillips looked his way and gravely nodded her head; in that breathless moment Charles wanted to believe that she was a lady, wanted to believe that he would spend his life with her.

Offer her marriage, he heard Lady Pamela's voice saying. Impossible. Never. But perhaps a waltz. . . . He moved to join the governess and her charges, making his way with some difficulty through the throngs of people beginning to fill the ballroom.

"Miss Phillips," said Lord Quentin. He bent over her hand. "You look quite lovely this evening."

"Thank you, my lord." The governess sketched a graceful curtsey. She held his eyes, her countenance serene, and Charles felt for a moment that her presence in this ballroom was the most natural thing in the world, that it was he himself who was out of place.

"Isn't she *beautiful?*" Alice was saying. "I think Miss Phillips is the most beautiful lady of *everybody.*"

"You are entirely correct, Miss Alice," he told the girl, and had the satisfaction of seeing Miss Phillips blush.

"Charles!" sounded a cry from the ballroom entrance. Was there the briefest flicker of protest in the governess's eyes? Lord Quentin didn't need to turn around to know that he was being hailed by Celia Sinclair. He would do well to placate the marchioness. But first—

"May I have the honor of the next waltz, *mademoiselle?*"

That flicker again. Charles held her gaze, the challenge in his words clear, daring her to accept him.

"*Certainement, monseigneur,*" she answered. Lord Quentin bowed and turned around quickly, lest she see evidence of the grin now threatening to spread over his face.

The waltz? Good heavens.

Helène dragged her attention back to Alice and Peter, and they managed to find a protected spot in which to watch as the ballroom filled with people. There were two enormous potted trees nearby; Peter was looking up at them in fascination.

"Oranges?" he said, pointing at the fruit. Helène frowned.

"Miss Phillips, look! There's Papa!"

Alice wanted to run to her father immediately. Helène allowed this, seeing that the marchioness's attention was still focused on Lord Quentin. The marquess smiled as he went down on one knee to greet his daughter.

So he *does* love his children, thought Helène. Why do the fathers of the *ton* pretend this stupid indifference?

Peter had followed his sister; Helène hung back, and was surprised when the marquess's next words were addressed to her.

"Miss Phillips, may I introduce Sir Alexander Northham?" said Lord Sinclair. Her employer was looking his most inscrutably genial. "Sir Alex, our governess, Miss Helène Phillips."

Helène found herself being presented to a young man of remarkably pleasing appearance. Fair haired, Sir Alexander had twinkling blue eyes, and Helène suspected that his smile had weakened many a young lady's knees. He was smiling at her now, apparently unconcerned that his host had just introduced him to the lowliest female in the ballroom.

"*Enchanté,*" said Sir Alexander Northham, and Helène stifled the impulse to giggle. She heard the first strains of the orchestra and realized a quadrille was about to begin.

"If I may?" The young man held out his hand. Helène turned in consternation to Lord Sinclair. What was she to say? She couldn't dance! Alice and Peter—

"Ah. Splendid, splendid," the marquess replied. "The children can remain here with me."

"But—"

"Now, Miss Phillips," admonished Lord Sinclair, his eyebrows raised, "I assure you that I can manage a creditable job of watching Alice and Peter. I am their father, after all."

"Yes, my lord," said Helène. She turned to Sir Alexander, and they glided out onto the floor.

"What a magnificent creature," said Lady Detweiler. Her eyes were on Sir Alex as he and the governess walked through the first steps of the quadrille.

"Too young, I should imagine," said Lady Pamela. "He would bore you to tears."

"Boring?—hmm. The boy's quite wealthy, they say."

"They," said Pam, "are correct. His father left India at a highly propitious moment, and old Northham was a pinch-penny. Never wasted a grot." She watched Helène execute the steps of the *chaîne Anglaise* with polished grace. Clearly the governess had not been spinning tales when she said she could dance.

Glory, but it was warm in the ballroom; even with the dancing just begun, and in the middle of winter. Pam raised her fan, indecisive. Was it too early to take a turn in the garden?

"Put that silly thing down," said Lady Detweiler. "You'll catch your death of cold from the draught. D' you suppose Miss Phillips's attentions will be turned by the handsome Alex?"

Lady Pamela had asked herself the same question. Sir Alexander was charming and kind—ideal, in a way, for Helène. She had seen her brother making the introductions and marveled at Jonathan's sudden display of amiable good sense. But why? Why should the marquess suddenly champion Miss Phillips? He'd all but ignored her for weeks.

Perhaps Helène's fate waited for her apart from Lord Quentin. And I was so sure those two would suit! thought Pam, in unspoken protest. The sparks flying between Charles and the governess were certainly not in her imagination. Besides, Alexander Northham was still a puppy, and Lord Quentin . . . Lord Quentin was a man.

"I thought perhaps it was true love between them."

Amanda seemed to know that she was talking about Charles and Helène. She shook her head at Pam. "Sometimes I think you are still fifteen," said Lady Detweiler.

True love. Pah, thought Lady Pamela. I must stop this ridiculous obsession with what I know so little about. 'Tis hard enough to recognize, and even if one could find it, how could one ever be persuaded to believe it would remain?

"Papa," Peter asked, "why doesn't Lady Celia like Miss Phillips?"

"Oh, Peter, be quiet," said his sister.

The marquess turned mild, questioning eyes on his son. It was not in his nature to dispute the obvious.

"Is it because she's the prettiest?" said Peter.

"Do hush!" said Alice.

"I think that Miss Phillips may remind your stepmama of

what it was like to be much younger," said Lord Sinclair.

This made no sense to the children, to whom all adults were of much the same age. But they said nothing more about the marchioness.

"So, my dear," Celia was saying, "how is your young bride-to-be this evening?"

"Miss Phillips is not—" Charles stopped himself and shrugged. Lady Sinclair brushed her hand along his arm, laughing, and he realized that although the dancing had barely started she was already quite tipsy. He admired her resilience; even after the blow of seeing Charles with the governess, Celia was evidently in high spirits. But, as he knew well, the marchioness was at her most predatory when imbibing. Lord Quentin could only imagine what she might be up to by midnight.

"Mmm, Charles," the lady purred. "Do as you please, of course, but save the waltzes for me." She leaned into him suggestively and Lord Quentin flushed, hoping that Jonathan was not looking their way. Lady Sinclair's ball dress was finely made—sea-green satin, cap sleeves edged with lace, rows of tucking and lace along the hem—but it pushed the limits of propriety, as usual. At his current angle he could see nearly everything of her breasts that there was to see.

Lord Quentin took a deep breath and turned his gaze elsewhere. *All* of the waltzes, had the woman said?

"I shall be happy to attend you later in the evening," he told Celia, "but I've promised the first waltz to Miss Phillips."

The marchioness's eyes glittered. "Oh, very well." She waved one gloved hand in the air. "Enjoy your time with the little slut. I shouldn't imagine she can even dance." She turned on her heel and walked away, leaving Charles frustrated and fuming. Celia calling Miss Phillips a slut? That was rich. But a gentleman was not allowed to throttle a woman in a ballroom, he reminded himself. No matter how much he might wish to do so.

Helène was enjoying herself, an astonishing fact considering the circumstances. Sir Alexander had proved to be a marvelous dancer, charming to a fault. During the times when the steps of the quadrille had brought them together he had entertained her with amusing comments about several of the other guests present. Sir Alex seemed to know everyone of the local gentry. He is not the least puffed up with himself, Helène realized, and this pleased her. She remembered Lady Pamela's words—

Don't damn us all. 'Tis an individual you would marry.

Marry? Helène blinked, wondering why her mind had decided to wander off in such a treacherous direction. Fortunately, her partner now interrupted her thoughts to inquire tactfully about her own circumstances as a governess.

"I imagine Alice and Peter are a delight," said Sir Alex. "I've always found children quite relaxing."

"Relaxing!" Helène laughed. "Then I should imagine you have none of your own."

"I've not yet married," he told her, "but I have more younger cousins than I can count—"

"Ah—cousins. And are they all quiet, studious children, never turning the household upside-down, or falling out of trees?"

"Well . . ." He smiled down at her, blue eyes crinkling. "They don't run riot *all* the time."

"Then," said Helène, "you must count yourself lucky."

Sir Alexander protested. "Alice and Peter are well behaved!"

She looked up at him and laughed again. "Well . . . not all
the time."

He grinned and—good heavens, was that a wink? But the
music was now parting them for a *pastorelle* and Helène's concentration fixed for a moment on the sequence of steps. She
presented her hand to Lord Burgess *pour s'élever* and they advanced. It was so comfortable to talk to Sir Alex, thought
Helène. She did not feel as she did with Lord Quentin, as if
they were engaged in battle and each word could mean—vic-
tory. Or defeat, conquest, utter surrender.

And her partner for the moment *was* handsome. Helène
watched Sir Alex as he advanced with Lady Dreybridge.
Handsome, charming, and possessed of blue eyes in which
one might drown. But her heart did not seem to be skipping
any beats at the sight of his smile.

Ha! scoffed the little voice. *Sir Alexander Northham can be
any number of very nice things. He is simply not Charles Quentin.*

Helène gave an inward sigh. Enough, she told herself. And
thinking about marriage, of all the nonsense! A pleasant
young man is willing to dance with you. Don't make it into
more than that. The marquess all but commanded him to do
so, after all. No doubt Sir Alex is willing to stand up with any
number of young ladies. And as for Lord Quentin—

As for Lord Quentin, there was always the first waltz.

Or was there? The quadrille was now coming to an end,
but it had taken up quite some time, as did many of the country dances. Alice and Peter would soon be sent to bed, and if a
waltz was not played soon, it might be too late. Helène was
half convinced that the marquess had not been serious when
he suggested she remain at the ball. Perhaps, once the children's bedtime had arrived, Lord Sinclair would gently sug-

gest she accompany them to the nursery.

The children . . . She looked for them during the last bars of the quadrille, only to find Alice and Peter nowhere in evidence. Concerned that they might be disturbing one of the guests—or worse yet, their stepmother—she asked Sir Alex to return her to the marquess. When Lord Sinclair saw their approach he merely shrugged.

"Lady Pamela has taken Alice and Peter to see the ice sculptures," Lord Sinclair told Helène, looking distracted. "I believe Peter could not be dissuaded of his opinion that the swans were real. Something Cook said, no doubt. At any rate, 'tis close on their bedtime."

"Very well, my lord." So soon? Helène felt disappointment threading through her veins. There would be no waltz with Lord Quentin, no chance to feel his strong arms at her back—

She curtseyed to Sir Alex, and received a smiling, courteous bow in return.

"Ah, here's Cecil," the marquess was saying. "I believe, Miss Phillips, that Lord Taplow has requested the dance following your *menuet italien* with Viscount Dreybridge."

Damnation! Would he have to bribe the benighted orchestra to play a waltz? Charles watched Helène as she took the floor once again. What was Jonathan thinking? The marquess had introduced her right and left, until it seemed the Winter Ball at Luton Court was arranged for the sole purpose of Miss Phillips's debut. He'd barely been able to get near the girl for the best part of an hour.

Carte blanche was one thing; as his mistress she would appear in society to a limited extent, and Lord Quentin easily admitted that Miss Phillip's deportment lacked nothing. But here, at Luton—the chit was a governess, for heaven's sake! She had no business dancing with the likes of the viscount or, even worse, Cecil Taplow. Why, the man was a rake of the worst sort, he couldn't believe Lord Sinclair had sent a young girl off in his arms—

"A charming couple, don't you think?" said a voice in his ear. He turned to see Amanda Detweiler standing at his right hand, smiling dryly.

"Lady Detweiler," he acknowledged, with a small bow. He was in no mood right now for thinly veiled sarcasm.

"Charming, as I said. Cecil will lead her right out the terrace doors, and we'll have no more trouble with pretty young governesses for the rest of the night."

How dare she? Charles felt his fists clench, the blood roar through his veins.

"Madame," he told her, "if you are impugning Miss Phillips's honor, I must tell you that I take great exception."

Amanda laughed. "Dear Charles! Even tempered to a fault as usual. But there's no need for formality between us," she added, "after I've done you such a favor."

"A favor?"

"Yes. The first violinist is an old acquaintance, you see. I believe the next dance will be a waltz."

Helène relaxed against Lord Quentin's strong arms and thought—so this is waltzing. They swept around the ballroom in easy, measured circles, and any worry she may have had about stumbling soon faded. It seemed almost impossible to make a misstep in *his* arms.

"You've had a fine dancing instructor," said Lord Quentin. It was said without a trace of question, but Helène realized he must find this very odd.

"My father . . ." Helène hesitated. "My father danced." Lord Quentin raised one eyebrow, but had no reply, and she wondered if he thought she was spinning a tale. It was the truth, in fact, although she neglected to mention that Aunt Matilde had instructed them both. Perhaps her mother had enjoyed dancing as well—

Helène had a sudden, sad image of her mother and father in each other's arms, waltzing alone through a silent house. Perhaps Matilde had played the pianoforte for them. Her aunt said there had been such an instrument in earlier, better days, together with money for gowns and parties, perhaps even enough to hire a few musicians. Helène was too young to remember any of it.

"But not your mother?" He was smiling and Helène realized, with gratitude—or was it regret?—that Lady Pamela had been as good as her word. He must know nothing of her history.

"My mother has been dead these eighteen years. My father passed away last autumn."

Silence. They whirled through another figure of the waltz, Lord Quentin regarding her with grave attention. "And you were left with nothing? No family at all?" His eyes flicked downward for a moment, and Helène realized he had seen the ring. How could she ever explain that? The truth, she decided. Or something close to it.

" 'Tis a family heirloom, so I was told," she said to Lord Quentin, "and the only thing of value that was never pawned." That was plain speaking, and as much as it pleased her to say. The man thought Helène below his touch, and she would not rework her existence in London to win his favor.

"It is a fine piece," commented Lord Quentin. "A sapphire, I assume?"

She nodded.

"And your father taught you Latin and French as well?"

Helène sighed, more aware than she wanted to be of Lord

Quentin's warm hand against her back, the strength of his forearm under her own hand. Her body had no questions about what felt right, but her mind . . . that was a different matter. Lord Quentin would never love her for herself, thought Helène. He might applaud the refinement of her French, her Latin conjugations, a costly ring—but not her, herself. And all this interest in her family, what could he possibly mean by it?

Her father was a tradesman and, at the end, with his illness, a drunk. Those particulars would never change.

Lord Quentin was still waiting for her answer. "No. My . . . aunt," Helène told him. "Matilde."

She dared say no more, and a part of her was cursing even this. Fool! All he needs do is ask her last name!

Would that be so awful?

"And your parents?" she heard herself asking. Lord Quentin looked down at her and something passed between them, the barest hint of sadness, unacknowledged regret—

She would have been perfect for him. If she had been a lady.

Lady Sinclair watched Lord Quentin and Helène through narrowed eyes. As they glided through a turn she noticed the ring on Helène's hand, its huge sapphire glittering in the candlelight.

Another hand-me-down from Jonathan's sister, thought Celia, with a sour smile. Although, she reflected, with dear Lady Pamela's inclination for expensive jewelry, you'd think I would have seen *that* piece before.

"The governess! Celia, I really can't believe you are allowing—"

Beatrice Harkins, of course. The marchioness turned to greet her, donning a small, tight smile.

"The marquess's instructions," she told Lady Harkins. "Such a soft touch, you know."

"It's shocking! Putting herself forward, and the gown is positively indecent!"

This was dangerous territory to explore, considering Lady Sinclair's own neckline. When all was considered, Beatrice Harkins was sometimes an ally, but no real friend of the marchioness. Celia said nothing.

"And those pearls!" added Lady Harkins. Her enormous, laquer-red turban waggled as she stuck one stubby finger in Celia's face, jabbing the air. "Wherever could she have gotten them? I shall making a thorough check of my own jewelry case tonight, I will tell you that!"

Celia pursed her lips. The ring might still be a mystery, but the string of pearls twined through Miss Phillips's hair was not; it belonged to Lady Pam and she had seen both her sister-in-law and Amanda Detweiler wearing it on many occasions. Would Beatrice take offense if she pointed that out?

Probably so, thought Celia, with an inward sigh. And it wouldn't do to offend Lady Harkins. The marchioness was aware that her own claim to *ton* respectability was somewhat tenuous; it depended in large part on the continued presence of people like Lady Harkins at Luton Court. Celia had been lucky that Beatrice was a notorious pinch-purse; the free food and drink extended by the marquess's hospitality ensured her return year after year.

No, 'twas probably best to say nothing further about the pearls. But there were other ways—

"I understand your concern," she told Lady Harkins. "Have you seen the ring the chit is wearing? I'd wager any amount 'twas stolen—"

"My dear marchioness," said Beatrice, "what you put up with! It's in their blood, you know—you can't trust a single one of that class. Now when Henry was alive . . ."

The conversation moved to other topics, but Celia's eyes continued to stray to the dance floor. As Lord Quentin and Miss Phillips circled the room, as she saw his arm tighten, just perceptibly, around the governess's waist, as she sensed the fire that consumed him growing hotter—

As she saw all this her determination to strike back at the girl intensified, and her attention turned again to Helène's ring.

Chapter Sixteen

To Helène's dismay, the waltz was coming to its end. She felt she could dance forever as long as it was Lord Quentin's steps guiding her, Lord Quentin's arm at her back.

She wasn't being sensible. She knew it. A few minutes in this man's company, and she had forgotten . . . everything.

Stupid to forget. He insulted you with *carte blanche,* called you a dirty little nobody! Helène reminded herself. And he is as good as Lady Sinclair's lover. You'll never be good enough for the likes of him.

She tossed her head, willing these thoughts to be gone.

"Miss Phillips?"

Lord Quentin seemed no happier than she. His arms pulled her closer, and Helène could sense his agitation increasing as they made a final circuit of the ballroom. How could I have thought him arrogant? she asked herself. Or pompous, or over-bearing, or—

The last notes of the waltz faded away. They stopped, silent, and Lord Quentin stepped back.

"Perhaps . . . perhaps a moment's breath of air out on the terrace?" he asked. It was little more than a whisper.

Helène nodded, wanting this as much as she'd wanted anything in her life but worried all the same. She had seen Lady Celia's eyes following them during the waltz. Fortunately the terrace doors were wide open by this point—even in cold weather any ballroom got stuffy—and other couples were wandering in and out. True privacy was impossible with so many people, but at least the end of the dance could no longer part them. She didn't think she could stand that. Not yet. Not so soon.

"You will drive me mad," said Lord Quentin. It was little more than a murmur, but Helène was startled into looking up, directly into his eyes. She saw a hunger that robbed her of her own breath. He must care for me, she told herself. He must.

He wants *you,* the little voice pointed out. *Not the same thing at all.*

But—

"I can't endure being apart from you," Lord Quentin said. His hand moved up her arm, trailing fire over her skin. Helène was silent, wondering—what do I say? What do I do? She was afraid that if she opened her mouth there would be no end to what she would admit to, what she would be willing to do to hold his attentions. Her own body was warm, shaking, traitorously weak.

"Lord Quentin, I don't . . ."

"Let me come to you tonight, I beg you." His body shielded her, as she leaned against the balustrade, from the view of others on the terrace. His hand moved from her arm to the side of her bodice and his fingers traced the line of one breast.

Helène's eyes closed against her will, her head tipped back just slightly, the long curve of her neck vulnerable and pale in reflected moonlight. Lord Quentin's breath was harsh, his lips close against her hair, she could feel his hands touching her in places that, in truth, they did not. Not here, not almost within sight of the Luton Court ballroom—

Time slowed. For a few, untold moments no one else shared their corner of the terrace, and Lord Quentin crushed her to him, his mouth hard on hers. They swayed together, and he moaned her name over and over, his voice hoarse. She heard him telling her that he would care for her forever, they could be in London within the sennight, in her own beautiful townhome, her own bedroom, with him, with him, with him—

A dirty little nobody.

Helène's breath caught in her throat. I don't care, she told herself. Why should I? I'll never be more than a glorified servant to these people and I've no home anywhere else. Why should I care what *anyone* thinks? She had forgotten, for a moment, the many kindnesses of Lady Pamela, and Lady Detweiler, and even Viscount Dreybridge and Sir Alexander. The hurts of a lifetime gathered like storm clouds, and tears threatened, snuck under her closed eyelids, trickled down her cheeks. She didn't know they glistened like white fire in the moonlight, didn't know that Lord Quentin could see them and guess their cause—

She didn't know that his own guilt—unbidden, unwanted—threatened to overwhelm him. And that he very much did not wish to feel guilty, or acknowledge himself to be little better than any pompous lobcock of the *ton*, smug and sure and overly concerned with his own consequence. People he had always affected to disdain.

People like him?

Passion had robbed Charles of reason. He had been on fire since the first steps of the waltz. And then, feeling Helène's resistance weaken as they embraced, his mind had raced ahead to the nights to come. He had seen the delicious Miss Phillips unclothed, beneath him—It had all lasted far too long for Lord Quentin's self-control. And now, to see the girl in tears.

What about the disrespect of offering carte blanche to an innocent of not yet twenty years? He heard Lady Pamela's voice yet again, for what seemed the hundredth time, and inwardly cursed all the interfering busybodies of the world. Would they keep her from him? Would they have her spend a lifetime alone? Fury rose inside him, an anger commensurate with desire. He stepped back from Helène and heard a harsh voice, speaking almost in his ear—

"Don't be a fool. How much can you possibly think your low-class virginity is worth?"

Only when her eyes snapped open and focused in stunned outrage on his face did Lord Quentin realize the voice was his own.

Miss Phillips's hand flew up and she slapped him, hard, across the cheek; then she pushed past him and ran.

"Helène! No!" Charles ran after her. "Miss Phillips! Helène!"

What had he said? He *couldn't* have said that—

She stopped, turned to face him.

"I do apologize," began Charles. He extended his hand.

"Leave me alone!" hissed the governess. She ran.

Lady Detweiler was the first to notice that Helène was absent from the ballroom. Another quadrille had begun and, to Amanda's disgust, Lady Pam had consented to partner the ox-footed Jeremy Burgess. This was taking one's duties as the host's sister entirely too far, in Lady Detweiler's opinion. The man could hardly perform a *tour de main* without falling on his face, most likely taking his partner with him. Recalling the last time she had danced with Lord Burgess, Amanda felt the toes of her right foot curl under in protest.

Well, it was just too bad. If Lady Pamela would insist on partnering every ham-fisted chucklehead in the room there was nothing she could do about the matter. Amanda turned her attention to the other guests, watchful for likely sources of gossip. She noticed a group of the younger local bucks passing around a silver flask, and wondered which of them would be the first caught relieving himself in a potted palm. It was astonishing how much mischief people could manage to get into. . . . And in Bedfordshire, of all places.

A high-pitched giggle floated across the ballroom, and Amanda identified Lady Sinclair as its source. *There's a cat drinking cream,* she thought, watching the marchioness flirting shamelessly with Lucinda Blankenship's brother. But, of course, Celia did love her champagne. She was clearly half-sprung, and Miss Blankenship's brother—Rodney?— was wearing an almost comical look of alarm, as if he had just realized that the Marchioness of Luton might be visiting his bedroom at some time during the night.

Good luck getting rid of her, Amanda silently wished him. Just then something seemed to catch Lady Sinclair's attention, and she looked up, a brief, predatory smile crossing her face. Young Blankenship was forgotten as Charles Quentin, his countenance grim, his neckcloth slightly rumpled, crossed the dance floor. He was headed, perhaps unwittingly, in Celia's direction.

What was this? Lady Detweiler had last seen Lord Quentin at the end of the first waltz, his hand firmly underneath Miss Phillips's elbow as they made their way from the ballroom to the terrace. An expression of barely restrained passion had colored the gentleman's face, and Amanda had not expected either of them to return for some time.

But here he was. Where was Miss Phillips?

Damn Jeremy Burgess, thought Lady Detweiler. I suppose I shall have to do something about this myself.

She would really need to say something to Lady Pamela about her absurd matchmaking schemes. True love! What nonsense! So much fussing over an adolescent sentiment. Still, she liked Helène. And if it would annoy Celia Sinclair . . .

For the marchioness had now intercepted Lord Quentin, claiming him as her partner in the quadrille. They moved hand-in-hand across the square of dancers, his steps measured and sure, Celia's catlike, seductive.

I'll wager he's offered the governess *carte blanche* again, thought Amanda. What a cawker. Men are such idiots sometimes that it's a wonder the species manages to reproduce at all.

Now, where would I go if I was a young woman desperately in love with a man who has just insulted me? Out to the gardens, decided Lady Detweiler, and she made her way toward the terrace doors.

How much can you possibly think your low-class virginity is worth?

Lord Quentin's words rang in her ears as Helène, skirts in hand, ran along the terrace to the one outside staircase she knew had been brushed clear of snow. Her hands were beginning to numb with the cold, her nose—she assumed—was now a bright, unappealing red, and her shoes were in no way meant for this kind of use. Still she kept on, determined to find her way through the parterres of the formal garden and around the west end of the house to the kitchen entrance. She was *not* going back into that ballroom.

How much can you possibly think—

Crack. She felt her hand fly up, once again, and Lord Quentin's face twist with the force of her blow. How dare he? But Helène thought, miserably, that she knew exactly how he dared. She'd behaved like a wanton—a light-skirt. Allowing him to caress her, knowing all the time that he never proposed anything beyond making her his mistress. If even that. Helène had a sudden, horrible suspicion. Perhaps a few days' dalliance before he returned once more to Tavelstoke was all that Lord Quentin had intended from the start. Perhaps the rest had been a lie.

'Tis not like there's to be suitors banging at your door—

For once she could think of no other maxim of her father's that might apply.

The staircase leading down to the French gardens loomed in front of her, its steps glistening with the remnants of ice. She ran toward it, not slowing, not thinking of anything beyond reaching the safety of her own rooms. Half-way down the slippery steps one toe caught the hem of her gown and the governess fell, awkward and twisting, ending up at the bottom in a jumble of grey silk. She managed not to cry out, and sat for a moment, shaken, hearing faint strains of the orchestra descending from the ballroom above. Helène felt her legs and decided that, although her right ankle was sore to the touch, no serious injury had been done. No doubt she would be sporting a number of magnificent bruises on the morrow.

She limped back to the staircase and sat carefully on a spot free of ice, reaching down to brush a bit of crusted snow from her satin slippers. The bedraggled shoes had never been fashioned for running—or falling, for that matter—and the grey silk gown was torn badly where her toe had caught the hem.

She remained there for several minutes, catching her breath, but the stone was no warmer a seat than the snow had been, and her hands and feet were becoming icy cold. For an odd, disorienting moment Helène was not sure why she had descended the steps at all. Where had she been going?

Oh. Yes. Back to her rooms. Unbidden, Lord Quentin's voice sounded once more in Helène's ears, and she attempted to block out the sound with nerveless, shaking hands. It was a vain exercise. Her eyes now brimming with silent tears, the governess rose slowly to her feet. The music of a quadrille drifted down from the ballroom, and Helène imagined the fancy lords and ladies as they took to the dance floor.

Including, quite doubtlessly, Lord Quentin and Lady Sinclair.

Have your dance, thought Helène. Have them all. *I* shall have nothing to do with another adult male ever again.

"Good heavens," a familiar voice complained. " 'Tis little better than a death-trap."

Helène turned around to see Lady Detweiler standing at the top of the staircase, looking distrustfully at the steps in front of her.

"I suppose," added Amanda, "that I shall have to manage the descent if we're ever to get out of the cold. I assume you've no intention of returning to the ball."

Helène shook her head silently, wondering why Lady Detweiler was out-of-doors.

"Well, then, there's no help for it," said Amanda. "D' you suppose you could stand just over there, to break my fall?"

Charles Quentin moved smoothly through the steps of the quadrille, hand in hand with the marchioness. He was kicking himself for not avoiding this situation, and wondering what his chances were for escape. Lady Sinclair had claimed him the moment he returned to the ballroom, and—distracted, still feeling the sting of Helène's hand against his cheek—he had been unable to concoct an acceptable excuse not to dance with her.

"Dear, foolish Lord Quentin," said Lady Sinclair, as they swept out another figure. The marchioness pressed against him at every opportunity, her movements practiced and sly.

"Celia—" Lord Quentin began.

"Oh, don't inflict another one of your speeches on me," said Lady Sinclair, beginning to pout. "*Honor,* of all the nonsense! What is that to do with anything?"

"I don't believe you understand—" Lord Quentin stopped, having no idea of what he had intended to say. Celia sniffed, and the quadrille parted them, the marchioness moving off with Viscount Dreybridge.

She was drunk, of course. Drunk, and jealous, and even fighting mad. A passionate woman—

He would admit to an appreciation of that facet of the marchioness's personality. Charles's mind turned to his first year back from the Peninsula, the months in London spent partaking of the enjoyments offered by, among others, his current dance partner. Lady Sinclair was no hypocrite, and this had attracted him to her from the start. After the nightmare of Spain, the last thing Charles had desired was a dewy-eyed miss protesting his every advance. Celia was refreshingly open about her enjoyment of . . . physical relations.

Women are just like men, she had once told him. *But you insist in keeping all the fun to yourselves.*

Fun, thought Charles. Is that what they call it?

After an endless trek through drifts of snow on the west side of the house, Amanda grumbling loudly with every step, Helène and Lady Detweiler reached the kitchen door. They hurried past startled cooks and scullery girls to the back staircase and—taking care to avoid the ballroom—soon reached the haven of Amanda's suite. 'Twas like her last few months in London, thought Helène. Sneaking past the hapless landlady when her father had not paid the rents.

Come along, child, come along. 'Tis a scandal to even charge for such a sorry dwelling. The next one will be vastly improved, just you wait and see. . . .

★ ★ ★ ★ ★

The outcome in this instance was rather more pleasant. Her sodden slippers were now drying in front of a blazing fire, her feet were no longer numb, and Lady Detweiler had poured them each a large snifter of brandy. This was an unfamiliar drink to Helène, but—even while gasping each time the fiery liquid reached her throat—she thought she might rather learn to like it.

"I don't believe," began Amanda, "that I shall venture outside again before June. How the poor cows survive I can't imagine."

Helène smiled. "I suppose," she told Amanda, "that animals become accustomed to the weather."

"Nonsense. Not even a cow could become accustomed to snow. Such a sad variant of rain, I can't see why 'tis allowed."

"Mmm."

"Charles Quentin is still determined to offer you *carte blanche,* I take it," added Lady Detweiler.

"Ah. Well . . ." began Helène, and then sputtered to a halt. She blushed.

"My dear girl," said Lady Detweiler, "if we are to make any progress at all you must put away this silly notion of being embarrassed. The last time *I* was embarrassed was a decade ago, and I can assure you that you will not miss the experience."

Helène laughed. Amanda was like Lady Pamela, the governess realized. One could talk to her about anything, and she would understand. But why should the affairs of an impoverished governess be of interest to anyone?

Amanda tipped her head to one side. *"C'est carte blanche, n'est-ce pas?"* she repeated.

"Yes," Helène told her. "Lord Quentin has offered to make me his . . . mistress. But sometimes I believe he just wishes to . . ." The governess took a gulp of brandy and felt it trickle fire down her throat. She coughed.

"What?" said Amanda. "To bed you? That would rather be the point. Why should you be surprised? He *is* a male."

"They can't all be like that!"

Lady Detweiler eyebrows went up a notch. "Well," she told the girl, "perhaps not all of them."

"It's too horrible!" cried Helène, warming to her subject. "How could anyone—even a man—never wish to be settled and have children? I can understand that he will not marry me, but surely he wants to marry someone!"

"My dear young innocent," said Amanda, "he undoubtedly will."

Helène looked up in shock, the color draining from her face. Lord Quentin—married? To someone else?

Lady Detweiler was shaking her head. "Helène," she said gently, "you must have known. A gentleman who takes a mistress will take a wife as well. It's simply the way society is."

"I—I know," said Helène. And she did, of course. What a fool she had been, even to consider a life with Lord Quentin, all the time knowing the reality of the situation. He will have a wife. And children. Imagining Lord Quentin with Lady Sinclair was bad enough, but his *wife* would likely be a dainty young miss of the *haut ton,* well-bred and virginal. Impossible to even think of it.

"Lord Quentin is not yet thirty, of course," said Amanda. "It may be some time before he marries. Within ten years, though—" she mused, "—at most."

"And then," the governess said softly, "what will become of me? I should think the attraction of a mistress is that they can be disposed of."

"Quite true," said Amanda, "but it hardly signifies." She poured herself another glass of brandy, adding, "Whatever his faults, Charles is no scoundrel. You'd be well provided for."

"Provided for!" As if I were a child, Helène reflected—but this thought, uncomfortable as it was, was accompanied by an even deeper stab of pain. Her own father had not been able to provide for her nearly as well as Lord Quentin proposed.

It wasn't his fault! The *ton*—

"Yes." Lady Detweiler shrugged. "The usual arrangement, I should imagine. Lord Quentin is traditional in his own way, much as he pretends otherwise. You would receive an assortment of gowns, jewelry, no doubt a quarterly income as well."

Helène's eyes widened. It sounded awful, but she didn't want to admit this to Amanda. The mistress of a well-borne gentleman was as likely to be a member of the *ton* as a common light-skirt, and it was conceivable that Lady Detweiler had a more than theoretical knowledge of the matter.

"I suppose I could move into a small country cottage—"

"—and live quietly for the rest of your life. Yes," said Amanda, "it could easily be done. And I understand some people actually enjoy that sort of thing."

Nothing more was said of Charles Quentin for some time. The fire crackled and sparked and, with the brandy working its magic from within, Helène relaxed into her armchair, warmed through and through. What was it that he had said to her on the terrace? For the moment it hardly seemed to matter. The governess pulled the pins from her hair as Lady Detweiler—a born storyteller—regaled her with one piece after another of outrageous London gossip.

"Countess Renfield," Amanda was saying, "has never met a groomsman she didn't like. I believe there is a wager recorded at White's on the subject. . . ."

"Oh, no!" said Helène, giggling helplessly. "How dreadful!"

"Indeed. Something to do with hay lofts. Or," Lady Detweiler added, frowning, "was that Lady Breton?"

"But what do their husbands say? Surely they would object to seeing their wives' names in a betting book?"

"Hmm? Dear me, I don't believe so," said Amanda, who had apparently never considered this aspect to the matter. "Lord Breton generally spends the Season closeted with a fan dancer—"

"Good heavens."

"—and I can't imagine the Earl of Renfield has spent a sober moment at White's for years."

Helène thought about what it might be like to be a member of the *ton,* your behavior always on parade. . . .

"What an unappealing way to live," she told Amanda. "I mean, to be so . . ." She trailed off, unsure of what she meant. A bad thing, to be wealthy? Certainly not—a moment's true hunger would put that to rest. But—

"To be under society's thumb?" said Lady Detweiler. "Or to be uselessly idle?"

"I suppose that's it. I don't know. . . ."

"Idleness can be deadly," agreed Amanda, "for a weak-minded person. Renfield for example. Drinks out of sheer boredom, most likely. A good day's work would put it all to rights, but there's no chance of that happening."

"Lord Quentin does not seem idle." There. She had said his name without blushing.

"Charles? No, but then he has a large estate to oversee, and a good man for a father."

A father? Helène realized that she had thought of Lord Quentin as alone in the world. Like herself. The idea of him as a member of a family was somehow unnerving, and she had never heard any mention of his mother—

"Is . . . ? Mmm." Helène hesitated, not wanting Lady Detweiler to guess that she might be interested in Lord Quentin's relations. But Amanda, of course, needed no further cue.

"No brothers or sisters," she told Helène, "and the countess—his mother, not the earl's new wife—is long dead. But speaking of Lady Quentin—"

The marchioness was insisting that she and Charles take a walk on the terrace when Lady Pamela appeared. Jonathan's sister rested one elegantly glove hand on his shoulder and favored them both with a blinding smile.

"Come now, Lord Quentin," said Pam gaily, " 'tis bad form to ignore the host's sister. I *must* have the next dance. Dearest Celia, I know you won't mind."

Lady Sinclair's expression might have said otherwise, but Lady Pamela was already pulling him away.

"Thank you," said Charles, as they reached the dance floor.

Pam sighed.

"Charles's father, of course, is the present Earl of Tavelstoke," began Lady Detweiler. "He is a very pleasant gentleman these days, but was quite the rowdy in his youth. Women, drink—the usual sort of thing. I even recall hearing about a duel."

"Good heavens."

"When Edward was close to Charles's age he fell head-over-heels in love with an Italian opera singer. Signorina Francesca something-or-other . . . I can't remember the family name now. Anyway, they were secretly married in Europe, but when the happy couple returned to England all hell broke loose."

"Was his father still alive?"

"Father *and* grandfather. The old earl promptly died of apoplexy—"

"Oh, no!"

"—and the father—Charles's grandfather—absolutely refused to meet Francesca. He sent them back to Italy, where Charles was born, and where Lady Quentin disappeared posthaste with a Venetian glass-blower. Edward raised his son almost entirely on his own, rattling around Europe with scarcely a nanny in tow, and it was only after Charles's grandfather died . . . five or six years ago, I can't remember exactly when . . . that the two of them returned to England."

Helène considered this. The arrogant, top-lofty Charles Quentin was the son of an opera singer? It might have been almost amusing had her own circumstances been different. He had the nerve to call her low-class! But Lady Detweiler's story did, she supposed, explain why Lord Quentin was so touchy on the subject. She wasn't sure whether she now thought his behavior toward her better—or worse.

"I suppose the earl would not appreciate another female of questionable background as the Countess of Tavelstoke," she commented to Amanda.

"Quite right," replied Amanda, "and that, my dear girl, is why you must set Charles straight on the matter. Your own breeding is equal to his own by anyone's standards, and at least *your* mother never—"

The door flew open and they looked up to see Lady Pamela, hands on hips.

"What," she said, "are the two of you doing? The marchioness is foxed, she's already had one dance with Charles, and would have taken a second had I not practically wrestled the poor man from her grasp. He's a marvelous dancer, by the way,"—this was addressed to Helène—"but I can't follow him everywhere. And now Jonathan has disappeared into the card room and won't come out until dawn."

Lady Pamela flopped into the nearest armchair with a martyred sigh.

"Poor babe," said Lady Detweiler. "Have some brandy."

"Yes, well—" Pamela reached for the glass and then stopped, seeming to focus on the governess's appearance for the first time since she had entered the room. Her forehead wrinkled.

"What on earth," she asked Helène, "have you done to your gown?"

A number of gentlemen had now abandoned dancing for the cardroom, and the marquess, of course, was among them. Lord Quentin thought that gambling large sums of money on the luck of the draw was an especially pointless way to lose one's shirt, but in this he was in disagreement with most of his breed. *Vingt-et-un, chemin de fer,* even the new fad of whist—Charles sighed, wondering how much his friend had already lost. Jonathan had little head for cards even when he wasn't drunk, and it was fortunate he could afford to lose frequently.

Charles's thoughts returned once more to Miss Phillips, and his—as yet—fruitless wait for her reappearance in the ballroom. Had she retreated instead to her chambers? Charles's single desire was to seek the girl out and apologize, but if she was to return while he searched elsewhere—

The sound of female laughter interrupted Lord Quentin's thoughts. Lady Sinclair was deep in conversation with Mrs. Henley-Jones and the squire's wife, two women who were among the worst gossips in Bedfordshire. She gestured widely, to more shrieks of laughter, and Lord Quentin grimaced. The marchioness was often tipsy, but he had never seen her as intoxicated as she was tonight. He could almost predict the scene soon to come; Celia taking a pet over an imagined slight, her voice climbing higher . . .

Damn Jonathan for abandoning the ballroom—and his wife—for a game of loo.

Of course, it might be even worse than a fit of pique. He had seen a few of the younger men looking speculatively in Celia's direction during the last hour or so, and this boded very ill indeed. If the marchioness could be trusted to confine her intimacies to one lusting mooncalf at a time—

No. There was no help for it. Still fretting over Miss Phillips, Lord Quentin felt compelled to intervene with Celia before there was real scandal. Whatever he might think about the marchioness, he would not allow Jonathan to be embarrassed in such a public way.

A burst of masculine laughter drew Charles's attention, and he noted that Terrence Farley had now joined the marchioness's group. He looks, thought Lord Quentin with disgust, like a stag in rut. Bedding your host's wife in private is one thing, but to advertise one's intentions so brazenly . . .

He could delay no longer, decided Charles, thinking to take Celia back to her rooms, tuck her into bed, and say a quiet good-night. If past experience with other inebriated females was any indication, she would be asleep within minutes.

So be it. Lord Quentin strode confidently toward the group and was greeted with bills and coos from Mrs. Henley-Jones and the idiotic Brigsby woman. The marchioness was watching him with hooded eyes; undaunted, he smiled widely.

"Lady Sinclair, if I might have a moment of your time?"

The marchioness needed no other convincing. Leaving

Farley without a glance back, she attached herself smoothly to Lord Quentin's arm.

"Charles," said Celia, her voice low and inviting, "I trust that at least *now* I will have your undivided attention."

With Lady Pam's arrival the second decanter of brandy began to disappear at some speed.

"I've never seen a woman so bosky," Pamela said. "Men, yes—Jonathan still casts up his accounts regularly—but not a woman."

"Nonsense," said Amanda. "Don't you remember Viscountess Kelley?"

"Viscountess Kelley," retorted Lady Pam, "had reason. Her husband preferred her clothes to his own."

"I can't imagine why. She had the most abominable taste in evening gowns."

"Heavens, you're right. Do you remember that chartreuse satin—?"

They went on in this vein for some time, Helène contributing little. She was thinking, unhappily, about Lord Quentin dancing with a drunken Lady Sinclair. Oh, *why* had she left the ball?

Because, came an impatient little voice, *he insulted you dreadfully.* But the governess had by now finished her second glass of brandy, and this argument was wearing thin. She loved Lord Quentin. 'Twas unfortunate but true. And Helène believed that he cared for her . . . in some way. Wasn't that enough? What was her dignity against a life of happiness and love?

Or if not a lifetime, at least a few years.

Amanda and Lady Pamela had moved on to a spirited discussion of "that odious Squire Brigsby" before Helène plucked up enough courage to interrupt. Her voice, when it came, sounded strained and forlorn.

"Do you think I should accept Lord Quentin's *carte blanche?*"

Conversation stopped abruptly. Lady Detweiler frowned. Lady Pamela took a sip of brandy and blew out a deep breath. She seemed about to speak, when—

"No," said Amanda. "I do not."

Both Helène and Pamela looked up at her in suprise. "But—"

"I believe Lord Quentin should marry you. *Et donc alors,* I believe that you should tell him the truth."

Chapter Seventeen

*A governess must grant that the ways of a great house
and its inhabitants are beyond her question.*

As Lord Quentin half expected, Lady Sinclair managed only a
few wobbly steps down the ground floor hallway before becoming ill. Fortunately, a large potted palm stood directly before
them; he held her hand and offered soothing words until Celia
had emptied her stomach. All attempts at seduction now left
her, and they continued at a somewhat slower pace up the grand
staircase and to the marchioness's rooms, where Charles hoped
to find her abigail waiting.

No such luck. He considered the situation at some length
while helping Celia to wash and undress. Would the marquess look in on his wife later? Would Mrs. Tiggs still be
awake? Like most men of his class Charles was no stranger to
extremes of inebriation, and he knew that someone should remain with Lady Sinclair until all danger of further sickness
had passed.

"Oh, Charles," whimpered Celia.

But that person was not going to be him.

He rang for a footman, and presently James scratched on
the door.

"Milord?" said the footman, not batting an eye to find
Lord Quentin in the marchioness's suite. Charles was afraid
that the young man's understanding would be inadequate to
the task before him, but as soon as he caught sight of Lady

Sinclair, bedraggled and moaning on the bed, James hurried to the washstand and found a cloth to dip in the cool water of the basin. He sat on the bed next to marchioness and gently dabbed at her forehead.

"Everything is spinning about horribly," moaned Celia. "Make it stop."

"Open your eyes a bit, milady," said the footman. "You know it always spins worse if you keep your eyes closed."

James, it seemed, was no stranger to Lady Sinclair's present circumstance. The footman turned to Lord Quentin. "She'll be fine, milord," he said. "I'll ring for Aggie and we'll keep her quiet 'til she falls asleep."

"She should be watched—"

"Don't you worry, milord. Aggie'll stay with milady all night. More'n likely t' get sick another time or two," added the imperturbable footman. Charles noted that he already had a basin placed strategically close to the bed.

Helène opened the door and peered out. The brandy, combined with the evening's varied excitements, had caught up with the governess, but in her case the major consequence was simple exhaustion. She was too tired to worry about anyone who might be offended at the sight of a young woman in dirty shoes and a torn grey silk gown. Yawning, she trudged along the hallway to her own room.

The slow scrape of a door being cautiously opened caught her attention. She stopped, momentarily confused as to the source of the sound. Bother. She would much prefer to reach the sanctuary of her bedchamber without the need for uncomfortable explanations—

Creak.

Another soft scrape, answered by the whisper of a sharply indrawn breath and a muttered imprecation of some sort.

Helène turned around to see Charles Quentin standing in the doorway of Lady Sinclair's bedroom. Of course. He seemed about to say something, but the governess turned her back on him and continued on without a word. She wouldn't let him have the satisfaction of seeing her in distress. She didn't want to see him at all.

Damnation! thought Charles. If he could only explain.

But the stunned look on Miss Phillips's face had made things entirely clear; there would be no talking to her tonight. And after what had happened earlier on the terrace . . .

Don't be a fool. How much can you possibly think your low-class virginity is worth?

Lord Quentin grimaced, hoping he would not continue to hear those words replayed in his mind indefinitely. How could he have said something so patently offensive? It was only that the chit was so provoking and infuriating and . . .

. . . and arousing. Charles normally thought of himself as a master of the chase, but he had never before played the game under the influence of strong emotion and flooding desire. And now it looked as if his advances had been checked.

Well, 'twas not to be helped. Lord Quentin was not given to regrets when regrets would do no good, and, perversely, he felt a surge of renewed hope. A good argument, hurtful words, a slap in the face—it all sounded like the opportunity for an impassioned scene of reconciliation. At least Miss Phillips could no longer pretend there was nothing out of the ordinary between them.

A few days for emotions to cool, and then he would find the right setting for his apology. In fact, thought Charles . . . Ah, yes. I have the exact spot in mind.

★ ★ ★ ★ ★

Lady Pamela stared at her brother across the breakfast table. She could hardly believe her ears.

"What!" exclaimed Pam. "A 'nice, quiet Winter Ball'! Is that what you would call it?"

"I won fifty guineas from Lord Burgess at loo," said Jonathan, grinning smugly. All of Bedfordshire would soon be aware of the marquess's winnings, thought Pamela; it happened so seldom that it was real news.

"Cards—pah! Are you aware," she said to her brother, "that Miss Phillips left the ballroom in tears? Or that Amanda was so worried that she actually went *outside* to look for her?"

"Good heavens," said Lord Sinclair. He was clearly startled by this intelligence, but it didn't seem to affect his appetite. Another thick slice of ham had vanished as they conversed, followed by several links of sausage.

"I suppose," said the marquess, "that you will now tell me that Charles is at fault. Well, I did my best—"

"Your best!" said Lady Pamela, exasperated.

"Yes, indeed. Besides, I rather thought Celia would keep him occupied." Lord Sinclair paused, fork in air, and sent his sister a wounded look. "Can I help it that he insisted on asking the girl for a waltz?"

Pam stared at him. Celia—keep Lord Quentin occupied? What fresh nonsense was this?

"Jonathan," she said, carefully. "You cannot understand what you are saying."

"My dear sister, I assure you—"

"Celia is your wife. You cannot have intended to throw her at another man!"

Lord Sinclair set his fork down on the plate and waved for the footman to take it away. His expression was hard, his tone abruptly serious. "Pamela. This is neither the time nor place

232

for this discussion. Lady Sinclair's activities are none of your affair."

It was as much of a set-down as he had ever offered, and Lady Pamela was both astonished and more than a little pleased. Perhaps the marquess wasn't as indifferent to his wife as he had recently appeared. But if so, why not pay her the attention she craved? Ignoring Celia was asking for trouble, and Jonathan must know it.

"But—" she began.

"Milord?" Telford had entered the breakfast room without brother or sister noticing; the butler held out a silver tray with the morning's post. Lord Sinclair handed one of the envelopes to Pam and, as was their custom of long-standing, conversation ceased while the marquess read his mail.

Lady Pamela slit open her own envelope with impatience, the precise hand of its address marking it as a letter from her man-of-affairs.

My lady, wrote Mr. Witherspoon,

Regarding the person of interest. He does, in fact, exist and is the acknowledged heir, being the third brother's only son.

He is presently somewhere in the Americas—

Bother! Of all the ill luck.

—although sources expect him back in England at almost any month. Does my lady wish to be kept informed of further developments?

Yes, thought Pam. My lady most certainly does. Forgetting the argument with the marquess, along with the rest of her breakfast, she rose from the table.

"Hmm?" said Jonathan.

" 'Tis nothing," replied Lady Pam. She hurried to her rooms to pen a reply, and Lord Sinclair, immersed in some interesting correspondence of his own, only noticed her absence several minutes later.

Two days after the *bal d'hiver,* Helène received a message of her own. The envelope must have been slipped beneath the door in the early hours of the morning; it was the first thing she saw upon awakening and she regarded it from the distance of her bed in all the anticipation with which one might regard an uncoiling snake.

A letter? This boded no good.

The address gave her only a small clue to the writer; a man's fist, she decided, and her mind leaped immediately and painfully to Lord Quentin. Helène placed the envelope on her nightstand, imagining that it felt hot to her touch, or that she could hear the soft susurration of skin against skin. She sat on the bed and brushed out her hair, determinedly counting the strokes.

Ten, twenty, thirty—

And what if it *was* from Lord Quentin? What could he possibly have to say that would interest her? She had thrown herself into the children's studies ever since the morning after the ball, spending most of her waking hours in the nursery. *He* had not approached her there, and she had strictly avoided the library.

Forty, fifty, sixty—

Helène glanced at the fire. Burn it, she told herself, but after a moment's reflection it was clear that she could no more destroy even a *possible* letter from Lord Quentin than she could swim to the moon. It would be, in fact, only a matter of seconds before she tore the thing open. . . .

Seventy. Eighty.

Helène forced herself to complete one hundred strokes, then slit open the envelope and laid the sheet of heavy cream vellum on the bedspread. Three short lines of a vigorous, scrawling hand—

The stables at nine o'clock tomorrow.
I should like to show you the Pantheon
—and apologize.

—Q.

Helène stared at the note, wondering what to make of it. Did he really wish to apologize? And what did he mean by the *Pantheon?*

No, she thought. I could never forget what he said to me out on the terrace. Helène sat at her writing desk to pen a refusal, but even as she wrote she knew that the paper would soon be crumpled and tossed into the fire. She was going on that ride with Lord Charles Quentin. She was going to change her mind.

I must confront him, Helène told herself. I refuse to spend my days hidden away, afraid to set foot outside the nursery door. This is his fault, not mine!

Let him face me and apologize. Let him see, once and for all, that I do not care.

Lord Quentin was carefully combing a few last burrs from Alcibiades's coat, confounded as always by what the stallion managed to pick up in the dead of winter, when he heard Miss Phillips's soft, musical voice calling out to the groom.

"Mr. Jennings?"

"Good morning, miss," answered Jennings. "Milord's asked for Ha'penny to be saddled for you. Won't be but a trice."

"Thank you," answered the governess, and Lord Quentin grinned. It appeared that the stubborn Miss Phillips did intend to ride with him and had not arrived at the stables merely to ring a peal over his head. As Helène came into view he saw that she was dressed in the wine-red habit that he had found so pleasing before. Charles's eyes took in every detail, noting appreciatively that the governess's lithe curves were only partly obscured by the added protection of a redingote.

Lord Quentin took a deep breath and sternly reminded himself that his mission today was one of apology. *Today* he would make no disreputable suggestions to the governess and do nothing to frighten her away. It was difficult. . . .

And suddenly she was there, standing directly before him with eyes flashing green fire, challenging his resolve. Charles fought to control his racing heart. Helène Phillips was beautiful, intelligent, and full of spirit—and very desirable.

Lord Quentin concentrated on putting the final touches to Alcibiades's coat, his body keenly aware of the nearness of hers.

"The Pantheon, my lord?" The governess cocked her head to one side, her expression dubious and wary.

"Ah. Ah, yes," managed Charles.

" 'Tis far from here?"

"A quarter hour's ride, perhaps."

"A long way's ride for an apology." The words were spoken softly, her eyes never wavering from his.

"Miss Phillips," said Charles, reaching out—

The governess turned away, shifting her attention to Alcibiades. The set of her shoulders spoke eloquently of her distrust, even if he could not see her face.

"Miss Phillips, I apologize abjectly here and now. My behavior was inexcusable—"

A shrug of those elegant shoulders.

"—but if you will give me the chance . . ." Charles trailed

off, wondering if she would now go—or stay.

The girl murmured softly to the stallion and stroked the blaze on his forehead. The horse nickered and sent a look to Charles as if to say, why has this delightful human not accompanied us in the past?

Faithless beast.

"I assume we are talking about a folly of some sort," said Helène finally. "In miniature, no doubt—though I hope it's more than the size of a henhouse."

"A bit more," said Lord Quentin. He was trying not to grin. She would stay!

"Well, then, I shall . . . I shall accompany you. You have managed to pique my curiosity."

Ha'penny was brought round and he threw her up into the saddle. The feel of her waist under his hands threatened to break Lord Quentin's composure; he quickly turned away to mount Alcibiades.

For her part, Helène was far from sure why she was even here. How could she forget the humiliating words Lord Quentin had said to her at the ball? How could she have agreed to ride out with him? She should have refused his company, apology or no.

So the little voice had argued for most of that morning. But Helène—sitting on her bed, close to tears, her heart faltering under the grip of a giant fist that was trying to squeeze out every last drop of blood—had found herself unable to bear the thought of never seeing Lord Charles Quentin again. In the end, she had negotiated a settlement with the little voice.

She would ride with him this morning. Even a folly Pantheon, so she insisted, was worth the blow to her pride. And really, it would hardly matter. Lord Quentin would disappear, like the other houseguests, when the party broke up in another week's time. She would continue to refuse his *carte blanche,* he would leave, and that would be the end of it. A morning's ride could hardly affect the inevitable outcome of their association.

Refuse his *carte blanche.* She would refuse it. She would.

Lord Quentin hoped that their departure had gone unnoticed by any of the other guests. The rules for a Bedfordshire houseparty were relaxed compared to those of town, and it was accepted that a gentleman and lady might ride out together of a morning, but he did not care to push the point too far. At least 'twas a pleasant morning, and Miss Phillips seemed suitably impressed by the scenic qualities of their route. A cobalt blue sky rose above the brilliant white of the snow, and the temperature—which had hovered below freezing for much of the early part of January—was now warm enough that they were comfortable, but not so warm that the lanes had turned to muddy slush.

First skirting the wooded hills that made up a substantial portion of the marquess's property, Charles led them into a wide valley run through with the river Lea. Water sparkled in the distance and quail darted in and out among the sheltering trees. As they neared the river a loud rustling sounded from the bushes to one side, followed by a series of sharp cracks.

"Oh!"

A huge buck bounded across their path in a flurry of snow, no more than three or four yards away. Miss Phillips was enthralled; Alcibiades and Ha'penny both disdained to take notice.

Her seat had much improved since the first lesson with Lady Pam, noted Lord Quentin. Nervous riders made for nervous mounts, but Ha'penny was clearly at ease, and Miss Phillips handled the reins with the light touch the mare deserved. Charles had thought to watch the governess closely, as one did a novice, but his attention seemed continually diverted by the sight of the snugly tailored wool of her costume. Searching for something to distract his thoughts, Lord Quentin decided to pay the governess a compliment.

"For a inexperienced rider," he said, "you have a natural rapport with horses."

"They are marvelous animals. My father always—" She broke off.

"Yes?" He encouraged her with a smile.

Helène regarded him levelly, as if considering whether or not to continue. "My father," she said, after a moment. "My father knew everything there was to know about horses."

"But you did not ride."

"No." A longer hesitation, then—"He was a carriage-maker."

"Ah."

"Father loved horses," added the governess. " 'Twas all he talked about. I think he would have happily bred them for a living, but that . . . that wasn't possible."

"So he built carriages for them."

"Designed and built. Yes. He wanted each animal to have the best."

They rode on in silence for several minutes. It was, of course, no more than what Charles might have expected, and it was perhaps to his credit that Miss Phillips's father even had an occupation, or indeed, that she knew a father at all. Still, the reality of her background was a jolt, and Lord Quentin realized that he had begun to think of Miss Helène Phillips as a young woman of quality. But with a family in trade, the father *selling* carriages to members of Charles's own class. . . .

Something nagged at his memory. Phillips. A

carriagemaker. Lord Quentin did not recall the name, but he and the earl had spent little time in England before these last five years, and the governess had told him that her father had since passed away. A carriagemaker . . .

A sudden gasp of pleasure brought Lord Quentin back to the here and now.

"It's *magnificent,*" breathed Miss Phillips. They had reached the top of a small hill, and she was staring in delight at the sweep of terrain before them. "And how extraordinary that the lake be so perfectly situated."

Lord Quentin smiled, wondering if he should tell her that the landscape, although every bit as beautiful as she said, was the product of merely human design. The far end of the valley had once been mostly swamp, but at some point an earthen dam had been contrived, with the result that the river widened into a lake. Groves of birch and willow had been planted at its edge; their empty branches now reflected white and cream against both ice and quiet water.

"It is quite . . . unusual," he allowed.

"But where is the folly?" Miss Phillips twisted around in the saddle, looking for the promised Pantheon.

"It is a scenic spot for Roman ruins," he twitted her, "but hardly authentic. The real Pantheon is nowhere near water."

"Yes, of course, but—" The governess looked dubious, and Charles wondered if she thought he had lured her here with false promises.

"Oh, ye of little faith. The pride of Rome 'tis just over there behind that group of trees. Watch the ice at the edge, now—"

He led them along the eastern shore of the lake to a large copse of pine. Beneath the sheltering trees the drifts were not so deep, and in the clearings Charles caught sight of a few snow crocuses braving the late January thaw.

"Dear heavens," said Miss Phillips. She clapped her hands in delight, like a child, and Charles leaned quickly to catch the reins as she dropped them.

A much larger clearing had opened before them and there it was, the ancient dome arching improbably into the blue of an English sky.

Jonathan was never clear as to which of the several marquesses of the past two centuries had built the folly, but whoever it was had not cared overmuch for subtlety. The ersatz Pantheon was enormous. It had been built of brick and concrete, like the Roman original, and sat solitary and majestic in the middle of a snow-covered meadow. The portico, with its distinctive triangular pediment and Corinthian-topped columns, presented an oddly welcoming face.

"Good gracious," added the governess.

Charles grinned at her. " 'Tis some forty feet high."

"Good gracious—" she caught herself and stopped. "That's nearly a third of the original! But why build it here where no one can see?"

"I believe that was rather the point. The marquess says that his grandfather would take unsuspecting guests out for a 'day at the lake,' and then bring them here, feigning surprise. On occasion the more gullible could be convinced that it was really Roman, and that they had just stumbled upon a major archeological find."

Miss Phillips laughed. "Oh, no! How disappointing to discover the truth!"

"The truth is evidently not so romantic," replied Lord Quentin. "Jonathan claims that there are still a few ladies from one summer's houseparty who are in no hurry to believe it."

"I can almost see why."

The dome loomed ever higher as they approached the portico, and Lord Quentin kept a sharp eye on the governess, who had now tipped her head so far back that she was in some danger of falling off Ha'penny. He found his heart again racing at the prospect of time spent alone with the enchanting Miss Phillips, sheltered under the coffered dome of a fanciful Roman ruin.

You are nearly thirty years old, he reminded himself. Stop behaving like a cub of seventeen about to steal a kiss from the milkmaid. Dismounting from Alcibiades, he reached up to assist Miss Phillips, his hands firmly around her waist.

"Oh," said Miss Phillips and blushed. She stepped quickly away from him, only to find herself backing into deeper snow.

"Careful," he said, extending his hand. "Come, 'twill be dry inside." The governess hesitated. She is shy, thought Charles. Shy and vulnerable. A sudden, brazen confidence overtook him, a conviction that he was master of this situation. The naive young governess and an earl-to-be . . . Lord Quentin flashed Miss Phillips a charming, boyish grin. Her blush deepened and she returned the smile.

She smiled at him—Charles's heart slammed into his rib cage, and several moments passed before he was again in control of his breathing.

No, he realized, with chagrin. Not master of the situation at all.

Helène had forgotten that she was determined to be cross and distant with Lord Quentin. She studied the enormous bronze doors of the folly, recognizing that they were exact replicas—albeit at a third the size—of the doors of the real Pantheon. Heavy, as well; Lord Quentin took a firm grip and pulled one open wide enough for them to enter. Their steps echoed against the polished marble floor as they walked to the center of the structure. The rotunda stretched in front of them, the dome above, the sky visible through the oculus in its center.

"We're much farther north, of course," commented Lord Quentin. "But in Rome, one sees a perfect circle of light against the ceiling."

Incredible. " 'Angelic, and not of human design,' " whispered Helène. She was overwhelmed by the emotion of seeing even this one tiny piece of her dreams. To visit the Pantheon of Rome, or the ruins of Athens, the cathedrals of Paris . . .

Lord Quentin looked at her curiously.

"Quoting Michelangelo?" he said. "Your education continues to be most unaccountable."

Indeed. "For a carriagemaker's daughter?" retorted Helène, her voice sharper than she intended.

"Truthfully? Yes. But I've known many a duke's daughter—"

Helène started; Lord Quentin seemed not to notice.

"—with far less learning. I don't understand—"

"As a girl I spent many days walking about London," Helène said hurriedly, hoping to deflect the subject onto a safer path. "I visited St. Paul's Cathedral often. . . . I would hide in the chapels. I can't explain it, really. I guess I was enthralled by the idea of great buildings. Their size, and their beauty—"

She paused, but Charles's attention had been caught by her first words. "You were about in the city *alone?*" he asked. "Now that 'tis a folly. What could your father have been thinking?"

His voice had grown concerned, but Helène only shrugged.

"That may be true for the Quality," she told him. " 'Tis not so for the rabble."

"Helène—"

"Father was often occupied," she continued, ignoring his interruption, "and my aunt had a crippled leg. She was unable to accompany me." She did not mention that Matilde had protested nevertheless, and at some length. Helène had disliked upsetting her aunt, but she had not been able to bear confinement for long. The city, for all its dangers and filth, could give at least the illusion of freedom.

"I'm sorry," said Lord Quentin. "I didn't know."

Another shrug. "It was a lifetime ago." Helène walked over to one of the smaller columns of the rotunda wall, running a gloved hand along the smooth fluting of marble. The folly was much smaller than the original, and she supposed it was considerably less imposing; still, she seemed to feel something of the magic and aura of the ancient Roman temple itself.

"I've often wondered what it would feel like to walk through the real Pantheon," she told Lord Quentin. "Or any ancient building—"

"And to think about the people who've walked in the same place, seeing the same things, thousands of years before?"

Helène gazed around her at the ornamented brick of the rotunda interior, the precise lines of the coffered ceiling above.

"Yes," she said. "Yes. That's exactly it."

"That's exactly it." Miss Phillips's face, had she known it, was alight with that same dreamy, enraptured look that Lord Quentin had seen once before, during their discussion in the library. He found himself engulfed by longing, drawn to her, unable to resist. Just one kiss. One kiss, one caress, a single touch of his hand against her breast . . .

She brushed her hand once more along the fluting of the column and Charles felt the soft caress on his own skin. He was unaware that he had moved toward the governess, or that she had moved toward him. They stood apart, then not apart, barely touching, and then they were pressed together with implosive force, Charles's one hand at her waist, one against the back of her head as he crushed her lips to his own.

He could feel the whole of her body pressed against his, and he was engulfed by passion within seconds, brought back to logical thought only when Miss Phillips sagged in his arms, her legs no longer able to hold her upright. Charles held her against his chest and scanned the interior of the building.

As with the real Pantheon, there was a niche opposite the portico entrance, flanked by marble columns and topped with a relieving arch; unlike the real building, it held a large garden seat. He carried the governess to the bench, thankful it was wood and not iron, and held her in his lap. Their kisses deepened until Lord Quentin no longer felt the cold.

"Helène," he murmured. Her answer was muffled against the wool of his coat.

If only the folly was a little warmer. If only he had thought to bring a number of blankets along.

Of course, the little voice pointed out, *that might have made your intentions rather less obscure.*

But I never intended to make love to her! Charles protested. Not today!

The little voice was unconvinced.

Helène tried to remind herself that she was angry with Lord Quentin, very angry indeed. He had insulted her in as many ways as possible, offering her *carte blanche,* speaking to her as if she was a low-caste light-skirt out on the streets—

But I could spend my days like this. Days and nights, engulfed in his arms, feeling like this.

★ ★ ★ ★ ★

The marchioness, perched in her sitting room window, happened to be watching as Charles and Helène returned to the house. They walked slowly from the stables, seeming to barely acknowledge one another's existence, but Celia immediately sensed the change between them. A new intimacy, thought the marchioness. Surely Charles could not have bedded her in the cold!

Rivals in love were nothing new to Lady Sinclair, but losing was. And to lose to a governess—

Bad enough that Jonathan had brought the girl into the house under odd circumstances, and without a satisfactory explanation. Celia had abandoned any notion that the marquess had hired the girl for improper reasons, but the situation was most peculiar, and to be shown up by some girl from the streets, with her French, and fine gowns, and dancing, and Lord only knew what else.

It was unsupportable. And then, another blow, to see Charles's interest in her—

Botheration. Celia rummaged through the contents of her wardrobe, becoming more annoyed by the second. She should have thrown every last one of these dresses out ages ago. It was shocking—she had not a single decent day gown to wear. And until they returned to town . . .

It had been a frustrating houseparty, to say the least. Lord Burgess would have been easy pickings, as would that Blankenship boy. But she had been so convinced that Charles would come around, that he could no more refuse the offer of a woman's body than he could refuse to breathe.

At least, not the offer of *her* body. Celia thought back to the year before her second marriage, to the young men she had entertained in that London townhouse. None of them had been as passionate, as fierce, as purely commanding as

Charles Quentin. He had engulfed her with raw, insistent need, and for a time Celia had exulted in the glorious experience of being claimed.

None of the others had taken the emptiness away.

That awful feeling, thought Celia. That awful feeling of being alone in the world and responsible for one's own fate. Young men were so foolish, thinking she wanted to be the aggressor, when she was simply playing the only hand she had ever been dealt. But when Charles had bedded her . . .

The marchioness sighed. When Charles had bedded her there had been no doubt as to who was in control.

If only Jonathan—

Lady Sinclair shook her head, unwilling to travel again down that particular path. Jonathan was who he was. Her husband, whom she cared for despite everything. Lord Sinclair was a good man, and she willed the belief that he loved her still, but she could see that he would stand in support of this governess, and that Charles was infatuated with the girl as well. It was all too much for Celia's fragile pride. She needed to feel wanted again, she *must* feel wanted again.

Steps in the hallway outside—

The sound of a man's voice, a soft female laugh. Celia felt a stab of anger as she realized that Lord Quentin was accompanying the governess to her room. Fah! Everyone treated the chit like she was the blessed answer to prayer. Alice and Peter adored her, her sister-in-law treated her like a bosom beau—and Lord Quentin wanted her as his mistress. Lady Sinclair felt growing outrage at the whole situation. It was one thing to be without amusing company. But to be stuck with the darling, simpering Miss Phillips, immured together in the country, bored senseless until the marquess could be persuaded to take them to London—

Celia slammed the door of the wardrobe shut and began to

pace. Oh, her poor nerves—where was that stupid maid, any-way? She felt another headache coming on, and Aggie *knew* she would need one of Cook's tisanes.

Where was that benighted decanter of sherry? It seemed to disappear each time she left the room, she'd accused the maid more than once—

Ah. The marchioness, in a moment of inspired recollec-tion, found a second decanter she had hidden in the back of the wardrobe. She poured herself a large glass and, sighing with pleasure, sank into the chaise lounge.

Once in London she would rid herself of the entire diffi-culty, decided Celia. 'Twill be the work of a day. Like Lady Pamela, the marchioness had great respect for town gossip. The tiniest piece of misbehavior could, with little effort, be amplified until the chit couldn't find employment as a scul-lery maid, let alone as a governess.

The gossip would need to be chosen carefully, of course. She could claim the girl was Lord Quentin's lover but, as Charles had warned her, that particular scandal might reflect poorly on the marchioness herself.

Celia's expression grew thoughtful. Something at the back of her mind, something she should have remembered . . . She saw Charles and the governess once more gliding through the steps of the waltz, the sapphire ring glittering on the girl's hand as they swept past.

The ring. Of course. Stolen, she had suggested to Beatrice Harkins. Now, 'twould be delightful if that were true, but—

Celia shrugged. With a bit of patience, the sapphire ring it-self would not be needed for the gossip she had in mind.

Chapter Eighteen

Snow and more snow. Helène looked out her bedroom window at the drifts piled high atop the knotted plantings of the kitchen garden, at the mounded shapes seen dimly in that strange half-light of a night snowfall.

She had seen plenty of the stuff in London, of course, though never so clean and . . . fluffy. There was nothing picturesque about the city in winter. Helène remembered plowing through the grey slush of some revolting alleyway, her hands chapped and bleeding, her feet numb with the cold—

Carrying a packet of medicine for her father. 'Twas good for the liver, the leech had claimed, though Helène sometimes wondered if the bitter powders were what had killed him. At least he had been more comfortable toward the end.

Don't be a clunch, gel. Back you go an' take the money. Don't make no mind for me, not now.

She sighed, hugging the robe closely around her, wondering whether sleep would continue to elude her for the remainder of the night. Flakes of snow sparkled in the candlelight from her window and Helène imagined she could make out the faint glimmer of the Lea in the distance. Luton Court was so beautiful in the winter. . . . And every other time of year as well, no doubt. She wondered what Tavelstoke Manor was like. Lord Quentin had spoken little of his own home, which she understood to be not far away.

Lord Quentin, she reminded herself, generally has interests more pressing than mere conversation.

Helène sighed again. There seemed to be no end to this argument, and she was bitterly tired of it, wanting nothing more than to settle back into her quiet life with Alice and Peter, to wake each morning free of the pounding misery of an impossible love.

Ha! said a voice. 'Tis misery indeed! Tell him you are a duke's granddaughter.

But Helène had already considered this. And if he then did *not* offer marriage? Lord Quentin's behavior toward her—the strength of his hunger for physical intimacy, the growing need she saw in his eyes—had convinced the governess that her body was that gentleman's single goal. It was not likely that Lord Quentin would ever intend more than *carte blanche*. Duke's granddaughter or no, her father's name was hardly incentive, and there must be plenty of young, eager misses with no such blot to their name.

Then accept the offer that he can make. Live with him and be happy.

This was the more difficult argument to ignore. To spend your days with the man you loved . . .

Helène's face flushed as she considered those days . . . and nights. Even if it lasted no more than a year or two, what more could any woman hope for? And perhaps she might have a child by him. A bit of him to keep for all time, a part of Lord Quentin to love forever.

But at the thought of a child, Helène knew what her final answer must be. It didn't matter what Charles Quentin might settle on her, it didn't matter if she could live in comfort for the rest of her life, she would not inflict the disgrace of bastardy on her own child. Unfair as it was to an innocent babe, it was the way things were, and 'twould not change.

Never disagree with bread on the table, her father had always said. Never argue with what *is*.

So be it. A weight fell from Helène's shoulders and, feeling suddenly drowsy, she crawled back into bed and fell immediately asleep.

Lord Quentin's night was less restful. An auburn-haired beauty haunted his dreams, and he woke time and time again, heart racing, arms clutching the air, only to have his thoughts turn immediately to the memory of his interlude with Miss Phillips in the folly. The bewitching Miss Phillips. Helène. Her happiness at seeing that ingenious replica of old Rome had charmed him, the sound of her voice had delighted him, and the curves of her body . . .

I must have her. I *will* have her.

The girl had been close to surrender, Charles knew. So close. If it had only been a bit warmer, if he had thought to bring blankets—

—if he had not seen the tiny spark of fear in her eyes.

What could Miss Phillips be afraid of? Did she fear that he would tire of her and cast her out, that she would die of hunger or cold on some miserable back alleyway of London?

Much as he had tried to reassure her, Charles could not deny these were reasonable concerns. His years on the Spanish peninsula had given him an appreciation for the necessities of life that most of his class lacked. There was nothing missish in worrying about hunger. Hunger could bring strong men to their knees, and Lord Quentin recalled once more Miss Phillips's gaunt figure when she first arrived at Luton Court, the feel of each rib under his hands.

His promises had failed to convince her, thought Charles. She still anticipates being abandoned to the streets.

Charles threw back his bedding. He stood up and began pacing about the room, combing his fingers through his hair in agitation, his breath forming small clouds in the freezing air of his bedchamber. Cold and hungry. No. It was impossible, he could not stand to think of the governess on her own, without his protection. Not for a single hour, a single day.

Damnation. She must be made to face reason. Perhaps he could convince the marquess to dismiss her—

You are a bloody-minded bastard. The little voice condemned him, and Lord Quentin was at once ashamed. Of course he would do nothing of the kind. But Charles could think of no other leverage he might use against the stubborn Miss Helène Phillips, no reason he could give her to live with him beyond the usual arguments one made to one's prospective mistress.

A life of luxury and ease, gowns and jewelry, a furnished home in a respectable yet out-of-the-way part of town—

There was travel, of course. Charles's upbringing had made him as comfortable on the Continent as in England itself, even with the complications caused by the war. Fortunately that was over now, and Rome—a city which seemed to particularly intrigue the governess—was a favorite of his as well. They could rent a villa on the Ligurian coast, where he knew several likely situations, and visit Florence and Pisa as well. Perhaps somewhere near La Spezia . . .

Lord Quentin's mind was soon immersed in a gratifying daydream. He pictured the two of them fleeing the drab cold of London winters for a sun-washed villa in the south. The blue of the Mediterranean sparkling below them, the heady scents of coastal flowers perfuming the air—a few servants at their disposal, but otherwise alone. Alone to spend his days showing Miss Phillips the glories of a country where love was its own excuse, where no one spent a moment's worry on such stupidities as whether this chattering young miss or that received vouchers to Almack's. No one, in fact, would think twice about the young woman at his side, or treat her as anything other than . . .

Than his wife.

Yes, absolutely. Lord Quentin smiled to himself, the sheer rightness of this solution presenting itself full paid. Miss Phillips would be received as his wife and they could remain in Italy for the best part of the year. 'Twas perfect. He would need to spend much of the spring and early summer at Tavelstoke, of course, but perhaps Helène could remain in Italy for his return.

Charles closed his eyes for a moment. No. It was impossible. He could never last a week without her. Circumstances were bad enough now, but once she belonged to him, when he knew that it was only miles separating him from the delights of their bed—

No, his mistress must always accompany him to England. It was settled. Lord Quentin climbed back into the icy sheets of his bed and lay there until the dawn, planning his next moves against the redoubtable Miss Helène Phillips.

Alice frowned in concentration, her chalk poised above the slate.

"I can't do this!" she wailed. "I'm a *girl!*"

Helène's eyes widened. A girl? "Nonsense," she told Alice. "You are as capable of maths as anyone else. Subtraction is no more difficult than sums. It only takes practice."

"Papa says Lady Celia can't add two plus two! He says ladies don't need maths!"

The governess made a mental note to strangle Lord Sinclair the next time he poked his head into the nursery. "Ladies may not," she replied, "but little girls do. Now the five is bigger than the three, so remember how we borrow—"

"Miss Phiwips! I need to visit the prinnie!"

There was a burst of laughter from the doorway, and Helène turned to see Lady Pamela, outfitted for a late morning's ride in a tailored habit of charcoal grey. The governess was reminded of the first time she had seen the marquess's sister. The goddess Aphrodite, Helène had thought then, with that perfect face and the crown of white-gold hair.

"Run along, quickly," she told Peter, and then, to Lady Pamela, "If you have come to tempt us with visions of fresh air and snow, you will get no argument from me."

"I have just now realized," said Lady Pam, "that we have allowed a serious deficiency in your training to go unremarked."

Helène rolled her eyes. Lady Pamela's last complaint of a "serious deficiency" had involved the governess's lack of experience in taffy-making. Alice was now giving the two adults her full attention, all attempts at subtraction forgotten.

"Sledding, my dear," said Pam. "With all the snow last night, Crabtree Hill is begging for attention."

Sledding? Helène knew what a sled was, of course. She had seen a drawing of the strange contraptions in a London shop-window; sleds topped with rosy-cheeked boys, girls with their pigtails flying—

"Oh, please, may we, Miss Phillips?" begged Alice. The girl pushed her chair back and began to jump up and down. Her eyes were shining.

"I'm sure the children will enjoy—" began Helène.

"I'm sure they will too," interrupted Lady Pam, "but 'tis good sport for everyone. Put on your riding costume. We'll take the horses."

They made their way down to the stables to find Jennings fitting Ha'penny and Duchesse, Lady Pamela's mare, with a curious sort of harness. Helène eventually realized that the device was fashioned to allow the horse to drag a sled without tipping the front end up into the air. Alice and Peter were obviously no strangers to this arrangement. They ran in and out of the stables and generally made a nuisance of themselves until Jennings set them to work pitching hay.

"Don' ye be fergetting the ponies," said the groom. The children nodded, delighted by this responsibility and were well-occupied as the adults finished preparations.

A soft nicker—Helène turned to see Alcibiades being led from his stall by one of the grooms.

"I've asked Charles to join us," said Lady Pamela, holding out her last carrot to Duchesse. She did not meet the governess's eyes. "I tried to convince Lady Detweiler—"

Helène snorted.

"—but she has declared sleds to be the work of the devil."

"I believe Amanda thinks winter itself is of hellish instigation," interjected a deep male voice. "But one still assumes Lucifer cannot abide snow."

Lord Quentin emerged from Alcibiades's stall and was in front of them, sporting a smile that threatened to turn Helène's knees to water. Why did men always appear to such advantage out-of-doors? The governess was sure that her own curls had already begun their untidy escape from the tyranny of hairpins, but Lord Quentin was turned out to a trice, his thick brown hair held neatly back by a ribbon. The effect, especially when added to the wool muffler wrapped around his lordship's neck, was to make him look startlingly young, almost boyish.

Did he just wink at her? Helène flushed, and thought she must say something. Something sensible and collected.

"Ah," she managed. "Yes, well—"

"Charles, be a darling and see to Ha'penny's cinch," broke in Lady Pamela, to Helène's relief. "I'm going to organize another sled."

She left, and Lord Quentin was at Helène's side in two long strides. He cupped her chin with his hand and bent down to kiss her. A few breathless moments went by before the governess, blushing even more furiously, summoned the strength to push him away.

"Someone will see us!"

His smile widened, and Helène felt herself trapped, rooted to the spot, unable to move from the hunger she saw in his eyes.

"If that is all that bothers you, *ma petite*," said Lord Quentin, "I will take you someplace where no-one will see anything at all." He moved forward again to take her in his arms. She tried to step away but found herself backed against Ha'penny. The mare snorted and sidled away, and Helène would have lost her balance if Lord Quentin's arm had not steadied her. His hands went around her waist, the muscles of his forearms like a band of iron.

"Please, don't," said Helène.

"I will agree," said Lord Quentin, "for now. But you must see we have much to discuss. "

The governess looked up at him, confused. Things to discuss?

Carte blanche again, you little fool. He's leaving in a matter of days—

Helène sighed. It was quite true. The houseparty was breaking up and Lord Quentin would be gone before the week's end. She might not see him again for another year. Or perhaps never, for who could predict what might happen before next Christmas? It was impossible to contemplate, and she found herself weakening, ready to agree to whatever he might have in mind.

"Tonight, in your rooms," said Lord Quentin. He was

watching her face carefully.

Waiting, thought Helène. Waiting for some sign.

Never to see him again . . . Helène found herself nodding. "Tonight," she agreed, although for a moment she was not sure if she had spoken aloud. Only the look she saw on Lord Quentin's face confirmed that she had uttered that one word. It hung in the air between them.

Tonight.

Alcibiades was persuaded to accept the sled harness, although his demeanor clearly expressed disdain for the arrangement. He bucked and shimmied, forcing Lord Quentin to say a sharp word in his ear.

"Alcibiades! Stop this at once!"

The stallion's head jerked up, his nostrils flared—and the horse was obedient from that moment forward. Helène smiled privately, struck by the contrast between Lord Quentin and the horrid dandies of London, who cursed their mounts and used the whip against them at every opportunity. Her father had enjoyed that same understanding of horses.

Jennings helped her onto Ha'penny and the small group rode off with sleds trailing behind. Alice sat in front of Lord Quentin on Alcibiades, and Peter rode with Lady Pam. The sun shone almost warmly on Helène's back, and she began to relax, realizing how comfortable she felt in present company.

Lord Quentin was apparently no stranger to the day's activities; his running commentary on youthful sledding adventures with the marquess produced paroxysms of giggles in the children. Helène felt a twinge of anxiety, knowing that once Alice started to laugh it might not end until she had fallen off the horse, but Lord Quentin kept a steady hold on the girl.

"Miss Phillips! Look!"

Alice pointed at the hill looming in front of them. Good heavens, were they planning to sled down *that?* Surely it's too high, thought Helène. It looks like a mountain.

She had herself climbed the other side of Crabtree Hill only weeks before, but the view from this angle was alarming. The slope rose in front of them, smooth, unmarked—and steep.

They dismounted, settled the horses, and began to organize the sleds. Helène turned and caught Lord Quentin watching her, his eyes alight with mischief.

"Would you like to join me?" he asked. "The largest sled can hold two adults."

"Oh, no—"

"Or, of course, you can try it alone."

Alone? "Perhaps . . . perhaps I might observe for a few minutes," she allowed.

"Miss Phiwips! Watch me!"

Peter was climbing up the hill as fast as his feet would carry him, falling face first into the snow every few steps of the way. Alice followed at his heels. They dragged the two smaller sleds behind them and had soon reached, to Helène's eyes, an appalling height.

"Miss Phiwips!" rose the tiny cry. She saw the boy aim the sled downhill and fling himself on top as it started to move. Slowly at first, then gliding with increasing speed, until Peter was careening toward them at breakneck pace.

Directly toward them—For a heartstopping moment Helène thought they would be bowled over. But the sled ploughed into the deeper drifts at the bottom of the hill, throwing a fountain of snow into the air and stopping so abruptly that Peter tumbled off. He shrieked with laughter and then jumped to his feet, hurrying to drag his sled out of

Alice's way. His sister hurtled down the slope even faster, having given her sled a tremendous push at the top, and the horses whinnied and stomped as gobbets of snow flew everywhere.

"Come *on*, Aunt Pamela!"

Helène was startled to see the marquess's sister already half-way up the hill. Lady Pam pulled the larger sled through the tracks already made by the children and soon reached the top. She stood there with Alice and Peter, waving down at Helène and Lord Quentin, calling something the governess could not make out. Then, unlike the children, Pamela *sat* on the sled with her feet tucked to one side. Even at this distance she made an elegant, ladylike figure. Helène could see that Pam's cap was still perched at a jaunty angle, the brilliant peacock's feather brushing her forehead—

"Aieeee!" Alice had given her aunt a push and the sled began its long descent. The track, Helène realized, was becoming faster each time, as the snow was packed down by the sled runners.

"Aieeee!" continued the drawn-out cry. Lady Pamela's speed was astonishing but, against all expectation, she reached the bottom of the slope in good order, barely a single golden curl out of place.

"That," said Pam, tromping happily over to Lord Quentin and Helène, "was exhilarating. But mind the trees."

"Indeed. Miss Phillips, if you please?" Lord Quentin had taken the sled's rope from Lady Pamela. He held out his arm for Helène.

"Oh, but I don't think—" began Helène. Then—"What trees?"

"That clump there, don't you see?" Lady Pam pointed half way up the slope, ten yards or so to the side of the track.

"But—"

"Sleds," explained Lord Quentin, "are very difficult to steer."

"Then how—?"

"The trick is to get them pointed in the right direction. Don't worry," added his lordship, eyes twinkling, "I'm accounted an expert in the field."

She followed him up the slope as Alice and Peter shouted encouragement from above. The children were too impatient for the slow progress of the adults, however, and halfway to the top Helène was startled by a whoosh of snow as Peter flew by, followed seconds later by Alice. The governess turned to watch their descent and immediately felt Lord Quentin's steadying hand at her waist.

The governess looked up.

"Be careful," was all he said.

The top of Crabtree Hill afforded a magnificent view to all sides. Luton Court lay below them to the east, the village with its various small cottages in the opposite direction, with the Lea a somewhat more distant ribbon of glitter. She picked out the burnished copper of the parish church's steeple, and the roof of a larger dwelling nearby that she had not noticed before.

"What's that?" she asked Lord Quentin, pointing to the house.

"The church?"

"No, over to right—"

"Oh, that—" he said, with a dismissive flick of his hand. "That edifice is Noble Oaks Manor, the home of Squire Brigsby." There was a pause. "And the charming Lady Brigsby."

His distaste was so obvious that Helène, who had never heard of the squire and his wife, was immediately curious. Was this another example of Lord Quentin's arrogance toward members of any class lower than his own? Perhaps the Brigsbys were simply not *haut ton* enough for his lordship's refined sensibilities. Despite never having met the couple in question, Helène found herself ready to argue the point.

"Well, I can imagine that country gentry may not be up to the standards of elegance *you* require," she began, but Lord Quentin interrupted at once.

"The squire and his lady could be no worse associates if they dressed in sacking," he told her. "And you would find them no better company in cloth-of-gold. Now. I shall sit first, on the back of the sled, and hold you exactly so—"

"Ah . . . mmm. I suppose—"

Helène sat down gingerly, as directed. She found herself immediately blushing red, for it was remarkable how intimate the arrangement seemed. Out here in plain sight of Lady Pamela and the children below, swathed in layers of wool, she could feel the heat of Lord Quentin's chest and his thighs, as if his body was pressed to hers within the warm comfort of a bed. Her bottom seemed nestled shockingly close to—

"Lean back," Lord Quentin said gruffly.

Lean back? Slowly, Helène relaxed until she felt his breath warm against the top of her head.

"Now, do not move," he told her. "Are you ready?"

"Oh, I'm not sure—" She tried to turn around.

"Sit still! Here we go—"

Lord Quentin managed a push, and they were at once gliding headlong down the slope, faster and faster, the only sound the whisper of sled runners against the snow. Trees flashed by at both sides, and she saw the tiny figures of Lady Pam, Alice, and Peter, shouting and waving miles below.

It was thrilling. Helène felt the wind cold against her face and thought that not even flying could feel this free. It seemed impossible that they would ever stop, they would glide and glide until they fell off the edge of the world. She laughed out loud—

"Hang on!" Lord Quentin shouted, and he pulled, hard, on the rope attached to the right side of the sled. Helène felt a sudden lurch, a change of direction—and more trees flashed by to their left, very close. She paid little attention, heard herself yelling into the wind and wondered what she might be saying.

Faster and faster—

"Ooof!" said Lord Quentin, as the sled, thrown from the previous tracks by their near encounter with the trees, burrowed itself headfirst into a drift. Helène pitched to one side as the sled tipped, and a white fountain erupted around them. She and Lord Quentin tumbled from the sled in a tangle of arms and legs, and were immediately covered by the cascade of snow. After a moment's dazed silence Helène, as delighted as any child at this outcome, began to giggle. After one glance at the sophisticated and aristocratic Lord Quentin, who was trying to extricate one of his boots from a foot of snow, the giggles turned into helpless laughter.

He grinned at her.

"Miss Phillips! Miss Phillips!" That was Alice. The governess began brushing snow from, seemingly, every square inch of her clothing, as Lady Pamela and the children ran forward.

"Are you all right?" Lady Pamela. "I seem to recall warning you about the trees."

"Didn't get a proper start," said Lord Quentin, gasping as melted snow began to drip down his neck. "My aim was off."

Pam looked at him, nodding. "Indeed," she said, and helped the governess to her feet.

★ ★ ★ ★ ★

That afternoon remained ever afterwards in Helène's memory as one of the happiest of her life. They climbed to the top of Crabtree Hill time after time, the track becoming smoother and their descents faster. She doubled with Alice or Peter, sometimes with Lady Pam—and again with Lord Quentin. Only when the children's clothing had become thoroughly soaked with melted snow did any of them entertain thoughts of returning home.

"Oh, no, Miss Phillips! We aren't cold at all!"

"Mind your governess," said Lord Quentin, and that was the end of it. Lady Pamela had the foresight to bring blankets, and each child was bundled from head to toe before being thrown up onto a horse.

"Mmph!" complained Peter. "I can't breath!"

"Try," said his aunt, "and you may live long enough for hot chocolate."

They began the trek home as the sun touched the horizon and the evening's chill began to descend. Alcibiades led the way, and Helène found it hard to take her eyes from the stallion's rider. Tonight. Tonight. Tonight. The insistent drumbeat had begun to invade Helène's every thought, and she wondered if Lord Quentin could hear it too.

Chapter Nineteen

It bears repeating: a governess takes no interest in men.

The knock, when it came, was so soft that Helène wasn't sure she had heard it. The governess stood with her back to the window and stared at the door of her bedchamber. She was willing the sound to come again, both afraid to move and afraid not to.

Then, a whispered "Helène?" as the door cracked open of its own accord. Lord Quentin was inside the room in an instant, his arms around her in the next. Helène looked up into his strong, craggy face and felt the breath catch in her throat. His eyes were the deepest brown she had ever seen, and the warmth of his smile penetrated even to her toes.

His mouth—

Lord Quentin bent down to kiss her, his arms crushing Helène against his chest until her feet left the floor. She was at once at sea, sensations pounding against her like waves, tossed and buffeted until coherent thought was lost. She thought she heard him sigh, softly, thought she felt a hand gently stroking her cheek.

Abruptly, impossibly, he broke off the embrace. "Excuse me," he said to the governess, and swiftly crossed the floor to throw the bolt on her bedchamber door. In that moment of respite Helène's reason reasserted itself and she lifted her chin, shooting him a look of admonition as he returned.

"You said—" began Helène.

Lord Quentin laughed and tried to catch her up into his

arms. She backed away, feeling like very small prey indeed.

"What did I say?"

"You said we had things to discuss."

"Yes. I did, didn't I?" He had captured one hand and turned it upwards, stroking the palm with his fingers. Helène's toes curled into hard little knots. She forced a swallow and began again.

"I've no doubt you could bed me without further ado," she told the startled lord. "But I would prefer to have certain things made clear first."

"Ah." Lord Quentin's smile widened to a grin as—without further ado, indeed—he picked Helène up and tossed her onto the duvet. She squeaked in outrage, afraid to make any more noise. "I will make everything perfectly clear on the instant. But it will be much more comfortable doing so in your bed."

"My lord!"

"Charles."

"Lord Quentin," said Helène severely, propping herself up on her elbows. "I cannot think we will accomplish much *talking* in my bed."

"I can assure you I have no intention of doing so." But a look at the governess's expression seemed to changed his mind. He took a deep breath and extended his hand to her. "Very well," he said. "We shall talk."

Helène knelt on the small rug in front of the fire, drinking in the solid, relentlessly male presence of Lord Quentin at her side. It was comforting, somehow, even if she knew she was unlikely to see him again after tonight. Her hair, unpinned, cascaded to her waist and she felt his hand fingering its length. The touch was mesmerizing, addictive; Helène felt that she could happily sit there for hours if only he would not stop the soft caress.

Talk—pah! She had been the one to insist they discuss the situation, but Helène could think of nothing, after all, that she might be willing to say.

Would it be so impossible to marry me?

But some questions, if you must ask them, were not worth the answer.

"I am leaving for Tavelstoke in a few days," said Lord Quentin. Helène nodded, unable to meet his eyes. "You can give Lord Sinclair your notice tomorrow and I shall return for you in a month's time. It will give me a chance to make the necessary arrangements."

"Why?" said Helène.

He hesitated. "Why wait a month? I suppose it isn't necessary. Alice and Peter have survived nicely without a governess before. I'm sure—"

"No," said Helène. "Why me? You have your pick of the available *ton* females, I should imagine. What makes you think that I should suit as your mistress?"

"Ah. Well . . ."

Lord Quentin seemed to be having difficulty framing the response to this question and Helène felt herself blushing. *You are a little peagoose,* scolded the voice. *What did you expect? A declaration of undying love?*

"I can't quite explain it," he said finally, sounding honestly perplexed. "You are beautiful and kind and . . . desirable, of course. I feel we would rub together very well."

His eyes held hers, and she could see her own regrets mirrored there, genuine and profound. He might marry me, thought Helène. He really might, but only if I told him. She took a deep breath, knowing that her decision had been made.

"I am aware that you . . . compliment me with this offer,

Lord Quentin," said Helène. It was no *compliment* to a respectable female, of course, but she could not say the real
word between them, could not give that truth a name. "However . . ." She hesitated. "I will not go to London with you. I
will not be your mistress."

With these words, time froze. Charles Quentin sat there,
smiling at her still, having yet to register her reply. She tried
to imagine how she would feel on the morning he left Luton
Court. She thought to the years ahead, years spent alone,
without him—

Something had been stretched within her, tighter and
tighter, and in that moment it snapped. Steeling herself, feeling a hot blush color her cheeks, Helène spoke again, abruptly.

"As for tonight—"

Charles stared at Miss Phillips, his mind racing, certain of
what she had said but in no wise able to understand why she
would have said it. He had been so sure that the governess
would agree to his *carte blanche*. And now—had he heard
aright? She would not be his mistress, but would invite him to
her bed for the night?

Miss Phillips was looking at him curiously and Lord
Quentin assumed that his face had turned a rather alarming
shade of red.

"Tonight?" he hissed. "What on God's good earth are you
talking about?"

"Have I not made myself clear?" she responded, a little
tartly. "I am willing to be . . . intimate with you for the night.
But I will not be your mistress."

"Why?" he finally asked her. "Why would you want to . . .
do that? What would be the point?"

The governess shook her head, apparently exasperated.
"Surely it is obvious that I am not indifferent to you," she

said. "But I will not risk getting with child."

Charles was at sea. Pregnancy was a hazard of these circumstances, certainly, but the complication was rarely discussed between a gentleman and his mistress. There were certain ways to avoid it—Lord Quentin frowned at the thought—but he had assumed . . .

"With child?" he managed.

"Well, I heard people talk. In London, you know. On the street. The ladies—"

"The ladies on the street?" His voice sputtered, and rose to such a pitch that the governess looked up in alarm.

"Hush," she told him. "You'll have Lady Sinclair at my door again."

"You spoke to the ladies on the street?" he hissed. The conversation was spinning out of Charles's control.

"No, of course I didn't *speak* to them. But several of the . . . ah . . ."

"Prostitutes?" suggested Lord Quentin.

Miss Phillips nodded. "Yes, several of . . . them seemed to spend a great deal of time on the sidewalk below my bedroom window. I could hear their conversations—"

Charles groaned.

"And it was obvious that they were all concerned with this . . . issue. I just thought that—"

She faltered, but Lord Quentin felt sudden enlightenment. He lifted one eyebrow and fixed the governess with what he hoped was a schoolmaster-ish eye.

"Let me guess. You've somehow assumed that a woman is unlikely to get with child—the first time?"

"Exactly." The girl sighed, relieved that no further elaboration of the subject would be necessary.

"I see." Lord Quentin was caught between desire and laughter. He was loathe to pursue the topic further; still,

Helène deserved the truth.

" 'Tis no less likely the first time than any other," he told her. "If you understood the . . . arrangement of the endeavor, you would know this to be true."

"Oh." She rose to her feet, looking confused.

He stood as well, and caught her hand before she could back away. Some unknown pain flickered in her eyes, and Charles saw clearly that Helène was passing from his reach for all time, saw her inexorably slipping away.

How had it happened? He had been so sure—

"I would love to live with you in your beautiful world," said Miss Phillips. "But I could not live with myself."

Helène did not sleep for the rest of that night. She kept to the nursery the next day, and for several days after that, and saw nothing of Charles Quentin. The houseparty was nearly over, and with the exception of Lord Quentin and Lady Harkins—who Amanda claimed would manage to stay until she was booted out the door—most of the other fine lords and ladies were preparing their return to London. Each morning the children ran excitedly to the schoolroom windows when the general clatter and commotion of horses announced another departure.

One morning the departing guest was Lord Quentin, setting out for Tavelstoke in the company of the marquess.

"Lord 'Wentin! Papa!" called Peter, then—"He waved!"

Who waved? Helène never knew, for she refused to join Alice and Peter at the window. Eventually there came the sound of hoofbeats, first clearly heard, then receding slowly into the distance until they were finally, irrevocably gone.

That evening, exhausted, Helène prepared early for bed, and it was by sheerest luck that she had not yet removed her day dress when the magistrate arrived, for her bedchamber door burst open, and two burly men of uncertain provenance and foul breath dragged her from her room, down the grand staircase, and through the front hall of Luton Court.

At least the children were already asleep.

Chapter Twenty

"Ahhh," sighed Lord Sinclair, stretching his legs out onto a large ottoman, "my feet don't want to see the inside of another pair of boots for days."

"Then we are agreed," said Lord Quentin. His own legs were slung over the side of an armchair. Rufus, the earl's ancient Irish setter, occasionally roused himself from his bed in front of the fire to sniff worriedly at Charles's feet.

The two friends sat in the Tavelstoke library, weary from the long ride and enjoying their second—or third—glass of Lord Quentin's best port. It had been the custom for years, even while Jonathan's first wife was alive, for Charles and Jonathan to make this trip at the end of the Luton houseparty. Their journey this year meant pleasant company as usual, but an uncomfortable ride. Temperatures were warm for early February, and with the amount of snow fallen, the roads had turned to slush.

Slush kicked up from the horses' hooves, slush falling from the branches above them— knee deep in slush, sometimes, when they dismounted for the necessaries. Both men had been thoroughly chilled by the time they reached the gates of Tavelstoke, and they had consumed several glasses of port in the effort to warm themselves.

Perhaps the drink was the cause of his present, cheerless mood, thought Charles. It could hardly be anything else. He had always enjoyed these two weeks with Jonathan, two weeks where he and his friend counted themselves free from every social obligation. They would tramp for miles through the surrounding countryside, play game after game of bad chess, and sit up until all hours of the night drinking, with never a female to say them nay.

It was one of the highlights of his year, so why did he feel so . . . bereft? *This* was what he wanted, freedom from every worry and claim upon his affections.

He felt fine, actually. Altogether fine. He and the marquess would have a splendid time, and at the end he would make a brief trip to town and treat himself to the most beautiful courtesan in all of London. He would stay at the Tavelstoke townhome and be satisfied for days on end. Yes. That was clearly the plan.

"A fetching chit, I should say," commented Jonathan.

"Your pardon?" Charles realized that his attention had been wandering.

"Miss Phillips."

At the sound of her name, Lord Quentin's careful logic collapsed into a hollow, dreadful pain. Miss Phillips. Miss Helène Phillips, whom he was not likely to see again until Luton Court's next houseparty, and if Celia had her way, perhaps not even then. Charles imagined her lovely, smiling face as if she were standing in front of him and remembered the feel of her skin under his hands—

He heard the delighted cries of Alice and Peter as they pelted their governess with snowballs, and Miss Phillips's laughing response—

Never to see her again.

"Yes," said the marquess. "I think she'd be perfect for you." There was a short pause, then Jonathan added, "And a splendid countess."

"What in heaven's name is all this ruckus?"

Lady Detweiler threw open the door of her bedroom, snifter of brandy in hand. She and Lady Pamela had both heard the commotion, but Pam was faster to respond and had already thrown on her robe as she hastened toward the grand staircase. She motioned for Amanda to follow, and they reached the hallway's end in time to see Helène Phillips being half carried, half dragged down the marble steps by two very large and scruffy-looking men. The men were sweating and swearing, lurching from side to side and banging into the balustrade as the governess struggled frantically against them. Helène's cries were muffled under the beefy hand of the larger of the two men.

Below they could see James barring the way to the front door. The footman's fists were raised, and he was clearly prepared for a fight.

"James, *no!*" cried Lady Pamela, charging down the staircase. She had recognized the two men holding Helène. Petrus and Torvin Emory! The two had a reputation in the village as rough trade indeed and would likely be armed with knives.

Which they might not hesitate to use against a poor servant. Lady Pamela reached the bottom step, Amanda at her heels, and they sidestepped the thugs to stand at James's side.

Pam tried to give Helène a reassuring smile, but the governess's eyes seemed not to focus, and her face had taken on an ashy hue. She was wedged tightly between the two men, continuing to struggle weakly against them.

"It's all right, Helène," Lady Pamela told the governess. "I don't understand what's happened, but we'll set it to rights."

The footman had not lowered his fists, and Pam gently touched his shoulder. "You've done very well, James," she whispered. "Now, don't worry. I will see to the matter." He nodded, and Pam realized that for once there was no trace of uncertainty or confusion on the footman's face. James, it seems, was a man to be counted on in a crisis.

"Now," said Lady Pamela to the Emory brothers, "what is the meaning of this?"

Petrus and Torvin halted. Without relaxing their grip on Helène, they eyed Lady Pam uncertainly. Not quite stupid enough to attack the marquess's sister, she decided. Petrus glanced to one side and only then did Pamela notice that there was someone else present, another man. He had been hiding, by the looks of it, standing in the shadow of a huge Kentia palm.

"Eh," snarled Petrus, "scullery slut, y' said. Weren't to be no gentry coves."

"No gentry coves!" echoed his brother.

The third man seemed to shrink against the palm. "I paid you! Do your jobs!" Lady Pamela immediately recognized the frightened, nasal bleat of Malcolm Brigsby.

What was the squire doing at Luton? As Pam's eyes adjusted to the dim light of the entry hall she saw that it was indeed Sir Malcolm, the identification confirmed by his short stature and a pair of breeches that were, predictably, several sizes too small.

"Gracious, an overstuffed sausage," murmured Lady Detweiler, snorting her distaste.

"Sausage?" said Torvin, looking around.

Sir Malcolm coughed nervously.

"Helène," said Pam, giving the girl a worried glance, "give me a moment to talk to these . . . people." Miss Phillips's face was drained of all color and Pam realized, with horror, that the governess's wrists were manacled.

This was outrageous.

"Sir Malcolm, explain yourself immediately," ordered Lady Pamela. She was uncomfortably aware that she was dressed only in a silk wrapper, and that the Emory brothers were leering at her. "Are these ruffians at your hire?"

"Well—"

"Ruffians she calls us!" said Petrus. He seemed pleased.

"You see—"

"Ruffians!" said Torvin.

"Not enough wit between the two of them for even a single ruffian, I should think," commented Amanda, *sotto voce*.

Lady Pamela's attention was fixed on the squire. "This young lady is governess to Lord Sinclair's children," she informed him. "I insist that she be unhanded at once."

Sir Malcolm's face was beet red and his forehead shone with perspiration. "Ah, well, I don't know about that," he said to Pam. "I was told—"

This was unbelievable. Who did the little mushroom think he was talking to? "Do not argue with me!" Pamela said, stamping her foot. "You have no right to be in this house. Release Miss Phillips and get out at once!"

There was a moment's silence, and Sir Malcolm seemed to be weakening. Then—

"*I* asked . . . asked him to come."

The marchioness's voice, unsteady with drink, floated down from the staircase. All eyes turned to see Lady Sinclair at the balustrade. She was flushed and, against all previous habit, disheveled.

"Celia," said Lady Pam, "what in heaven's name is going on here?"

"I sent for Sir Malcolm's services as a magistrate," said the marchioness. "In the absence of the marquess, of course." Celia held up a piece of jewelry, large green stones flashing along a gold chain. She pointed a shaky finger at Helène. "This woman stole . . . stole my emerald necklace. I found it hidden behind some books in the nursery."

Helène's head jerked up, outrage evident in every line of her body.

"What!" cried Lady Pamela.

"Yes," said Amanda. "I just bet you did."

Lady Sinclair had been waiting for this moment, planning for it—but now that she saw the harsh facts before her, the governess manacled before her eyes, doubts arose in force. What had she done? That spineless Sir Malcolm! And those two dreadful men he had brought with him, of all the *nerve* to bring such riffraff inside her home.

An empty decanter of sherry in the marchioness's suite was testimony to Lady Sinclair's current state, and she wished for another glass even now. She'd only thought to cause gossip, she'd never intended—

Celia hiccoughed, and swayed. Speaking of gossip, where the devil was Beatrice? The marchioness had assumed Lady Harkins would be up as long as there was still wine and *les petits aliments* to be had. She was counting on Beatrice to carry the story to London. The marchioness, even when sober, had spared little thought to the potentially serious consequences of an accusation of theft. Her intention was only . . . was only . . .

Celia was suddenly confused, unsure of why it had seemed necessary to ruin the reputation of Helène Phillips. Something about speaking French, and Charles Quentin's interest in the girl, and her own husband—

Lady Sinclair felt her resolve waver, the tears start to her eyes. Then she saw Helène standing below, dressed in a day gown of fine cambric, her jaw set in defiance. Showing not an ounce of shame . . . Celia's back straightened. She was a marchioness! The girl was a nobody, plaguing her without end in her own home. It was insupportable, and she'd been given no choice, really, the girl must go.

But it seemed that the odious squire couldn't manage the job himself. Those two revolting hooligans he had brought with him were really the outside of enough. . . .

"What is happening!" A shrill cry came from behind the marchioness. "My heart—I cannot bear it! Are we all to be murdered in our beds?"

Celia turned, and ventured a tipsy smile. Lady Harkins had arrived.

The entry hall erupted in a babel of speech.

"There is some mistake," Lady Pamela was saying. "You must wait until—"

"Well, like her ladyship says—"

"We're ruffians!" crowed Torvin.

"Celia—"

"I knew she was a thief the moment I set eyes on her! Why Lord Sinclair would ever hire such a—"

"I didn't steal anything," cried Helène. "I didn't steal *any-thing.*"

Sir Malcolm swallowed the discomfort growing in his gut. This was no scullery maid, he could see that now. Dressed fine as a lady, and friends to his lordship's sister, by the looks of it. Damn Lady Sinclair for getting him into this. She had assured him that the marquess would approve his actions, but here was the sister, taking exception. It wasn't his fault! He was only doing what he was told!

What was he supposed to do now?

Squire Brigsby wasn't entirely a fool. He understood that Lady Pamela was a power to be reckoned with on the Luton estates. But Lady Sinclair was the marquess's wife. Surely she was the more important—

"Telford! Where the devil is the blasted butler?"

"Just look at her, standing there pretty as you please! I will be inspecting my own jewelry case, and if—"

"Celia, will you please explain— "

Difficult decisions were not Squire Brigsby's strength. He swallowed again and tried to think, but the ladies were arguing loudly and the footman looked as if he had designs on Sir Malcolm's neck. It was too much to consider all at once. He should leave immediately—yes, leave. The squire puffed out his chest, thinking to announce his departure, but as he did so, a button of his weskit popped and fell to the floor, rolling off into the darkness. He heard a snort of feminine laughter and felt anger surge.

So be it, thought Sir Malcolm. *I am the magistrate of this township, and the Marchioness of Luton has accused this young woman of theft.*

She is coming with me.

Lady Sinclair and Lady Harkins descended to the front hall, and the noise level rose another notch.

"A crime has been committed," declared Sir Malcolm. "It is my duty—"

"I didn't take Lady Sinclair's necklace," said Helène, who had recovered her color and was protesting angrily. "I don't know what you are talking about!"

"A criminal! I knew it all along."

"I can assure you that Miss Phillips would never—"

"It was missing from my jewelry box this morning. I've searched—"

"The only crime *I* see," said Amanda, "is those breeches."

The squire glared at Lady Detweiler and began backing toward the front door, one nervous eye on the footman. He motioned for Petrus and Torvin to follow with Helène.

"It's the law," he said. "You can't stop me."

"Leave her alone!" cried James. He moved toward the brothers, but there was a sudden flash of metal and a knife appeared in Petrus's hand.

"James," said Lady Pam. "No." If there was a fight, the person most likely to be injured was the footman himself.

"But, milady—"

Amanda stepped forward, glaring at Petrus. "Put that ridiculous thing down!" she said, motioning toward the knife.

Celia spoke again. "This is none of your affair, Lady Detweiler," she cried. "Leave him to do his job."

Lady Detweiler rounded on the marchioness. Her eyes flashed mayhem, and Lady Pamela saw, for the first time, the blood of the French king that flowed in her friend's veins.

"You do not tell me what I may or may not do," said Amanda. "You do not tell *me* anything at all."

Petrus Emory had little tolerance for the gentry, especially the female gentry. Remembering the time that Lady Pamela had caught him with the fishmonger's daughter, he scowled at her and Amanda. Interfering busybodies! Always stickin' their noses where they ain't wanted. The girl's clothing might be that of a lady, but she was only a governess, wasn't she? And a thief.

Bloody hell, thought Petrus. The stupid coves'll be crownin' the slut queen if this goes on. An' we know where that'll be going. Be going where we don' get our pay, that's where.

"Bunch'a gobs, the lot a' ye," said Petrus suddenly. He turned and, without warning, struck Lady Detweiler hard across her cheek. She crumpled soundlessly to the floor.

Torvin jumped up and down in excitement. Celia and Lady Harkins both screamed.

"Oh, now, I do say," protested Sir Malcolm.

Lady Pamela tried to reach Amanda, only to be stopped by both Emorys. "Get back!" said Petrus furiously. "Or I'll cuff 'er again." Giving Helène's arm a vicious yank, he addressed Sir Malcolm.

"Come on then," said Petrus. "You wanted the silly chit, you got her."

Lord Quentin could not believe he had heard his friend correctly. What was Jonathan talking about? Miss Phillips—his wife?

"But," sputtered Charles, "but she's a *governess*."

"Ah, yes," said Lord Sinclair. "Yes, she is, isn't she? One tends to forget. The fine deportment and all that, you know. Excellent French—"

"If you will recall, I am the future Earl of Tavelstoke. I cannot marry a . . . a chit of no breeding whatsoever." Lord Quentin almost flinched at his own words. *I sound so pompous,* he thought.

"—and such an elegant wardrobe. Superb taste. Can't you imagine her at a fine London *soirée?* Put a few duchesses to shame, I dare say."

Her *wardrobe?* Even Jonathan must realize that Lady Pamela had bought Miss Phillips every stitch of her present clothing, thought Lord Quentin. But the marquess's words had released another flood of memory, and this time the pain was tinged with despair.

The future Countess of Tavelstoke. Marriage. It was inevitable—and sooner rather than later, given the state of his father's health. The earl would love to see grandchildren, love to see the title fixed on a third generation before his death. It was common decency to oblige him if he could. Charles had assumed he would pick a likely girl from some year's crop of *ton* debutantes, a decorative young miss of good family.

Someone it would not be a trial to face over the breakfast table each morning.

When I marry, Lord Quentin thought, *I will need to spend time with my wife and my children.* His own father had never abandoned him to the care of nannies, and Charles would do no less.

But what, then, of Miss Helène Phillips?

Petrus and Torvin dragged Helène out the door. She did not resist, judging it fruitless for now and a waste of her strength. A battered coach stood in the front drive, and behind it an even sorrier-looking hayrack. The two men motioned toward the rack, and Helène, sneezing, climbed onto the straw.

The men followed her into the rack, leering at Helène, but evidently Sir Malcolm drew the line at rape.

"If you touch her," he warned Petrus, "you won't get a penny."

The squire produced a heavy wool blanket from the coach and threw it at Helène. Shivering, she drew it around herself and shrank into the straw. It was perhaps a half-hour's drive from Luton Court to the squire's home. To the governess's relief, the brothers took Sir Malcolm's warning to heart; Petrus glanced at Helène from time to time, and spat, but otherwise left her alone. When the hayrack and coach finally arrived at Noble Oaks Manor, the two men jumped out and approached the squire for their pay; they then disappeared without a word.

Helène stretched cramped legs and looked around her in the gloom, remembering Lady Detweiler's comment about the Brigsby home. "Noble Oaks, my aunt Fanny," Amanda had remarked. And indeed, what she could see of the place in the dark—a square brick building overgrown with ivy—was far from reassuring. She started to climb out of the rack.

"Malcolm!"

The squire's wife had appeared on the front steps. "Malcolm!" she screeched again. "What do you think you are doing with *her?*"

James carried the unconscious Lady Detweiler to her rooms; Lady Pamela hurried alongside, torn between her worries for Amanda and Miss Phillips. Celia had disappeared along with Beatrice Harkins. It was a small favor, as Pam was not sure what she trusted herself to say to her sister-in-law.

A stolen necklace, indeed! Lady Pam hadn't believed the marchioness's story for a moment; nor, she knew, had Amanda. She must send a groom to Tavelstoke with a message for her brother, but the first priority was to call for the doctor.

"James," she began, but the footman was already out the door and on his way to the stables. At the moment there was nothing more to be done, and Pam turned her attention to Lady Detweiler.

Amanda's right eye was swollen shut and cheek horribly bruised, the skin broken in one spot and seeping blood. Lady Pamela fought down a moment's panic at the sight. "Amanda?" she whispered.

"Where's the bleedin' brandy?" was the faint reply.

Helène stood on the front steps of Noble Oaks Manor, waiting in the cold as Lady Brigsby berated her husband.

"I won't have her in the house!" declared the squire's wife.

"Come now, Edith," said Sir Malcolm, " 'twas the marchioness's express direction. The girl stole a necklace, and I *am* the magistrate—"

"Pah!" said Lady Brigsby.

What were they planning to do with her? wondered Helène. She remembered a fragment of conversation from her father—

"There are no true gaols in the countryside," Mr. Phillips had said. *"The nobs take their turn plaguing the likes of us."*

So. It seemed that Sir Malcolm Brigsby was the local magistrate, and she would be held in his home on the charge of theft. Helène felt somewhat reassured. Lady Pamela would surely inquire after her, and the house could hardly be as bad as what she had heard of London prisons.

"She'll be put in the cellar room, like the rest of them," Sir Malcolm was saying.

The cellar?

"Well . . . I suppose—" said his wife.

"Don't worry, my love," said Sir Malcolm. "I'll send her on to town straightaway."

Lady Sinclair allowed Aggie to help her out of her gown and then sent the girl off with a curt word. The evening's arrangements had dissolved into fiasco, and Celia was sure someone else must be to blame.

Her head ached so abominably she could hardly think—

How dare that upstart Sir Malcolm bring such men into Luton Court! Celia realized that she had thought nothing about *how* Miss Phillips was to be arrested; only that Beatrice Harkins hear of it. And why did they take the girl away? Surely the marchioness could not have expected anyone to take her complaint so seriously. 'Twas only a necklace, after all, nothing more than a trifle.

And how could she have known that either Pamela or Lady Detweiler would put themselves to real trouble on Helène's behalf, let alone stand up to those thugs! The girl was a governess, for heaven's sake. Little more than a *servant*.

But now there had been a fuss, and Amanda Detweiler—*Lady* Amanda Detweiler, of the Clairveax-Detweiler clan—had been injured. Even badly injured, perhaps, and this was scandal-broth of a far different flavor. Her own name, Celia knew, would not fare well when stacked against that of Amanda and Lady Pamela Sinclair. Eyebrows would be raised, and although Miss Phillips would assuredly still be ruined, the marchioness's reputation would suffer as well.

Jonathan will be furious, thought Celia. Tears came once again, and she sat on the floor at the foot of her bed, burying her head in her hands. Oh, Jonathan, what have I done? She could not bear to think of it, didn't wish to think of anything at all—

More sherry. She must have another drink or there would be no sleep at all this night.

Charles and Jonathan, both staggering slightly from the combined effects of exhaustion and drink, found their beds sometime after midnight. There had been no more talk of governesses or marriage, and Lord Quentin was beginning to think that he might be able to find an approximation of contentment in the next weeks at Tavelstoke.

Women, thought Charles fuzzily, as sleep claimed him, were only a pleasant *divertissement* in the life of a true gentleman. Really, how could one think otherwise? Apart for the need of an heir, females were hardly a necessity. Now, as to the more important things in life . . .

Despite his fatigue Lord Quentin tossed restlessly through much of the night, dreaming of Miss Helène Phillips as he had first seen her; dirty, ragged, desperate with hunger and the cold. There was nothing in his mind's figure of her that suggested a lady. Nothing at all.

★ ★ ★ ★ ★

The doctor arrived within the hour, and clucked at the sight of Lady Detweiler's eye and the broken skin of her cheek. Amanda showed signs of a fever; Doctor Howorth cleaned the wound and prescribed a dose of willow-bark powders, promising to return first thing the next morning.

It was now the middle of the night and, worried as she was about Helène, Lady Pamela would not ask a groom to attempt the journey to Tavelstoke before morning. She spent the wakeful hours at Amanda's bedside, composing one message after another to the marquess and discarding each one as unlikely to provoke her brother to the needed haste. Celia's involvement complicated matters, as Pam could see no tactful way of informing Jonathan that his wife was the author of the trumped-up charge of theft. Lady Pamela would have preferred that Charles Quentin hear nothing about a stolen necklace, or discover that Helène had been arrested, but in the end she decided that there was no help for it.

My dearest brother, wrote Pam—

Miss Phillips has been arrested by Malcolm Brigsby—and taken to his house—after being falsely charged as a thief. Please return at once.

—*P.*

Shortly before dawn Lady Pamela pulled on a woolen cloak and walked to the stables, treading quietly as she passed Celia's door.

Chapter Twenty-One

A governess in disgrace expects no help from her betters.

"I'll send her on to town straightaway."

Hearing this, Helène thought for one frantic moment of simply turning around and running. Sent off to a London gaol, with no one having any idea where to find her, even if they cared enough to help—

Of course Lady Pamela and Lady Detweiler care, she told herself. *Of course they don't think I stole the necklace. Lady Pam will write the marquess.*

But what if Lord Sinclair did not believe her? The impulse to flight grew stronger, tempered only by cold reason. At night, unable to find her bearings, floundering helplessly through the snow—

Patience would serve her better, decided Helène, and she did not protest as the squire led her to a back staircase, and then down to a dusty, foul-smelling room.

"In there," said the squire curtly, unlocking the door with a large iron key. He seemed embarrassed to meet her eyes.

The room was filthy. Helène once again fought the impulse to flee—what if Petrus and Torvin Emory were her gaolers?—and decided she would not make the situation any easier for Sir Malcolm.

"Lord Sinclair will not be pleased with my treatment," she told the squire, nose in the air and waving one hand in front of her face at the smell.

"Get in," was the only reply. The squire locked the door behind her and, from the sound of his footsteps, left the cellar nearly at a run.

Helène examined her new surroundings. A small window high up on one wall provided ventilation and a faint shaft of moonlight. A cot was pushed against the opposite wall; next to it was a small table boasting the stub of a tallow candle but no way to light it. The floor was covered with rush matting, which was a fortunate circumstance, as the stone would otherwise have been intolerably cold. London bred, Helène noted the quantity of rat droppings underfoot with a practiced eye. Her current lodgings apparently boasted a vermin population of considerable size.

The cot was equipped with a tattered wool blanket, and she hoped that it, at least, was free of droppings.

She was both cold and very thirsty, but could see no likely vessel for water. A slop-bucket was partially hidden under the table. It was empty, noted Helène with thanks.

The silence of the place was eerie, and she wondered if anyone would answer should she cry out. Would they leave her down here to starve? She felt tendrils of panic slipping around her heart. Stop playing the dainty miss, Helène told herself sternly. Fine airs 'twill not unlock that door.

The moonlight was growing fainter as the night wore on. Helène looked up at the small window, judging it both impossible to reach and too small to use as an exit in any case. Panic threatened again, but even her brief exposure to city poverty now proved its worth, for the last months with her father had given Helène an appreciation for the practical and the necessary. She could stand here and bemoan her fate, or she could save her energy and get some sleep.

Resolutely ignoring the look and smell of the cot, she curled up on it and covered herself with the blanket.

She was very thirsty.

"I'm going to marry Miss Phillips."

Jonathan barely looked up at Lord Quentin's entrance into the breakfast salon, his attention concentrated on an enormous plate of roast beef.

"Well, yes," said the marquess finally, between mouthfuls. "I should think so."

I should think so? "Did you hear me?" asked Charles. "I said—"

"—that you are going to marry Alice and Peter's governess. Yes, I heard. Come have some of your cook's *boeuf miroton*. It's delicious."

Lady Detweiler's fever improved somewhat upon a second dose of willow powders and, although her eye was still swollen shut, and her bruises an interesting mix of purple and green, the next morning found her strong enough sit up in bed.

A groom had been dispatched to Tavelstoke at early dawn; Amanda and Lady Pamela were now contriving how Miss Phillips might be released from the custody of Sir Malcolm and his wife even before Jonathan's return.

"Bribe her," said Amanda, who was aware of Lady Brigsby's penny-pinching ways. "I'll wager a monkey that ten pounds would do the trick."

"Mmm," said Pam. "What if Celia has bribed her first?"

" 'Tis possible," admitted Lady Detweiler. She paused, then added, "Have you told the children anything?"

"I said that Miss Helène has gone to see some acquaintances for a visit and will return within a few days. Unless Celia speaks to them I don't think they need ever know more."

"Celia keep her mouth shut? 'Twill be the first time," said Amanda. "And between our dear marchioness and Beatrice Harkins spreading tales, I think Helène's chances of a good marriage may be greatly harmed."

Lady Pamela sighed. "I know." She shrugged. "I think it's time to pay a visit to Noble Oaks Manor. Squire Stupidity may not agree to release Helène, but perhaps his wife can be persuaded to treat the Marquess of Luton's governess with particular care."

Sir Malcolm enjoyed his small sphere of authority as a magistrate. Not that this authority was widely appreciated in the shire. Local villagers had never accorded the squire near the consideration they paid Lord Sinclair, and it rankled. He might not be a marquess, but he was gentry, fair and square. They ought to show him proper respect. And as a magistrate, oh, then he could make 'em hop. Rousting drunks on the new year's, thrashing the cobbler's son for stealing a bit of candy— It had all been quite satisfying.

Until today. The squire now wished he had never heard of that benighted emerald necklace. He had meant to ingratiate himself with the marchioness, but a quarrel with the marquess's sister had never been part of the bargain.

And here she was sitting in his own parlour, cutting up nasty and making all kinds of threats—

"My dear Lady Pamela," he began, risking a glance sideways to where his wife sat smiling fixedly at their visitor. "I can assure you—"

"Don't bother," said the woman. Then, to Lady Brigsby— "Here is a ten pound note."

His wife sat up a fraction straighter.

"Ah, yes?" she said to Lady Pamela.

"I assume it will more than cover any *expenses* involved in moving Miss Phillips to decent accommodations on one of the upper floors."

"Well . . . you see—"

"And I have another thirty pounds—"

Lady Brigsby stifled a gasp.

"—which I will put into the hands of Miss Phillips. Should there be any . . . misunderstanding about the new arrangements, Miss Phillips will no doubt be inclined to keep this money to herself."

"Oh, but—"

"Now, please show me to the . . . cellar. I wish to have a word with my *friend*."

He was going to marry Miss Helène Phillips.

Lord Quentin was torn between spending the next weeks at Tavelstoke with the marquess as they had planned, or returning at once to Luton Court. He was going to marry Miss Phillips! He wanted to be with her this very minute. And yet . . .

What would his father—the earl—say? wondered Charles. Not to mention the rest of the family; his stepmother, and the various aunts, uncles, and cousins that were regular visitors to the earl's townhome. What would they think? Perhaps he should send a message to his bride-to-be, informing her of her happy fate, and then journey to London, to speak with his father.

"Are you completely daft?" was Jonathan's reaction to this idea. "Offer for the girl in a *letter?*"

"Well, it's not as if the outcome is in any doubt," said Charles. He truly wanted to see Miss Phillips again, but he was also aware of his responsibilities as the earl's son. The road might be smoother for Helène if his family had some chance to adjust to the thought of a governess as the newest

Tavelstoke bride.

Jonathan was adamant. "It simply isn't done," he told Lord Quentin. "Besides, you must ask permission from—ah, from someone, I'm sure."

"She has no family," said Charles.

"Nonsense," said the marquess. "Everyone has family."

No one had been down to the cellar since Sir Malcolm had locked her into the room last night, and Helène was beginning to consider screaming for help. At least the noise might keep the rats at bay. If she stood the cot on end, perhaps she could reach the window—

Footsteps sounded in the hall and, to Helène's relief, she heard the rattle of the key in the door lock—and Lady Pamela's voice.

"Good heavens," said Lady Pam, holding up her skirts, "what a disgusting room."

"Ah. Ah, yes," stammered the squire.

"And you say you actually keep criminals in this? I should think even sots would turn their noses up at the smell."

Helène hid a smile.

"Yes, well, you see—" began Sir Malcolm.

"Miss Phillips would surely die of some ghastly fever within the fortnight if she stayed down here," Pam continued, "although you, my dear squire, might expire much sooner."

"I beg your pardon?" The man sounded startled.

"I have already sent a groom for the marquess. If he had found his children's governess being held in this squalid pest-hole, I should imagine he would have been most displeased. And if Miss Phillips should happen to take ill . . ."

"Surely, you can't expect—"

"But, as you say, you *are* the magistrate. And Lord Sinclair hasn't fought a duel in years. Perhaps he will not start with you."

"Oh, Lady Pamela—but—"

"Now, get her out of here."

Sir Malcolm sat in the library and downed another glass of port. Emerald necklaces—fah! Damn Lady Sinclair, and damn the marquess's interfering, butter-won't-melt-in-her-mouth sister. Miss Helène Phillips, a low-class nobody and accused thief, was now residing in one of the squire's guest rooms, and it vexed him no end.

He'd be the laughingstock of the shire, thought Sir Malcolm, once it came out that he'd arrested Lord Sinclair's governess, only to have Lady Pamela sitting at his doorstep the very next day. Not to mention—and here, the squire shifted uneasily in his chair—what the marquess himself might have to say about matters.

Lady Brigsby had made her thoughts on the subject exceedingly clear. "You were a fool," she told Sir Malcolm, "to cross Pamela Sinclair."

"But Celia Sinclair is the marquess's wife!" Sir Malcolm had protested.

"That she is," said Lady Brigsby, "and he may love her, for all I can fathom. But he don't take her word over that of his sister, and he won't be thanking you for it, neither."

"Oh!" moaned the squire. "What are we to do?"

"Send her back to Luton," his wife rejoined. "First thing on the morrow."

"But my dearest—the marchioness—"

"A pox on the marchioness. Tell her I've taken ill with the grippe and cannot bear any more commotion. Tell her anything. Just get rid of that girl."

So he had been left with no choice, and the pretty little

miss would be on her way tomorrow, right enough. The squire poured another glass of port, and smiled sourly. Not that she knew it, of course. Let her stew another night. If he had to release Miss Helène Phillips, at least he could scare her a bit first.

Jeb Carnath, one of the Luton Court grooms, arrived at Tavelstoke early that evening, shivering with cold and so exhausted from his ride that it was several minutes before Charles and Jonathan could make any sense of what the man was saying.

"Lady Pamela," gasped the groom, finally. "Lady Pamela says you must come back as soon as ever you can, milord, there's awful trouble."

Lord Sinclair went white. He staggered and would have fallen if Charles had not reached out a steadying hand. "My children?" asked the marquess, his voice a whisper.

"Oh, no, milord," said Jeb, "there's nothin' wrong with Miss Alice or Master Peter. It's Miss Helène what's in a fix."

The groom only then remembered the note from Lady Pam. He fished in his pocket and handed it to the marquess, who frowned as he read the short lines. It took some time before Charles and Jonathan elicited the complete story—or as much as Jeb knew of it—and by the end of the tale Lord Quentin was ready to saddle Alcibiades and leave at once. Lord Sinclair, however, kept a cooler head.

"It will do Miss Phillips no good if you freeze to death on the way to Luton," said Jonathan with a huge yawn.

"Every minute's delay is a minute she is in the hands of that—that blithering jackass!"

"Sir Malcolm may be a jackass," said Jonathan, "but he's passingly honest. She'll come to no harm for another day."

The marquess turned to the young groom.

"Jeb," said Lord Sinclair, "get yourself something to eat and find a bed. Lord Quentin and I will be departing for Luton at dawn."

Lady Pamela fingered Helène's sapphire ring, turning it over and over in her palm. She had gone to Helène's chambers to assure herself that nothing of Petrus and Torvin's presence lingered there. Pam felt responsible for the girl's welfare, and as she sat quietly, pondering the current predicament, her attention was captured by Helène's remarkable ring.

The center stone was large and uncommonly brilliant, almost as if it shone with its own light. Pamela had felt a strange fascination with the ring from the moment she had first seen it, and she now succumbed to the temptation to try it on herself.

'Twas a perfect fit. She held her hand up, turning it this way and that and marveling at the flashes of dazzling blue light.

It must be worth a small fortune, thought Pam. Enough to buy a modest cottage, perhaps, and live for some time. But Helène said that the ring belonged to the Duchess of Grentham, and not to her. Would she even be willing to sell it?

Pam wondered if there currently was a Duchess of Grentham. Her man-of-affairs had instructions to contact her the moment the duke returned to London, but she had heard nothing as yet.

The ring shouldn't be left lying around, thought Pam. I'll put it with my own jewelry for safe-keeping—

"Milady?"

Lady Pamela turned to see James standing in her doorway. She smiled.

"Sir Malcolm has sent word that Lady Brigsby is quite ill,

and Helène must be removed from Noble Oaks first thing on the morning."

James snorted, but said nothing.

"I'd like you to fetch her. I'd go myself, but—" Pam hesitated, not wanting to mention the real reason, which was to make sure that the marchioness organized no interference.

James seemed to understand. "Never you worry, milady," he said, grinning. "I'll make sure Miss Helène gets back safe 'nd sound. We'll keep it all quiet like," he added, with a wink.

Helène sat on the four-posted bed and looked around her. A second-floor guestroom, not to be compared to the governess's chambers at Luton Court, but reasonably clean—and a vast improvement over the cellar.

She was not terribly happy to be there, nevertheless. The squire had been in a foul mood as he had shown Helène to her new accommodations, almost pushing her into the chamber.

"Don't get any ideas that you are a guest," Sir Malcolm had snarled. "I may have the chance to send you on to London, yet. And I'm sure Petrus and Torvin would enjoy keeping you company on the way."

Helène had made no reply, wondering if this was bluff. If the squire was the shire magistrate, could Lady Pamela, or even the marquess, stop him from doing as he wished?

She was still locked in, of course. Helène began to pace around the room. She examined the window, noting that it was a long drop to the ground, with no ledge or other means of climbing down conveniently at hand.

But, as at Luton, the snow was very deep. One might jump.

And then? She unfolded the three, crisp ten-pound notes Lady Pamela had pressed into her hand earlier that day and stared at them, thinking hard.

"Use them to keep the squire's wife happy," Pam had said. "It should be enough for a day or two—until Jonathan returns and this is all sorted out. I've told Alice and Peter you'll be home before they know it."

Helène sighed unhappily. *Home.* She had said nothing to Lady Pamela, but Luton Court was not home, and she could never, ever go back there. She would miss the children dreadfully, of course, but—

I have no home, thought Helène. Perhaps it is time I find one.

She closed her eyes, seeing a scrap of paper with its three short lines of address—

Benjamin Torrance
27 Emmet Street
Charlottesville, Virginia

Aunt Matilde's handwriting. Helène recalled the days spent with her aunt as she lay dying, and heard her own voice, protesting Matilde's wishes.

"I can't leave England."
"I know you wish to stay with your father. But the man is your cousin. He can help you."

Helène had memorized the address, not leaving the paper around for her father to discover, to ask questions, perhaps to insist that his daughter do as her aunt had asked.

And then, a year later, Nathaniel Phillips's death as well. But not before arrangements had been made for Helène to become a governess, her father insisting to his daughter that *this* was Aunt Matilde's dying wish. And so she had arrived at Luton Court, in Bedfordshire. Only to fall in love with a man who would not marry her, and who insulted her, and who had gone away.

She would never see him again.

The guestroom boasted a small writing table. Helène sat down and, finding a few pieces of paper and the necessary implements, began to compose a letter.

My dear Lady Pamela—

Chapter Twenty-Two

Charles and Lord Sinclair had spoken little for most of the day. They rode hard, stopping only twice for food and to give the horses a rest. Alcibiades and Pendragon—the marquess's gelding—were lively and game, but even the strongest animal had limits, and it would do no good to run them into the ground miles short of their goal.

The groom had explained the circumstances of Miss Phillips's arrest, but Jonathan appeared unperturbed by the theft of the marchioness's necklace. *He doesn't believe Helène stole it anymore than I do*, thought Charles, *but this left the question of who did take it, or if the necklace had really been stolen at all.* That last was an awkward thought.

Would Lady Sinclair really have fabricated such a grave accusation? For what purpose? Lady Pamela had told him that Celia was out to ruin Helène socially—but an *arrest*. That was a far more serious matter. Charles found himself bitterly angry with the marchioness, and he nursed that feeling, perhaps as a shield against his own guilt.

I left her there, thought Charles. I left her alone at the mercy of Celia Sinclair.

Helène wrapped the blanket firmly around her shoulders, took a deep breath, and jumped. She landed awkwardly, up to her hips in the snow, and pitched forward onto her face.

Mmph. After a moment's floundering she was able to stand up. Brushing snow from her face and neck, Helène struggled away from the house as quickly as she could, thinking that anyone who looked out the window would have no difficulty in discovering what had happened to their prisoner.

She headed in the direction of a nearby copse of trees, sinking deep into the snow with each step and hoping that it would be easier going once she was in the shelter of the woods. The months at Luton had given her a tolerable knowledge of the local countryside, and Helène knew that Cotter's post was less than a mile away.

The mail coach stopped there each day on its way to London, and with any luck Helène would be on the coach before the squire or Lady Brigsby noticed she had escaped. She didn't want to think about what might happen if they *did* notice. She was feeling guilty enough about taking Lady Pamela's money, about deserting Alice and Peter, and about leaving the marquess's employment without a word of goodbye.

Her letter to Lady Pamela was sitting on the guestroom writing table, and Helène hoped that Sir Malcolm would be honest enough to send it on its way. She had been in tears last night as she wrote, as she apologized for taking Lady Pamela's thirty pounds, even as she promised its eventual return. She wept as she sent her love to Alice and Peter and told them she would never forget them, as she tried to explain—

Her behavior was, on the face of it, inexcusable. But, after examining every other possibility, over and over throughout the long hours of the night, Helène had unhappily concluded that she had no choice.

She had been accused of a serious theft. False as the accusation was, Sir Malcolm had told her that he could send her on to London at a moment's notice. And once in town—

Helène knew entirely too much about the justice to be expected from the London courts for those not of the *haut ton*. She would drown there, disappear utterly, and not even the marquess would be able to fish her back out.

Yesterday, Lady Pamela had tried to reassure Helène that every difficulty would vanish upon the return of Lord Sinclair, but the governess remained unconvinced. Who would the marquess be more likely to believe? His own wife—or Miss Helène Phillips, the penniless daughter of a carriagemaker?

Lady Pamela paced up and down the entry hall, hoping that Celia would sleep, as she often did, until the mid-afternoon, and worrying that James was late in returning from Noble Oaks Manor. That morning had produced a maddening series of delays in sending the coach for Helène.

First, a winter's fog had rolled in off the Lea, so thick that one could hardly see the stables from the house. James was eager to go, but Pamela had insisted he wait until the fog lifted and the danger of running into something, or running off the road entirely, was past.

Then, one of the carriage traces snapped before the coach had gotten beyond the drive, and repairs were complicated by the cold. Finally James had left, and Lady Pamela had started counting the minutes.

Too many minutes, by now. What could have happened to them?

Helène was exhausted and lost. The fog seemed to be getting thicker by the minute, and she was no longer sure which direction she had come from, or in which direction the road lay. Each step was an effort. Twice now her shoes had remained behind as she dragged her feet forward, and she lost precious minutes digging them out.

She had no coat, and the blanket that she had taken from the guestroom—I *am* a thief, thought Helène miserably—was little help in keeping her feet warm. Her hands were numb, and her nose dripped.

Worst of all, however, was the resurgence of self-doubt.

Last night, when she was locked into a room, Sir Malcolm's threats still ringing in her ears, running away had seemed like the only solution to her present difficulties. But this morning fatigue and hunger had taken their toll. Helène worried that she would walk around in circles until she froze, and returning to Luton Court was beginning to sound attractive.

What could she do in London, after all? Helène tried to fight off the doubt and stay focused on her plan. She was to find cheap lodgings in London—a task easily accomplished, as she knew *those* parts of the city well—then seek out a ship bound for the Americas.

D' you think thirty pounds will buy you passage? scoffed a little voice.

Well, no—but Helène had heard of people signing marques of indenture, in return for passage overseas. If she could only get to the Colonies, surely she could find her cousin—

Hoofbeats in the distance, becoming louder. Helène was immediately cheered, knowing that if she could find the horse—without being seen herself, of course—she would find a road. She picked up her skirts and tried to run but immediately lost her right shoe. Swearing, she bent down to dig it out of the snow as the hoofbeats sounded closer, then faded away.

Bother it all. But she had a good idea of the sound's direction, and now better hopes of finding the road.

Lady Pamela was arranging flowers in the entry hall—anything to pass the time—when she heard a firm rap at the front doors.

"Telford?" called Pam.

She was annoyed with the butler for not consulting her before he followed Celia's instructions to admit Sir Malcolm and the Emory brothers on the night of Helène's arrest. And then to conveniently disappear, leaving James alone to assist the ladies—!

Telford had been avoiding her ever since and was nowhere in sight. Pam sighed and went to open the door herself.

A man stood there. A tall and very handsome man, nearly as blond as Pamela. He was perhaps thirty years of age, clean-shaven, and with cropped hair. Pam's eyes took in the broad shoulders, the firm jaw, and the clear, deep blue eyes. Goodness. The man's riding coat was a simple affair, without capes, and his boots looked well-worn. Not a gentleman's dress—

The man gave her a crooked smile, and Pam's knees, unexpectedly, turned to water.

"Can—can I help you?" she managed.

"I certainly hope you can," he replied. His voice was deep and strong, with a slight twang that Lady Pamela could not immediately place. "I'm looking for Miss Helène Phillips."

"Miss . . . ah, Miss Phillips?" She took a deep breath, mentally kicking herself for reacting like a moonstruck girl. Handsome or not, this was only a man. But why was he looking for the governess?

"Yes. A young lady of about twenty, I believe." Seeing Pam's confusion he added, "Miss Phillips is my cousin."

Lady Pamela felt the stirrings of alarm. Something was wrong here. Helène's Aunt Matilde had been childless, and she had no uncles, no family at all on her father's side—

His *cousin,* the man had said? Lady Pamela's eyes opened wide as she realized who this young man must be.

"You are the Duke of Grentham, sir?" she asked him.

The man grinned again. "Mmm, yes," he replied. "So they say."

"Your grace," said Pam, dropping into a curtsey. "I am Pamela Sinclair, sister to the Marquess of Luton."

The duke was silent for a moment; Lady Pamela saw that he was staring curiously at her right hand. What was he looking at?

"Benjamin Torrance, at your service, ma'am," said the man at last. He removed his hat and swept her a wide bow. "Now, have I come to the right place? Is my cousin at home?"

"Ah, well . . . hmm. Not at present, I'm afraid," said Lady Pam, beckoning him to enter. "But please, do come in. I'll ring for tea." Good grief, this was a pickle! Pam's mind raced through a number of possible explanations she might offer for Helène's absence, but she saw no easy way of telling the Duke of Grentham that his cousin had recently enjoyed the hospitality of their local magistrate.

"But she *is* living here?" asked the man. He had not moved from the doorway. "I understood that Lord Sinclair had employed Miss Phillips as a governess."

"Yes, yes, indeed," Lady Pam answered. If only James would return with Helène! Lord Torrance was standing there like a rock, and if he couldn't be convinced to sit down and take tea, she was going to have the devil's own time stalling. "I must thank you for responding so quickly to my inquiries," she added, wondering why her man of affairs had not informed her that the duke had returned from the colonies.

"Your inquiries?"

At that moment, to Lady Pamela's relief, she heard the clatter of a carriage rounding the drive. Thank goodness.

"Here's your cousin, now," she told Lord Torrance brightly. Smiling, the duke strode toward the coach with

Lady Pam at his heels.

Charles and Jonathan took a final, short rest before crossing the Lea. Traces of fog still lingered next to the river, but Luton Court was only a few miles distant now, with the squire's home not far beyond that. Lord Sinclair wanted to stop at Luton to speak with Lady Pamela, but Charles said he would press on to Noble Oaks Manor.

"Are you sure, old man?" asked Jonathan. "Won't take a minute to talk to m' sister."

"I'm sure," said Charles grimly. He spurred Alcibiades.

"She was gone, milady! She was gone!"

James had at first been close to incoherent. Lady Pamela and the duke—who had quickly grasped that the footman had been sent to retrieve Miss Phillips from . . . somewhere—managed to sit him down in the small parlour and were now plying him with a soothing glass of brandy.

"I got there quick just like you says. The squire, he went up to the room, but Miss Helène wasn't there!"

"Miss Helène?" said the duke. "You mean Miss Phillips?"

James looked at Lord Torrance in confusion—no one had told him who this strange man was—and repeated, "She weren't there!"

"Well, perhaps she was somewhere else in the house," said the duke, impatiently. He is assuming, Lady Pam realized, that Helène was a guest at Sir Malcolm's house, free to walk about at will.

"The squire says the door was still locked," said James. "He says she musta jumped out the window!"

"Jumped out—! What?" exclaimed Lord Torrance.

Lady Pamela sighed, but was spared further explanation

as just then the parlour door burst open, and her brother walked in.

Lord Quentin stood at the entrance to Noble Oaks manor, his fists clenched at his side.

"As I told you before, my lord," said Sir Malcolm, licking his lips nervously, "Miss Phillips is no longer in our charge."

Charles fought the temptation to box the man's ears. "And she left when? How?"

"Ah, well, that is the question, you see," said the squire, "but I can assure you that, however it may have happened, she is no longer here."

Of all the dunderheaded, half-witted—

"She walked right out the front door into the cold?" hissed Charles.

"Ah. Well, I believe—"

"Show me where she was being held," demanded Lord Quentin.

"Oh, now, my lord, I can assure you—"

"*Show me.*"

Squire Brigsby led him to the second floor room. The bed had not been slept in, and Charles—remembering a certain evening when he had been unable to leave Miss Phillips's bedchamber by the door—immediately crossed over to the window.

He opened the window, the squire sputtering behind him, and looked down.

Lord Quentin was seized with a number of conflicting impulses; to strangle Sir Malcolm, to strangle Helène—and to burst into laughter. Jumped out the window, did she? And managed not to break any bones, either, from the looks of those tracks in the snow. My resourceful little half-wit!

Charles turned toward the squire. "And you have no idea

where she went?" he inquired amiably.

"No, my lord. But—"

How stupid *was* the man?

Or perhaps he knows well where Helène has gone, thought Charles. Someone must have closed that window. But he doesn't want to admit he's lost her or go to the trouble of getting her back.

An envelope on the writing table, addressed to Lady Pamela, caught Lord Quentin's eye. He pocketed it and turned to the squire.

"Very well," said Charles. "Good day to you, sir. I'll show myself out."

He left Sir Malcolm gaping at him. Charles took the staircase by twos, and strode out the front door, yelling for the boy to bring Alcibiades.

"Not to worry, Pam," said Lord Sinclair. "Lord Quentin is already on his way to Noble Oaks Manor. Be back with Miss Phillips in a trice."

"Have you heard a single word I've said?" said Lady Pamela. "She isn't there!"

"Why," said the duke, with exaggerated calm, "was my cousin locked into a room?"

Jonathan looked around as if he had just noticed Lord Torrance. "Grentham," the marquess said genially, "glad you're here."

Pam frowned. "How do you know Lord Torrance?" she asked her brother.

"Don't know him," said Jonathan, "but if he's Miss Phillips's cousin—" Lord Sinclair turned to the duke. "Heard you were back in England. I take it my message found you."

"You're Luton?" asked the duke.

"Indeed, indeed," said the marquess. "Now, Miss Phillips

should be returning with her fiancé at any moment—"

Fiancé?

"Good heavens, Amanda, what happened to your eye?" inquired Jonathan.

Lady Pamela turned to see Lady Detweiler standing in the doorway to the parlour.

"Have I missed any of the fun?" asked Amanda. She was regarding the duke quizzically.

Finally, thought Pamela. A woman. Someone who makes sense.

Helène—miserably cold, and once again engaged in pulling a shoe out of the snow—never heard the rider until he was a scarce ten yards away.

She ducked down behind a bush but it was too late. The man jumped off his horse and was in front of her with a few strides. It happened so fast that she had only just recognized Alcibiades when Lord Quentin hauled her unceremoniously up out of the snow and kissed her. She sputtered as he threw her over his shoulder.

"What are you doing? Let me down!"

Lord Quentin did not reply. He tossed her up onto the stallion's back; as she continued to protest and squirm, he said—

"Sit still, my absurd little ninny. The poor horse is tired enough as it is."

"I am not your absurd little anything. Now let me go!"

Lord Quentin laughed. He jumped up behind her and clucked to Alcibiades. The stallion began to trot off in the direction of Luton Court.

Charles sighed, tightening his arms around the bedraggled Miss Phillips. The girl had looked too cold to be making so much of a fuss; if she would only stop squirming . . .

He had found Helène at almost the same spot they had first met, Lord Quentin realized. He wondered if she remembered it, too. She had been even more bedraggled those months ago, of course—in rags, nearly, and hungry as well.

I should have seen what she was worth even then, thought Charles. No matter what she looked like, I should have known.

And what if he had not found her just now? What if she had become lost walking to Luton in that snowstorm, or if the squire had manage to send her on to London, accused of theft, to rot in some miserable prison—

Never again, thought Lord Quentin, shuddering. I will take care of her forever. She will never again have anything to fear.

"I've been in Virginia for the past several years," the Duke of Grentham was saying. "If I'd known I had a cousin—"

"I understand that Miss Phillips's father refused the connection," Jonathan said. "He was bitter and wanted nothing more to do with Matilde's family."

Lady Pamela looked at her brother, puzzled. Matilde? How did the marquess know anything about Helène's aunt?

"Jonathan—" she began.

"We have guests?" The petulant female voice sounded from outside the parlour door. "Why was I not informed?"

The marchioness. Pam looked at Amanda in alarm as the door was flung open and Lady Sinclair entered. The marchioness spared a glance for Lord Torrance—clearly dismissing him as poorly dressed and therefore of no account—before seeing her husband. She turned pale.

"Jonathan," she said. "Why . . . why are you here?"

"My dear, may I introduce—" said Lord Sinclair.

"Jonathan, it was all an awful mistake! That horrible

squire, and those men he brought with him—"

"Celia—"

"And I'm sure the necklace must have been misplaced by accident. But what," added Celia, "what if I *had* been robbed? No one seems to care for my feelings at all!"

The marquess regarded his wife without a word, one eyebrow cocked.

"Lady Sinclair," began Pam, "I don't know how your necklace came to be in the nursery, but I can assure you that—"

"Well, keep—keep her as governess then, for all I care!" cried Celia. She seemed to be on the edge of hysteria, and to hardly know what she was saying. " 'Twill be all she ever does! If you think Lord Quentin will be willing to take her as his mistress after *this*—"

There was a short, shocked silence. The duke bounded to his feet.

"*Mistress*—?" shouted Lord Torrance angrily.

"Your grace," interrupted Lady Detweiler, smiling as if nothing untoward had been said, "may I present Lady Celia Sinclair, the Marchioness of Luton?"

"Sit still, my love," said Lord Quentin.

His love? "I can't go back to Luton," said Helène, trying to turn in the saddle. She wanted to be off this horse, out of this man's arms, and on her way to London. Whatever dangers town might hold, they would be far easier to bear than seeing Charles Quentin again.

"Nonsense," said Lord Quentin.

"You don't understand, and I don't wish to explain. Please let me down."

Lady Sinclair's eyes widened; she turned to Lord

Torrance in bewilderment.

"Your . . . your grace?"

"Lord Benjamin Torrance, the Duke of Grentham, as I believe," added Amanda helpfully.

"Lady Sinclair," said the duke, nodding coolly. "I have the honor to be the cousin of Miss Helène Phillips, your governess."

Confusion warred with panic on the marchioness's face; she looked at her husband—at the duke—and back at her husband again.

"I . . . I beg your pardon?"

" 'Tis a long story, my dear," said Jonathan easily. "Now, come, let's have some tea."

"What is it that I don't understand?" said Charles. "That you were arrested for stealing Celia's necklace? Or that you would run away from Luton rather than trust to the loyalty and common sense of your friends?"

The girl looked away from him, silent.

"Just let me down," she said finally. "I'm going to London, and—"

"London!" sputtered Charles. "I think not."

Another silence, that stretched on until he felt her shoulders shuddering against his chest and realized that Helène was weeping.

"Will you not leave me alone?" she cried. "I cannot stay at Luton. And I will not be your mistress."

"My mistress?" said Charles. "What a shocking idea."

"But—"

"Of course you aren't going to be my mistress. You will be my wife."

The tea arrived. Lady Sinclair poured, her face still pale,

saying nothing. The duke seemed to have forgotten about Celia's outburst and was chatting amiably with the marquess concerning Miss Phillips. They had determined that the governess was actually the duke's first-cousin-once-removed as he was the son of the old duke's youngest brother.

Amanda had eschewed tea and was sipping brandy. She and Lady Pamela conversed in low tones, both still concerned—despite Jonathan's assurances—as to the whereabouts of Lord Quentin and Miss Phillips.

Nobody mentioned an emerald necklace.

Lady Pamela wanted to speak to her brother privately and ask him what he had meant by Helène's *fiancé,* but she hesitated to bring up the subject of Lord Quentin with Lady Sinclair still in the room. And was Jonathan even referring to Charles?

Celia made a tiny hiccough, and Lady Pamela looked over to see—

Good grief, the marchioness was *crying.*

"Jonathan," said Lady Pamela. Her brother looked up, then rose and walked over to kneel beside his wife.

"Now, what's all this?" he said gently, taking Celia's hands in his own.

"I'm sorry! I didn't mean—"

"Sorry about what?"

"The necklace! I didn't think—I didn't know—"

The marchioness was staring at the ground. Jonathan tipped her chin up with a finger.

"What about the necklace, my dear?" he said.

"Miss Phillips didn't take it," said Lady Sinclair. "I hid it in the nursery myself."

The marquess was nodding. "Why would you do that?" he asked his wife.

"I don't know!" cried Celia. "I don't know! But everyone

thought she was so wonderful! The children, Lord Quentin—even you! Everyone thought so much of her, and she was so pretty, and—" The marchioness broke off, burying her head in her hands. Her shoulders shook with sobs. "No-one cares about me at all!" came the cry, faintly, from between beringed fingers.

The duke was regarding the marchioness gravely; Lady Detweiler hid a smile behind her hand. Jonathan took one of Celia's hands and raised it to his lips.

"I care about you, my love," he said. "I care about you very much."

"Oh!" Sobbing, the marchioness collapsed into her husband's arms.

"You don't want to marry me!" Miss Phillips said. "I'm not good enough for your—your name, or your family—or your *anything!*"

"You are more than good enough," replied Charles. "Helène, I am sorry. I was a fool to think any of those things important. I love you and I want to marry you. That's all that counts."

The girl was silent for a moment. She twisted around in the saddle to look directly at Charles.

"You want to marry a 'dirty little nobody'?" said Helène softly.

"Who dared speak to you in such a manner?" said Lord Quentin, outraged. "I'll call him out—"

"*You* did."

"What?" Then Charles remembered one night, in the library, with Lady Sinclair. It seemed like a lifetime ago, and had he really said—?

Oh. Yes, he had. Lord Quentin chortled. "In the library? Don't tell me you were hiding behind the *drapes?*"

312

"As a matter of fact, I was," the girl said indignantly.

"Well, my love, I do apologize," said Charles, and he kissed the top of her head. Helène said nothing. "But if you will insist on sneaking into libraries and hiding where you ought not be—"

"I might hear the truth?"

"No," said Lord Quentin. "You might hear a very foolish man, saying something very stupid about a woman he should have admired from the beginning."

"Mmm," said Helène.

"Do you forgive me? Or," said Charles, "perhaps I should ask you another question. Do you love me?"

Miss Phillips had turned forward in the saddle, away from him. She said something Charles could not hear. He leaned forward and whispered the question once more, in her ear.

"Well?" said Charles.

"Yes," said Miss Helène Phillips. "Yes, I do."

The marquess was about to take Celia back to her rooms when the parlour door opened once more. Miss Phillips and Charles Quentin stood there, the girl looking wet and tired, her shoes in tatters.

"Helène, thank goodness—"

"Ah, here's Miss Phillips now," said the marquess. "Lord Torrance, your cousin—"

Lord Quentin was frowning; the duke rising to his feet—

"My—my cousin?" said Helène.

"Benjamin Torrance, yes, indeed," said Jonathan. Helène was staring at the duke in confusion as the marquess continued blithely. "Your grace, this is my friend, Lord Charles Quentin—"

Lord Torrance had moved forward to sweep a bow to

Helène; he stopped now, frowning. He looked at Helène, then at Charles.

"Lord Quentin?"

Oh, no, thought Lady Pamela, realizing what had happened. If Celia had only kept her mouth shut—

"Lord *Quentin?*" roared the duke, and cocking his fist he knocked Charles to the floor.

Celia started to cry again and Lady Pamela had caught one arm of the duke and was trying to explain that the marchioness had been quite mistaken—Miss Phillips would never—

Lord Quentin came to his feet, looking more puzzled than angry.

"I'm sorry, I don't believe I caught—" Charles hesitated. "You are Miss Phillips's *cousin?*"

"Charles." The marquess stepped forward. "The Duke of Grentham arrived from the Americas just this past week. I asked him to Luton for a visit. With Miss Phillips being our governess and all—"

Everything made sudden, perfect sense to Helène. The Duke of Grentham had arrived unexpectedly in England. Heaven only knew why he'd picked this particular time to leave the Colonies, or how he knew she had been employed at Luton, but—

And now Lord Quentin, asking her to be his wife—

"You *knew!*" cried Helène. She turned angrily to face Lord Quentin. I'll knock him down myself, she was thinking. All that nonsense about a foolish man saying foolish things—

The marquess stepped between them. He took Helène's shoulders gently in his hands.

"No," Lord Sinclair told her. "No, my dear, as it happens, he knew nothing at all."

★ ★ ★ ★ ★

And so, the future Earl of Tavelstoke found himself on one knee before the Marquess of Luton's governess, in front of the gathered company of Lord Sinclair's parlour, once again offering her his hand in marriage.

"You certainly do not have to accept him," the Duke of Grentham said helpfully. "I will be remaining in England and you will always have a home with me."

"Is it true love?" asked Lady Pamela.

"Heaven help us," said Lady Detweiler, rolling her eyes.

"True love? Yes," said Helène. "I believe it is."

Chapter Twenty-Three

The governess may well ask if she can marry . . .

'Twas a beautiful morning. Helène was enjoying the late winter sunshine streaming through the windows of the *petit salon* while she held two small children in her lap. The governess was to be married to Charles Quentin within the fortnight, and Alice and Peter chattered excitedly about the upcoming wedding, asking Miss Phillips if she *really truly* had to leave.

She would miss them, of course, and she had extracted a promise from the marquess that the new governess was to be approved by Lady Pamela. Helène had tried to explain this to Alice and Peter.

"*You* can still be our governess!" said the girl.

"Lord Quentin has asked me to marry him," said Helène. "I cannot marry him if I am to remain as your governess." She and the children had already discussed this at some length, but Peter, especially, was unconvinced.

"Yes, you can!" he protested.

"Your papa will find someone *much* nicer than I am," said Helène, in mock seriousness. The children giggled. "And Tavelstoke is not so far away, you know. We can visit each other."

"A visit! That's not enough!"

"And then, when we have babies of our own,"—Alice and Peter quieted suddenly, their eyes opening wide—"you will have them to visit, as well."

This, it seemed, was quite satisfactory. Soon they were discussing the number of children Miss Phillips and Lord Quentin should have—"Ten!" said Peter—when the Duke of Grentham walked in, Lady Pamela on his arm.

They are a striking couple, thought Helène. Blond on blond, with the duke's rustic simplicity a counterpoint to the elegance of Pamela Sinclair.

"You have a lapful, cousin," said the duke, laughing.

"Indeed."

Helène was not yet accustomed to having such a powerful man claim kinship with her. Yesterday, after she had finally accepted Lord Sinclair's assurances that Charles had certainly known nothing of her family connections prior to that very moment, the duke had stepped forward to insist that Lord Quentin ask his permission before paying his addresses to Helène.

"I find I do not like this talk of mistresses," said Lord Torrance. "You, sir. Are you worthy of my cousin?"

"Your grace, I am quite sure—" Lady Pamela, alarmed, had begun to expostulate when Lady Detweiler burst into laughter.

"Hoisted on his own petard!" Amanda had cried. "Oh, Charles, I do so *love* irony."

The day past had provided a surprise from the marquess, as well. After Jonathan had escorted Celia to her rooms, he had returned to face a number of questions from his sister. Yes, the marquess had explained, he had known Helène was the granddaughter of the old Duke of Grentham from the beginning. Did Pamela think he would hire just anyone as governess for his children? And yes, he had written Lord Torrance, asking him to visit Luton upon his return to England.

"But how did you know Miss Phillips even existed?" asked Lady Pam.

The marquess turned toward Helène, and the governess wondered how she could ever have mistaken the gentleness in his eyes for indifference.

"I knew your aunt," said Jonathan softly. "Matilde. When I was a younger man. She refused me, you understand. Your father was so bitter against all *ton* society by that time that he would never have allowed you to live with us. And Matilde would not leave you."

Tears rose in Helène's eyes. She knew that her poor father, angry at the death of his wife, had been determined to provide for her on his own. And he had done so, well enough, until near the end. But her aunt, giving up her own chance of marriage—

"But I made her a promise," said the marquess, "that if Mr. Phillips died with you still unmarried, I would bring you to Luton Court. As it happened, when your father knew he was dying, he contacted me himself."

Peter was squirming; Helène lowered both children to the floor and sent them off to the kitchen with a promise of cocoa. She turned to the duke and Lady Pamela.

"Oh!" she said suddenly. "Oh, your grace! I have something for you."

Lord Torrance looked at Helène curiously. "You have something for me?"

"Indeed. From my grandmother, you see—your aunt. I never knew her, of course, but before she died—"

Lady Pamela, who had forgotten about the sapphire ring in all of yesterday's excitement, at once realized what Miss Phillips was talking about. Pulling the ring from her finger, Pam handed it wordlessly to Helène.

"Here it is!" Helène offered it to Lord Torrance. "This ring," she said, "belongs to the Duchess of Grentham."

He took it from her hand and then glanced at Lady Pamela.

She blushed. "Yes, I was wearing it. How did you know?"

"Know what it looked like?"

Pam nodded.

"I've seen portraits of several of the duchesses. They were all wearing that ring." He smiled at Lady Pamela. "It does look very nice on you."

Lady Pamela's blush deepened, and she turned to Helène. "I spoke with the marchioness late last night," she told the governess. "I believe she is truly sorry for the trouble she has caused."

"That will have to do, I suppose," said Helène.

"Someday she may even tell you so herself. But at the moment, Celia has focused her efforts on mending fences with her husband."

"I dare say."

"And I believe that Jonathan has fences to mend himself."

Helène's face showed her surprise.

"I think you will find that the typical male can fix his attention on only one subject at a time." Lady Pamela shot a quick smile at the duke. "And for my brother," she added, "it has been the estate."

"Ah . . ."

"But Charles has convinced him that the steward should take on most of those duties. Jonathan will have the chance he needs to convince Celia that she is cared for and loved. Now, as for Beatrice Harkins—"

Helène grimaced.

"My brother has had a talk with her as well, and I think

you can be assured there will be no gossip. Lady Harkins very much wishes to continue a welcome guest at Luton Court—"

"Indeed," said Helène.

"And," added Lady Pamela, favoring Lord Torrance with another wry smile, "she has high hopes of forming a favorable connection with the illustrious Duke of Grentham, as well."

Lord Quentin now entered the *petit salon*. He crossed immediately to Helène's side and took her hands in his. She rose to face him.

"I vow to you that I shall spend the rest of my life proving myself worthy of a carriagemaker's daughter," he told her, his eyes twinkling.

"I should hope so," said Lady Pamela. Lord Torrance looked on without comment, his lips twitching.

"And I," said Helène, "proving myself worthy to be a Tavelstoke wife."

Lord Quentin bent to kiss his bride-to-be, but for a moment she held him at bay.

"In truth, my lord," said Helène, "I find all this talk of ancestors to be quite beside the point. Does not true nobility lie in the soul?"

"Indeed."

"Then let us strive only to be worthy of each other," said Miss Phillips, "and of our love."